Praise for *In the Dark We Forget*

"*In the Dark We Forget* is a hair-raising high-wire act.
Wong gives us a hero whose search for her identity, and the truth
of what happened to upend her life, reveals more than she wants to
know and leaves the reader gasping as much in admiration as in fear."
SARA PARETSKY, award-winning author of *Dead Land*

"[A] fiercely original and stunningly written thriller."
P. J. VERNON, author of *Bath Haus*

"Wong's brilliant prose will keep you riveted until the very last,
shocking page. An outstanding psychological suspense."
JENNIFER HILLIER, bestselling author of *Little Secrets*

"[A] pulse-quickening story about the complexities
of family, memory, identity, and luck."
LORI RADER-DAY, award-winning author of *The Lucky One*

"The wonderfully talented Sandra SG Wong gives us everything a
book lover could want—brutally honest social commentary,
rich cultural details, deft psychological suspense, and often-
heartbreaking family dynamics. The result is a story that will stay with
you long after you get to the last word. I couldn't stop reading."
KELLYE GARRETT, award-winning author of *Like a Sister*

"Wong works wonders with *In the Dark We Forget*,
a gripping psychological thriller that hooks you from page one
and never relents. The characters and setting ring true in this
powerful, haunting story about family, memory, and loss."
SAM WIEBE, award-winning author of *Hell and Gone*

IN
THE
DARK
WE
FORGET

Also by SG Wong

Die on Your Feet
In for a Pound
Devil Take the Hindmost

IN THE DARK WE FORGET

A NOVEL

SANDRA SG WONG

HarperCollins*Publishers*Ltd

In the Dark We Forget
Copyright © 2022 by Epiphany EKOS Incorporated.
All rights reserved.

Published by HarperCollins Publishers Ltd

First edition

HarperCollins books may be purchased for educational, business or
sales promotional use through our Special Markets Department.

HarperCollins Publishers Ltd
Bay Adelaide Centre, East Tower
22 Adelaide Street West, 41st Floor
Toronto, Ontario, Canada
M5H 4E3

www.harpercollins.ca

For information in the U.S., please email the Special Markets Department
in the U.S. at SPsales@harpercollins.com

Library and Archives Canada Cataloguing in Publication
Title: In the dark we forget : a novel / Sandra SG Wong.
Names: Wong, Sandra SG, author. Identifiers: Canadiana (print)
20220192405 | Canadiana (ebook) 20220192413 | ISBN 9781443465564
(softcover) | ISBN 9781443465571 (ebook)
Classification: LCC PS8645.O464 I52 2022 | DDC C813/.6—dc23

ISBN 978-1-4434-6556-4 (Canada) | ISBN 978-1-4434-6604-2 (U.S.)

Printed and bound in the United States of America

LSC/H 9 8 7 6 5 4 3 2 1

For Kevin, my always

ONE

I awake with a shiver. Full on, from toes to the tingling roots in my scalp.

Sharp corners dig into my shoulders, down the length of my spine, underneath one set of ribs. My feet twitch. I feel the backs of my shoes slip on something wet.

Shoes. Why am I wearing shoes while I sleep?

I push up on my elbows, can't hold myself up, fall back with a thump onto those sharp corners again. I blink up at a murky sky. My head aches, like I've taken a chill. I hear a soft rustling of leaves, a lone chirping bird. My ears are cold. A slight breeze blows grit into my cheek. My eyes widen. Why am I outside?

This time, I roll to hands and knees first, then push up to kneeling. Those sharp rocks now dig into my palms. My knees hurt, like they're bruised, deep. I catalogue stiffness and aching all over—my body like a muscle stretched too far, now snapped back. I rest my hands on my thighs, stare down at them while I catch my breath. Too dark. I lift them up, close to my eyes. I don't know what I'm looking for. A few more chirping birds join the first. I scan the dimness around me. The sky seems lighter to my left.

The skin at the nape of my neck tightens into gooseflesh. I turn, slowly, feeling a weight on my back. A black silhouette rises impossibly high. A mountain. Scratch that. A mountain *range*. Peaks and long angular lines run as far as my incredulous eyes want to look. A thick forest of tall trees skirts its base, dark and impenetrable. The shiver returns as I stare into the depths of the darkness. How silently it would swallow me whole.

I pull my gaze back to the ground around me. No tent. No campfire ring. No sleeping bag. So . . . I'm not camping. A slope in front of me, heading upward. It looks green . . . ish. I check the sky to my left again. Is this dawn? I push to my feet, wincing at the sharp pain in my shins, brushing off dew from the slippery fabric of my pants. My seat doesn't feel damp. Just cold. I rub my arms, encased in a similar slippery, light-weight fabric. I unzip just enough to feel the two layers of (cotton?) shirts beneath. At least I dressed for a night out of doors . . . I guess. I don't understand this. How am I here? Where is here? What—

I scramble up the slope, slipping a few times on the damp grass, desperate to do something. My head is suddenly pounding, my mouth foul and gummy. The grass beneath my feet gives way to gravel and asphalt. Two paved lanes on either side of a faded yellow line stretch away from me, left and right. East and west, then, judging by the rising light of the sky. I hold my face, willing the cold of my hands to seep down into my chest, slow my racing heart. Should I recognize this place? I should. I must. I got here somehow . . . right?

I stare down the dark road, first one way then the other. The sun may be rising, but it's mostly behind the enormous mountains that seem to cut off the left end of the long ribbon of highway. I strain my ears. Birdsong, louder and more insistent now. More leaves rustling in a light breeze. A pressing silence in between.

A shudder runs through me, uncontrollable. My toes curl painfully inside my shoes. My mouth fills with saliva. I swallow several times. My guts twist a second before I bend over abruptly and heave. Nothing but a thin stream of bile and spit. I stand, knees apart, propping myself up with my hands, panting like a sick dog, and stare at the slick patch of vomit on the asphalt in front of my battered running shoes.

Walking. I should be walking. Somewhere. I need to move. I need to find help. Need to get away. My skin pebbles with goosebumps, the hairs standing on end. I swivel my head every which way, trying to pinpoint where this sudden foreboding is coming from.

There's nothing. Nothing and no one.

Clumsily, I wipe my mouth, my chin, my cheeks, then scrub my sleeve on the dewy grass. I scrub my fingers along my scalp, trying to get rid of the sensation of ants, feel the pull of a ponytail, gone loose now, the elastic pulled almost to the end. I undo the tail fully, tearing out strands in my haste. Hair past my shoulders, heavy, sweeping along the synthetic shell I'm wearing. I pull it all back into a tight bundle, secure it with the elastic, put in a few twists, tuck in the ends. I feel something like familiarity as I tap the bun riding high at the back of my head. It loosens suddenly, slipping through my fingertips. I redo it all into a loose bun at the nape of my neck instead, grasping at the small bit of comfort from how normal it feels.

I stare again down the still-empty highway, fighting the distress just behind the insistent thud of a worsening headache. A wave of fatigue hits me. I blink against the rush of pressure behind my eyes. My brain fills again, this time with questions. Where am I? How did I end up here? Why is this happening?

I scour my memory for any hint of a clue, find nothing but a thick blankness, shot through with threads of unease. Chest tight, I pat at my pockets, fumble stiff hands inside, come up empty. No phone, no wallet.

How do I get home with no money? Oh God, I don't even know where home is. I close my eyes, prodding at the blackness in my head for an address . . . an image of a house . . . anything, a bill, or a . . . or a driver's licence—

Sweet Jesus. I don't know what I look like. *I don't know my name.* Frantic, I spin on my heel, my gaze everywhere, hummingbird-like, as though a name might be darting just past my field of view, if only I could snatch it, quickly, before it disappears.

I'm panting again. My stomach flutters. I press a hand against my abdomen, take slow, deep breaths, grimace at the smell of my breath in the morning air.

Who the hell am I?

No, stop it. I need . . . I need to be in motion. I know precious little right now, but—damned if I'm going to stand here, waiting for someone else to save me.

Ignoring the trembling of my limbs, I turn myself away from the bright sky. I put one foot in front of the other, toward the still-grey west.

TWO

"Hi, um, can I speak to someone please? I need help."

My eyes can't seem to stay on any one thing, jumping from the plastic-framed glasses perched on the receptionist's nose to her grey-blond hair to the round, gem-encrusted brooch winking from her sweater. I feel the strain of shoulders hunched too long, try to straighten myself up, but it's hard to overcome the sense of foreboding.

The white woman behind the counter blinks, then looks past my shoulder before returning her gaze to me.

"What's the nature of your problem? Once I have that, I can get the appropriate help." Her voice is pleasant and soothing, a contrast to her pursed lips and cool, pale gaze.

I hesitate, pushing aside my wobbly fatigue. What choice do I really have here? I need the police to help me. I think I may need them to . . . protect me. From who, I don't know, but I get the sense it doesn't matter if I know. That feeling of being unsafe . . . it's not going away. That sends a shiver through me, though I try to hide it with a grimace. I just . . . I hate the thought of displaying weakness to this woman. Anyone can tell from looking she's not inclined to help. She has a judgment about me, I can feel it, like cobwebs against my face. I just don't know if I can afford to care. I grit my teeth for a second, then dive in.

"I woke up at the side of the highway and I have no idea how I got there." She raises one light-brown eyebrow. I take a deep breath, finish the rest. "Also, I don't remember who I am."

Even seated, she manages to give the impression of looking down her nose at me. I resist the urge to straighten up. I don't need to *impress* her, for chrissake. As if to remind me it'd be a long shot anyway, all the aches in my body throb in unison. Another full-body shudder. The pain reminds me what I have to lose if she throws me out on my sorry ass. I wrap my hands around myself, trying to warm up from the chill of being on my own against—

From behind me, my good Samaritan steps up. She places a long-fingered hand, tipped with immaculate bedazzled purple nails, on the desk's edge. "I saw her just outside of Field, walking on the Number 1. We all know that's not a safe place for a woman alone." A short pause. "She looked safe enough, so I stopped. Then she told me her story." Another pause. "What there is of it, I mean. So I brought her straight here."

"And you are?" The receptionist's expression remains coolly judgmental as she tips her head up, looking through the bottom half of her glasses.

"Thea Halford. I live here. In Golden, I mean. I was coming back from Lake Louise. Worked a bachelor party." She rattles off an address, tossing her sleek dark ponytail. "Do you need my ID or something?"

The receptionist puts up a hand. "Let me start a file and capture all this. Then I'll call a constable, okay?"

Thea pats my shoulder. "It's gonna be all right."

"Thanks." The skin around my eyes feels tight. I manage a shaky whisper. "I hope so."

Despite her aloofness, or maybe because of it, the receptionist is fast and efficient. I tell her everything I can, which accounts for the fast part. Thea is patient and articulate, breezily forthcoming with her personal info, and the fact that she's a stripper. My gaze flicks between Thea and the older woman. I note the way the receptionist speaks to Thea in clipped tones, her mouth downturned. But Thea only appears amused, her expression just this side of a smirk.

My chest constricts suddenly, goosing my heart rate, pumping blood in a roaring wave that buzzes in my ears. I survey the waiting area again with a jerky gaze, see the same empty hard-plastic seats as I did minutes ago. Dread creeps up my spine as I stare at the sliding entry doors, replacing the roar in my head with the static of growing panic. Oh God. Will it be . . . now? Or . . . *now?* The doors, Jesus, the doors. Anyone can stroll right in. Any stranger. Or worse—someone who knows me, someone who did this to—

I force several deep breaths, gripping the counter with clumsy fingers. I focus on my gratitude for Thea's kindness this morning, on her refusal to let the receptionist's attitude needle her. I focus on the fact that I'm inside, at a police station. I'm not alone. I repeat that to myself as many times as it takes while the receptionist types rapid-fire into her computer. She then dismisses Thea with curt instructions that a constable will likely be in contact.

Thea sweetly requests a blank piece of paper. She writes out her phone number and address, finishing her name with a flourish. I find myself surprised at Thea's beautiful penmanship. I turn my face away, hiding my flush of shame. I'm no better than the receptionist, with her blatant disdain.

Thea folds the paper into a perfect square, hands it over with a genuine smile. "Promise you'll contact me as soon as you figure it all out. Write, call, text, I don't care. Just let me know, okay?" She holds onto the paper, her dark eyes intent, until I give my word. We part with a hug. Thea squeezes my hand and wishes me luck.

I watch her leave the RCMP detachment building, then turn back to the woman at reception. She's not wearing a uniform and there's no nameplate for reference. Her chilly demeanour doesn't invite questions. And there's no one else in the waiting area to talk to. Not that I would.

Shoulders hunched again, I move to sit far from the door, next to a fern of some kind in a bright blue ceramic floor planter. I rotate the square of paper in my hands over and over and over again, handling it by the corners. The receptionist stands, ignoring me, to move to a printer farther back behind the desk. Pocketing the paper square, I grip the sides of my seat, swing my feet back and forth, trying to burn off my jumpiness. The tips of my shoes barely scrape the heavy-duty linoleum floor. I stop when my knees twinge sharply all of a sudden, leaving me breathless from the pain.

A door opens to the right of the reception area. A Japanese Canadian woman steps out. There's no mistaking her position. Thick-soled boots, trousers with the stripe up the sides, green-grey shirt, full duty belt. She holds out her hand. I take a breath and stand, stumbling a bit as my toe catches. I have to crane my neck back a bit to look at her face properly.

"I'm Constable Naomi Aoki. Lenore's started a file on your situation, and I'm here to help you fill in some of the gaps if I can." Her handshake is firm, dry.

I stare at her gun in its holster.

"Right now, I'm going to take you to the hospital and get some tests run. You need to be examined for injuries and sexual assault." Aoki's voice is low and no-nonsense. "Do you feel any bruising? As though you've been assaulted?"

I feel the blood drain from my face. "No." I swallow. "I . . . No."

Aoki nods. "All right. A nurse and maybe a doctor will examine you, gently. But if they believe something's happened and they advise the full sexual assault exam, it's best if you agree." She pauses. "I also advise a drug screen in addition to the physical exam, miss. Your amnesia could be drug-related."

Frowning, I say, "I know I might not be the best judge right now, but I don't think I'm a drug addict."

Aoki nods, once. "What I mean is, let's get the drug screen done and see if it can help us determine why you've lost your memory. They'll draw a little blood and analyze it at the hospital. They'll have a form for you to sign—consent to have your exam and test results shared with us."

I open my mouth. Aoki nods, gestures with a hand, stalling my question.

"We'll have the hospital people witness, since you'll have to be a Jane Doe for now." She ducks her head slightly, maybe to put her eyes level with mine. "And I'll be at your side at the hospital, wherever you want me. You won't have to do this alone. All right?"

I notice my hands are aching. I look down. My fists press tightly against my thighs. I force them to relax, open up. I watch the crescent marks on my palms going from white to an angry pink, darkening to red indentations in my dry skin. I suppose I should be grateful for short nails.

I breathe out slowly, meet her determined grey gaze with what I hope is a show of confidence. "Let's go."

The hospital is a short drive in a buffed, shiny RCMP truck. Aoki takes me through Emergency, and it's all a blur from there. Forms and questions. Signatures and witnesses. Needles and vials and cool, searching hands encased in latex. Drawn curtains and the illusion of privacy. I answer as truthfully as I'm able. The nurse leaves a lot of blanks on the forms. Through it all, Aoki keeps her promise, her tall shadow against the curtains a steadying presence.

In the end, the full sexual assault test isn't necessary, just some awkward minutes on my back, atop an exam table with my heels in grey plastic stirrups while the Filipina nurse makes a visual assessment. But serious bruising on both knees and my left shin. Deep black-purple swells, speckled red. Like I banged them against something really hard. Added to the soreness in my arms, shoulders, and back, the nurse wonders in a murmur if I got in a fight. The doctor, a slender brown man, finds a tender spot behind my left temple, too. He jokes they won't have to shave my head, at least. I feel stupid for laughing as soon as it's out of my mouth. I take the offered pain meds, averting my gaze.

Sobering, the doctor warns me I might also be in for some nightmares as my brain works to put me back together. Once he leaves, the nurse touches me gently on the shoulder, asks if I'd like to clean up a bit. Handing me a rough towel and an individually wrapped toothbrush, she leads me to a nearby restroom. I can't change clothes, but I do scrub all my grimiest bits, using the coldest water I can stand. I discover the toothbrush comes prepped with a harsh mint toothpaste. It burns a little in my mouth, making my eyes water.

When I exit, the same nurse tells me she hopes I get what I need to heal. I thank her and clumsily hand over the damp, dirt-streaked towel. Far from a fair trade for her unexpected kindness, but it's all I have.

Aoki grabs us coffee as we wait for the blood-work results. I take a sip, swallow with difficulty. It's burned and overly sweetened. I force myself to finish, if only to distract from the unpredictable, frightening bustle of so many strangers surrounding me. I pull my legs up onto my chair, settling my feet flat on the seat. When a nurse arrives to hand over a single sheet of paper, he immediately shuffles me off to a staff therapist, an Indigenous woman with a sharp gaze. It's a quick consult, no-nonsense questions, some discussion of the test results, and an off-hand caution.

I find Aoki finishing a phone call in the hallway as I exit the therapist's small office. I thrust the sheet of test results at her.

"Rohypnol." Aoki's expression turns grim. "Drug of choice for rapists. Causes short-term memory loss." She looks at me sidelong as I drop into a chair along the wall.

I grimace at the bitter taste in my mouth, fight the urge to vomit, silently curse the burned coffee from earlier. "I'm sure I wasn't raped." It comes out a rough whisper.

Scanning the corridor, Aoki gives a curt nod. "You'd be the best judge of that, for sure. You gotta—" She breaks off, pinning her gaze on a white man in street clothes as he passes, dragging a shaky hand across his haggard face, oblivious to her scrutiny. "You should trust your body and what it tells you." She sits next to me.

I feel unwanted tears prickling the skin around my eyes. I stare at the floor, blinking back panic as though it were only salt tears. "Am I . . . in danger? Someone did this to me? That's what this means?" I tighten my hands into fists to stop the trembling. "What do I do? Where do I go?"

Aoki straightens her shoulders. "For now, back to the detachment. I'll see how long I can keep your file."

"I'd like that," I say, words tumbling out without time for careful consideration. "I didn't exactly have any expectations, I mean, I didn't think I did, not until I saw you come out and I realized I felt . . . relief." I shrug, awkward. "Guess I was expecting some big strapping white guy. Or something."

Aoki quirks her lips, just a little. "You're not the first person to say so." She pauses. "Not even to my face."

I cock my head to one side. "It's weird that I don't remember my name or anything about my life, but I know somehow that another Asian woman will take me seriously better than a white man will."

Aoki's gaze sharpens. "Did you *know* you were Asian? I mean, without thinking about it? Without seeing your reflection somewhere?"

I stare at her. "I just . . . knew." I comb what little there is of my memory. "I just thought, when Thea's car pulled to a stop ahead of me this morning, on the side of the highway, I thought, *I hope it's a woman,* and I knew I'd look safe to her since I was Chinese." My eyes widen as I realize what I just said. "I'm Chinese."

"Do you know any Mandarin? Or Cantonese? Um, maybe Taiwanese? Or, uh, Fukienese, even?"

I gape at her, brain suddenly on whiteout, digging for a reply.

Aoki puts her hands up, palms facing out. "Sorry, that was rude." I see kindness behind her joking expression. "I should know better than to ask that of any Asian Canadian. It's a sore spot for a lot of us, eh, the *mother tongue,* yada yada."

I blink at the taste of truth in that. I push aside the unease that follows.

Aoki looks intent again, all joking done. "Don't worry about it. I know this is difficult, and you'll be hearing it a lot, but something's sure to come back. You just have to be patient."

I give a short laugh. It sounds like a bark. "I don't think you're supposed to say that. Shouldn't give the patient false hope." I hear the bleakness in my voice.

"Not that I should ask." Aoki pauses. "Is that what the hospital psychiatrist said?"

I swallow instead of spitting. "Don't get my hopes up too high. Some people never recover their memories. But I might experience potentially disturbing and confusing flashbacks. It's not exactly a science." I think back. "She said my amnesia is . . . unusual. If the . . . Rohypnol caused it, then it should look a different way. Like you said. Short-term. Not this gaping emptiness—but, I still *know* things, random things about how stuff works." I pause, guts roiling coldly. "It looks like the only thing I don't remember is who I am or how I ended up on the side of the Trans-Canada." I press my lips together, tight, and remind myself Aoki's virtually a stranger. It's her job to help. Doesn't mean I should tell her everything I'm afraid of. I chafe my arms, glancing up and down the hallway.

"Well." Aoki gathers herself to stand. "Let's get started on what we *can* do, okay?"

Back at the RCMP detachment, I get fingerprinted. Another surprise: it's all electronic. No ink or stamp pads. I blush when I realize I was expecting a black ink pad. Maybe I watched too many TV cop shows as a kid.

Aoki runs the freshly scanned prints. "Well, you're not a criminal."

"Awkward otherwise, right?"

She allows a small smile, barely a twitch of her lips.

Another database. Another search. "Not a Missing Person either."

I rub at my sternum. "So that means . . . no one's looking for me." I try to blink away the stinging in my eyes. I breathe carefully past a sudden panic pushing up against my diaphragm. "Could we—" I swallow, try again. "I want to look for the place I woke up. Can we do that? Now?"

"If you're sure you're up to it. I was hoping we could get a start on that." Aoki checks the wall clock, an old-fashioned analog with multiple hands. "Are you hungry? Why don't we grab something from the Tim's on our way out?"

I suppose it's a sign I know where she means. I wish I knew good or bad.

THREE

Where do I go afterward? How are you or the hospital going to keep tabs on me? I mean, *I* don't even know where I'll be."

"That's probably in our favour right now. We don't know enough about the situation, but we need to keep you safe."

Aoki merges the truck smoothly onto the highway. I hear the tires rolling over asphalt underneath, the sound of air whistling past. The sun shines bright and strong, past its zenith now. There's a rattle just behind me, but I can't place what it is. I sip my warm tea. Too many tannins or something. So bitter.

Or maybe it's just me. I replace the tea in the cup holder. Should've asked for cold water.

"I'll ask Lenore to contact a few of the churches, find you a safe place to stay overnight. They're good like that." She glances at me. "Non-denominational, if you want."

I shrug. "Sounds fine. Do I have to stay there, whatever charity billet you dump me? So you can reach me by phone or whatever?"

Aoki gives me a sidelong look.

"Sorry. I sound like a snotty teenager." I crumple the takeout bag on my lap, compressing the remains of a bland turkey sandwich into a tight ball.

"Are you all right?"

"I guess?" I throw my hands up. "I don't even know. I should just be grateful I'm fine. Just some bumps and bruises, right?" I sink back into the seat.

"You change your mind, we can skip it. Head right back to town. No problem."

I stare out at the brilliant landscape unfolding around us. There are precisely two white fluffy clouds in the stunning blue of the sky. The mountains are as massive as they've been for the past millennia, impassive and aloof.

I open the window, feel a sharp wind. The rattling behind me intensifies. I give myself three deep breaths of cool, fresh air. I depress the window button again. My ears pop slightly as the air pressure inside the truck readjusts.

"Just nervous, I guess. Sorry." I press back the stray hairs around my face, redo my ponytail, remind myself of my manners.

Aoki remains silent for a few more kilometres. "Nothing to apologize for. However you deal with this. Everyone's different, and you're entitled to freak out or not freak out." I can see her hesitate. "Just know we're here to help best we can."

I watch the kilometres roll past in an undulating sea of plant life. Trees, flowers, grasses, weeds, shrubs. And undoubtedly, animals invisible to my ignorant eyes. The highway twists, ascending and descending through the rock and dirt and thousands of hectares of trees. I try to envision the toil taken to break this trail. . . .

I can't. It's literally unimaginable to me. Who takes a look at these mountains and thinks, *Yeah, we can cut a railroad through that.* I mean, I can imagine someone thinking they want to climb up and over. They want to see how far they can push themselves. They want to explore. They want to migrate westward. But to believe you can make your mark with thousands of kilometres of steel and other people's blood. That's just . . . unbelievably . . . arrogant.

I shake off the distraction, tap my to-go cup. "Hey, uh, I'm not sure I'd know exactly where I . . . woke up."

Deciding against more bitter tea, I sandwich my hands between my knees, but I only end up reawakening the pain from the deep bruising.

Aoki gives a short nod. "I'm estimating from Ms. Halford's statement. We'll pinpoint it best we can once we're closer."

She's good as her word. We slow down maybe ten minutes past Field, lying alongside a CN train station on the south side of the highway. The town is so tiny, I think I could count its streets and buildings from here, if I wanted to. I can't tell if the train station's still in use. As we continue eastward, I spy an access road off the north side of the highway, heading east along the foot of one of the mountains. It must lead upward. There's nowhere else to go. I squint at the small sign at the intersection. *Yoho-something-something. Road,* perhaps?

"Ms. Halford said she picked you up at about seven o'clock this morning from the north shoulder around Yoho Valley Road. She said she was driving west. Did you cross the highway before you started walking west?"

I shake my head. "I remember passing Field in the car with her, but I can't say. . . ." My attention catches on a curled piece of shredded rubber laid out on the left shoulder of the highway. I point it out as we pass. "I think I walked past that. I remember wondering how big the truck must've been." I remember I checked over my shoulder, too, nervous all over again about walking with my back to high-speed traffic.

The Trans-Canada Highway leads on, clear of any roadside turnouts for as far as I can see. Aoki checks her rear-view mirror, pulls over onto a generous patch of shoulder to let a stream of cars roar past. We resume our comparative crawl.

We pass a sign for an outdoor exhibit overlooking a deep, dark green valley to the left.

"Did you walk past this?" asks Aoki. "Lower Spiral Tunnel viewpoint."

I nod. "Used the facilities." I consider. "Where I woke up . . . it's flatter. Not the side of the mountain, like this. I was in a, like a shallow dip. I had to climb up a little before I even saw the highway."

We pull over, allowing a few cars to pass, then continue round a very slight bend.

My scalp tingles again, like ants all over it. I straighten up abruptly, the seatbelt pulling against my collarbone.

Aoki flicks a glance at me. She slows, aiming the truck toward the shoulder, checks the highway in both directions, then makes a smooth U-turn.

I find my voice. "How far is this from where I got a ride?"

"We're about ten klicks east of Field." Aoki turns off the engine. "Let me go first, okay? I'll signal when you can come out, too." Seeing my alarm, she says, "I don't think it's dangerous, but I'm cautious by nature."

She gets out, scanning our surroundings carefully, her hand at ease at her side, close to the pistol in its holster. I want to curl my legs up onto the seat. I settle for undoing my seatbelt and rubbing the tops of my thighs to dry my palms. I watch as Aoki steps away from the truck and slowly circles around the rear. She ends up outside my door, gives me a shallow nod. She steps just far enough away to allow the door to open.

The air smells of pine cones and hot grass. Now that we're not encased in the coolness of the AC, I can feel the full afternoon sun on my head.

I leave my jacket on the passenger seat. I hear the click of a camera, look over to see Aoki with her phone in hand.

"Getting a screencap of the coordinates." Aoki slides her phone into a pocket. She opens the small door behind me to grab her official cap.

"Are we supposed to be doing this?" I swallow. "Alone, I mean? Like, aren't you supposed to get a crime scene team or something for this?"

"We need to find where you woke up first." Aoki rounds the hood of the truck, fitting her hat on snugly, her lips quirked up a little. "I get some leeway since I'm the constable who started your file." Her expression sobers. "Since the tests found Rohypnol, and you were apparently physically assaulted, this is definitely a criminal offence file. It'll go to Serious Crimes, out of Kelowna. But I'm here now and I can gather some evidence, so that's what we're going to do." She looks at my face. "Don't worry. It's not like in the movies. There's no jurisdictional fighting or anything like that. We just want to do the best we can for you. Whoever's in charge of the file."

Aoki pauses to assess me again. "Are you ready to take a closer look around? I'm going to stick right next to you."

I nod, my mouth abruptly dry. I run my tongue over roughened lips.

Turning, I face the mountainside. It's not a huge bit of land between me and the dark evergreens that skirt the foot of the mountain. But it's not tiny either. How am I supposed to find the spot again?

"Take your time," says Aoki. I glance at her. She looks back at me, bland. "The spot's not going anywhere."

Right. I look down. There's a very slight dip downward leading from the gravel toward the trees. Too shallow. I pivot and walk east along the shoulder until I find more of a slope. Is this it? I squint farther eastward, down the line of the highway shoulder. Is *that*? How am I supposed to distinguish one patch of grass from another?

I feel my shirt sticking to me, at armpits and the small of my back. My head feels too light. Everything hurts. A spear of light strikes my left eye and I slap a hand to cover it. Flashes of disjointed things bomb my brain. Blackness and screaming, terror, anger, despair—

I gulp in air, mouthfuls and mouthfuls, like I've been drowning. I feel tears against my palm and uncover my face. My eyes dart every which way, searching for what, I have no idea.

"Hey, it's okay. You're okay." Aoki hovers next to me, careful not to touch me, her palms facing me.

My hands are trembling. This is useless. *I'm* useless.

"No, no you're not."

"Jesus, did I say that out loud?" Hearing the tremor in my voice, I wrap my hands around my shoulders, squeezing tight.

"It's natural to have flashbacks or to feel panicked. Just . . . take as long as you need." Aoki's tone is level and calm, her face kind. "Then we'll start again. Whenever you're ready. We don't need exact coordinates. Just an idea of a search area. Somewhere to start."

I clench my hands into fists, rest them against my forehead. All right. I can do this. Another deep breath, this one maybe a little less shaky. I let my hands fall to my side, flick them to dispel the lingering panic. I try for levity. "Well, I did throw up on the side of the highway, once I climbed up and started to freak out. But yeah," I gesture vaguely at land and sky, "that's not gonna be a reliable marker now." A thought bubbles up through my shame. "I can't have walked that far, right? Before Thea—Ms. Halford—picked me up. And I know the sun was just rising." I look up at Aoki again. "What time was dawn?"

"About six, give or take."

"So, is this a reasonable distance for me to have walked?"

Aoki taps at her phone, snaps another screenshot. "Yeah, I'd say so."

We spend another few minutes walking back and forth along the highway shoulder. Despite my embarrassment, I look for a patch of gravel with the contents of my stomach still on it. No go. It's been hours after all, and it's a sunny day. Aoki makes some notes for herself. We get back into the truck. She hands me a bottle of water from a cooler behind her seat.

On the ride back, she explains next steps. Serious Crimes, higher-ups, investigators. I don't have anything to say. I wonder if I'll end up with the strapping white RCMP officers of my imagining after all. I rub my temples. That sounds wrong, even in my head.

We pass the Lower Spiral Tunnel viewpoint again. It was still cool when I stopped there earlier in the morning. I remember shivering inside the smelly facilities, then rubbing my hands with a triple dose of hand sanitizer as I skimmed the outdoor exhibit. Tired, I read the signage and peered at the facing wall of tree-clad mountainside, trying to find the tunnels, playing at tourist while I fought off another stomach-churning wave of panic.

I realize now how right I was when I told Aoki I "just knew" my heritage. Earlier this morning, I searched the exhibit text and the scattering of contemporaneous camp photos for any mention of the Chinese men sent in to fire the dynamite, their lives considered disposable by the white overseers and engineers tasked with carving a figure-eight of tunnels into these daunting mountains and, really, across this whole country. And I remember I wasn't surprised when I failed to find a single image of any Chinese labourers, not even unidentified ones.

I suppose expendable people don't get names.

FOUR

Back in Golden, I hesitate before exiting the truck.

Aoki stops with her hand on her door handle. "Feeling okay?"

I stare through the windshield at the dark brown siding on the RCMP building, the darkish green roofing, the flags hanging motionless on the pole. The pale yellow stone cladding the bottom half of the building looks like it has minerals embedded in it. I frown as I move my gaze over it, puzzling at the play of sunlight. "Is your detachment *sparkling*? Or am I seeing things?"

Aoki lets out a laugh. "It's the minerals and the little fossils in it. I mean, that's what I've been told. Apparently, it's a big deal, don't ask me why." She looks at me, her smile fading. "You all right?"

"Not sure how I'm supposed to answer that. I don't know my name, where I live, how much money I have in the bank, how I got here, if anyone's missing me...."

The truck's engine ticks, trying to cool itself down in the afternoon heat.

"Not that you've asked me." Aoki turns slightly to face me. "But you're handling it all remarkably well, given your situation." She pauses.

I keep my gaze fixed on the ugly building. "In my experience, people hate uncertainty. Your circumstances are the very definition. It's like that saying *There but for the grace of God.* Do you know it?"

I press my finger against my temple, shake my head.

"Sorry," says Aoki. "Thoughtless."

"But I can guess. Better me than them?"

She nods. "*Everyone's* going to be asking how you're doing. Either they genuinely care about your well-being or they're curious how you're handling it or they're gaining some weird satisfaction that it's not their problem."

"Or some combination." I resist the urge to clutch my stomach. "I'd better get used to it, in other words."

"And that's just normal people. I'm not even talking about the press or social media. Once they get a sniff of this, they're going to be all over you. They'll have your face plastered all over the internet, which might be a good thing, but they'll also spin your story whatever way they want." She stops abruptly, her intense expression flattening out. "I'm sorry. That was uncalled for. Probably overwhelming, too." She settles back. I hear the scrape of something hard against the black fabric of her seat.

"You're trying to help me, right?"

My deadpan tone startles a grin out of her.

"Yeah, in my clumsy, ham-handed way." She runs a hand through her short hair, leaving parts sticking straight up.

I swipe at my hairline, pull my hair up off my neck, and tie it up high.

Aoki takes a breath. "Okay, it's like this. It's not just the press I'm thinking of. I don't know everyone out of Kelowna detachment, but I do know there aren't any Asian women there. Outside of the Lower Mainland, it's just me out here."

I work through what she's *not* saying. "And you think whoever they send from higher up, they'll treat me a certain way. Like, they won't help me or something?"

She cocks an eyebrow. "Once any of those big strapping lads gets one look at pretty little Chinese you, they'll be falling all over themselves to help you. I mean, even *I* feel protective, and I should know better than to jump to conclusions." She speaks over my sputtering. "No, I mean it. They're conditioned to see us as vulnerable and helpless, right? That's how Asian women get . . . fetishized in our society. Demure and meek and all that. Me being five-eleven and broad-shouldered messes people up, every time. You know what I'm talking about at some level, even if you're not conscious of it. You said it yourself, earlier. You knew I'd pay better attention to what you have to say."

Her gaze sharpens. "So, I'm gonna say this, just between us, because I think . . . I think you need to know someone's in your corner. Someone who knows what it's like to be Asian in this country, and to be forced to depend on people who might not understand our different cultural nuances." She pauses, mutters, "I'm probably breaking some unspoken cop code or whatever by saying this." On a huff of breath, she continues, "I have to hand over your file now. I have no choice. But it's not that I don't trust they'll do their best for you. I do, completely. It's that I want to make sure you can advocate for yourself. Don't let them stonewall you for your own good or some crap. You don't have to slap them upside the head or anything. Just . . . let 'em know you can handle yourself. You don't need them to protect you from the truth."

Unease stirs in my gut.

She fishes a business card out of a shirt pocket, then a pen from the glove compartment. "Here. I'm putting my cell phone on here. You can reach me anytime. I won't step on anyone's toes, and especially not Serious Crimes, but I'm happy to listen to whatever you have to tell me, okay?"

I give her a quick nod, queasiness making me clamp my lips tight together, rendering me speechless.

Dawn again. My second in this limbo. A creeping sense of foreboding prods me out of my borrowed bed. I wash as quickly and quietly as I can, put on yesterday's clothes. My only clothes, now laundered and left folded for me atop the hamper in the guest bathroom. Pastor Susan's home is beautiful, and I stop for a moment at the wall of tall windows, staring at the fingers of sunlight behind the mountains.

I find Pastor Susan in her kitchen, her short grey hair curling damply around her ears and the nape of her neck. She turns as I enter, light flashing off her silver wire-rimmed glasses. "Good morning. Good sleep?"

"Morning. Yes, thanks." I inhale deeply to paper over the lie. "That doesn't smell like instant."

She smiles, her lined face softening. "That's because I keep the good stuff to myself. Fair trade Guatemalan. I buy the beans whole, grind them fresh before brewing."

I approach the counter, the terracotta tiles cool under my socks. "What can I make you for breakfast?"

Susan gestures with a hand. "As if. No, you're my guest."

"In other words, nobody messes with your kitchen." I hold up my hands. "I get it. I was just being polite." The coffee maker gurgles on the counter.

"Be polite by sitting down, enjoying this gorgeous coffee, and keeping me company while I cook. Scrambled eggs, toast, and fruit okay?"

"Sounds great. I can wash and cut up the fruit."

She gives me a look.

"Just trying to earn my keep."

"Maybe this is your chance to accept help. Gracefully."

"Am I allowed to fetch my own mug?"

"I see you're a lover of sarcasm."

I can't help the grin. I fill a mug that says *Cup-o-Heaven* on it, pre-empting the old coffee maker while the pot is still only half-full.

"Cream and sugar?"

I take a sip. Scalding. I shake my head. "It's divine. Er, sorry."

Susan chuckles. "No worries. I'm not Evangelical."

I smile, uncertain.

"Never mind. Inside joke."

Susan pours her own coffee, drinks it as she makes our food. She seems wholly unselfconscious about me watching her.

"What's on your agenda today?" she asks.

I take another sip. Not scalding anymore. Just this side of hot. "Actually, I should be asking you the same thing."

"You need a ride somewhere?"

I hesitate, then nod. "Back over by Field. Past it, actually. I want to take another look at, uh, at the place I woke up yesterday."

Susan pauses over the pan, her spatula hovering above the eggs. She looks over at me, then goes back to cooking. Her tone unchanged, she asks me to fetch cutlery and the fruit bowl. Toast, eggs, hot sauce, apples, bananas, and oranges. Salt and pepper. The table is ready. She motions for me to start eating before she replies.

"I'm sorry. I can't do that." She watches my face. "I'm happy to take you back to the detachment, though, like we agreed. Ten o'clock."

"Of course. Thanks."

The fluffy eggs turn to chalk in my mouth. Is this what charity tastes like? I shift in my seat, trying to escape the chafing inside me. Is this what'll happen if I never remember anything? What if I never discover where I'm from or who my family are? Will I have to rely on the whims of others for the rest of my life?

Susan clears her throat delicately. "Please understand. I want to help. I just don't think I ought to get mixed up in police business. Surely the RCMP are searching the area. What if we mess something up?"

"No, of course not. I understand. A ride to the detachment will be great." I finish my coffee, tasting a slight edge of bitterness. I get up for more, tipping in a little cream to smooth out the hidden sharpness.

After breakfast, after I wipe the table of crumbs, I excuse myself to go for a walk.

Susan eyes me silently as she finishes washing the frypan. I watch her careful hands, sturdy and strong. "I'm guessing," she says, "since Naomi popped by, plus we had a car sat out front most of the night, that it would be better if you stayed in. Until it's time to drop you at the RCMP."

My jaw tightens. I force aside mean-spirited thoughts, replace them with the reminder that I'm here on nothing more than Susan's forbearance. I reach for a cheerful tone. "Well then, you'd better put me to work. I'm no good at sitting around."

"Are you sure?" Susan frowns slightly. "I noticed you're a little stiff, and Naomi mentioned that you'd been hurt somehow. The last thing I want is to make you worse."

I nod, determined. "It's just aches, some soreness. I'll get over it." Maybe it'll help me slough off this foul mood, too. I don't share that, though. The last thing *I* want is for Susan to start counselling me or something. It probably comes naturally for pastors. She wouldn't be able to help it, and I'd be nothing but a stone wall for her to bash against. Better I endure some discomfort. I may not know everything about myself anymore, but I know a little pain won't scare me.

FIVE

At precisely ten o'clock, I sit in the same hard plastic chair, beside the same potted plant, with arms crossed and my face screwed into a proper scowl. Lenore-no-last-name taps rapidly on her computer and shuffles some papers. After about five minutes, Aoki strides out from wherever they squirrel away constables here and introduces me to the Serious Crimes team assigned to my file.

The woman is white, blond, taller than Aoki by noticeable inches, square-shouldered, and lanky, her hair pulled back into a ponytail of curls. She smiles as she reaches out a hand, her light blue eyes warm. "Hi, I'm Inspector Shae Miller. I'm sorry it's under these circumstances, but I'm glad to meet you. How was your night?"

"Awkward." I take a moment, rub my temples, rein in my sharpness. "Pastor Susan was kind to take me in." I loosen up a little more. "And I appreciate that Constable Aoki stopped by."

Aoki gives a shallow nod. "Heard the rest of the night was quiet, too. That's good."

A dark-haired white man stops beside Miller, assessing me intently, gaze opaque, neither warm nor cold. He's somewhere between Aoki and Miller in height, but wider by a good margin. I guess by the way he holds himself that he's just as athletic as Miller seems. "Better safe than sorry, eh?" Low voice, curiously flat. Dry hand, strong grip, quick handshake.

"I guess." I stand up straighter as I reply. "I didn't notice anything, though. My guestroom is at the back of the house."

Miller pokes a thumb in his direction. "Staff Sergeant Chuck Pendelton, my partner."

Pendelton replies with a sort of low grunt. Lenore takes that moment to start signing me in. Once I'm kitted with a visitor badge, they escort me into the secrets of the building through the same door Aoki stepped through yesterday. We adjourn to a proper boardroom, with a line of windows facing a stand of dark evergreens and tall poplars across the staff parking lot. I choose one of the high-backed, padded chairs near one end of the oblong table, glad not to be crowded by their height any longer. Miller takes the end chair and Pendelton settles across from me, his dark brown eyes turning a shade deeper in this light.

Aoki sits next to me, setting down a drink. "Same order as yesterday. Hope that's okay."

Abruptly aware I'm still scowling, I flush hot. "Sorry." I smooth out my face. "Thanks." I wrap my hands around the band of cardboard halfway up the red to-go cup. "So, I guess you need to hear my story."

Miller nods. "We've read Naomi's report, but yes."

Pendelton puts a laptop on the table. Where he was hiding it, I have no idea.

"I'm going to take notes while you talk."

Something about his demeanour. I flutter between nervous and . . . something else.

Flushed, I keep my gaze on Miller. I tell them everything I told Aoki, then add in the search for where I woke up yesterday morning. Pendelton's a fast typist. Maybe he uses shorthand. He's done almost as soon as I falter to a stop.

I watch Miller watching me, her expression thoughtful. She shifts, asks Aoki something, but I don't understand the terms or codes she's using. Also, there's a roaring in my ears. It's more than just the lingering headache I woke up with after the series of disjointed nightmares. Rubbing at my temples, I say, "I want to go back. Today. I asked Pastor Susan to take me earlier this morning, but she refused." Miller stares at me, closes her mouth. "Sorry. I'm just . . . I need to *do* something."

"Hey, we understand. It must be really hard right now." I have a hard time reconciling Miller's patronizing words with the genuine warmth in her gaze. "Chuck and I wanna get the situation straight in our own heads, then we'll take you back out with us."

"Is there a . . . like, a crime scene team out there?"

Miller shows a small smile. "No, just us. But if we find something warranting techs, we'll make it happen. Okay?"

I glance at Aoki. She's wearing a serious expression, but she gives me a smile of encouragement. I focus back on Miller. "Okay." I shift farther back on the seat, my feet dangling. I sigh and pull them up, manoeuvring to sit cross-legged in the chair instead.

Once I'm settled, Pendelton clears his throat. "Let's get some of our questions out of the way first."

It's another half hour before we all stand up. I rub at the back of my neck, trying to release the tension. It's like touching a thick cord of steel. My skull feels about to burst and my throat's dry from saying essentially the same three words. *I don't remember.*

Aoki says, "This is where I get off." She offers her hand to me. "If you're staying with Pastor Susan again, I'll give you a ride there. I'm off shift at six today, but I can come get you from wherever. All right?"

"Oh, uh, okay. Thanks." I try to smile through my alarm and disappointment. She's leaving me with these two? Really?

Miller says, "We'll let you know where we're at." She and Pendelton take turns with handshakes. Aoki walks us out to the front reception area, then turns and disappears back through the door. I return my visitor's badge at reception. Lenore taps away at her keyboard, bright blue glasses settled on the bridge of her thick nose.

With a silent apology—to what or who, I don't even know—I dump the to-go cup, cold tea and all, into the waste bin next to the exterior door. I hear it land with a dull *thunk*. I put on a confident face that belies the unease in my belly as I turn to Pendelton and Miller. "Ready?"

They take me back out in their grey, four-door sedan, using Aoki's GPS readings to pinpoint my best-guess estimate. Like Aoki yesterday, they make me wait in the car until they're satisfied there's no one else lurking about. I ignore the drum of worms spinning around in my stomach as I watch them assess the far trees and passing vehicles. I clamp my jaws tight together. No way am I throwing up in front of these two.

Miller opens my door, gives me a kindly expression. "Hey, so Naomi told us about your panic attack yesterday."

I can't grit my teeth any tighter, but I try. Her gentle tone . . . like fingernails on a chalkboard.

Next comes encouragement. "So, if you need a break or some time to gather yourself, just let us know, okay? We're not here to make anything worse for you."

I manage a stiff nod as I clamber out. Lucky for me, my dignity, and my shoes, I feel much better in the fresh air. I breathe in as much as I can without getting light-headed. I grab a bottle of water from the back of the car. "I'm ready."

They let me help them walk the wide expanse of heated grass, Miller carefully spacing us out by arms-widths so we cover as much ground as possible. We walk at a slow, measured pace, our eyes scouring the earth in front of us.

We repeat this five times, back and forth, switching places, moving slowly eastward from our starting point. Nothing but grass and rocks, weeds, flowers, and bits of tree. At least the ground is fairly flat and clear, all things considered. I'm surprised there's not more trash.

Everyone gets water back at the car on the highway's shoulder. I finish my bottle, start on a new one. Miller has us repeat the walking pattern, heading west instead. By the time Miller calls a final stop, my stomach is growling and my shoulders are tight from expecting another flashback that doesn't come.

Miller eyes me for a moment. "How're you holding up?"

"Thirsty. Hot. Hungry." I gesture with my empty water bottle. "Grateful you brought a cooler." I swipe my forehead with a cuff, scrub at the back of my neck. "So, you're sure it's okay for me to do this with you? I'm not gonna mess up evidence or whatever?"

Pendelton shifts. Miller grins. "Not entirely. But I'm willing to take the flak for it. You're our best lead. *Your* best lead. Why wouldn't we take advantage of that?"

I bump the empty water bottle against my leg, listening to its hollow impact as I watch a big semi heading westward. I realize I can see it before I hear it. A neat trick of the topography, I suppose.

I ask Miller, "So, what's farther east?"

"Lake Louise. Then the whole Banff area. A bit farther north is Jasper. All in Alberta."

Pendelton says, "We're in Yoho National Park. That's the BC side. Banff National Park starts as soon as you cross the border into Alberta."

He pauses. "Just names, though. The mountains and trees don't change."

I pivot to face west again. "So, from here, it's Field, Golden—and then?"

"Glacier National Park. Next biggish town would be Revelstoke. Sicamous is right on the Shuswap. That's a lake. And a provincial park." Pendelton shrugs. "Eventually, you hit Kelowna. Where we're stationed."

Miller watches me, expression thoughtful. "What are you thinking?"

"Just hoping something would sound familiar." I brush away a huge black fly darting toward my nose. "What about closer?" I frown. "I saw a . . . Yoho *Something* Road. Like, just around Field. What's up there? Does it go to another town?"

Miller recaps her water bottle. "There's an RV campground, at the foot of the mountain, close to the entrance. Another Parks Canada campground higher up, no RVs allowed. It's named Takakkaw, for the waterfall up at the top of the road." She stops, searches my face. "Something there?"

I feel the skin between my eyebrows bump up, I'm frowning so hard. I tone it down a notch. "Maybe? I don't know."

"But it's made more of an impression than any other place?" Pendelton's gaze seems bland as ever, but his shoulders seem to bunch beneath his pale green dress shirt.

I nod. "Can we go there? Up that road?"

Pendelton opens the passenger-side door for me as Miller gets into the back. A question occurs to me as we come up to the Lower Spiral Tunnel exhibit. I force myself to stop fidgeting with the bottle cap.

"I don't know. If I came eastward, *from* this Taka . . . Takakkaw water-fall," I swallow, hard, "then if someone . . . dumped me, wouldn't I be on the other side of the highway?"

Miller is all business. "That's impossible to know at this point. I say if Takakkaw sounds familiar, then that's where we check next."

A small, crystal-clear lake bounds the south side of the highway, to our left, as we near the turnoff. Pendelton slows to take a right. I'm able to read the sign clearly this time. *Yoho Valley Road.*

I stare at the mountain face to the left, clefted with vertical cuts in the granite at irregular intervals. A sign points to the RV campground. I see one large vehicle, white with teal accents, parked far from the entrance. Glimpses of dark brown picnic tables flash through the thickening trees before the road climbs in earnest. The posted limit is thirty klicks. Pendelton's doing fifty.

The road climbs and dips several times, curving around soft bends. We drive over a small bridge made of concrete and metal. Just past it, the Parks Canada campground appears on the left, the entrance marked by what looks like a green-brown toll booth, its windows papered with notices. Across from it, on our right, we pass a large building with wood siding painted deep red. I see a peaked roof, tall windows, a large deck, and an outdoor fireplace next to the river we just crossed. It's in much better shape than the Parks Canada booth, that's clear even to me.

"The Lodge," says Miller. "Luxe mountain resort. There are cabins behind the main building there. About thirty, I think. Fireplaces, private decks, the works."

"Called *The Lodge at Yoho*, actually," adds Pendelton.

I swivel to look at Miller. "Have you ever stayed there?"

She shakes her head with a rueful smile. "They start at four hundred bucks a night." She shrugs. "Never say never, though, eh. Maybe for something special."

After a pause, Pendelton adds, "Good restaurant, though."

I think about presumptions as we continue upward in silence.

SIX

I'm not sure if *ironic* is the right word, but Yoho Valley Road clings to the side of a mountain. I don't see much, if any, valley. Trees to the left. Trees to the right. I suppose they're obscuring the bigger picture.

Pendelton slows. I see a small turnout to the right up ahead. A large sign, painted a fading orange-brown, with words carved into the wood, the letters still bright yellow. *Meeting of the Waters*. I turn in my seat, trying to figure out what it means, as the car follows the road's curve to the left.

I'm abruptly jerked sideways, the seatbelt cutting into my neck. I let out an involuntary hiss.

"Sorry." Pendelton points through the windshield. "Gate's up."

It's really just two metal bars, set about four feet up from the ground, attached to two metal poles set into the shoulders and locked together in the centre of the road with a simple padlock. My guess is, when not in use as a barrier, the long bars swing outward, parallel to the road. Right now, though, there's no getting a car any farther.

"What's past here?" I crane my stinging neck, looking past the barrier.

"Takakkaw Falls, but not for a few more kilometres." Miller moves up, pushing slightly into the space between my seat and Pendelton's. "Is this familiar to you?"

I stare at the paved road, at the trees lining the shoulders, at the impassive mountain. "Can we park? I want to get out."

Miller slides back into her seat. After a beat and a quick survey with narrowed eyes, Pendelton gives a short nod, backs the car up into the cleared turnout area by the sign. He stops with the car in the only spot of shade. When I get out, my ears fill with the sound of running water. I walk over to read the signage properly. The confluence of the Yoho River and the Kicking Horse River. I peer through the trees, catch glimpses of grey-green water and whitecaps. I walk to the barrier, stare up the road, but the asphalt continues up a slight rise without yielding anything.

Miller joins me.

"How long has this gate been up?"

"Chuck's calling to find out." Miller points to the sides. "It's made to keep cars from passing, but anyone could walk through." She gestures. "You think you did?"

"I don't know." I skirt the pole grounding one side of the gate. The water is a steady roar on my right. Miller pulls even with me to my left.

"Looking for anything specific? Anything I could also keep an eye out for?"

"I wish I could say." I squirm internally. "It sounds stupid. It's just a feeling. But that's pretty much what I've got to work with here."

"Hey, it's okay. I understand." She pauses. "Well, I can *guess* how you're feeling, at best. I'm just gonna call that understanding, if that's okay with you."

I look over, catch a glint of humour in her expression. She sobers as she returns my gaze. "I've never had amnesia, so I can't say I know exactly what you're going through, but I can say I'll do my best to help you." She points a thumb over her shoulder. "And so will Chuck. It's our job."

I think I'm supposed to feel bolstered by her commitment. I offer a small nod. If anything, I feel a deep unease I can't explain to her. It threatens to overwhelm my veneer of calm. I take a deep breath, look up at the mountainside to our left, let my gaze trail down and up. I can't help the slight shudder. It's impossible to feel anything but utterly inconsequential amid the sheer denseness of forest around us.

Over to my right, occasional breaks in the trees show me huge chunks of broken-off bits of mountain, some still squared, others rounded and smooth. Fast-moving water rushes over and around them all, in the direction where we left Pendelton and the car.

We walk the paved road. I can imagine, if you were out with a friend or a lover, and no strangers crowding you, this would be a beautiful, comfortable stroll. With the gentle curvature of the roadway, I can imagine you'd want to keep going just to see what's around the next bend. More trees, more mountain, more road ahead of you, all incredibly peaceful. And at the end of your jaunt? An awe-inspiring waterfall. You might even prefer to walk instead of drive.

If things were different.

Miller remains silent beside me, perhaps thinking the same thing, though her restless, observant gaze tells me otherwise. After a while, though, I start to feel the damp spots under my arms again and a sore spot on the arch of one foot. My head is itchy with perspiration. I motion to a thinning in the trees. "I need to stop. Shade." It's not much, a patchy spot beneath a thin fan of evergreen branches, but it's out of the full sun. I hope the sight of the crashing river below us brings on thoughts of coolness.

"We should get back," says Miller, watching the water with me. "Chuck will be cranky if I make him hike up to find us."

"He should've worn his hiking shoes," I reply, distracted, mesmerized by the white water tumbling over and around the handful and more of huge boulders in its path. Here, the rocks are mostly sharp, their edges jutting out, darkly gleaming and wet. The edges of my vision grow inward, blackening, thickening until I can only see the crashing water through a diminishing circle.

I think I hear screams again.

"Hey." Miller grabs my arm. "Careful."

I blink, come back to myself. I'm staring down at the river twenty feet below, my shoe tips right at the edge of the pebble- and twig-strewn dirt. Swallowing my thundering heart, I turn back to Miller. Her face is tight with alarm.

"You're right," I say, tongue clumsy. "I think I'm about done in this heat."

The return always seems faster than the journey out. *How do I know that?* I keep silent the whole way. Miller watches me from the corner of her eye, but she seems content to let me be for now. We find Pendelton standing under the trees, in the shadows, just to the right and behind the signage. He gestures downward. "A few paths down to the water's edge. Checked out a few of them, but it's shaded, hard to pick anything out except stones and dirt and fallen leaves."

I shake my head before I realize he's addressing Miller. I walk a few paces away, searching for viable paths among the trees. It's probably easier than it looks, though definitely only for the able-bodied. It must be cool right next to the water, though. *The confluence of two mighty rivers.* All that water, smashing together and rushing onward over the remnants of the very mountains surrounding us. White water. White noise.

Miller says. "Did you find out why the gate's up?"

"Avalanche a couple weeks ago. Road's closed before the Falls."

"An avalanche?" I force myself to engage. "In May?"

Pendelton shrugs. "Still spring, isn't it?"

Miller watches our exchange. She says, "Let's get back to Golden. Time to check in with the Missing Persons bulletins. Maybe grab a quick lunch." She pauses to give me an assessing look. For all that, it's mild. "Listen, this is a tough time, no two ways about it, and our first priority is to ensure your safety." She tips her chin toward Pendelton. "Some of the things Chuck and I do might not make sense to you. But we need you to trust us. To trust that we're doing everything we can to help you. Can you do that?"

I shift my gaze from one to the other, my gut clenching. "What do you mean? What are you talking about?"

Earnestly, she says, "We need to canvass area churches, hostels, hotels, restaurants, gas stations. Get your photo out to the media. It's key to find out who you are, where you're from. Might be nearby, might not. But if we figure out your identity, we'll be able to figure out who did this to you."

I cross my arms, gripping my shoulders hard enough to bruise. "But then my attacker. . . . They'd know where I am."

"The media might be our best chance for someone who knows you to come forward," says Pendelton.

"But then why hasn't anyone reported me missing?" I push my chin downward, hard into the space between my wrists. Is that a headache pounding in my skull? Or just panic?

Pendelton's expression is unreadable. "They might not know it yet. You could be on vacation. There are a lot of possible explanations."

"The media can be really helpful to us. There are a lot of good people who just want to help." Miller's tone is gentle. "We're not going to stake you out like bait. We know there's an unknown perpetrator out there, somewhere, and we'll be searching for them. I promise you, we *are* considering your safety. But this is the part where you trust us to know our jobs."

I flinch at the admonishment, then fist my hands. "Please, I know I sound unhinged, but I, I don't want my face all over the news. I can't explain why. It's just a . . . a bad feeling. Please, please don't put my photo out. Not yet." My brain scrambles for a reason, anything plausibly rational. "Just give me a chance to remember something, anything that might explain why I—why I'm so scared about this."

Miller assesses me for long seconds, her gaze clear as blue glacial ice. "Okay."

"We'll wait," says Pendelton with an abrupt nod. "But when we say it's time . . ."

Relief floods me, making my knees shake. "Okay." I breathe out slowly. "Okay. I got it. Thanks." I rub at the sweat along my temples, my steps wobbly as I follow them and return to the car.

Pendelton runs the AC in the car for a few minutes, then motions for us to get in. We retrace our route down Yoho Valley Road with no further conversation. I clasp my hands tightly in my lap, hiding the trembling, and keep my face turned out my window, away from the interior of the car. I feel light-headed and yet heavy in the pit of my stomach. Muscles down the length of me twitch involuntarily, synapses firing without rhyme or reason. I want to sleep for a week.

But I can't. I can't let others make decisions for me.

SEVEN

After I convince her yet again that I'm up to it, Susan cautiously puts me to various tasks at her church building, from tidying up a cobweb-clad storage space to helping set up lecterns for an evening choir practice to moving furniture for the next day's mums-n-tots session. With every task, she asks me if I'm sure, as though I would honestly decline. Every time, I answer in the affirmative, as though I'm not a charity case, eating her food, drinking her imported organic coffee, intruding into her personal spaces. Maybe it's cultural or maybe I'm really a selfish person, I don't know, but it chafes, this feeling of dependence. Of powerlessness.

A day and a half of constant physical labour ought to do me good, right? Keeping my body in motion, bleeding off stress, taking my mind off of exhaustion and uncertainty, getting me involved in the community. But for a good cause or not, it's still mind-numbingly boring. Maybe I should do something fun. Oh, wait. I have no money and I've been wearing the same clothes for days now, laundered every night while I wear borrowed pyjamas to sleep. Pastor Susan regularly offers me a paw-through of the donated clothes boxes, but I just can't bring myself to admit this limbo may not have a specified end date. The thought of wearing musty castoffs only makes me queasy.

At least Naomi discreetly gave me a couple multi-packs of underthings and socks. Just some cheapie stuff from the local bargain store. I opened my mouth to promise I'd pay her back, but the sentiment stuck in my throat and the moment passed. Is this normal for me? Getting emotional over twenty bucks?

Miller and Pendelton have left Golden for the time being, following up on something for another case. To be fair, they wore out their borrowed desks, calling all over the area as promised. In addition to learning that investigators usually have more than one file going at a time, I've discovered they watch their budgets closely. So instead of driving all over the area to show people the picture Pendelton took of an unsmiling me, they use the phone first. If someone thinks they recognize my description, Miller or Pendelton texts or emails them the image.

They haven't sent my photo to anyone in the media.

I begged a couple more days from Pendelton before they do. I ought to be grateful my blubbering and sudden flop sweat netted me his reluctant agreement. Or maybe he had his other cases top of mind and no time to hand-hold. I should be relieved that the police still watch over Pastor Susan's house during the night. Naomi still checks in on me at all hours, when she can. Susan thinks Naomi is sweet on me, but I think she's just kind. Naomi feels like a big sister to me. Though I can't recall if I know what that even means. Of course, it could also be a result of our height difference, but . . . something in her steady gaze and careful attention helps me feel safe. Like she means it when she says she's here for me.

They say human beings can adapt to anything. I never thought that having some faceless person after me would be one of them.

Never mind. I can't say that, can I, because I have no freaking idea what I've ever thought or not thought.

There are a lot of reasons for gratitude. I know it, I do. It just feels a lot easier to be angry.

I have a lot of time to speculate, that's the problem. That's mainly what fills my head while I stack chairs and collapse tables in the church sanctuary. What am I even doing here? But since talking to myself doesn't seem quite the healthiest thing for me right now, and I feel an irrational need to keep up a cheerful facade, I play a game with Pastor Susan as we work. So far, I've made her laugh out loud a couple times with my outlandish theories.

Maybe my people are all shady criminals and the last thing they want is to dial up the cops. Maybe I'm involved in some byzantine criminal plot and they'll be coming for me once they corner me in a dark alley. Maybe I'm a theatre star and no one recognizes me without my makeup.

Susan is tactful enough not to mention the most viable and likely alternative, and I'm eager to avoid the obvious: no one's missing me.

It's foolish and irrational, but I feel ashamed when I notice the square of paper again, the one with Thea Halford's contact information. It's been sitting on the nightstand since the first night Pastor Susan took my clothes for the wash. Thea. My good Samaritan. So certain someone out there would claim me. How long will I have to hang on to her info to make good on my promise? I seriously contemplate crumpling it up and tossing it in the church recycling bin when Susan's on the phone. In the end, I don't. It feels a poor way to repay Thea's kindness.

Thursday morning, I ambush Naomi when she comes to pick me up for a late breakfast on her day off. "Can we go back today? I want to drive up Yoho Valley Road again. Is it still closed due to the avalanche? Can we go up to the Falls, do you think?"

"Guess you're a morning person, eh?" She looks at me askance before returning her attention to the road. "How are the headaches? Getting better?"

"They come and go." I hesitate, unsure how much I want to share.

"Do you need to see a doctor? I can take you to the hospital again."

I'm shamed by her concern. "No, they're fine. I can handle them. They're not any worse than the weird dreams."

"Are they flashbacks? Real memories?"

I shrug, abruptly worried I've revealed too much I'm at a loss to explain.

Naomi pulls to a stop in a half-full parking lot outside a diner. She turns the engine off and faces me. "Can you tell me about them? Recovering from trauma's tough, but maybe it can help to unload a bit of the burden."

I don't know if she's right, but what have I got to lose? Shoving aside the nagging unease, I sift through the images that remain from the dreams. "I think I'm in a car. It's dark out. Like we're driving somewhere deep in the trees. I'm in the driver's seat. But the car's parked. There's someone in the other seat. They sort of . . . loom at me out of the dark. I'm panicked. There's no sound, though. I feel like I *want* to scream, like I can feel it as a physical thing . . . and then I wake up."

"Sounds more nightmare than just weird dream." She waits until I meet her eyes. "Do you need to speak to the therapist?" I shake my head. She says, "How many nights now?"

"Since I woke up on the side of the highway?" I tamp down on the sarcasm, reaching for calm. "All . . . three of them?" I frown. "It feels a lot longer." My voice trails away, weighed down by a sudden exhaustion.

"I'm sorry. That's . . . rough." She taps the steering wheel. "I've had some experience with victims of trauma, though I don't have any training in how to help you directly, but a therapist would. I really think you should consider it." She hesitates, her gaze thoughtful on me. "You could find one who specializes in hypnosis, even. I don't have the stats on hypnosis helping victims of Rohypnol who've lost their memories, but it's worth researching. Don't you think?"

My mouth goes abruptly dry, weariness blasted aside by a pulse of fear. "Honestly?" She nods, encouraging. "I feel sick at the thought of being so . . . vulnerable. And with a stranger." I shudder so unexpectedly I'm shocked. I rub my arms, feel the skin pebbling even through layers of clothing. "There's got to be other ways to jump-start my memory. I'm willing to try every single one of them before I try . . . that."

I expect her to get offended, defensive. Instead, she says, "Okay."

"Really?"

Nod. "Yep. Your life, your call. I'm just trying to think of things that might help."

Relief pulses through me. Guess Naomi's agreement means more than I thought. Am I always this . . . starved for approval?

She cocks her head, eyes narrowing. "Is that why you want to go up there again? Yoho Valley Road. Takakkaw Falls. You think you've been there before?"

"Not exactly. I mean, I'm not sure of anything. But I feel . . . like I'm missing something and it's out there, up that road." I make a face. "I don't know. That sounds idiotic when I say it out loud. Plus, Miller must've included that lodge up there, right, when they were calling hotels and places with my description? Nobody recognized me." I take a deep breath, smooth out my scowl. "Probably a good idea to at least have some coffee before spouting woo-woo theories with zero backup, eh?"

Naomi takes the hint. We exit her silver SUV and go in to breakfast.

With its shiny chrome accents and rounded oblong shape, the diner looks like an old Airstream trailer, supersized. Inside is classic greasy spoon, upgraded. Jukebox accented in reds and golds and ambers, lit up from within to showcase its playlist. Clean, sparkling windows the length of the place. One counter stretching down half the space, with bolted-down stools. Cut-out window with shelving for orders between the kitchen and service area. One set of swinging doors into the kitchen. Vinyl-upholstered benches, booths under the windows. Waitresses in jeans, black T-shirts, and pink aprons. Pies under glass, two coffee machines with four burners apiece.

Naomi gets smiles and affectionate greetings, with friendly spill-over for me. An older white waitress with fuchsia-framed glasses and her silver hair in a ballerina's bun leads us to a booth at the end away from the washrooms. She pours our coffees, brings glasses of water. I tell Naomi to order whatever she thinks I should try. I'm too agitated to focus. The food comes fast and hot. I can't speak for shovelling it in my mouth with barely enough time between to breathe.

When the carnage is over and the dishes cleared, the good constable says, "Okay. I'll take you." She pulls out her phone. "Just lemme rearrange some things. I'll be right back. Gotta make a call."

I stare after her, my face flaming. She steps outside and down the small flight of stairs, moving to one side as she puts the phone to her ear. I smile woodenly at the waitress, decline another refill, finish my water, fidget. I do my damnedest not to watch Naomi. I take the opportunity to visit the restroom. When I return, she's waiting for me at the cashier.

"Ready?" she asks.

Even though my agitation crests well beforehand, I wait until we're at her SUV. "I'm so sorry. I never even thought to ask if you're free. I'm treating you like my personal taxi service and," I exhale heavily, "I'm sorry. If you have other plans—"

"It's okay. I just had to push back an appointment. It's a minor

inconvenience. You've got much bigger problems. If I can help, I will."
The SUV unlocks with a beep. I follow her lead and get in.

"Thank you. I mean it."

She gives me a distracted nod, navigating around the now much busier
parking lot to the street. "Can I ask you something?"

"Yeah, of course."

"What's it been like, staying with Pastor Susan?"

I frown. "Fine. She's kind. I don't really get her sense of humour. But
I'm grateful for her generosity. Why do you ask?"

"Just wondering. I don't know her well. I'm not Christian. Do you
think you are?"

"No." The answer comes immediately. "Can't see myself putting that
much faith in something totally without proof." I force a lighter tone.
"You worried she's trying to convert me?"

I get a faint smile for my half-assed joke. "But she's treating you all
right?"

"Aside from all the sneezing from shifting dusty furniture and stuff in
storage, yeah. I don't even mind the extra-sore muscles. She's been really
kind. Especially about not telling people my situation, like I asked." I
pause. "Plus, she's really getting good at avoiding calling me by name."

Naomi looks blank for a moment. "Oh . . . yeah, I've had that problem
a few times, too. Yeah, that's kind of tricky. I didn't think I said people's
names all the time, but . . ."

"I've been toying with the idea of giving myself a name for the fore-
seeable future." I press on with the lighter tone. "So, let's brainstorm.
What's the absolute worst name you could see me going by?"

She wears a half-frown, half-smile, clearly bemused. "What? Like . . .
Marge?"

"Yes, exactly! Or, ah, Maryann."

"Mary-Sue."

"Mary Ellen."

"You sure the pastor's not getting in your head? That sounds like a nun."

I surprise myself with a genuine laugh. "Mary Louise. No, wait, that's just as nunnish."

"I think that's someone famous."

"By all means, let's avoid famous names, then. What about . . . Clementine?"

"So, onto fruit? Um . . . Kiwi?"

We work our way through fruits, aristocratic Euro names, and unisex monikers before we drive past Field again. I fall silent, suddenly unable to hold up my end of the silliness. I crane my neck as we continue east, staring at the pristine blue lake lying to the south of the highway. I shiver, imagining its chill water, wondering if it's connected to either of the two big rivers we're about to see soon.

Naomi takes the curve off the highway smoothly. I shift in my seat, my brain a scramble of thoughts and what I think might be anticipation. I watch every passing tree as though the answers are about to leap out in a flurry of motion, filling the shadowed parts of me with bright colour.

"Oh," says Naomi. "It's closed." She pulls onto the gravel shoulder by the Meeting of the Waters sign.

"Pendelton said there was an avalanche. Farther up somewhere." I tap my fingers on my thigh. "I thought maybe it would be cleared by now. I really want to see the Falls." I sigh. "Damn."

Naomi checks her mirrors. I follow suit. The road stretches empty behind us. "What do you want to do?"

"God, I don't know. I thought . . . I had a feeling, but now I'm not sure what it means." I scrub my face with both hands. "It's as bad as the nightmares. Nothing makes any sense."

"Why don't we get out for a bit? Maybe clamber down to the water. Clear our heads. If I remember right, it's an easy climb, down and up." She manoeuvres the SUV into the same spot Pendelton did, encourages me to get out. My limbs feel leaden as I comply, as heavy as the thoughts sitting in my head. She leads me past the signage into the dimness under the canopy of foliage. Scattered among the roots of the thick trees, rocks large and small give footholds down the steep path made by hundreds if not thousands of feet before us. The roar of the rivers grows in my ears. Not quite loud enough to drown out the buzzing sense of yet another failure. But I only allow myself a few more moments of self-pity before I force my gaze to turn outward.

Fathomless mountains, a blanket of majestic trees, boulders rough and smooth, thousands of litres of icy water, and the sun shining down through a break in the clouds. We're the only people in sight. Spectacular.

"Isn't it?" says Naomi. I blush when I realize I spoke out loud. "Sometimes, I can't believe I actually *live* in the Rocky Mountains," she says on a smile.

I take a deep breath of fresh air. "Can I just stay here forever, do you think? Tell everyone I decided to meditate on the mountain. They can come get me in a hundred years. By then, I shall be known by my chosen name: Marge Persimmon Carol-Ann Smythe-Belmont."

Naomi gives me a mock salute.

We sit companionably on some flat boulders, in the middle of the river above the flow, content for the moment simply to exist. I listen to the river water. I shiver as a slight coolness settles once the sun disappears behind the growing cloud cover. I feel the tiny sprays of water on my face.

I know there's a lesson in this for me. Patience. Persistence. Calm in the face of immense, unknowable forces. So maybe this time a hunch didn't pan out. Maybe the next time it will. Maybe it will take an untold number of wrong turns before I find my way. The trick is to remember there's always another way.

Rain starts without fanfare, driving us off the rocks and back up to the road. The humidity seems to take an exponential leap once we're inside the SUV. I fan my face with a hand, pull my collar away from sticky skin. I envision the sweat stains. Even with the good pastor's laundry machine, my clothes—and I—must be pretty smelly from all the embedded stress sweat. Maybe it's all right to take Naomi up on her repeated offers to loan me the money for fresh clothing. God, at this point, maybe even musty castoffs *would* be better.

I count the time on my fingers. Four days. When I go over the timeline so far, I can't complain, precisely. It took time to get checked out at the hospital. It took time for Miller and Pendelton to get here. It took time to call all those hostels and gas stations and motels and whatever. But I can't help feeling cheated. Am I the only one needled by any urgency?

Why is it taking so long to find out who I am?

Naomi turns on the air conditioning, lets it run for a few seconds, windows partway open, then puts the SUV in gear. I cross my arms, holding my impatience close. As we wind our careful way downward, I feel an increasing pressure at the back of my skull. Something different from the intermittent headaches. Maybe my ponytail's too tight. I scratch my itchy scalp, redo my hair into a bun to keep it off my neck, hope that manages the sweat until I acclimate.

The rain peters out as we near the part of the road that runs between luxury lodge and campground. I feel suddenly itchy again, my brain filled with buzzing, my feet tapping an anxious tattoo on the car mat. I swing my gaze from the Parks Canada booth to the lodge's main building. Right to left to right to left again.

"Can we stop?" I blurt out, pointing. "Here. At this lodge place."

Naomi eyes me sidelong. My body jerks as she brakes to make the left turn into the narrow driveway. She parks facing the road. "You remember something?"

I shrug, frustrated, unable to attempt an explanation I'm not sure I have.

She follows me out of the SUV and across the gravel area that passes for the parking lot, which sits mainly empty. I see signs, low to the ground, faux-rustic, with cabin numbers and arrows painted on them, pointing away, toward the river. At the end of the long lot, farthest from the main lodge, sit a couple of large sheds and a handful of dirt-streaked cars.

I take the few steps up to the main door, which is more than half window. I see warm yellow paint and decorative items through the clear glass. The air inside is cool. To the right, a large room—high ceilings and three walls of windows create an airy, welcoming space. An indoor/outdoor fireplace anchors the far wall. Through crystal-clear windows on either side, I see a deck area, and beyond, the small bridge over what I now know is the Kicking Horse River. This must be the restaurant Pendelton mentioned. I recall too clearly the small secret smile on his face.

I swivel to my left in the small entrance, more a foyer than a proper lobby. A young white woman with light brown hair smiles from behind a narrow counter. Her name tag says *Kayleigh*. Behind her is an open door, through which I can see a slightly cluttered desk and a shelving unit.

"Hello, how may I help you?" Her smile falters as she focusses on me, her expression morphing into alarm. "Ms. Li! Oh gosh. Um, uh . . . this is . . . okay, wait, let me call Nola for you. She must have finally reached you?" Her voice tapers off into a quivering question.

"Reached me?" I gape at her. "I . . . I have no idea what you're talking about. Who is Nola?"

"But," she splutters, "aren't you here about your parents?"

EIGHT

My mouth drops open, though I can't think of a word to say.

Naomi touches my arm, just enough to slide me slightly to my right. She flips open a wallet-type thing, showing her work ID. "Hi, I'm Constable Naomi Aoki, with the RCMP out of Golden. I'm a friend of Ms. Li. If you'll just bear with me, let's take it one step at a time. You know Ms. Li?"

Kayleigh frowns as she looks from Naomi to me and back again. "Um, well, Ms. Li stayed with us last summer, er, ah, fall. Just before we closed for the winter." She flicks a look at me, eyes widening. "I'm sorry, but I really need to call Nola to speak with you. She's on the grounds. She should be right over."

"You said my parents are here?" My voice squeaks. I'm not sure I care. "Where are they now?" I step forward. "Are they on-site? Which is their cabin?"

I can see her swallow. "Please, let me call Nola. She can explain everything to you, okay? She's the manager."

"Yes, sure." Naomi speaks firmly, a pen and notebook at the ready. "Can you tell me Mr. and Mrs. Li's first names please?"

"Stephen and Glinda." Kayleigh picks up a walkie-talkie unit, speaks some sort of code into it. I hear a reply in the affirmative, low and clear. Kayleigh sets the little black unit down, clearly relieved. "Nola's on her way." She gestures toward the restaurant area, a deep crease still settled between her brows. "Please take a seat anywhere. I'll send someone to you with coffee and water."

I know my lips are moving soundlessly, repeating the name, *my* name. *Li.* It should ring some kind of bell, shouldn't it? I try *Stephen*, then *Glinda*. An ache grows to fill my head.

Naomi hesitates, perhaps weighing the option to push Kayleigh for more answers. In the end, she says thanks and gestures me to precede her into the restaurant. Instead of taking a seat, I walk once around the space, mostly staring out the windows. The road, green trees, a bit of the river, the small bridge, and slices of granite mountains against partly cloudy skies. Naomi remains standing near a second door leading to a partially glassed-in patio, her clear gaze assessing the space methodically.

I choose a table for four, take a chair facing the large fireplace. Shifting on the soft cushion, I scrape my wrist on the chair arm. I realize the entire thing's made from what looks like rough-cut branches. I run my hands over knots and bumpy red-brown wood, willing my sore head to behave.

A freckled young woman with light brown skin and thick dark hair pulled into a high ponytail approaches, carrying a tray with two glasses of ice water. "Would anyone like coffee?"

I shake my head. "No, thanks," says Naomi.

The waitress sets the glasses on the table with a soft thud, the ice cubes circling lazily within the clear water. I shiver. With a faint smile and an uncertain nod, she departs the way she came.

Naomi pulls out the chair opposite me. "Do you remember any of this? Remember meeting anyone here? What about the name, *your* name, Li?"

She puts her small notebook on the table, a black ballpoint pen jammed into the coils.

I stare at the fireplace, noting the partially blackened rocks just above the hearth. There's a sitting area in front of it, with couch, chairs, low table, magazines, checkers board. Everywhere I turn, I can see blue, grey, green, white through the tall windows. Sky, trees, mountain. An incredible day outside. I realize every stick of furniture in here is meant to complement that view. How could anyone forget a place like this?

I look back to Naomi and shake my head. I know we're still worried about whoever drugged me, but I can only take on one thing at a time. For now, that has to be this latest . . . situation. I clasp my trembling hands together in my lap.

To the right of the fireplace, through the glass door, I see a lean Indigenous woman with grey-streaked black hair out on the deck. She enters the restaurant with a clatter. Her smile is warm and quick, white teeth bright against her brown skin. She reaches us in five steps, her hand out before step three's done. Naomi and I rise to meet her.

"Nola Cardinal. I manage The Lodge at Yoho." Her hand is wrinkled and thick-knuckled, her grip firm. Her eyes size me up, though I can't tell what their dark brown depths come up with. "Ms. Li. I'm so sorry about all this. I wish I could be happy to see you again, but under these circumstances . . ." She turns her focus to Naomi, assessing her from top to bottom, her look of genuine regret turning to polite coolness. "And you are?"

Naomi bears the look with a bland expression, though she retains eye contact with Cardinal. "Constable Naomi Aoki. RCMP out of Golden."

Cardinal's expression thaws slightly. "And did Ms. Li call you in? Are you a family friend?" Cardinal gestures at Naomi's cargo capris and long-sleeved tee. "You're not in uniform. Do we need to call someone on duty?"

Naomi gives her a small frown. "Actually, I'm involved with Ms. Li's file on another matter. We're not sure yet if her parents' . . . circumstances are related. Can you please fill us in?"

Cardinal presses her lips together, runs a hand through her short hair, clearly reviewing her options. "Okay." She takes the chair next to me. We all sit. She twists to face me more squarely. "Your parents arrived as scheduled on Friday, May 25th, but . . . I'm sorry to tell you that they haven't been seen on the property since Sunday. The closest I've been able to confirm is afternoon tea time that day. One of the staff *thinks* they recall seeing Mr. and Mrs. Li returning from dinner off-property, perhaps around eight that night. They're not sure."

I inhale so sharply it feels as though a piece of ice has lodged in my throat, cutting and cold. I clamp a hand over my mouth. The room whirls around my slowly narrowing field of vision. Is it possible to swoon while sitting down?

Cardinal grips my arm, hard enough to hurt, but her other hand gently takes hold of my shoulder to set me upright. Someone places my hands around an icy column of glass. I realize my eyes are closed. I force them open. Naomi peers into my face from her crouch next to my chair.

"You okay?"

I squeeze the glass of ice water, concentrate on the cold seeping into my fingers, calming my mind though not my heart. "I'm not even sure what that looks like at this point." I hear the shakiness of my voice, clear my throat. "I don't understand. How could no one notice until now?"

Cardinal grimaces. "I had Monday off, and Tuesday I was dealing with a large booking. I was in meetings all day with my events staff." She pauses, angry displeasure tightening her face. "I'm sorry, none of my staff mentioned this to me until this morning. I don't know what they were thinking." Her expression softens as she catches my gaze. "Let me explain. We don't keep tight tabs on our guests, for their privacy. As you may recall, all our guests usually eat breakfast here, unless they're leaving before we open, because we're really the only place close enough. Plus, breakfast is included in the room rate. So we usually see our guests at least once a day, in the morning."

Naomi looks grave, writing swiftly as she glances from her notes to Cardinal and back again.

"Today, I asked one of our wait staff if she'd seen Mrs. Li at breakfast yet because I'd made sure to put aside a particular type of tea for her." Cardinal's frown deepens. "One question led to others, and I soon realized something was wrong. I canvassed my entire staff, then. I thought I should know when someone last saw the Lis before calling any police in." Her lips twist a little before she continues. "I also called the numbers we have on file for both Mr. and Mrs. Li. It's a precaution I instituted last year. We ask for cell phone numbers for all members of a party of guests. Many guests go hiking in the area and we want to make sure we can reach them in case of emergency."

"What was the result of your calls?" asks Naomi intently.

"*Customer not available* messages." Cardinal shifts back to me. "Then, I thought of you and started calling *your* number and got the same message. I thought perhaps you'd surprised them with a side trip, as you'd surprised them with their stay here." She looks at Naomi. "I've been trying all three numbers regularly since. I was just about to check their cabin again, before calling the RCMP, when Kayleigh caught me on the radio."

I down half the water, holding the glass with both hands. Something akin to despair threatens, but underneath it, I feel a slow swirl of dread. A cold, cold ache starts behind my eyes. I set the glass on the table, press my chilled hands against my cheeks, my forehead, the back of my neck. I push back, away from Cardinal's concerned gaze, scrambling to a stand. "I'd like to see it please, their cabin."

Naomi's out of her chair before I speak the last word. "Let's hold off on that for now. Ms. Cardinal, I need a list of the staff you spoke with about the Lis this morning. Can you please work on that for me right now? Names and positions, home addresses and phone numbers. They're going to need to be interviewed."

"Wait. I'm sorry." Cardinal flushes, rises to standing. "I should've done this sooner, but do you have proof of your ID? That you're with the RCMP?" She looks from me to Naomi, her expression hardening again. "I was fine to share what I know with Ms. Li here, but I'm not comfortable giving out staff personal information. I need to perform my due diligence."

Naomi shows her ID again, but also gives a set of instructions. Cardinal gives me a nod, then steps away, pulling out a phone. She walks over toward the door leading into what I guess to be the kitchen area. There's a small alcove there with bottles of wine and spirits on shelves. Cardinal steps behind the bar counter, facing us as she calls the Golden detachment, as per Naomi's suggestion.

"Why are you making me wait?" I grip the chair back with both hands, pressing my flesh hard against the wood. Maybe I'm being unfair to Naomi, but for chrissake, aren't they supposed to be helping?

"Procedure," replies Naomi calmly. "I don't want to mess anything up. Especially since I'm not on duty. I need to call Miller and tell them to get back here now." Reading the anger on my face, she sighs. "We can't get a look at that cabin without Miller's say-so. She's the lead on your file, and we have to treat this as related until we discover otherwise. I don't want to mess anything up for her. Or for you." She hesitates. "For what it's worth, I'm really sorry this is happening."

I wave away her sympathy. If I let it in, I might start feeling everything else, too, and I just . . . I can't. Not now.

I clench my hands. "I can't believe nobody noticed they were missing. It's been four freaking days. I might not remember anything else right now, but I'd sure as hell remember if my parents were *invisible*. What the hell's wrong with the staff here?" I think Cardinal's doing her best, but this is seriously messed up. And I can't do anything to fix it. Frustration boils up, like bile in my throat.

Naomi shifts her feet, straightens up, getting taller. I grimace at the reminder of my size. "Look," she says, "everything's moving real fast right now. Which is the best reason to slow down. I don't want to miss anything because I didn't think it through properly. The timeline—" She halts abruptly.

I narrow my eyes, trying to extrapolate what she didn't finish. "What about it?"

Her expression shutters. "Like I said, I can't just barge into their cabin and start tossing it for clues or something. That's not how good police work happens."

"Okay, but promise me you'll ask Miller if we can see their cabin. Now."

Naomi searches my face, perhaps signalled by the urgency in my voice. "Is this your intuition again?"

I release my hands, flexing them to get the blood flowing properly. "I don't know what I'm supposed to do. I just know I need to do *something*. If seeing their things can spark a memory, then that's something, isn't it? It may lead to more answers. It may lead to *them*."

"And more questions." Naomi's expression changes, her tone gentling. "This must be a lot to take in, and you might not like the answers we find or the questions that get raised. You've got to be ready for all that."

"Aren't you the one who told me to stick up for myself? I don't need babying. I want to know the truth."

If she's bothered by me using her words against her, she doesn't show it. She only pauses, as though to give *me* time to settle. "It's only been a few days since you woke up on the side of the highway. Do you honestly think you're done processing all of that? All I'm saying is, we should proceed cautiously. Not just for the sake of the investigation, but also for you."

I realize then how much I hate that calm, reasonable tone of hers. I know she's right. I know she's being kind to help me, outside of her official duties. I know she's generous to rearrange her day, to offer her company and reassurances. I know all of this, and I still want to slap her.

I whirl around, away from her, and walk to one of the windows. "Just ask her, all right?" I ram my hands into my pockets, stare unseeing at the river in the distance.

"Okay, sure." Her professional impassiveness returns, rebuilding the distance between us. "Excuse me." She crosses to the door Cardinal entered through. I lose her to view as she exits onto the large outdoor porch on the other side of the fireplace. A few moments later, she reappears, standing at the farthest porch railing, facing the small bridge over the river. Is she standing away from me deliberately, to hide what she's saying? Not that I can read lips, as far as I know. Hell, maybe I can and she's taking precautions 'cause she doesn't know for sure either.

Rain clouds thicken overhead. I watch them over the crest of the facing mountain.

Or maybe I'm just being melodramatic and paranoid. Maybe Naomi needs to do her job and I'm only making it harder. I bet she just doesn't want to see my pissy face right now. And honestly, who am I to blame her?

NINE

After the call is done, Naomi stands staring at the river for a few seconds, tension riding the broad line of her shoulders. I watch, frustration pushing me forward two steps before I catch myself. Perhaps she senses my impatience, perhaps she doesn't want to deal with it, because she hurries down the steps at the side of the porch and doubles around to the right, toward the parking area. She doesn't look over at me once.

I debate whether or not to follow. I can't tell how far I can push.

Looking around, I catch Kayleigh watching me from behind the reception counter. She shifts, fixes her gaze firmly on her monitor, expression unmistakably guilty.

Thoughts splintered by worry and indecision, I grasp for anything to keep from exploding out of sheer frustration. There's got to be something I can *do*. Seeing Kayleigh's furtive gaze, I recall how she recognized me . . . and why. I approach the reception counter, abruptly aware of how chilly my palms are from holding on to the water glass earlier. I wipe them on my pants.

"Is there something I can help with, Ms. Li?" Kayleigh asks stiffly, eyes wary, cheeks a faint pink.

I fix a smile on my face. "Thank you for taking an interest in my parents. I heard from Ms. Cardinal that you were the one who noticed their absence."

Her face shades to red. "I'm really sorry this is happening. They're such nice people. So cute together in their little matching outfits. I hope they're okay." She peers past my shoulder. "Are the police getting involved now?" she asks in a low voice.

"Yes. Constable Aoki's spoken with the Serious Crimes unit. I think they're probably on their way here."

Her eyes grow even wider. I wonder how old she is. I say, "Um, I know this is going to sound weird, but would it be possible for you to print out a copy of the details from my stay? Last year?"

"Oh, sure. Let me see." She taps at her keyboard. "Is there a particular reason you need it? Do the RCMP need to see it?"

I'm deeply reluctant to explain my amnesia. I hew to the truth as closely as I can. "Actually, I literally just lost my wallet and all of my ID. My phone, too." At her wide-eyed look, I say, "It's been . . . a really weird week. Anyway, I'm hoping I can see my credit card information on the receipt. You know how you have to give them the number when you call?" She nods. "Well, I don't have that number memorized, so . . ." I shrug instead of blabbering on. Lies are best kept short. Didn't I read that somewhere once?

I feel an excited flutter in my stomach at the thought of seeing my name on the printout. At discovering my full name. On my own. Doing more than the RCMP have in four days.

"Oh . . . I'm sorry. Any statements I'd have here would have the credit card partially starred out. Like, it wouldn't show. And I don't have access to bookkeeping records. Plus, I think the system's already off-loaded the transaction records from last year." She pauses, her brow furrowed.

"What about the receipt for when I booked this stay for my parents?"

Her cheeks redden. "I'm so sorry. I need my manager's authorization for that, since it's not technically your stay. Even though it's your credit card . . ." She looks momentarily confused, but her red-faced shrug tells me pushing her would be too far out of her comfort zone. Or maybe her pay grade.

I know I could appeal to her sympathy, but something holds me back. Is it only pride? An aversion to looking foolish and helpless? Maybe I just can't bear the thought of being patronized again, and this time by a well-meaning child.

"Thanks anyway." I try for an "oh-well" smile. "For checking. Guess I'll have to do it the long way round."

"Sorry."

I step away before turning back. "Do you know where Ms. Cardinal's gone? I'd like to speak to her again. Get a rush on that authorization."

"No, sorry. But I saw your friend? Constable . . . Oakey? She went back there—maybe to find Ms. Cardinal?"

I hesitate a fraction of a second, think better of it, and exit through the main door. I'm just not up to that fight right now. Naomi can make the correction herself when poor Kayleigh mangles her name again.

Outside, at the bottom of the short flight of steps that lead up to the front door, is a small area with three parking slots. They sit empty. I walk on toward the main lot, the one bounded at its farthest edge by the large shed and dirty cars I guess must belong to employees. I listen to the small sounds of crushed gravel beneath my shoes. The way is just slightly uphill, graded like the road beside it. I'm embarrassed to be a little out of breath when I stop next to Naomi's SUV, its silver exterior already dulled by a thin layer of dirt like the staff cars at the other end of the lot.

I reach out to try the door, realize it's probably locked. I pull my hand back. I'm sure there'll be an alarm. I carefully place my hands behind my back, wondering how, precisely, I'm going to get my jacket now. I rub at the sudden goosebumps on my arms, scowling at myself, reflected in the dark glass.

Wait. Naomi doesn't have tinted windows. I take a hurried step back. This isn't her car. I look around. What are the odds? There are only two cars in this guest area of the lot—early days yet in tourist season, I guess. Naomi's car is parked opposite this one. It looks so similar, but I can see now hers is a Honda. This one's a Toyota. As if it wasn't enough of a clue that this car's parked facing the cabins, you'd think the tinted windows would be a giveaway. Or the layer of dirt. Clearly, this car's been here a few days.

Jesus. Naomi might be right. I need to take it slow if this is how well I'm thinking.

Where is she? And where's Cardinal? I glimpse a few people walking amid the trees and cabins, carrying linens and vacuum cleaners. None of them is either woman I'm searching for. If I approach the employees, it's likely they'd just redirect me to the main lodge and Kayleigh.

I sigh, blow at the strands of loose hair around my face. I look at the little ground-level signs. They point the way to cabins 1–16 and then 17–31. How long would it take me to wander around the grounds, searching out thirty-one cabins? Would Cardinal even stay put long enough for me to locate her? Or would I just be walking around futilely, just missing her, like in some demented game of hide-and-seek?

Then it strikes me that I've got nothing but time right now. The signs seem to line up with faint paths tamped down among the cabins. I can't get totally lost, right? And Naomi won't leave without me. She might be pissed, but she won't abandon me outright. It wouldn't be professional.

I resist the abrupt urge to rap the car beside me for good luck. As I move away, I catch a glimpse of a small business card displayed on the dash. It sports a logo and the name of the lodge, along with a printed number. This one says *28*. Lucky number. Judging by its placement, clearly visible through the windshield, it's meant to act like a parking pass. Matching vehicle to guest, I'd guess, using the cabin numbers—

My brain stutters at the implication. A chill runs up my spine, multiplying the goosebumps on my arms. My ears fill with a noise like static, a low scream building as though coming from far away. I shake my head, clearing it, forcing away the nightmare images. *Concentrate. Do something other than stand here shaking.*

I follow the barely-there footpath, wending between patchy grass, small-limbed trees, and compact faux-log cabins with inviting front porches, my quick jogging steps emphasized by the sound of crushed stones beneath my shoes.

As I near the river, the sound of its rushing waters fills my ears. These cabins look larger than the ones close to the parking lot, though they ought to be dwarfed by the surrounding trees, snugged up, as they are, tight against the mountain side. I see only a few lodge staff, no one that looks like a well-pampered guest. The cabin numbers are displayed at the foot of the stairs to the porches, which each feature a pair of Adirondack chairs.

I see a familiar figure at the door of Cabin 28.

I pitch my voice so she can hear me over the walkie-talkie at her ear. "Ms. Cardinal."

The lodge manager whirls around from her position at the open door. Her unguarded expression turns carefully neutral. "Ms. Li."

I look closely at her, see her rigid shoulders and the tightening around her mouth. That's disapproval I'm seeing. She's not happy with something. Or some*one*.

I try for a placating tone. I need her help, not her scorn. "I saw my parents' car—what I guessed is their car. It had this cabin number on its dash." My heart chooses this moment to try to escape the cage of my ribs, drumming its every hard beat through my body. "Is this . . . ?" I swallow. "This is my parents' cabin, isn't it?"

Cardinal hesitates, then pulls herself taller. "Yes, and you have every right to be here." Her voice grows louder.

Frowning, I grasp the rough-hewn rail of the steps onto the porch. I stare at the large window to the left of the door, growing larger as I approach. The darkness behind the glass reveals nothing, no matter how much I will it otherwise. All I see is my silhouette, like a shadow growing in a mirror. My heart rate soars. My skin feels tight.

Behind me, a large shape suddenly lurches up. I spin around with a gasp.

"Steady," says Naomi. "It's just me."

"What . . . what are you doing here?" My voice comes out like I've just finished a set of wind sprints. "I thought we were supposed to leave this for, for Miller and Pendelton." In my periphery, the cabin door looms. Have I been here before? Inside?

Naomi grimaces. "I'm sorry, I wanted to tell you, but there was no time. They want me to take a preliminary look around. They're on their way as fast as they can."

"But—" I scowl. Anger feels good right now. Safe. I grab onto it.

"I'm sorry," Naomi repeats, stressing the last word. "It's like I said, we can't afford to screw up. Any mistakes will cost us more time, and that's one thing we need to stay on the right side of in a file like this." She shifts past me smoothly and I realize she's holding something in her hands. "Ms. Cardinal, thank you. If you would stay out here, please, with Ms. Li." It's not a request.

Naomi pulls on thin gloves made of latex or plastic, something inorganic.

I grit my teeth and lean against the door frame with my arms crossed over my chest. Fine. I know how to follow the letter of the law, too. Cardinal moves to stand beside me. I hear her mutter under her breath.

Naomi turns on every light available, adding to the filtered daylight coming in through three sets of windows: the large picture window at front, one above the bed across the cabin from the front window, and one on my right, at right angles to the door where I stand. Opposite this window, a fireplace, clearly made of the same rocks as those of the main lodge. As for furniture, I see a fluffy-looking bed with a headboard of dark metal bars, a seating area with a loveseat, tiny dining area, mini-fridge, tall standing wardrobe. The cabin's cozy, especially with two pieces of luggage, closed and sitting on the floor neatly beside the fireplace. There's not much room between them and the bedframe. Two night tables with reading lamps flank the head of the bed. One holds an old-fashioned alarm clock, complete with double bells at the top. The other has a short stack of books.

Naomi disappears into what must be the bathroom, its doorway a step and a half from the side of the bed. She steps back into the main space. "Toiletries are still here." She points to the suitcases. "It doesn't look like they're getting ready to check out or anything."

She meets my eyes, her expression one of resolve, but also somehow . . . expectant.

What? Am I supposed to be grateful she's talking to me? These are *my parents* we're talking about. I have more right than anyone else to be here.

"They're scheduled to stay until Sunday, June 2nd," Cardinal says in a low voice. I catch her giving me a soft look.

If that's pity, she can shove it. I let my scowl deepen.

Naomi opens the wardrobe doors. One side is full-length, filled with hanging garments. The other side has shelves. She checks the hanging items of clothing, running her hands down their lengths, reaching into pockets. She turns to the shelves, squatting to look into their depths, then smoothing her hand over the empty surfaces. She pulls out a shelf on a runner that holds a tea and coffee service and examines each item. She's empty-handed as she closes the doors.

"What about their car?" She turns to Cardinal.

"It's a silver Toyota." I explain in flat tones how I ended up at this cabin on my own. "But I don't know the licence plate number."

Naomi's frown passes so swiftly I barely catch it, but I know what she must be thinking. Where would an elderly couple go out here in the mountains without their car?

I rub my arms, straighten up in the doorway. I feel the anger and outrage drain away, revealing the real emotions beneath.

"This is bad, isn't it?" I ask her.

Her mouth thins as she surveys the room. "I don't see a purse." A pause. "Or any electronics."

Cardinal clears her throat. "Service is better than it was, but it can still be spotty for some. We encourage our guests to leave their laptops and tablets at home."

Guess that explains the stack of books on the bedside. I wonder if it's my mother or my father who's the avid reader.

Naomi seems to follow my thoughts. She picks up the top book. I can see the cover has Chinese characters. She flips through the pages, right to left. A quick flash of something white falls to the floor.

I ignore any thoughts of caution. Their crime scene techs or whatever will just have to deal. I stride to a stop at the foot of the bed. "What is it?" I hold my arms tightly against myself.

"Stop," shouts Naomi, throwing a hand out toward me. She's still holding the book. I can't decipher the title. "You can't be in here."

I point, my eyes riveted to the thing at her feet. "*What is it?*"

I hear Naomi blowing a breath out. "Just . . . stay there. Don't come any closer." She crouches quickly, gingerly picks up a rectangle of flat white cardstock.

I reach out my hand, palm up.

She scowls. "You are not touching this." She positions it face out toward me, holding only its edges. "Look familiar at all?"

I stare at the bright blue ink.

Cassius Li, M.A., Ph.D.
University of Lethbridge
Department of History

I meet Naomi's shadowed gaze. "I need your phone."

TEN

Of course, it's not that easy.

Naomi asks Cardinal to lock up the cabin and to keep all staff out until further notice. Seeing Cardinal's expression, she says, "Inspector Miller and Staff Sergeant Pendelton from Serious Crimes will be here late this afternoon. This is their file now. But I'd guess there'll be a forensics team along soon, too. I'll have to put up some tape on the doors and the porch. I'm sorry, it's likely the cabin will be off limits to you for some days." She glances at me.

Cardinal adopts her coolly professional mask. "Of course. I'll tell my staff now. Excuse me." She gestures for Naomi and me to exit the cabin, then locks up behind us. Without another word to either of us, she departs, murmuring into her walkie-talkie.

"May I borrow your phone please?" I make sure to enunciate clearly.

Naomi stands a few feet from me. She shakes her head. "I'm working to help you, you know. I'm not ordering you around for kicks. You can't contaminate a crime scene like that. You have no idea what it could mess up—"

I make an impatient gesture. "He could be an uncle or cousin or even my brother. If I had my *own* phone, I'd already have called by now. So what difference does it make if I borrow yours? You can't stop a private citizen from making phone calls."

"If you had your own phone, I'd still make the same request. Miller or Pendelton will want to contact him first. Like I said, I don't want to mess this up."

"But you're not even on duty right now."

"Technically, that's true, but I'm going to act as though I am, as far as procedures are concerned." She speaks calmly, rationally, and entirely without rancour.

I clench my hands, fighting for control. "How will it mess anything up for me to call someone *in my own family* and tell them I've lost my memory and oh, by the way, please, *what's my fucking name?*"

Naomi remains silent a moment, her gaze steady on me. "I have to call into my detachment, to Golden. Will you please stay here with me until I'm off the phone?"

I realize the roaring in my ears isn't wholly born of rage. "I'll be down at the river." Before she can remind me to be careful or something equally patronizing, I turn to follow the rising sound of the water, grinding my heels into the gravel underfoot with every step. I find a path between foliage, part the greenery, slap at slender tree limbs in my way, kick at unwary rocks. A vibration hums within my chest, building in intensity with every small act of pique, a low note of violence I find deeply satisfying. If someone comes for me now, I will fucking rip them apart, swear to God.

At the river's edge, I come upon a half-ring of Adirondack chairs, set around a firepit. I make a face, imagining well-to-do travellers roasting marshmallows here in a beautiful, warm orange glow, soaking in the view of stars and the moon above the silhouetted peaks of the surrounding mountains. How impossibly romantic.

Jesus, did I do that when I stayed here? Is that what I'm seeing in my mind's eye? Not sour conjecture but a real memory? I can't imagine being so content.

Right now, clouds obscure the mountain tops like a woolly blanket wrapped around enormous immovable shoulders. I can't decide if I wish it would rain, to compound my miserable state, or if I wish it would rain to wash away my turmoil. Not that it matters. It doesn't smell like impending rain. Another thing not going my way.

I think of running to the lodge, begging the use of their phone. I'm certain I can wheedle for privacy, in that space behind the reception counter. I've memorized the phone number from the business card, I'm proud to say. I could do it. I could call that man and find out who I am. I don't need anyone's goddamned permission.

I hear footsteps approach at the exact moment that I realize I don't know how to introduce myself to him. *Hi, I'm, uh, Ms. Li. I don't remember my first name or my identity. It's a long story. But my parents are Stephen and Glinda. Who are you?*

Or maybe I could start by alarming them. *Hi, Stephen and Glinda Li are missing and the cops found your card in their cabin. Who are they to you? And by the way, who am I?*

The sheer ludicrousness of my situation strikes me solidly in the gut. Any sane person would hang up. I hurry away from the footsteps, heedless of any potential danger, and head away from the lodge, following the worn path in the bank toward a bend in the river. In only a few minutes, I end up on a broad flat plain, perhaps carved out by the river when it had a different shape here. In the distance, I see cars and large semis a considerable height up, speeding by on what looks to me to be the very side of a mountain. It must be the Trans-Canada, winding downward to the plateau where the small town—Field—nestles.

I feel my shoulders slump, bowing under the weight of my own idiocy. Running away like a bratty teenager, unhappy with some adult's dictates. Thinking I have a better way, that I'm smarter than the actual trained police officer working to find my parents, and who's only here because I dragged her here on her day off. All to help me.

Jesus fucking Christ. I'm such an asshole.

Admitting defeat, I turn around, retrace my steps to the firepit and its semi-circle of empty chairs. I don't have the wits to light the fire, but I take a seat, pulling my legs up and holding my knees tight against my chest. I ignore the pain that flares up once more. I grimly push aside the cold fear and the unnumbered worries, and I wait.

It might be minutes or hours, but I watch the sky and listen to the river. Eventually, Naomi arrives, calling out a soft greeting. I raise my head from my knees.

"Okay, Constable Jankowski was in the area. He's setting up the tape around the cabin. He'll stay there until Miller and Pendelton arrive. In the meantime, I thought we could look up this Professor Li on my laptop. It's in my car. The lodge has wi-fi in their main building."

A spike of adrenaline zings through me as I see the implications. And just like that, I'm back on the upswing. I'm sure there will be a cost to this insane emotional roller coaster, but for now, I'm hanging on for the upward ride with all I've got.

I stand with a wince, brushing off my pants, and offer a conciliatory smile. "Hey, I, uh, I'm sorry for throwing a fit back there. I'm sorry for walking into the cabin like that, ignoring your instructions."

Naomi watches me for a beat, her expression tinged with wariness. Then she sighs, rubbing at her eye. "It's a stressful time. You're forgiven for losing your shit now and then." She pauses, the wariness replaced with briskness. "But we *will* have to let Miller know, and the forensics team. It's likely going to add to the time they take to process the cabin. It's our job to help you, but you've got to help us, too."

Chastened, I follow her on a path traversing the riverbank, passing a small display explaining the naming of the river and the looming mountain beside us. I find myself scanning the photographs and illustrations accompanying the text. I guess it's a habit now. Something in my messed-up head urging me to remember the thousands of Chinese men who helped break through these mountains. From there, my mind jumps to the glaring lack of Indigenous representation in these so-called historical plaques and displays. It's the twenty-first century, for chrissake.

I shake myself. Where did all of *that* come from? Am I some kind of academic, too? A historian? Oh God. I hope I'm not some fake woke ally. . . .

How do I even know that's a thing?

I kick half-heartedly at a thin branch of shrubbery, flushing at the resulting satisfaction as much as at my childishness.

We emerge at the foot of the main lodge's outdoor porch. I wait at the steps to the main door, staring at my parents' car, discomfited by the ground-level pylons and yellow tape around it, while Naomi strides to her Honda for her laptop. She leads me inside again, seeming perfectly at ease claiming a four-person table in the still-closed restaurant. I glance at Kayleigh, wondering about our welcome. If anything, she looks relieved.

"So, Cardinal's cooperating?" I take a chair beside Naomi.

She nods, like she didn't just scold me ten minutes ago. "She's got a healthy distrust of the RCMP, not that I blame her. And she didn't like me entering the cabin, but I think that was more habit than anything else. Or maybe she was thinking of unhappy guests. Under the circumstances, she's being incredibly helpful." Naomi pauses, turns to face me squarely. "I'm sorry. I had to tell her your situation." She keeps her voice low.

My scalp prickles with unease. "Why? What did you say?"

"That you have amnesia. That you don't recall how you got into the area. That your situation is likely connected to your parents' disappearance. I emphasized that we want to keep it under wraps for now."

I give my shoulders a shake, trying to release their tension. "I understand." I huff out a breath. "I don't suppose she wants the negative publicity anyway."

Naomi opens up the laptop, a matte black rectangle barely an inch thick. Something about its sleekness makes me think it must be expensive. A personal machine. She bends down to plug it into a discreet wall outlet, hidden near the floor on a section of wall between two tall windows. "All right. Let's start with the University of Lethbridge website. Maybe the sight of the professor's face will jog your memory."

I shove down the abrupt return of my resentment, make an effort at a placid tone. "Doesn't hurt to try."

She navigates the university website with quick efficiency, and within minutes, I'm staring at a square photo of myself, made male.

"That's him." Naomi makes a small noise in the back of her throat. "The resemblance is startling." She glances at me. "I'd guess he's your brother, given the years on the degrees listed in his bio. . . ."

I stare at the screen. "Can't argue with that." I sound faint even to myself. Or is it *only* to myself? I'm not sure I've spoken aloud. I shift on the cushioned chair. "Have they called him yet? I want to speak to him."

"I'm sorry. They didn't say." She studies me.

I nod with ill grace.

"Constable Aoki?"

I look over as Cardinal nears, her gaze pointed and tone brisk. "Sorry to interrupt, but I've got that list for you. I need to talk to you about it. I have some questions." She pauses, expectant, her mouth downturned slightly.

Naomi stands, says to me, "I'll be right back."

"Okay."

She hesitates, narrowed eyes assessing me for a beat.

"Constable?" The lodge manager's expression tightens.

"Yep, I'm coming, Ms. Cardinal."

I don't have to wait until she's out of sight. She left me with her laptop. She must know I'll tool around while she's gone. And if she didn't consider that possibility, she'll learn from her mistake for next time, and with a much worse offender than me, I'm sure.

I stare for a few moments at the bright screen. Jesus. How is it that I can't remember my parents' faces, but I know exactly what to do here?

I type his unusual name into the browser. I ignore the university listing, drawn to the social media accounts this time. I choose Facebook, flinching at his wide grin in the profile photo that pops up. Is that what I look like when I smile? Scrolling down, I feel increasingly unsettled by the endless array of bright photos and group shots. Nobody's that relentlessly happy, are they?

I click on his friends list only to find that I can't access because I'm not logged in. Frowning, I open a new browser window and continue my search on two other accounts, but none of them net as many possibilities. I return to his Facebook page.

From behind me, Naomi says, "You have to be friends to see his other friends."

I jump in my chair with a curse, my head suddenly pounding.

"Sorry," she says, "thought you heard me." She gestures with her chin at the laptop. "What are you doing?"

I exhale sharply and try to calm my breathing. "I just want to see if I'm in there." I stop just shy of biting my lip. "I want to find my name. This one has the most photos. I thought it'd be easier than scrolling through all the names that end with 'Li.'"

"Good hunch." Naomi resumes her seat, pulls the laptop to face her. "I'll log into the law enforcement portal." She waits with her hands over the keys, expectant gaze squarely on me. I turn away. Over the sound of key taps, she says, "It's encouraging that you remember . . . how to search online and stuff."

"Normal stuff, you mean? Yeah, I guess so." I glance down at my hands. At her okay, I look back up to find her scrolling through the previously elusive friends list. "It's annoying I can't recall more things," I mutter.

She swivels the screen back toward me. "Do any of these people look familiar?"

I pull the laptop closer and start trawling slowly through . . . 972 names and attendant profile photos. Popular guy.

Naomi echoes my thought. "You'd be more likely near the bottom of the list. If you're on Facebook, that is. People often friend their families early on."

I continue my slow scroll. "Maybe I'll recognize some of these other faces."

And there they are. Well, one of them anyway. *Glinda Li.* My mother.

My stomach gives a slow, excruciating roil.

I click the link to her account and find a ton of pictures on her home profile. Plenty of Chinese faces, all around her age. Food. Restaurants. Flowers. Vegetable gardening. Before I have time to wonder why I'm not in any of the photos, I discover my father. Most of his photos show a stern face, lean like my . . . like my brother. There's a hint of a smile just behind it. I stare at Stephen Li's image, feeling anxious, feeling an unexpected desire to see that smile come out. I swallow down the lump in my throat, hover the cursor over the photo descriptions. He doesn't have his own account. Guess my mother posts enough for the both of them.

"I'll say." Naomi offers a faint smile. "A real social butterfly."

Oh. I spoke aloud. "Guess it's not really his thing." I pause. "My father. Being social, I mean."

"But you recognize their faces?" Her tone is hopeful, kind.

I relax the fist in my lap, shake my head. "But it's clear we're family." Is that what I'll look like in twenty years? I reach out a finger, trace the contours of my mother's high cheekbones, her small nose. She has lines around her mouth and at the corners of her dark eyes. Are they from smiling or worrying?

"What about your brother? Cassius is an unusual name. Did that spark anything?"

I feel off-guard, stuck in an emotional space I'm not sure how to escape. "It's *Cash*-us, not *Cass*-ee-us." My hand freezes over the laptop trackpad. I glance over, meet Naomi's warm, encouraging gaze. "I think so, anyway."

"That's a start, though, eh?" She taps the monitor screen. "Let's see if you're in there, too. Your mum's account might be faster. She's only got 581 friends."

Naomi's right. I'm near the bottom of my mother's list.

"That's you, right?" She looks from me to the face inside the small thumbnail photo. "Your hair's different, but . . ."

I stare at the pop-up as the cursor hovers above my photo. "Apparently, my parents like unusual names." Sudden static inside my head. My voice sounds like a weak echo from the deep dark bottom of a well.

Naomi shrugs. "Maybe your dad's a Classics scholar? Or a . . . Shakespeare fan?" She flicks the screen with a fingernail. "Great work, though. We've got a lead."

Cleopatra Li. I touch my lips with cool fingers as I mouth the five syllables, their contours made alien by circumstance—if not by chance.

ELEVEN

Finding my brother's work page online was one thing. But you really need social media if you want to dig into a person's life. For example, you can catch glimpses of their home. You can discover that my brother goes by *Cass*. That his wife is a psychiatrist, in private practice. Dr. Julietta Shen, but she goes by *Etta*. That the happy couple is expecting their first baby. That they're calling it *Beanie Baby* for now, *Beans* for short. That they really like nicknames.

In person, they're striking. He's trim and broad-shouldered, in dark grey jeans and a light orange hoodie, scuffed navy blue sneakers on his feet. She wears a loose-fitting maxi dress, patterned with gold and orange flowers entwined with bright green foliage, her stomach bumping out gently as she moves. Her shoulders look smooth and silky-skinned, burnished as though she's just been tanning.

I stand from my seat in the RCMP detachment waiting room, pushing off a little too hard and stumbling as a result.

"Sis." Cass breaks from Etta, striding toward me, and enfolds me in a tight hug.

I can't quite make myself relax. I have to turn my face to the side to avoid having my nose crushed into his armpit. Beneath the smell of perspiration, this man smells of oranges and something green . . . herbaceous. I blink against unexpected tears. On some level, it makes sense, this roller coaster of emotions, but . . . there's no sense of homecoming, no flash of recognition. I don't know this person. Why do I want to cry?

He keeps the hug brief, though he holds on to my hands. "Jesus, I'm so glad you're okay. You *are* okay, right?" He assesses me from head to toe and back up again. I thought his eyes were black, but they're actually very dark brown. "Right?" He gives my hands a slight shake. I fight the urge to pull away sharply.

His wife steps in, gently nudging him aside, forcing him to let go. She pulls me into a gentler hug, her stomach pressing against me, surprising me with its firmness. She smells like lemons. "We're so glad you found us, Cleopatra."

I count to three before extricating myself. "Please, just . . . just call me Cleo, okay?"

Cass looks surprised. "Uh, yeah, sure."

"Something wrong?" I take a small step backward.

"No." He hesitates. "I . . . Um, you asked us to stop using that name when we were teenagers."

I shrug, adding it to the growing list of things-I-don't-remember.

Etta takes his hand. "That's okay, babe. We can sort all that kind of stuff out later." She smiles at me. "We're so relieved you're all right."

I catch the evening-shift receptionist watching us, Lenore-no-last-name now long gone. This receptionist is a white officer in uniform, though I haven't sussed out the name tag sewn into his shirt. The man's curious gaze shifts to the interior door to his left as I hear it opening.

Pendelton comes through, his broad face set in a professionally neutral expression. "Dr. Li, Mrs. Li. We spoke on the phone earlier. Chuck Pendelton." He shakes their hands. "If you'll sign in and follow me, we can get started. I'm sure you must be tired from the drive. We appreciate you coming straight to meet with us."

"Sorry." Etta smooths her dress over her abdomen. "I'm a total walking cliché. I have to use the loo."

Pendelton's expression softens into a bemused smile I can't quite reconcile with his usual demeanour. Maybe he has a soft spot for pregnant women. Or beautiful women. Or beautiful pregnant women. I try to hide my scowl. He says to Etta, "Of course. Through there." He points her in the right direction and turns back to my brother. "We can take care of the sign-in for both of you while we wait." He walks Cass through the steps. When Etta returns, Pendelton makes sure we each wear a visitor's badge on a lanyard. Etta wraps hers around a wrist.

Pendelton says, "I'm sorry, Mrs. Li, but it has to be visible around your neck."

"It's Dr. Shen, actually." Etta unwinds the lanyard from her wrist. "No problem." From her tote bag, she pulls out a long linen scarf and wraps it around her neck, looking stylish and composed and entirely unconcerned that she's making us all wait on her.

Pendelton leads us to the rear conference room. I notice that though my brother may be a few inches taller, Pendelton takes those few inches back in width. Etta, slender and graceful in just her flip-flops, is still almost as tall as Pendelton. I guess I ought to be grateful I'm bringing up the rear. Otherwise, I might feel like the kid in trouble being herded to the principal's office.

At the conference table, Cass waits for me to choose a chair. Etta selects the one to my left, so Cass takes the one on my right. Great. Super. So much for not being the bad kid. I shake myself mentally. I must be getting loopy from fatigue. Or maybe it's stress.

Cass says, "Can we have a few minutes alone please? It's been a whirlwind since, uh, Officer Terada knocked on our door this morning to tell us about . . . all this. I mean, we're grateful you sent someone in person, but this is pretty nuts and I'd like to talk to my sister first." He flicks me a glance. "I don't even know if you remember us."

I swallow and look away, my face flashing hot.

Pendelton grabs hold of the tall chairback in front of him, offering a perfunctory smile. "I think the sooner we start, Dr. Li, the better. You and Dr. Shen had a five, five-and-a-half-hour drive? Ours was four, from Kelowna. It's been a long day for all of us. We're sure to have more questions as the file progresses, but we need to do this preliminary interview tonight. I'm sure you understand the urgency and I know this is a difficult time, but the more information we have, the better we can help."

Etta clears her throat, shifting so she sits taller. Before she can say anything, Miller enters abruptly, her slacks and blouse somehow looking freshly pressed, though her cheeks show spots of pink.

"Hi, I'm Inspector Shae Miller, Staff Sergeant Pendelton's partner. Thanks for coming in to meet with us, Dr. Li, Dr. Shen. Can we get you some water or tea or coffee before we begin?"

I catch a glimpse of wariness on Cass's face, swiftly hidden with a smile. "I think we're fine, thanks."

"Okay," says Miller, a bit breathless. "Something's come up, it might shed some light on things here, but I just need Chuck for a sec. We'll be back in a few minutes. Thanks for your patience." She doesn't wait for a reply before whirling around again to exit.

An eagerness comes and goes on Pendelton's face in the time it takes me to blink once. He releases the chair, sending it bumping against the table's edge, and follows Miller out of the room. The door closes behind them with a hard click.

Etta takes hold of my hand. "Cleo, there's something really important you need to know. About your parents' situation. We want to tell you before we have to tell the police." Her voice is high, breathy with tension.

I frown at her, my insides feeling squeezed all of a sudden. "What? What is it?" I slide my sweaty hand out of her grasp. What could make a calm-and-cool psychiatrist nervous?

On my other side, her husband stirs. "Sis, we don't know how it's connected. I mean, I'm on the outside of all this, to be honest. I don't even have most of the facts."

I wring my hands in my lap, grimacing in disgust at the slick perspiration on my palms. I rub them against my pants. "Just say it. They could come back any second." I hate how scared I sound. Like I really am the kid in trouble.

Cass flicks a look over my shoulder at Etta, then at the door.

"Okay, sorry. Okay." He takes a breath. "It's about Mum. Three months ago, she—"

The door opens with a clatter. I stifle a groan of frustration. Etta and Cass both startle, jumping away from me. As I look toward the doorway, I can see Etta in my periphery, bringing a hand to her collarbone, like she's pressing against the sudden pounding of her heart. Cass flushes, a deep pink highlighting his angular cheekbones. He clears his throat, shifting in his chair.

Christ. I'm sure we look guilty as sin. Maybe we're all in trouble now.

But Miller takes a seat without comment, giving us only a distracted glance. To my surprise, Naomi follows her inside, her expression smoothly unreadable, and takes a chair across the table from Cass. She places her notebook, pen, and a file folder in front of her. But she's still in street clothes. Is she on duty again? Should I ask what she's doing here if she's not? Why am I feeling so paranoid?

Pendelton closes the door, stony-faced, with a stiffness in his shoulders. He hesitates for a second before taking the chair across from Etta. Miller sits at the end of the conference table closest to Cass, forcing us to swivel to our right a bit. After a moment, I push back from the table, enough so that I can see Etta, even just a little. I don't like having anyone behind me, out of view like that.

"Sorry for the wait. We have a few things to accomplish this evening." Miller places a few file folders and a spiral-bound notebook down. "First, let me give you an update on the search efforts for your parents. We have parties out now, for as long as there's sufficient light. They'll be out again tomorrow, if needed." She looks at us all. "It's distressing, I know, but it helps that we know where their car is. It gives us a sort of ground zero to spiral out from in the search."

"But it's been days." I unfold my hands, the fabric of my pants now twisted and wrinkled from me clutching at my legs. "Would they have taken food and water with them? They wouldn't have gone very far off any clear trails, right? How will the search people know where to look for them?"

"They're professionals, Cleo." Miller studies me. I'm unsure how to interpret her expression. "Given your parents' ages, and any additional information you can give us now, they'll expand the search area as needed."

Pendelton clears his throat. A flash of irritation shows on Miller's tanned face. I sneak a glance at Naomi. She looks focussed and poised.

Pendelton says, "We have your father's age as sixty and your mother is fifty-five. Are they healthy? Do either or both of them suffer from a condition that would render them unconscious unexpectedly? One of the lodge staff said your father asked about the nearest pharmacy."

I give a useless shrug.

"You mean like a heart condition or something?" Cass shakes his head. He looks to Etta.

She says, "Not that I've ever heard."

Cass leans forward slightly toward Pendelton, tension riding his shoulders. "But listen, neither of them is what you'd call an experienced hiker. They're totally city people." He frowns. "I've never been up there, but we, uh, we took a look on Google Maps and the forest looks pretty thick around that lodge. Like, could they have gotten turned around or, or something?"

"How long will the search continue?" I ask. "They've been missing since Monday, right? It's Thursday night. We're coming up on four days." I rub at my arms, suddenly covered in goose bumps. "Did you find anything useful in their cabin?" I try not to flush with guilt. "Anything that could help?"

Miller replies, "Four days or four hours, we start the search as soon as possible. There's a reason we're in here right now, instead of letting your brother and sister-in-law catch their breath. Time really is of the essence. We want to capture as much information about your parents as we can. This will go a lot faster if you simply answer our questions, but I also understand your position, Cleo, so I'll let Naomi cover the cabin before we continue." She motions.

Naomi says, "The forensics team began their work at approximately 4 p.m. They're still processing. They have to photograph and catalogue everything. Carefully. It will take more than the three hours they've had so far to finish."

I shouldn't be surprised at Naomi's formal tone, she's in the presence of superior officers, but still, it sends up a red flag for some reason.

Maybe she knows something she wishes she could tell me. Then again, maybe she got a talking-to and she's pissed all over again that I went into the cabin. At least Miller's not taking me to task for it.

After a pause, Cass says, "Are there buses from the lodge, for sightseeing or whatever? Maybe they decided to leave their car and take a bus somewhere? The search would have to include wherever that might be, too, right?"

Pendelton shakes his head. "No buses go out that way. If they didn't catch a ride with someone else, and they didn't drive themselves, they must've walked from the lodge. Which Search and Rescue are aware of." He hesitates before continuing. "And you're right, Dr. Li, it is heavily forested up there. At night, and without additional light or any experience, it would be easy to get lost, I'm afraid."

I wrap my arms around myself, fighting a sudden shiver.

"We're following all possible leads," repeats Miller. "Talking to all the staff, with the lodge manager's full cooperation. It's a painstaking process, please understand. We're going over everything meticulously. Search and Rescue know their job. We'll depend on them to handle that aspect and we'll keep you updated on any information they discover." She pauses to give us a smile, meant to be reassuring, I think.

Pendelton opens up his laptop, his movements jerky. With anger? I'm not sure. Maybe he doesn't like Naomi being here. Though he looks pissed with his partner, not her. Maybe he didn't like Miller contradicting him right after he'd said no to Cass. I wonder what was so important she pulled him out of here.

I frown. Didn't she say it was related to our parents?

TWELVE

Miller's smile fades. "All right, let's continue with questions about your parents. Given the amnesia, it seems we may have to rely on Dr. Li and Dr. Shen, but if you remember anything at all, Cleo, please let us know."

I nod, alert to the sudden formality of her demeanour. Maybe, like Naomi, it's her automatic professional voice. Every woman in a male-dominated profession has one, doesn't she? Cass grasps my hand in his, shaking me out of my irrelevant thoughts. Etta makes a small movement, just in my periphery. When I check, she's fiddling with her scarf, resettling the lanyard's cord. She offers me a tight smile. I slowly pull my hand away from Cass.

Naomi taps her notebook with her pen, her attention on the page. Pendelton shifts in his seat, his expression stony again as he glances side-long at Miller. He catches me watching him and rearranges his face into an expressionless mask.

I try to parse the undercurrent of tension, which seems only to run between the Serious Crimes partners. What are they disagreeing about?

Their displeasure seems too high for a small miscommunication. Pendelton notes my frown, his gaze dipping down to my mouth. My cheeks flush hot. I stop worrying my lower lip between my teeth. He returns his gaze to his laptop.

"We don't know enough yet to even know what's important." A fleeting smile from Miller. "Let's start simple." She turns subtly to me. "We noticed from your address that you appear to live right next to your parents."

Cass gives a small swivel of his chair. "They share a duplex. Mum and Dad on one side, Cleopatra on the other."

"Your parents own the duplex?" Miller says.

Cass nods.

My eyes feel like they're jumping out of my sockets. I grip the chair's armrests. My palms prickle at the coarse, nubby fabric. "Please tell me I pay rent to them?"

"Of course." Cass gives me a lopsided grin. "You insisted."

"Do they still work?" asks Miller.

"Dad's been with the same engineering firm in Edmonton for decades. Targeted Engineering Inc. He began as a draftsman, doing all the hand-drawn blueprints and stuff, back in the day, then he learned the design software. They love him there, but," Cass glances at me, "he's about to take early retirement."

"And your mother?" asks Pendelton.

"She works at a friend's florist shop, a tiny little place in the west end. It's actually called West End Flowers. The building started as someone's house, decades ago, when it was popular to have those little pebbles as siding? Like, when was that? The '70s? It's pretty small—looks like a dump now, to be honest, all dingy on the outside. I guess they save their money for the flowers." He shrugs.

Is he always this talkative? Or just nervous right now? I sneak a look at Etta, but her ready smile shows me nothing but reassurance. I guess that means she's used to her husband's flow of talk?

"But Mum likes working there," continues Cass. "She loves flowers. And she says it's fun gossiping all day with Auntie Annie while they work. Anna Ong. She owns the shop."

"She's a relation?" asks Miller.

Cass shakes his head. "It's a term of respect for our parents' friends. Auntie. Uncle."

Naomi shifts in her seat.

My mind's still on the flower shop. I allow myself to imagine my mother, laughing as her quick hands bundle up a cone of bright blossoms into cellophane and paper wrapping. It's easier than I thought, seeing her smile. She didn't post as many bright smiling photos as Cass . . . as my brother did, and she seemed to prefer a small uptilt of her lips. Not a big-wide-grin type of person, but she certainly liked selfies with friends.

My . . . father on the other hand mostly looked like he barely tolerated those photos, dark eyes staring flatly from a stern face. Does he not like having his picture taken? Are my parents an opposites-attract sort of couple?

I guess I should be grateful at least half of my family likes to laugh.

My family. A thought strikes me with such ferocity, I fall back against the chair.

"What is it?" Naomi stares at me, voice sharp. "Are you all right?"

"No, I . . ." I feel sweat prickling at my hairline. "It's just—" I turn to Cass, feeling stiff and awkward. "I never thought to ask . . . do I have a family? Of my own." I swallow. "I mean, I don't feel like I do . . . but I should've asked . . . right?"

Cass says, "No kids, unmarried. No desire *whatsoever* to have kids. You've always been clear on that front."

"That's good." I blink, hearing how that sounds aloud. "No, I mean, it's good I don't have kids, since I don't feel, ah, maternal. Though I guess you could probably tell, though, huh, because I'd've asked about them sooner. I mean, if I were a decent mother—" I snap my mouth closed.

"It's okay." Etta gives my hand a small pat. "No one's judging you."

Miller says, with a trace of impatience, "We were able to access your income tax filings. No dependents. We would've asked you about a family sooner if it'd been different." She glances at Naomi.

"I'm sorry we didn't think to tell you." Naomi sounds genuinely contrite.

Pendelton twitches, his eyes firmly on his monitor, his mouth twisting like he's swallowed something sour. I look from him to Miller and decide it's time to say something.

Etta beats me to the punch. She leans forward, her elegant profile marred only slightly by the slight downturn to her mouth. "Excuse me, but is there something going on? I'm getting the sense that the two of you are in the middle of an argument of some sort. I apologize for my presumption, but if it's related to my parents-in-law or to Cleo, we deserve to know what's going on. At the very least, you seem distracted, which doesn't bode well for our case."

I realize my palms are over-sensitized from rubbing against the scratchy armrest fabric. I take my hands, press them against my pants, force them to still. I most definitely do not make them into fists. I add, "If there's bad news related to our parents or about my case," I swallow, "we don't need to be protected from it. I want to know what's going on. I need to know."

"We all do." Cass stops fidgeting in his chair and straightens up.

I think Naomi might have nodded, ever so slightly, but my attention's glued to Pendelton. His simmering resentment smooths out, his face becoming blandly handsome once more. Miller looks at us with something like wide-eyed innocence. It sits uncomfortably on her sharp features.

"We understand," she says firmly, "but we're also responsible for following and upholding standards and procedures. The last thing I want to see is someone in possession of preliminary information jumping to conclusions that are unwarranted and premature."

I scowl, interpreting the jumble of bureaucrat-ese. "We're not going to go off half-cocked. Like, what would we do, even?"

Cass's voice lowers. "Did the search party find something?" I sense Etta stiffening. "Is there news you're keeping from us about our parents?"

I shiver from an abrupt chill. "Or is this about my case?"

Pendelton turns to his partner. "Your call, Shae."

"Apparently not anymore," she mutters, mouth thinning.

"You can't *not* tell us now." The words come out more angry than I intended. Not that I can take them back. Miller narrows her pale eyes at me.

"One of the search party found a personal item." She pauses. I swear it's payback. I clamp my mouth shut, my hands gripping my legs hard, maybe even enough to bruise.

But Cass apparently doesn't care for pride. "What is it?" he asks, shaky.

"A wallet," says Miller. "We're still processing it, looking for prints, etc., but—"

Pendelton pushes aside his laptop, the harsh scrape of sound cutting into Miller's speech. "The ID and credit cards are your father's."

Naomi abruptly sits back in her chair. Did she not know? Why wouldn't they tell her? What's going on with this case? Why *is* she here?

Etta gasps. I stare at Pendelton, too many thoughts to corral into proper sentences.

Cass asks, "Where was it? Where did they find it?"

Pendelton subsides, gesturing to his partner. Miller nods, curt. "The Meeting of the Waters viewpoint, a few kilometres up Yoho Valley Road from the lodge your parents were staying at."

I watch them as if through wavy glass, blinking in vain to clear my vision. My body flashes cold then hot then cold again. I feel fresh sweat break out in my armpits and along my hairline, dripping down the nape of my neck. Goosebumps pop up along my arms, sending a shudder through me. This is bad. Really bad.

Miller gives a small shake of her head. "Not necessarily, Cleo."

Damn it. I spoke aloud again without thinking.

"It means we're on the right track, in a sense." She hesitates, her face hardening just a little. "Are you all right?" She narrows her eyes, peering at me. "Because this reaction is exactly what I meant when I spoke of jumping to conclusions. I'm not trying to play babysitter. But I am aware that it's an emotional time. I wanted to wait until we had a strong lead on their whereabouts before telling you about the wallet. I would hope considering your emotional and mental health isn't a bad thing."

"No one said it was," replies Etta smoothly. "I think my husband and Cleo and I are of the same mind, though. We'd rather have updates of ongoing developments than wait until the info's all tidied up. In my professional opinion, withholding information from us harms our mental health." She pauses. "Not to mention our trust in the process."

"Etta's right." Cass gestures toward me. "You've only known Cleopatra during a . . . vulnerable time, but believe me, she's more than capable of holding it together. And it doesn't serve us to be in the dark about this search. We appreciate your hard work, we do, but these strangers to you? They're our parents."

"I don't doubt your stake in this." Miller nods, though she looks exasperated. "But the fact remains that investigations don't move along at a linear and predictable pace. This isn't TV or the movies. We're bound by professional standards to communicate in specific ways, and I cannot promise anything other than that."

I wave a hand impatiently at her ass-covering, irritation focussing my thoughts. "Okay, fine. But what about the wallet? What can you tell us?"

"It was retrieved partway down the bank," says Pendelton. "You were up there with us, Cleo, you know there aren't defined paths down to the water from the viewpoint signage. There's just a long stretch of high riverbank. And some of it's sheer. The wallet wasn't close to the road, it was down on one of the steeper areas." He pauses, shifting to include Cass. "Credit cards and driver's licence were intact. No cash."

Cass gestures. "Dad didn't usually carry much cash. Maybe fifty bucks? His credit card collects rewards points. He charged everything and paid it off monthly."

Pendelton enters information as fast as Cass speaks. Naomi watches Cass, her gaze clear and sharp. Miller looks impatient again, her mouth a thin line.

"At least, that's what Cleopatra told me when they got these credit cards, a few years ago." Cass's voice lowers. "She said he'd gone charge-crazy. We thought it was funny. . . ." He trails off.

"So," I ask, careful to think it through before I speak into the weighted silence, "does this mean he might've . . . fallen down the bank? Into the river?" My throat constricts at thoughts of freezing cold water, of jagged boulders and the roaring current. I push the images to the periphery of my mind, try to keep my voice level.

"They only found the wallet," says Miller briskly. "But it's given us a focal point, as well as a lead. We now have reasonable confirmation your father was up there."

"But what about, uh, our mother? Was there any sign of—" I cough, my throat abruptly too tight to make the words.

Cass reaches for my hand again. I let him squeeze it once before taking it back, my palm clammy. Etta makes a low noise, I think in sympathy.

Miller sounds confident. "The teams will continue the search up at the viewpoint, around the lodge, and along the Kicking Horse River, widening the search from there."

I frown. "But are there caves or something on that bank, that area around the viewpoint? Where could they *be* up there?"

Cass runs a hand through his hair, leaving it standing on end in spots. "Be honest with us, please. Do you or the Search and Rescue people think our parents could still be hunkered down somewhere near where they found the wallet? I mean, I don't know that area, obviously, but . . ." He blows out a breath, like he's been holding it in for a while.

"I'm no expert," says Naomi, "but your parents might have wandered farther up that road, looking for help. They might've gotten turned around, disorien—"

Miller cuts in. "As Naomi says, it's not our area of expertise. But you can be certain that the Search and Rescue team is doing their best to find your parents."

I recognize a non-answer when I hear one. Not that I'm in any shape to cross-examine two RCMP detectives determined to stonewall. I'm not sure about the good constable. But she's probably got no choice but to follow where she's led.

My head fills up with too many worries and worst-case fears about my parents' situation—added to the ones about not remembering them or anything useful that might contribute to finding them.

"I know everyone's tired," continues Miller, curt, "but let's get back on track." Her gaze slides to Etta, then settles on Cass. "Dr. Li, about the living situation. You said your parents and sister share a duplex. But your parents own it."

"They wanted her nearby." He pauses. "They rely on Cleopatra for everything."

Pendelton rests his hands on his keyboard, a frown wrinkling his broad forehead as he leans forward. "Are your parents in need of extra assistance for some reason? You said earlier they're relatively healthy, but is there some kind of physical limitation or medical condition involved?"

Cass shakes his head. "Just the way our family is." He eyes the two white cops for a moment. "Like most Chinese immigrant families, our parents relied on us when we were young to translate things for them. Even now, though they've been in Canada for over thirty years, they still don't feel fluent. And I don't mean just language. Culture, too. So, they rely on us. I mean, on Cleopa—um, Cleo. I've been out of the picture for a long time."

Miller sharpens her gaze. "Why is that? You don't get along with them?"

Cass pauses before giving a shrug. "I was an arrogant little shit. I thought my parents small-minded, overly traditional. We didn't have much in common. I moved out as soon as I could and . . . I just kept a certain distance."

There's a beat of silence as Miller and Pendelton digest Cass's vague explanation. Etta clears her throat daintily, her version of fidgeting. Naomi writes something rapidly in her notebook, then turns to a new page, the sound crackling through the room.

"So," says Miller, "your sister would be the most likely person to have seen your parents before they left for this trip?"

Cass nods. "She set it all up for them. My mother was nervous, she's not very outdoorsy. She was happy for Cleopatra's help."

I hear something in his voice, a flatness in that last sentence. Neither

Miller nor Pendelton seem to note it. But I'm not so sure I can read them anymore. Or Naomi.

That last thought sets my insides squirming.

"The lodge people said your sister booked their stay as a surprise celebration." Pendelton's expression is intent, like a dog on the scent. "What was being celebrated? An anniversary? A promotion? Early retirement?"

My palms break out in a sweat. I resist the urge to touch my neck, to hide the pulse I'm sure is visibly pounding there. Where is this even coming from? Is this what Cass was trying to tell me earlier? I force my breathing to slow, to remain calm.

"Well, I mentioned Dad was retiring soon, right?" Cass shifts slightly, his shoulders stiff again. "A few months back, my parents decided to sell the duplex and move west. My mother had a condo picked out. On the North Shore."

"In Hawaii?" asks Miller.

"North Vancouver." Beneath the table, Cass bounces his knee once, twice. He rubs his hands along his pants, like he's drying damp palms, maybe. I can relate.

"What is it, Cass?" I ask.

"You . . ." He licks his bottom lip, flicks a glance at Miller.

"It's okay," says Etta, soothingly.

Cass fidgets, rolling his shoulders. "Um, Mum wanted you to move with them to BC, but you . . . didn't want to leave here. I mean, Edmonton."

I give him a frown. "So we argued?"

He nods. "That's what you each told me. Separately."

"But why would I set this trip up for them, then?"

His cheeks darken. "Ah . . . that was your, uh, sense of humour." I consider the expression on his face. He looks away, his gaze bouncing around the tabletop before returning to me. "Like, you wanted them to see what they'd be leaving behind. What they'd missed out on all these years, practically in their backyard . . ." I see him cross and recross his feet at the ankles.

"And?"

He ducks his chin. "And you wanted to show Mum you had the money for it. Like, you're an adult and have the money to spare, thank you very much." He looks back up at me. "You were pretty steamed Mum just assumed you'd move. This trip . . . it was like a, erm, a fuck-you." He grimaces. "She, uh, started making plans for you to live with them out there. And . . ." Another deep breath. "They sold the duplex without telling you."

I rub my newly aching head. No wonder he wanted to warn me first.

I can read between the lines. Surely Miller's got to consider the possibility of foul play. And in such cases . . . the cops always suspect family first, isn't that how it works?

Miller says, "So, you weren't exactly telling the truth? When you said your mother was happy for your sister's help?" Her tone confirms the sinking feeling in my stomach.

"I, uh, wasn't comfortable airing our family's dirty laundry. I'm sorry. I can see now you probably want to know as much as you can."

"Not *probably*. Definitely. What we don't know might end up being important, maybe even essential to closing this file." Miller flicks a narrow look at me and Etta before settling her hard gaze back on Cass. "Don't you want to know how your sister ended up drugged and abandoned hundreds of kilometres from her home? With your parents so close by? But now mysteriously gone? It must be clear to you by now that coincidence isn't enough to explain everything. Someone's got to know what happened. We need to figure out who. We need to figure out why. That's the game here. Those are the stakes."

THIRTEEN

Cass frowns, abruptly distracted, as though he's trying to recollect something. Even if I don't see myself when I wear that look, the one he's sporting now, I recognize that expression, deeply. I shouldn't be surprised, since we're siblings and all, but . . . it feels weird to see shadows of myself in his face.

Before I can decide whether or not to ask what he's trying to remember, Etta leans forward, her voice harder than I've heard it yet.

"I understand it's a figure of speech, Inspector, but just so we're all clear. We're not *playing* at anything. Even though it should go without saying, I'm saying it. We're here to give you as much information as we can and help out however we can. At the same time, we recognize that Cleo is your best source for information about Stephen and Glinda, something that might help in finding out . . . what's happened to them."

I decide not to dwell on the slight hitch in Etta's voice at that last part.

"We're well aware of that," says Miller coolly, "so why don't we continue?" She turns back to me. "Naomi's report indicates that you mentioned nightmares . . . or flashbacks. Can you tell us about them?"

"What? No. This isn't an appropriate place for this." Etta's outrage elicits a stiffening in Miller's body language. I don't think Etta cares. "You can't just poke around in her brain, hoping she'll cough up something useful." Etta turns to face me. "You need to speak with a trained and accredited therapist, Cleo, someone who can help you remember without harm to your mental health."

Cass's question sounds extra quiet in the aftermath of Etta's anger. "You're having nightmares, sis? Are you . . . are you okay?" He searches my face with his dark eyes, his earlier distraction completely gone now.

They all stare at me, a tableau of intense expressions in varying degrees.

I swallow, trying to figure out the best way to satisfy all the priorities in the room. The lie, it turns out, is easiest. "I'm fine. If I can help somehow, I need to try." I turn so I'm square with the table, eyes down, swallowing again at the sudden flood of saliva in my mouth.

"Um . . . the nightmare. Okay. It's, it's dark. Nighttime, I think. I'm in a car with . . . someone, but we're not driving. We're still. There aren't any lights outside the car." I close my eyes, try to stay level through the flashes of imagery, the close quarters, the press of imminence, of frightening eventuality.

"It's dark inside the car, but I can sort of . . . feel the steering wheel in front of me. I don't know if I have my hands on it or not. The seat, it's sort of high up. I'm looking down at the hood. Through the windshield." I shift in my chair, swivel slightly to my right. I feel my breath coming faster, feel it speed up in time with my heart rate. "There's a silhouette to my right. It's a . . . another person . . . a man. He's reaching for me from the other seat, lurching forward, lunging at me. I raise my arm to keep him away. I don't know what he wants, but there's a . . . an intent I can feel. I think I'm screaming." I open my eyes, though I don't look at the others. "That's when I wake up."

Cass takes my hand, holds it tight. I imagine I can feel Etta vibrating next to me, her desire to say something is so strong.

Miller clears her throat. When she speaks to me, she's gentle as the first time we met. "Does it feel like a memory?"

"Maybe?" I stare hard at the table's dark wood-veneer top as I listen to Pendelton exiting the room. "How do I tell?"

"I'm taking you to your doctor when we get to Edmonton," says Cass. His tone matches Etta's for implacability. "She can refer you for therapy. Etta can make a list of good therapists and you can cross-reference with your GP. That's the best way for you to work through this. It's going to take time and patience. It's certainly not going to happen overnight." I'm sure he directs this last comment at Miller.

She remains silent.

My eyes droop, I want to shut them so badly. Shut down and sleep for weeks.

Into the uncomfortable breach, Pendelton returns, setting six bottles of water on the table. He murmurs into his partner's ear. Miller stirs, clearing her throat. "We were able to clear the cabin."

I think of my father's wallet. What the cops must have decided once they found it. I forcibly repack my tears and my nightmares into their amorphous mental compartment and do my damnedest to reach for a calm tone. No one's going to tell me anything if they think I'm on the verge of collapse. For good measure, I release my hand from Cass's warm grip. "You packed up our parents' things?"

Through the open doorway, a uniformed constable wheels in a green suitcase, with a matching duffle bag clipped into place on its front, and parks the set against a wall. Soon after, he returns with a second green suitcase, a reusable cloth grocery bag slung onto the top, its handles threaded over the suitcase pull-bar.

Cass stands, face pale, as he waits for the constable to set the second case against the wall beside the first.

Pendelton addresses me. "After we dealt with your entry into the cabin, the suitcases and their possessions were prioritized by the forensics team. They photographed and catalogued everything we're returning now." He pauses, his tone softening. "Naomi thought you'd like to have them. We agreed it might help you with your memories."

Beside me, Etta asks gravely, "Is it true it took three days to notice Stephen and Glinda were missing?"

I turn away from Pendelton's grim expression as he replies. "I'm afraid so."

Naomi quietly tells them why, as Cardinal explained it, but I let their conversation fall to murmurs in the background. An almost-elderly couple in the wilds for four days with no food, no shelter, no knowledge of this immense, merciless forest. The roiling in my gut tells me what it likely means, but maybe, if I stop listening, I won't have to hear if it's true.

A roar slowly fills my head. Water rushing over boulders. Relentless. Cold.

Cass's orange hoodie flashes in my periphery, brings me back to the room. I wrap my arms around myself, squeeze against the shivering.

Cass takes the grocery bag, unpacks bottled juices, three packages of snack foods, two oranges, and a speckled yellow pear onto the conference table. Then he puts everything back inside. I get up, too, though once I'm standing, I'm uncertain what to do. Etta rises as well, staying beside me. I move away a little, unwilling to be touched.

Cass detaches the duffle, lays it on the floor to unzip the top flap. He doesn't take anything out, just peels the flap back, peering inside. I catch a glimpse of clothing before he rezips the main compartment closed, then checks the pockets on either end of the bag.

Miller's voice returns to briskness. "As you know, we weren't able to recover any electronics. We're assuming they had their phones with them. Can you say if they'd have brought a tablet or laptop with them on vacation?"

Cass and I mirror one another in the negative, he kneeling on the floor and I stiff next to my abandoned chair. Etta says nothing. I see a tightening around Miller's mouth before she turns away. "We have some paperwork for you to sign before we officially turn over everything to you."

"And it becomes my responsibility," I murmur.

Cass continues what looks to me like a cursory survey of our parents' things. I wrinkle my nose at a faint scent of mothballs. No one else seems to have a reaction, not even Cass, who's closest to the cases. Perhaps it's only in my head. I don't know what he's looking for. Maybe nothing more than reassurance. He finishes with the second case, closing it back up with a loud *zzzzbbbbrrrrppp* that fills the otherwise silent room.

Naomi offers me a single page on a clipboard and a blue ballpoint. I read the form, my thumb rubbing the cheap plastic pen along its hexagonal casing. Cass joins me, muttering as he reads over my shoulder. I glance at him. He gives a sort of shrug-nod. Without thinking, I sign the bottom of the paper, acknowledging receipt of my parents' possessions.

"Hey, that must be a good sign." Cass's voice sounds bright, overly so in this drab room and its undercurrents. He points to my signature. "I recognize that."

I stare down at the squiggle of blue ink.

"It's a good idea to keep track of all these things," says Etta softly, "the things you recall, as they happen. For when you talk to a therapist. It might help with understanding what can help you regain all your memories."

Cass squeezes my shoulder, then lets his hand fall away. He turns to the cops, arrayed in a line across the table from us, the windows behind them showing darkening blue skies and gently swaying trees with long shadows. "This means we can leave in the morning? Your giving us the suitcases and stuff?"

"We understand you're impatient to be on your way," says Miller, "but there's more we need to nail down before you can go." She nods at Pendelton.

"Dr. Shen," he says, "if you'd come with me, please. We just need to verify the information Officer Terada got from you this morning."

"Cleo," says Miller smoothly, "Naomi will escort you back to the waiting area, while I continue in here with Dr. Li."

Cass, Etta, and I blink at one another.

Naomi steps up close to me. "It's okay. They just need to confirm some details. Standard procedure." She angles her body, neatly blocking me from any other path but toward the door, her expression blandly expectant.

"I'll be out in a jiff," says Cass. "Promise."

Etta slides past with a brief touch to my shoulder and a reassuring smile. Cass gives her a quick kiss, his hand caressing her cheek. Head high, she follows Pendelton out into the corridor.

Naomi trails me out of the room and down the hallway. She holds the door open for me as I pass into the public space of the lobby. The uniformed receptionist gives me a quick glance from the side of his eye, his hands flashing over his keyboard without pause. Naomi nods at me from the threshold. "Please wait for them here." She holds out her hand. "Lanyard, please?"

I comply. I think maybe she'll say more, but she only releases the door. I hear it click shut.

Across from reception, three white men sit in the plastic chairs, empty seats between them. One of them eyes me silently, lined face harsh under the fluorescent lighting. I warily take my spot next to the potted plant. He returns his attention to his phone.

I consider leaving, but where would I go?

No one speaks. I wring my hands in my lap, then shove them into my jacket pockets. The room soon feels too close. I glance at the door and the fresh air available just on its other side. It's still light out, probably warm, too. I swallow, wet my dry lips.

The officer stands, papers in hand. He drops them into a wall-mounted file holder and resumes his seat. I shift my attention from him to the door again, imagining myself outside, alone in the growing shadows.

I pull my feet onto the chair and wrap my arms around my shins. I rest my chin on my knees. I wait.

The lobby gradually empties. Eleven minutes after the last of the men leaves, a sheaf of pink papers clutched delicately in his large hands, the interior door opens without notice.

Cass comes through, pulling the suitcase and duffle combination. He smiles wearily as his gaze finds me. Behind him, Naomi replays her role as escort, waiting patiently for Cass to give her his visitor's badge. She sets the other suitcase next to the door, offers me a nod, and disappears once again with a loud click.

Cass draws me up to standing and hugs me. It still feels strange.

I pull back first. "What did they want?"

"I need some air," he says with a sigh, turning toward the exterior door. As we pass the reception counter, he addresses the officer. "Uh, hi. We'll be back in ten minutes. Just going for a walk. My wife's still back there."

The officer nods sharply.

Cass leads me outside and across the bumpy parking lot to a deep blue station wagon, sleek and dusty. We wrangle the cases and duffle bag into the rear. He locks the car with a beep.

I was right earlier. It's lovely outside, warm with the slightest of fresh breezes. The sun casts stretched shadows on its way down below the horizon. I force myself to release the tension in my shoulders for one deep breath.

"C'mon. Let's get away from the road. It might not be busy," Cass glances up and down its packed-gravel length, "but we'll be eating dust if anyone does pass us." He steers me to the back of the building. We walk in silence along the bit of flattened earth that serves as access to the staff parking area.

We clear the parked vehicles, make for the stand of trees I've been staring at all evening through the conference room windows. On this side, they line a patch of grass overgrown with weeds. On the other, I see a chain-link fence and a neatly mown lawn, bordered by more of the same. Must be the safest neighbourhood in Golden.

I shake myself out of useless reveries. "So what did they want?"

His profile tightens briefly. "When the officer from the Lethbridge police came to the house to tell us you were here and that . . . that Mum and Dad were missing, she asked us where we were last weekend. What we were doing." He rubs at his eye with a finger. "Inspector Miller asked me about it again, a lot more in-depth."

"What did you tell her?" I wish I remembered our history enough to know if I should worry he'll take it wrong.

"Friday was the OB/GYN and then running errands all day. Groceries, prescriptions. Together," he replies with a quick sidelong glance. "Etta can send the receipts to Inspector Miller. We stayed home the rest of the weekend. I mostly read a book. Etta had some leftover work. They can probably verify her log-ins, her activity when she was entering patient notes into the system."

Cass huffs out a breath, running his hands through his hair. I'm struck by how much we look alike. High cheekbones, full lips, pointed chin. I think back to my mother's profile photo, the angle of her eyes. She gave us each that, too.

He waves his hand in the air. "Never mind that. Remember when I tried to tell you something earlier? I mean, remind you? It's related to the move. To Vancouver."

"Yeah, I figured it out when you mentioned us arguing about the move. Me and, uh, Mum." I clench my hands to hide their trembling.

He frowns at me for a second. "No, it's something else."

I blink at him for a moment. "Seriously, Cass, stop fucking around and just say it, then."

He lets out a laugh, short and truncated. "There's the ornery sister I know and love. I gotta tell you, I was worried in there." He points a thumb back over his shoulder, toward the detachment building. "You're usually a lot more . . . forceful."

"If dropping an F-bomb is what it takes for you to tell me, you're on." I grab his hand, give it a shake. "Just tell me, okay?" I drop his hand, wipe my suddenly damp palms on the legs of my pants. "The suspense is killing me already."

"Okay, okay. Here goes." He lets out another huff of breath. "Three months ago, Mum won the lottery."

I stumble, my foot landing in an invisible dip in the ground. I overbalance, hopping to regain even footing. "What?"

"The lottery. It was all over the news. A huge national jackpot." He returns my frown with his own. "You really don't remember any of this?"

"What do *you* think?"

"Yeah, sorry." At least he has the decency to blush. It's barely visible in the waning light.

I rub my temples. "Cass . . . You should've told them right away."

"I wanted to tell you first. We haven't done anything wrong."

"They're not going to see it that way. They're going to be suspicious. It's in their job description." I pause. "They have to suspect everybody."

"Sis. Cleo. Listen to me." He gestures around us. "We're *literally* in view of them. The time between when I tell you and when I tell them is practically negligible. I understand they might be suspicious. I get it, really. But Mum won the lottery three months ago. How can it possibly be related now?"

My stomach churns. I breathe deeply a few times, trying to calm my racing heart, the building headache. "That's how *you* think, not how the cops think. They always look at family first. That means us, idiot. It doesn't matter if we did something wrong or not. They're going to dig into our possible motives—" I glare at him "—like anger at having my home sold out from under me. They're going to check our alibis, like they've already done with you, but harder. They'll see this as reason for us to—" I clamp my mouth shut, bile rising up my throat.

"I'm *not* an idiot, sis. I get it. But we've got nothing to worry about. I'm sure I can prove I was home all weekend. Plus, I've done nothing wrong. And I know you've done nothing wrong, too. You—" He stops, mouth hanging open as his eyes widen with, I hope, realization.

"Do you get it now? I can only tell them *I don't remember*. Even if it's the truth, they're not going to just settle for that. They can't. If they're good cops, they have to follow through with a lot more questions."

He shakes his head. "You didn't do anything wrong, Cleo. You're a victim in all this. You were assaulted! They have to follow rules, right, the police? They can't . . . make up shit you didn't do." His tone matches the incredulous expression on his lean face.

"That's not the point." My mouth fills abruptly with saliva. I swallow several times, trying to relieve the unpleasant pressure building in my throat. "The point is, I can't defend myself. I don't have definitive proof like, like Etta does. And at least she can corroborate your alibi. Jesus, I don't even *have* an alibi." By now, I'm breathing shallow and quick, words coming fast and hard, my voice rising into the trees overhead. "I don't have an alibi, Cass. I can't remember where I was last weekend. Or what I did or didn't do. I can't even recall how I got here. How am I supposed to prove what I don't remember?"

Then it's too much for me to fight. My insides convulse and I grip my abdomen with both hands. Cass jumps back as I heave up every last bit of food and bitter tea I put in my stomach only a few hours ago.

All I taste is bile.

FOURTEEN

I don't think I've ever literally seen someone's vein throbbing at their temple before. I don't think Pendelton's head is actually going to explode—but I'm also not sure it isn't. If I weren't about to scream from the tension, I'd laugh.

My brother's chin rises a degree. "I take full responsibility if I made a mistake with this, but it felt important to me that I tell her first. Remind her, actually."

Pendelton's face twists into a nasty scowl. "Christ."

Naomi clears her throat, a small sound that still somehow expresses incredulity.

Miller's brows draw close together, ruining the fine expanse of her forehead. She shares a dark glance with Pendelton before refocussing on my brother. Cass's face is drawn, weary, but he meets her gaze without flinching.

Miller's blue eyes look even lighter, eerie ice chips in a face of stone. "Surely you knew it would change our line of investigation."

"Officer Terada didn't seem the right person to tell," he retorts. "I thought it'd be better for me to wait for the officers in charge of the investigation. *After* I spoke with my sister, of course. Like I said, I understand if you're unhappy with me about that."

I wonder, if I had my memories, would I still find my brother's naïveté as surprising? Is he always this trusting? If Etta were still here, I could ask her. But she left for the hotel and bed not long after I came back inside to rinse my mouth out and settle my nerves. With immovable patient obligations tomorrow, she'll be leaving early, with another five-plus-hour drive ahead of her. She looked less tired than Cass, but maybe Pendelton goes easier on pregnant ladies than Miller does on history professors with no corroborated alibi.

To be honest, I'm still wrapping my head around someone choosing to make an eleven-hour round trip, just to support me, in person, for less than two hours. I mean, they even came in separate cars. "We're family," Etta said. As if it were the most straightforward thing in the world.

Setting aside my disquiet, I watch Pendelton's face change subtly, the gears clicking away in his head as he no doubt calculates the new angles Cass's announcement creates. He says, "Who knew about the lottery winnings? You two, your parents, your wife. Who else?"

"Etta hasn't told anyone."

"You can be sure we'll check with her directly." Miller opens her notebook, the cover slapping the table with an audible smack. "We didn't see any kind of announcement on your mother's Facebook account."

"Or get any media hits on her name," says Pendelton.

Cass looks so earnest, despite his exhaustion. "She didn't want it made public. She wants to remain anonymous. She made us promise. That's why my in-laws don't even know, and we're gonna catch some serious flak for keeping it from them, too." He pauses. "Mum hasn't claimed the winnings yet. She has a year from the date of the draw. And when she does, she's getting her lawyer to do it so she can stay out of the media entirely. If her name and photo got in the news, then strangers would know, she said. And she didn't want to be a . . . target." He ends haltingly, his Adam's apple bobbing as he swallows.

Pendelton frowns. "That makes sense, but it's not up to her, unfortunately. Lottery corps require winners to go public. Names, photos, where they bought their ticket. They have to agree in order to claim their winnings. A family tried to stay anonymous, a few years ago, I think. But the lottery people refused them, so they had to go public to get their money."

Cass looks at me for a second before shrugging at Pendelton. "I don't know what to say about that. Cleopatra might know, but . . ."

I duck my head down and stare at my hands, useless again.

After a beat, Miller asks, "What about the rest of the family? Did your mother tell other relatives?"

"Both our parents are only children, far as we know. Our grandparents are all deceased. Before either of us were born." Cass aims a fleeting glance at me.

"What do you mean, *far as you know*?" Miller's iciness intensifies.

"I mean, our parents didn't talk about their past, in Hong Kong. I know they immigrated here in '82, but they didn't talk much about their life before Canada. Nothing beyond really general stuff, like being poor and how they did in school. A few funny stories about misbehaving."

"Where did they land, when they came?" asks Pendelton.

"But," Miller leans forward, interrupting, "you think they left something out? Like maybe more family? Back in China?"

Naomi shifts in her chair.

Cass shoots Miller an impatient look. "No, no. Nothing like that. And they were both from Hong Kong, not mainland China." He sits back.

"It's just something I always say in relation to my parents. There's so much they never talk about. It was aggravating, growing up, that's all. School projects about family history or whatever, and we'd have nothing to write about. We used to complain to each other," he gestures with his chin, "Cleopatra and I. Eventually, we made up this little joke. *As far as we know* was code. Like shorthand. A way to express frustration without it being a big deal."

I fidget in my seat. "I . . . don't remember that. Sorry."

"It's okay. It'll come." Cass turns to address Pendelton. "Vancouver. They arrived in Vancouver. November 1982. Mum was miserable from all the rain and grey skies their first winter. She told us that many times."

"Dr. Li," says Miller, "we need to nail down how many people would know about your mother's windfall. As she correctly thought, she could've been targeted for that ticket."

"It was *three months* ago," Cass retorts. "And no one knew it was her."

I barely hear his argument. "But my brother already said Mum was careful to keep it quiet. If that's what she wanted, I'm sure I wouldn't have told a soul, right, Cass?" I realize I've missed something. "Wait. What was the jackpot?"

"You really don't recall?" Pendelton's low voice raises the hairs on my arms.

I shake my head, helpless to fight the shiver.

"Forty-seven point three million," says Cass quietly. "She was the sole winner."

I blink, my brain stuttering out for a second or two.

Miller narrows her eyes, considering. "What about your father? Couples often share the claim."

Cass flushes slightly pink. "He knew, of course, but Mum said . . . She signed the ticket, uh, alone. It's hers. She's the only one in the family who likes to play the lotto. I don't know that Dad ever bought a ticket on his own. He's not much of a gambler." He turns thoughtful for a moment, then gives a half-shrug. "Doesn't matter. I'm sure he was supportive. He's just more, um, quiet about it. He never likes talking about money anyway."

I stare past Pendelton's shoulder, through the dusty glass. Leaves dancing in the breeze make momentary patches of bright green in the shadowy grove of trees. I focus on them, trying to predict the next flash of colour, trying not to think of my father in freezing cold river water, tumbling over sharp boulders.

Miller speaks, gentle but firm. "Let's return to the original question. Who else could have known about this?"

"Maybe Auntie Annie? They were best friends. But she was also a huge gossip, so I dunno." Cass runs his hands through his hair, leaving it ruffled in places. "Other than checking her Facebook, I don't have anything else to tell you. I didn't live close by. We only talked once a week or so. And that only began two months ago, after I called her to tell her about the baby news. Before that, I . . . avoided her calls. We talked maybe once a month, probably every couple months, actually. And I didn't talk to my father at all."

"About that," says Miller. "Can you be more specific about this . . . estrangement between you and your parents, Dr. Li?"

Cass eyes Miller blankly for a second. "Why?"

"Why not? I'm a big believer in gathering as much information as possible. You never know what will turn out to be definitive." At Cass's continued reluctance, Miller pokes further. "Surely spilling the beans on a family feud is worth it if we can find out something that might help with your parents' situation? With your sister's memories? Wouldn't it be worth it to guarantee her safety from another attack?"

Cass's lips thin at the blatant manipulation, but he says, "I came out to them right before I left for university. My father didn't react well. He disowned me." The words are level, given without inflection. I imagine he's said them often over the years, in exactly this emotionless way.

"And your mother?" asks Miller.

"I think she was too shocked to say anything, frankly. She let me hug her before I left, though."

"But . . ." Pendelton frowns at Cass. "You're married to a woman."

"I'm bisexual," says Cass, raising his chin slightly.

Pendelton's frown deepens. "And . . . your wife?"

"Not your business," replies my brother.

Miller raises a hand, pre-empting anything further from her partner. "Okay, let's start over. You said your mother won the lottery three months ago."

"So, you didn't know about the lotto win until a full month after it happened?" Pendelton asks sharply.

Cass nods. "Give or take a few days."

Naomi leans forward. "Excuse me, but . . . what was the exact date of the draw?"

My brother looks apologetic. "Should be easy to Google, though, right? Forty-seven-point-three-million jackpot?"

"And it was your mother, not your father, who won? She played regularly, you say?"

"Not every week, I don't think." Cass's expression becomes distant. "I think it was a bit of a lark. They didn't need the money. They were comfortable. They had the duplex, free and clear. They both had jobs . . . though, of course, the pay wasn't quite equal between them. Not that it mattered. They shared everything, financially speaking. One chequing account. Separate RRSPs, but that's just for tax purposes. Mum did

Auntie Annie's books for the flower shop. She kept track of her and Dad's personal finances, too. That's what Cleo told me."

"They didn't quit their jobs?" I ask. I don't know how to feel right now, hearing about information from some past version of myself. "After the lottery?"

"No. They didn't want to attract attention. You know them, always paranoid about people knowing their business." He stops. "Sorry."

Pendelton's clacking keys fill the brief silence. I can hear the scrape of Naomi's shirt over the back of her chair as she shifts again. Cotton against synthetic.

"You mentioned your grandparents are deceased. What about your parents' cousins? Any great-uncles, or great-aunts?" Miller taps a pen on her open notebook. "Any other distant relations?"

"None that I know of."

Miller's brows rise. "You've never checked those ancestry websites?"

"Those databases are mostly skewed toward Europeans," Cass says drily. "Plus, I don't fancy giving them ownership of my DNA profile to sell."

Naomi's expression abruptly smooths into blandness. Miller gives a curt nod.

Pendelton says, "We can check their landing documents, search for associated names. Can you confirm their full legal names?"

Cass's face reddens. "I remember Dad's passport, uh, it says Stephen Li, with a *ph*. I don't remember a middle name. And Mum's middle name is Chinese, but I never remember how they spell it out in English. Sorry."

I can hear the scratch of Miller's pen on paper. "Okay, so we're back to the question. Who knows of your mother's windfall and," she gentles her tone, "would they be the type of people who'd wish your parents harm because of it?"

"Does that really happen?" It's probably a bad idea, but I can't keep quiet. "This is starting to sound, like, really crazy. Like a movie or some-thing. Not real life." I look from Naomi to Miller, then turn to Cass. "I mean, our parents wouldn't know people like that, right? People who'd hurt others for money? They're just . . . ordinary."

"I'd like to say *of course not*." Cass's face tightens. "But we never know people as well as we think. And I don't know enough about their social circles to judge."

Naomi says, "We know this must be upsetting, but we need to ask these questions to progress with this file. What if—"

Miller taps her pen. "What about friends?"

I watch Naomi's face shutter as she cedes the floor to Miller again.

"There's Auntie Annie, who I mentioned already." Cass shrugs, looking helpless. "But other than that . . . I'm sorry. I don't know stuff like that."

Miller writes in her notebook. Pendelton types, rapid-fire. Naomi watches us.

I comb through my jumbled thoughts. "So . . . if I was their Girl Friday . . . was I helping her with all of it? The lawyer and everything?"

Cass nods. "Yeah. Appointments with the lawyer for estate planning. Appointments with the investment firm. The works. You even found people who spoke Cantonese, so Mum and Dad would understand everything." He nods, as though to himself. "That's right. Dad went with her to all the appointments. I think he was more comfortable with the legal talk than Mum."

"Okay," I say, drawing it out as I think. "As soon as I get home, I can look for their passports plus papers from the lawyer and investment people. I can pass their names to you. To interview or whatever . . ." Seeing Miller's cool gaze, I trail off.

"Mum may be the official winner, but they considered it shared money," says Cass. "I'm sure of it. These past months have been filled with estate planning and investment portfolios. They wanted to make sure it built a solid foundation. That the money would grow for us and our children. That's what Mum told me."

"Where's the ticket, Dr. Li? Do you know?" Miller taps her pen on the coiled spine of her notebook.

"In a safety deposit box at Mum's bank." Cass looks at each cop in turn. "What? You think my mum's going to carry it around with her in her purse or something? After all those other precautions?"

My chest floods with an abrupt looseness, a warmth that spreads upward to my cheeks. I let out a breath, swipe at the sudden perspiration at my temples. "That's . . . that's good. That she put it somewhere safe."

"And she signed it? On the back of the ticket, you're sure she signed it?" Pendelton says.

"Is that—" I frown at him. "Is that significant? Cass already said she did."

Pendelton nods. "Means no one else can claim the winnings. Whoever signs the back of the ticket is deemed the ticket's owner and entitled to whatever winnings are associated."

I'm stupefied at the thought of something so valuable being at the mercy of nothing more than a few pen strokes.

Miller says, looking down at her notes, "The passports, lawyer, investment advisor, etc., that will need to wait until you're back at your house and can find some documentation, Cleo. As will confirming the safety deposit box, etc." She returns her gaze to me. "Right now, let's return to your parents' cabin at The Lodge at Yoho. Now, the manager confirms you made the reservation for your parents last month. Dr. Li explained it was to celebrate the lottery windfall and . . . commemorate their move to BC. So, my question is, who knew they would be here at this time?"

"Obviously, I would." My face still feels hot. "Cass and Etta, I'd guess."

"Yeah."

"Our father's work, Auntie . . . Annie," I continue. "Maybe the lawyer? If they're handling stuff, my parents might want them to know? And maybe other friends."

"Mum wouldn't have posted on Facebook, though. I told her it's bad to post publicly when you'll be away from your house." Cass raises a fist to his mouth, stifling a yawn. "Didn't have to convince her too much. Like I said, they were super paranoid about stuff like that."

"What about any neighbours?" asks Pendelton.

"I'd guess . . . they were depending on me to keep an eye on their house and grab their mail?" I look to Cass for confirmation. He nods, his eyes now sunken, exhausted.

"Doesn't mean they wouldn't mention it in conversation with neighbours." Miller's gaze rests on me for another beat before she continues. "But we'll make the rounds up there ourselves, if it becomes necessary."

The silence after her statement seems weighted with something. Suspicion? Worry? Dread?

I shake myself mentally out of that downward spiral. "Do you have an update?" I ask. "From Search and Rescue?"

"Not at this time, I'm sorry." Miller turns a page in her notebook, clicks her pen once, twice. "But I promise we'll let you know as soon as we can. Now, it's late. We have even more to follow up on and an early morning, but before we let you go, let's revisit those flashbacks you described earlier."

I sit up from my half-slouch, eyeing Naomi, then her. "Okay," I reply slowly.

Pendelton also straightens in his seat, his gaze on his laptop screen. I hear the tapping on the keyboard quicken. I don't look directly at Cass, but he remains silent.

"You said it was dark, but you could see the hood of the car. Can you see the other person's face? How can you tell it's a man?" Miller's face shows concern, but I sense an underlying skepticism. I can't tell if it's habitual or targeted right now. Against my better judgment, I glance at Naomi, trying to gauge which side of the line she's on.

Not that I even understand what *the line* means right now. Everything feels so . . . uncertain.

Naomi, for whatever it's worth, meets my sidelong look with the tiniest of nods.

I look down at the tabletop, thinking. "I guess it's more emotional than an actual, visual memory. I feel . . . threatened, scared, like I'm trapped. I guess I associate that feeling with, uh, men. I just don't think I've ever felt that way with a woman, so . . . maybe I'm just assuming it's a man."

"But no details of the person's face? Or any sort of physical description?"

"If I knew something, I'd tell you." I'm careful to keep my gaze on Miller. "I told Na—Constable Aoki I was having bad dreams and *she* interpreted them as flashbacks. I'm not so sure. Until I can understand them, how can I be?"

"Fair enough," murmurs Naomi.

Cass makes a noise of impatience. "As my wife, *the psychiatrist,* already said, this is not the appropriate place for this line of questioning. My sister really needs to speak with a therapist about these nightmares, whether or not they're true flashbacks."

"That may be, Dr. Li," says Pendelton, "but no therapist will share anything from their sessions with us."

Cass scowls. "That comment assumes *Cleo* wouldn't share what she knows with you. Which is not my point. The point is she needs professional counselling and you pushing her for answers she doesn't have is inappropriate. Not to mention counterproductive. And potentially harmful."

"How about you allow your sister to speak for herself?" says Miller in a mild tone of reproach.

Cass snorts. "Cleopatra Li does not need anyone to give her permission to speak her mind, Inspector Miller, trust me."

Four sets of eyes turn to me. Déjà vu all over again, this time without Etta.

"Uh . . . I agree with my brother." I watch the cops' expressions flatten almost simultaneously. It would be comical, if things were different. "I can't say for certain what's a flashback or what's just . . . dreaming. I mean, that's a way to process stuff, right? Which means I don't know what's useful or not right now. I think, maybe, a therapist could help me untangle it all." I don't share my unease at the thought of spilling my fears to a stranger. Or to anyone whose literal job is to dissect every word I say . . .

Miller pounces on the uncertainty in my tone. "Hear me out for a second. Okay?"

Cass opens his mouth, but I place a hand on his forearm to stall his objections. "The more we know, the better choices we make, right?"

He subsides with ill grace, his mouth tight. I motion for Miller to continue. She lays her pen down with deliberation.

"Your parents have been missing since Sunday, probably late afternoon. The following Monday morning, you found yourself five hundred kilometres from home, but somehow close to where your parents were last seen. You have no recollection of how you got there or why you weren't home in Edmonton—or even that you live in Edmonton. Hospital tests confirmed Rohypnol in your system, which explains the memory loss.

"The fact that you were drugged with Rohypnol strongly suggests you were brought here without your consent. That's what it's mainly used for, to incapacitate and muddy the waters afterward. That's why Naomi kicked it up to Serious Crimes and how you ended up with Chuck and me. You're a victim of assault, Cleo.

"Someone gave you that drug. Someone brought you out here. The problem is, nobody saw you arrive." She points a long finger at me, then taps the tabletop with it. "At the lodge, nobody saw your parents leave. And, given what we now know about the lottery winnings as a possible motive, how plausible is it that your assault and your parents' disappearance are *not* connected?"

"But Mum signed the ticket and it's locked away at the bank," says Cass. "Why drag Cleopatra out here? How does that accomplish anything? And why now, three months after the lottery win?" He has that look again, like he's puzzling something out. A frown cuts deep grooves into his forehead.

Miller concedes the points with a nod. "We don't have those answers, Dr. Li—not yet. But let's be honest here. The clock is not kind on files like your parents'. If these are flashbacks, we have to pursue them. We can't afford to wait." She looks at me directly. "Memories degrade, shift, disappear."

A million and one thoughts fill the uncomfortable silence for me.

"All right. I get it." I rub my sternum. "Therapy is for healing—not police work."

FIFTEEN

Cass touches my arm. "Wait. Sis. I think I—"

I put up my hand. "Cass, I can take care of myself, you said so yourself. Don't start babying me now. It won't help me feel any better."

He rears back, as though stung, mouth set in a disapproving line.

I say to Miller, "Okay, what do you want to ask me?"

"Going back to this possible flashback, can you think again about the person in the other car seat? Man or woman?"

"Man." This time, I don't hesitate.

That garners me an encouraging nod from Miller. "Large? Average? Small?"

I close my eyes to focus my thoughts, feel my forehead wrinkling in concentration. "Larger than me, I guess. Like, more broad? I can't say about height. He's sitting and then . . . lunging at me." I open my eyes, concentrate on tracing the line of the faux-wood veneer with a finger. It centres my breathing, evens it out.

"Anything about his features? His clothing?"

Pendelton says, "Is there anyone else close by?"

I consider their questions, how best to reply. "There's not enough light to see colours. Just the green instrumentation lighting. Makes more shadows than illumination." I hesitate. "I can't say if there's anyone else in the car."

"Features?" Miller waits, her pen poised now over the notebook.

I repeat her question as I think it over. "Deep-set eyes? I mean, I can't see them." I fidget. "They look like deep holes. . . ." I reach for a bottle of water with a shaky hand.

Despite his earlier unhappiness with me, Cass grips my shoulder in support. I throw him a quick half-smile, but it can't withstand the building worry in me. Am I telling them anything useful?

"Anything about the car?" Pendelton's low voice sends a shiver down my spine. I clench my fists to focus. "Do you recognize it? Could it be your parents'?"

"The only thing I can really . . . see . . . is the dash, and the shape of the steering wheel." I hesitate, then exhale heavily. "I'm sorry, no. It's too dark to make out anything . . . familiar." Not that I'd know anyway.

"No other vehicles in sight?" asks Miller.

"No."

"Buildings? Landmarks?"

Pendelton interjects again. "Sounds?"

"The windows . . . they're closed. I think. The nightmares don't . . . they're silent." I meet Miller's gaze. "It's just blackness outside the windows."

"What about any smells?" Naomi asks, looking up from her notes. "Don't they say the sense of smell is the strongest way to evoke memories and emotions?"

I scour my brain for a way to explain. "That's mostly why I think they're just nightmares. Wouldn't a memory have more details, even if they're random?" I get unreadable stares. Okay. "I think Cass is right. I should return to Edmonton. Maybe the . . . familiarity will jump-start my memory." I pause, pressing my lips together briefly. "I just don't think we can depend on these nightmares or recollections or whatever they are right now. Since I can't separate what's true and what's . . . not." I let out a long breath.

"I know who I am now," I lie. "The best way for me to help my parents is to regain my memories. The best place for me to do that is home." It doesn't matter that I can't picture it right now. I feel its pull, yanking in increasing urgency, like a rope around my chest. "If I can just make it home . . . I know the memories will come back."

No one responds to my wishful thinking.

Cass breaks the building silence. "There's something else you need to know."

Pins and needles explode along my spine, cresting up my neck and over my head. I don't know if I should clutch my face or my chest, trying to stop what feels like an impending bomb.

My brother's voice is grim, taut. "I remembered someone at Cleo's work. Someone she told me hated her."

"In Edmonton, then." Miller raises a brow. "Name?"

"I'm sorry. Cleo never told me his name." Cass hesitates, a faint blush rising on his cheekbones. "She refused to say it, actually. Said it was like summoning him, like a demon. She only referred to him as, uh, *Asshole*." He takes a deep breath, as though bracing himself. "I'm sorry, sis. But . . . you don't work there anymore. You resigned six months ago. You said . . . you were forced out."

I can't feel my face, but I know I must be blinking because Cass is winking in and out of focus, like I'm looking through spinning fan blades.

"Were you holding this tidbit back for another *good reason*, Dr. Li?"

Cass flushes at Miller's sarcasm. "I thought I remembered something, earlier, when Etta was still here, but then I lost the thread. I only now remembered this guy. Honest."

Pendelton's voice breaks into my fevered paralysis. "You think this person hated your sister enough to assault her? Kidnap her? Why?"

Cass's face darkens. "I don't know enough to speculate. I just know Cleo mentioned a work . . . nemesis, some man who got his jollies by undermining her." He breathes in sharply. "Okay, wait. I remember he was an analyst. Like her. They were always competing for projects." He touches the back of my wrist for a moment. "For real, sis, you said you were always fighting with this guy."

He turns to Miller. "You should be able to find this guy, right? In Edmonton?"

Miller considers me for another couple beats, ignoring Cass. Then she looks over at Pendelton. They share something unspoken through their mysterious cop-partner bond. At the other end of the table, Naomi remains silent, intently watching the interplay between her superiors.

Pendelton asks Cass for the company name, finishes a spate of rapid-fire typing, and addresses me. "Can I show you the company website? There's a page of staff members, with photos."

My heart seems to lodge right in my throat. The cops wait me out with unreadable faces. Abruptly, I recall the water bottle in my hands. I fumble the cap, feel the painful scrape of the tiny ridges against the side of my finger. Somehow it centres me. I drink without spilling, take a moment to gather my wits again. "Okay."

I can tell that Cass wants to object, but he only grabs hold of my hand. I allow it for a few beats before disengaging. We watch Pendelton manoeuvre his laptop across the table. Naomi gets up, moves to the seat next to Cass.

"Take your time," says Miller. I think she might even mean it.

I scroll the web page slowly, my eyes lingering on every face, trying to recall anything about any of them. Trying to remember my time there. The static faces smiling back at me are mostly white. I count five East Asians. Three Black employees. About a dozen brown people. Out of sixty, maybe seventy, staff listings. Does that count as inclusive for a tech services company these days?

I go through them all twice. The third time, I focus on the men, which is still most of the photos.

"I can't . . . I don't recognize anyone." I fall back against the chair, bumping my ponytail against the tall back. The temptation to close my eyes is so strong, I know the tide of adrenaline must be ebbing again. I place my feet flat on the floor, forcing myself to sit on the edge of the seat precariously. There. I have to keep the chair from pushing back and out from under me or I'll fall on my ass. Either way, I'll be awake.

Naomi stirs. "Dr. Li, did Cleo ever mention the man's ethnicity?"

Miller gives the smallest of nods, though her face remains impassive.

Is that Naomi's role here? To play the race moderator? Cass flicks a glance at her sidelong. Maybe he's wondering the same thing.

He pulls a face. "I can't recall."

"HR would have documented every complaint between us if it was bad enough to get me fired." I have no idea how I know this.

Miller nods. "Can you tell us more about that situation, Dr. Li? Anything that Cleo relayed that you can recall, specifically?"

He pauses, reluctance clear in the set of his shoulders. With a sigh, he turns to me. "The truth is, you're kind of hard to get along with. I mean, we put up with it 'cause . . . *family*. But your co-workers . . . they weren't as . . . understanding."

I frown.

"You said your manager and the HR manager called you in about co-workers' complaints. They didn't name anyone specific, but you were certain that guy must've been behind it all." Cass pauses, scratching at a spot below his left ear, his eyes shifting away for a second. "And, um, you've never been good at patience really, especially for people not as smart as you. Which is most people, if I'm honest."

"Thank you . . . ?" I feel my cheeks heat. I avoid looking at Pendelton. Or Miller.

"But that's hard for people to take, day in and day out," says Cass. "And, uh, you've never been one to soften yourself to make others more comfortable."

"So they complained I was . . . a bully?"

Cass flicks a sidelong look at Miller. He gives me a cautious nod.

And Naomi thought I looked harmless and helpless.

"You do," says Cass, answering my inadvertently spoken thought. I flush even hotter in the face. He continues, oblivious to my slip. "That's why it took years of complaints before the company—"

"Fired me."

"Well, they asked you if you'd be willing to leave, without badmouthing them. They offered a generous severance."

Miller interjects. "What would that be? Six months?"

"Actually, a year. Cleo was great with clients." From his chagrin, I guess he's repeating the same words I used in order to frame something I ought to've been ashamed of.

"Hush money," I say quietly, staring at the surface of the table, trying to understand a version of myself I don't recognize. Or like.

What must the cops think of me now? If they're naturally suspicious of family first, then it's clear who's the better sibling. It's the person staring at me with genuine regret at outing me as an awful bitch, despite the fact it makes him look all the more innocent.

Into the pressing silence, the clack of Pendelton's keyboard. It pulls me back to the present with a nasty tug. "Will you be going to Edmonton? To investigate?" I wince at the vulnerability in my voice.

Miller regards me with something perilously close to pity. "It's a definite possibility." Her expression softens even further. "Listen, strictly speaking, what Naomi arranged for you here, in Golden, the nighttime drive-bys . . . it's not going to be possible in Edmonton. Chuck and I, we can pull in a few favours, I think, *maybe* get your address on a few patrol routes, have a slightly increased police presence seen around the neighbourhood. But you're going to have to take more cautious measures for your own safety."

"I'm always responsible for my own safety, Inspector," I say drily. "I'm a non-white woman living in Canada." In my periphery, I see Cass nod. A quick peek at Naomi shows she's wearing a neutral expression, tight around its edges.

Mildly, Miller replies, "Not to put too fine a point on it, but that didn't prevent you from being assaulted, Cleo." I gape at her, shocked. She barrels on. "And we want to prevent it happening again. We still don't know the motive. You've got to make sure they don't get another shot at you."

Cass leans forward, lays a hand on my shoulder. "We will."

Miller sits back, closing her notebook, clipping her cheap pen onto the cover.

"Is that it?" I look from Miller to Pendelton, back again. "We can go home?"

"Contrary to what you might think," says Pendelton, "we *are* interested in your well-being, Cleo. You'll get better faster if you're in your own home, seeing your own doctor, and a good therapist."

"Chuck's right. I think we've got as far as we can for now." Miller stands. "Of course, we'll be in touch. We'll have updates on the local search, and more questions as our investigations continue."

Cass pushes back from the conference table, as does Pendelton. Naomi approaches me as I wait awkwardly for Cass to move out of my way. She addresses both of us. "We had to tow your parents' car to the lab in Kelowna. Unfortunately, you'll be billed for that. I'm sorry."

I give her a vague nod. Cass says, "We're leaving for Edmonton in the morning." He and Naomi sort through whatever details she needs related to paperwork or whatever. I really don't care at the moment, though I know I should. The truth is, I can't take any more details right now. I feel my agitation rise, like a bubble of pressure shooting upward from my stomach. I really want to go home.

Miller hands over business cards to me and Cass. "If something happens, if it's an emergency, of course call 911. Like normal. When they arrive, let them know we have an open file on you and on your parents. Even if you're not sure it's related. We liaise with EPS all the time. Edmonton Police Service. Otherwise, call one of us directly. And email Chuck your parents' full names and the names of the lawyer and the investment people as soon as you can. CC me. If I don't hear from you, I'll be in touch."

It's not a threat—but it sounds like one.

I tap the window button in the door, just enough to hear my fingernail click against the hard plastic. We're on the highway heading east from Golden, toward Field and then on to Lake Louise and Calgary before we take a sharp left and go north. Cass is doing at least a hundred. I'm not sure I can take that much wind in my face right now, though I'm desperate for more fresh morning air.

It feels weird to be alone with Cass now. Weird, but also unexpectedly comforting. By the time I met up with him this morning, Etta was long gone in order to make her 11 a.m. appointment. Though, if I'm honest with myself, I'd probably have been more awkward if I'd had to see her off in the wee hours. The burden of gratitude sits poorly on me.

I do feel more at ease with Cass now than at our . . . reunion yesterday evening, but I keep finding myself darting my attention around the car, cataloguing the details. As though I might get to know him better if I understand why he chose to stick a bobble-headed anime figure on his dashboard. Is it a cat? A rabbit? I have no clue.

I glance into the back of the station wagon. Our parents' belongings sit tucked in tightly together. We even brought the bag of old groceries. I see the yellowed pear in my mind's eye and feel a pang of sympathy. I face forward again.

Cass gears down, slowing to avoid a camper van ahead of us, while a huge black SUV whizzes past us in the left lane. Then we speed up, gears shifting, pulling out to pass the van. I peer at the driver, a curly-haired ginger with a frizzy beard and a green ball cap. He meets my gaze with an incurious stare.

I wriggle in the car seat, thinking of the drive ahead of us. According to Cass, it's about five hours to Edmonton without breaks, so six or even seven with. If I allow myself to daydream about getting home, whatever semblance of it I have left, I think I'll go insane with anticipation. I focus on what's right in front of me instead.

"Thanks for the room last night, Cass. It felt so good to have my own space."

"Well, it was no Claridge's, but you're welcome." He pauses. "You've always been a pretty private person. We figured it was extra stress for you, staying with a stranger, no matter how kind."

I nod. After a moment, I say, "Can I ask you something?"

Cass keeps his attention forward, out the windshield. "Sure. Like what?"

"What else do you know about this mysterious co-worker of mine? The one who hated me?"

"What," he retorts, "you don't think I told the cops everything?"

"Um . . ." I decide this is too important to chicken out on now, so I say, "Yeah."

He spares me a scowl. "No, Cleo. I told them everything. You honestly only ever called the man *Asshole* to me. I have no idea who he is."

He's not angry like I thought he'd be, not really. I think. At least he answered. So I keep going. I need answers too badly to stop.

"How long did I work at that company?"

"Six years."

"Did I like it there?"

He shifts in his seat, does the round of checking his mirrors again. "You liked the work, and some of your clients, but most people . . . not so much." He seems distracted, cutting out into the fast lane, this time behind a bright purple truck with stylized flames on its flanks. We follow much too closely for my comfort. He passes three cars in the slow lane before switching back with a jerk of the steering wheel.

"Hey, is something wrong?" I swallow my pride. "I know I pushed you about holding back, I'm sorry."

I can see his knuckles go white. "I'm just . . . Mum and Dad are missing, and my worrying is through the roof, but I'm so . . . I'm also pretty fucking pissed at them."

I realize I'm clenching my teeth. I open my mouth, wide, stretching until my jaw pops. "Why? Is there something else, something about our parents you held back from the cops?" I don't care if this time he truly does get angry with me. The fear simmering in my gut won't let me stay silent. But how do I tell if I can trust what he tells me?

"It wasn't fair, what they did, sis. They shouldn't have assumed you would move with them to the West Coast. They shouldn't have sold the duplex to put pressure on you. It was wrong."

I sift through what he's not saying, speak slowly as I work out the implications. "Was it meant as . . . blackmail?"

Cass huffs out a harsh breath. "Mum thought you were done working in Edmonton. She reasoned your old employer would badmouth you to everybody else, get you blacklisted. But you still didn't want to move, so she . . . she forced the matter."

"So I could be their caretaker." I don't know why my brain is moving so slow. "Have me handle all the same stuff I do here for them?" I rub at a sudden hard knot just below my right earlobe. "Guess it's a pretty traditional expectation. What else do you do with an unmarried daughter." This tastes of an ongoing disagreement, like bitterness and ashes.

"I knew she couldn't see why forcing you was a bad idea, so I tried to reason with her. I told her moving to the Lower Mainland might make it harder for you to find work, not easier, but she had it in her mind that a larger city must mean more jobs. Dad agreed."

As usual bubbles into my head. "Did she praise you for being a good brother? For coming to my defence?"

He flushes bright pink even as a scowl furrows his forehead.

"Sorry," I say, shaking myself. "I don't know why I said that."

"Anyway." He loosens his grip on the steering wheel. "I feel shitty about being pissed, even though I have good reason. But I didn't say anything to the cops because—"

"It makes me look suspicious."

"I don't want to give them more fuel for that particular fire," he corrects me. "Even though you haven't *done* anything. I know you're not guilty of anything like they're saying. You can't be. You're my *sister*. I know you."

I wish I knew him well enough to let his conviction carry me forward. At some point soon, I'll have to make the choice, whether or not I'm ready. We'll be spending at least the next several days together, so . . .

Can I trust him? This man who looks so much like me, like our father. This man who asserts my innocence so vehemently, yet won't meet my gaze.

SIXTEEN

The landscape unfolds through the glass for long minutes. The sun shines, high and bright, daring any clouds to skim through the sky. We leave the mountains gradually, their grandeur slipping away behind us as we make do with foothills instead. We stop for a quick meal just north of Calgary, bypassing the central congestion by taking a ring road to get there. I think it's a bedroom community, though it looks like a glorified big-box-store complex with attached cookie-cutter vinyl-sided houses.

About ninety minutes after lunch, Cass pulls the station wagon over into a busy along-the-highway corridor of gas stations and fast-food places. I stare at the traffic rushing past, only a few hundred metres away.

As he climbs back in from filling the gas tank, Cass gestures to the right. In the next lot over, I see a large replica windmill atop a single-storey stucco building. "Wanna donut?" he asks. "It's kind of a tradition whenever we travel on the QE II."

I shake my head. "Too full."

He shrugs. "Okay."

It takes me until he's navigated back to the on-ramp heading north on the highway—the QE II as in Queen Elizabeth II—that I realize I missed something in our last exchange. "Cass."

"Hmm?" He accelerates the car, sending me back against my seat with a soft thump on the back of my head. Ouch.

We slide into a line of vehicles in the fast lane.

"It would've made more sense to stop for gas on *this* side of the highway, on the east side, but you crossed over to the west side. You must have wanted to go get donuts. You said it was kind of a tradition. You didn't say how important."

"Oh, that. Yeah, don't worry about it. It was just habit, pulling over there."

"Cass."

"What? Sis, they're just donuts. Nothing special. Honest."

"There's something I'm supposed to remember, isn't there?"

His reluctance fills the air between us. Then he sighs. "Fine. All right. We used to stop there with Mum and Dad every time they dragged us to visit their Calgary friends."

"Why did they have friends in Calgary? Did they know them from HK?"

"Dunno. Don't remember. The real attraction was Calgary had better dim sum than Edmonton then. Of course, every time we'd eventually fight over something or other in the car. So on the ride home," he gestured with a flourish, "donuts in Red Deer to keep us in check. And give the parentals a break from our bickering."

"Why didn't you just tell me this? We could've popped in, for sure."

He stays quiet as we pass a line of five cars in the slow lane. When he speaks, I have to lean close to hear him. "It wouldn't have been the same if you didn't remember."

I ignore the pinch in my chest at that.

The QE II unspools ahead, leading us north. I think about this strange, drawn-out conversation of ours, and where it started, way back somewhere on the Trans-Canada in BC. I think about my brother being kind.

"Am I really such a bitch?"

Cass startles. "Listen, it's not like that. I mean—okay, it's a little like that. But you're not . . . You're just . . . You can be abrasive. That's all. Also impatient. Sarcastic."

"I may have amnesia, but I remember enough to know that's what gets a woman called a bitch."

He lets out a feeble cheer. "Another thing you remember, that's great."

Jesus. "For fuck's sake."

"See? That's classic you. Zero tolerance for stupidity. We just think of you as . . . cranky." He grins, but it fades quickly. "Does it bother you?"

I consider that, truly consider it, for a few moments. In the end, I shrug. "It's out of my control, isn't it? What I said in the past, how I treated people, my behaviour." I pull the seat belt away from my neck. "Now I understand what you meant, though, back in Golden, about me acting so different."

His nod looks almost eager. "And I can understand why you want to be called Cleo now. It's like a clean break." At my perplexed stare, he gives a short laugh. "When I was, I dunno, about thirteen, you said you were *Cleopatra*. More mature. I tried to rile you up anyway, by using *Cleo*, but you just ignored me 'til I gave up. Took about three weeks. Mum and Dad didn't care. They mostly use your Chinese name." His ready grin dissipates.

After a beat, I say, "So, what? You're saying I'm a different person entirely now?"

"I don't know about *entirely*, but yeah . . . kinda."

"Because I'm nicer? That's really what you mean, isn't it?"

He accelerates, then switches out to pass a bright red minivan with a taped-over tail light.

I chew at my lip. "Guess I have to consider this seriously. If I don't recover my memories, I still have to live my life. So, if I'm not the same person, if I'm *not* Cleopatra, I've still got to be *someone*."

"Some part of you must already know." He glances at me. *"Cleo."*

I shrug away my unspoken doubts. "Better than *Marge* anyway."

"What?"

"Never mind."

We settle into an almost comfortable silence. I watch the intermittently pretty land slide past, my thoughts and fears a little too near to voice. When I eventually speak again, we're on the outskirts of Edmonton, passing the airport as we continue north toward the city proper. I scan the passing scenery, the ribbon of highway becoming just another major city thoroughfare, buildings and other vehicles increasing in density around us. After the wide open prairie, the big box stores and thickening traffic feel too close. Claustrophobic.

I straighten in my seat. "I've been thinking. About the move. I mean, about me not wanting to and, um, about fighting with Mum."

"Yeah?"

"Do you think the last thing I said to her was . . . was in anger?" Hearing my words, I shake my head. "That's not what I meant. I just mean, I'm worried, I'm—" I huff out a breath. "I hate thinking she's out there, lost and frightened, but her thoughts of me are only angry ones."

Cass takes a long time to reply. "You two had—have a complicated relationship."

I ignore his stumble. "Even more than you and Dad?"

"Wha—you remember that?"

"Not exactly, but c'mon, you said he disowned you."

He jerks to a stop at a red light, staring unseeing at the traffic passing through the intersection. I wonder if I should change the subject after all. But I want to know what he can tell me about my parents. I want to know why I feel so . . . torn and uncertain when I think about them.

"Dad couldn't handle having a gay son. He threw me out of the house, told me don't bother coming back." Cass shrugs. "I was already set up to go away for university. Scholarships, housing, the works. I timed it so I'd be, well, maybe not *fine*, but okay at least. I figured he might be unhappy, but I was shocked he was willing to cause a scene over it." He glanced at me. "Dad always tries to keep it low-key. Mum's more the drama queen. His reaction stunned her, too, though. She was totally silent, didn't even cry when I left. Probably couldn't compute that Dad ignored her when she told him to stop cursing at me." A pause. "I stayed away, as much because I didn't want to see him either as because of his edict." I flinch at the contempt in that last word.

"Please tell me we stayed in touch, though? I wasn't an asshole bigot on top of being a bitch?"

He lets out a sharp laugh. "You surprised me, actually. But in your oh-so-rational world view, it made no difference that I was gay. I was still the same person to you."

I feel the faint stirrings of a smile. "My annoying little brat of a brother?"

"Exactly." His face darkens for a second. "Mum would call once in a while, but that stopped, too, after . . ." He trails off, focussing on a large white van that's suddenly cut into the lane ahead of us. He checks the surrounding lanes on either side, but we stay where we are.

"What was I just saying?" He exhales. "Right. I met a lot of great people in the gay community. Some assholes and racists, too. I learned about navigating society as a gay Asian man. There are a *lot* of assumptions. Then, in my second year, I fell in love, hard, for one of my friends. Before that, I'd never once been attracted to a woman. It was . . . really confusing." He glances at me. "I didn't know anyone who was bisexual, no one I could ask. I mean, my gay friends were awesome in supporting and celebrating me, and I've dated women since then, of course, but it was a real adjustment for me then, those first years."

Another pause, this one weighted despite his light tone. "When I told Mum I'm bi, she just . . . short-circuited. Didn't matter how many times she asked me to explain, she just couldn't get it. I mean, it's not rocket science. And even if it were, so fucking what." He shrugs again. "She stopped calling me. I stopped trying."

"But . . ." I struggle to make sense of his generosity. "You called to let her know you're having a baby? Why?"

Another shrug, this one tinged with sheepishness. "I figured she'd want to know her first grandchild's on the way."

"That's so . . . kind. I'm not sure I'd've been as generous if they'd disowned me, windfall or not."

"Hey, that had nothing to do with it." He shoots me a sideways frown.

I chew on the inside of my cheek, trying to figure things out. "But I must've told you about the win, right? I can't imagine I'd have withheld that from you."

"Etta and I had already put Mum on the list to tell, asshole. We were waiting for her and the baby to pass three months. That's just how the timing worked out."

"I'm just messing with you." I gesture airily. "For what it's worth, I think you did the right thing not getting into all this with the cops. They'd jump all over you about ingratiating yourself with the baby news, trying to angle for a juicy cut of the money."

"Well, it's not because I'm guilty of anything. And I *did* tell them about the timing, so there's nothing for them to be suspicious about."

I marvel, yet again, at his breezy confidence in his innocence. What I wouldn't give to feel the same certainty.

Instead of obsessing over our differences, I say, "I'm glad Mum wanted to reconnect, though. A grandchild *should* be a big deal."

Cass shifts, pushing himself taller in his seat. "Actually, Dad did, too. Reconnect, I mean. He actually called me. I didn't recognize the number. I almost didn't answer." He pauses, a tiny smile lighting up his profile. "Some bullshit reason I don't even recall now, but he told me he has friends with gay children and those friends have grandkids now, and he understands better. So, hooray for progress, right?"

"Better than being disowned." Hearing the sound of that, I add, "You know this means your baby will have a crazy-ass Mah-mah and Yeh-yeh, right?"

He grunts, seemingly engrossed in changing lanes. But I see the upward curve to his mouth.

"Just don't expect me to change nappies and shit like that. I'm the spoil-her-sick-with-candy auntie, not the babysit-for-a-week auntie, okay?" I roll the words around in my mind, bewildered. Could this be possible for me? A future of teasing and lightness, maybe even joy?

Cass offers me a salute. "Roger that."

Over the course of the next fifteen minutes, the street we're on cuts through a number of busy intersections, curves around a bit of light industrial businesses, passes a mixed district of restaurants, bars, and apartments, then ends up high above a valley. Cass takes a sharp right and then a hairpin left, and we descend at a sedate fifty klicks down a curving roadway that leads us to a bright white metal bridge spanning a dark green river. The river valley looks beautiful and twisty, verdant with evergreens and deciduous trees with spotty white bark.

"Okay, so your neighbourhood's called Riverdale," says Cass. "It's sort of down low, on the flood plain." We take a right-hand curve off the bridge as he points the other way, where the road we just left goes straight from the bridge, up a steep street. "Look, that's downtown up there."

Before I can process how that works, we're on a different bridge, one nowhere near as pretty as the first, humping over a set of unremarkable streets. Cass takes us looping over and under and around and up, then we're heading down again on what appears to be the edge of downtown.

"Couple more turns," he says. We're suddenly in a dense area of houses and squared-off streets, in the shadow of a bluff we just drove down from. I note pretty, mature trees, older-looking houses, and all sorts of cars, some parked nose to tail along the curbs. Cass sighs. "No garage for us. Just street parking." He slows the car, craning his neck to peer ahead. "That's it."

It is a single-storey duplex with pale cream siding and a pebbled frontage. Two rectangular picture windows, one with drawn vertical blinds, the other with thick-looking draperies in a patterned frosty blue. Black wrought-metal railings for the five steps up to each of the twinned front doors.

Cass ends up parking a block away. He turns to face me. "So, I feel stupid even saying this, but we should be careful. That guy from your old company, he might know where you live."

I survey the street, the houses, the sidewalk empty of people. "It's Friday afternoon. If he's so competitive, he's probably at work."

Cass flushes pink. "But if he's the one who—"

I put up both hands to stall him out. "Listen, maybe you think I'm being foolish or not taking this seriously, but honestly, what are the chances someone's been following us all the way from Golden? Or that someone's been watching my house, waiting for me to return?" I gesture to the peaceful neighbourhood around us. "If you're really worried, we can talk to some of the neighbours, see if they've seen anyone weird around our place. Not that I can promise to remember any of the neighbours, but if it'll make you feel better . . ." I shrug.

"We should be cautious, that's all I'm saying. Keep our eyes open, that sort of thing."

"Cass, what do you think I've *been* doing for the past week? Or, like, my whole life?" At his deepening flush, I take a breath, pull back my temper. "Look. I'm doing the best I can in a really fucking weird situation. But I can't go around frightened of every shadow. I mean, I won't. Do you understand?"

He gives me a reluctant nod, his reply curt. "Fair enough."

We leave the suitcases and bags in the car. Cass makes a show of assessing the area, his face a dusky pink. The car locks with a beep and he motions me onward.

Despite my bravado, I walk slowly toward my home, alternating between eyeing the worn sidewalk and staring upward through the tree canopies, feeling distracted and strangely empty. My stomach abruptly lurches, taking my false courage and sense of balance with it. Of course, Cass grips my arm, murmuring reassurances I'm too disoriented to brush aside.

The property has a waist-high white-picket fence, of all things. He opens the little gate for the right-hand path.

"This side's mine?" I hear myself ask.

"Yup. And I've got keys. But let's go in the back. The front door's for visitors."

"Wait." My scalp prickles. I feel the inside of my head fill with pressure. I gesture to the other half of the duplex. "What if they're here? And we're worrying for nothing?"

SEVENTEEN

S is . . ."

I turn away from his cautious skepticism, from his pity, and the alarm underneath. Shoulders back, I cross the wide expanse of the front lawn. When I reach the bottom of the steps to my parents' front door, I look back at him. After a moment, he reluctantly joins me in climbing the concrete steps, fuzzy with some kind of green fabric, meant to suggest grass maybe. His expression settles into wary resignation.

We crowd the little stoop. I glance at my brother. Face tight, he reaches out to pull open the screen door, but it holds fast. Locked. I press the doorbell. I hear a peal of notes through the white door, like an off-tune harp. I strain to hear something after the notes die away.

Cass raps on the flimsy metal of the screen door with his knuckles, startling me. One-two-three. Quick and hard. I put my ear up against the door, its cold metal sending a shiver down my neck. Where are my parents? And what do I know about it?

Cass pulls me away, gently. "C'mon." He leads me back across the front lawn and along the side of my home, following a laid-concrete footpath. The gate into the back is taller than the one out front. I would have to stand on tiptoe, but Cass reaches over the top easily, yanks open the latch from the other side, and pushes the gate open. He enters cautiously, shoulders taut. Then he relaxes, holding the gate open for me.

There's a fence between the two backyards. I see a gate in it, too, but I'm not ready for that yet. I keep my attention instead on the slightly unruly lawn in front of me, framed by planters stuffed with small flowers still only showing buds. Along one edge of the yard sit two neat rows of terracotta pots. "Are those . . . tomato plants? And herb containers?" I turn a questioning look on my brother. "I garden?"

Cass shrugs from his place at the back door. "Guess so. Etta would know better than me." He tries the knob, then the door itself.

"I didn't think assholes gardened," I mutter.

"Even assholes need a hobby."

"Har, har." I watch Cass pull out a ring of keys, my throat abruptly dry.

"You gave these to me years ago, when you moved in, actually. I kept the key ring, too." He offers them to me on his palm. It's a metal snowflake, lacquered a bright pink. "You thought the colour would make them hard to lose." He grins, rueful. "You weren't kidding either." His grin turns uncertain. "Why don't you do the honours? I think it's safe enough."

I close my hand around the cool metal, press the bumpy teeth against my skin. The back door is on the side of the duplex closer to the fence running between by side and my parents'. I note the raised flower beds against the house, see tulip stems, a few strangely flat, dark green leaves, and some kind of low greenery sprouting tiny yellow-white blossoms. I may not know their names, but I've got a good hunch they must all be perennials. No one's been here to tend them. I swallow. I can't help a peek over at the other side, but from my height, the fencing hides their door entirely.

I fumble the key into the deadbolt with stiff fingers, manage to unlock the door. I turn the knob and push. The door slides back with a low *whoosh*, breaking the seal with the frame.

"Stuffy," I murmur.

Cass makes a non-committal noise behind me. I kick off my shoes, leave them on the back mat, take the three steps up into what turns out to be a kitchen. I peer around at the shiny white cabinets and stainless steel appliances, up at the bright ceiling, down to the smooth wood boards beneath my socks. I blink at the stinging in my eyes. I thought . . . I hoped . . . but no. I inhale sharply through my nose, forcing the tears back.

"So, um, this is you," says Cass. "Does it—do you recognize it?"

I hold my arms tight to myself, shaking my head.

"Oh, uh, okay. Well. This side's way different than Mum and Dad's. You had a few interior walls taken down to create an open plan." Cass points to the far-right corner of the living room. "That used to be a second bedroom. Now it's your office, but you didn't see the point of a full wall since you live alone. You also took out the eating nook. Put an island in."

Cass's tone is light, but I feel its undercurrent of unease. He clears his throat, says, "Hey, uh, I don't want to leave Mum and Dad's bags in the car. I'll just drop their stuff and come right back."

I swallow, harder this time, trying to keep my insides well down. "Can't we store them here, for now, I mean? I'm not, um . . . I know the cops are wanting that info, but I, I don't think I can go over there yet."

"But you don't have to. I'll take care of it." He smiles, puzzled, one hand already on the backdoor handle.

I stare at him, mute with a sudden premonition I don't want.

His smile disappears, like the sun gone behind clouds. "What's wrong?" A look of comprehension hits. "Do you remember something?"

I shake my head. "No, it's not . . . I wish I did. It's . . . I know it's been days already, but I don't want to go over there and not . . . and not see them." I stand, rigid.

He considers me for a long silence. I imagine I can see him weighing his options. Will I break under the strain? Lose my shit? Is it worth it to push me? Is it healthy? How important is it, really, to get those bags into our parents' house? I can tell the moment he makes up his mind.

He grins, a little lopsided. "You're right. We can store them here just as easy. Besides, do you even remember where you keep their spare keys?"

I shake my head, giving him a precarious smile in return.

"Okay. I'll be right back."

"I'll come help."

"No, you take a moment. I'll be right back." His grin broadens. "Open the front door for me, though, eh?"

So I let him go. He's right. I do need a moment. Or five or ten or a thousand. How long should it take for someone to remember how to feel safe?

Tentative, I touch the armchair and the sofa, press into the brightly coloured cushions, trail a finger along the book spines on the shelves that line this side of the half-wall separating the office space from the living room. I slowly pull aside the blue drapes, discover the picture window doesn't open. Frowning a little over the bookshelves, I note a narrow window next to my desk in the office space. How did I miss that from the outside? It's literally right beside the picture window.

I shuffle-step past the bookshelves, enter the office, and thread between a row of filing cabinets and a small, two-person futon sofa. At my desk, I crank open the window as far as I can. A cool breeze blows in, lifting the hairs on my arms. I breathe in so deeply my nostrils tingle and I feel like sneezing.

After that first hit, it's like I can't get enough fresh air.

I run to the kitchen and crank open the window above the sink, then whirl around, searching for the next target. From here, I see the guest bathroom to my right, jutting out into the open plan between the office space and the rear-entry steps. It shares the interior wall with the other half of the duplex, so, no, there mustn't be a window. I cross to the lone door on the left, across the living room from the guest bath and office.

My bedroom. A large bed, neatly made with a light, plum-coloured duvet, sits between two windows, blinds down. I pull them up, wooden slats clacking, and push up on both window sashes far as they'll go. To the left of the bed, I find the master bathroom, its window overlooking the backyard. Once I have it open, I take a deep breath, imagining I can smell the tulips outside.

I slip, bump the wall with my shoulder. I tear off my stupid cheap socks and toss them on the floor of my bedroom. I am so throwing those goddamned things away. I pass back through to the living room. I press my soles deliberately as I walk around the open space. I spread my toes and revel in the cool, smooth, waxed flooring. I place my feet onto the large dove-grey rug that helps define the living room area.

In front of the bookshelves lining the half-wall to my office, I slide my feet over and over the rug's softness. I stare at the sofa to my left, coffee table in front of it, and armchair on the opposite side of the room. Tucked into the corner, past the picture window, the armchair sits on just this side of another half-wall that marks the boundary of the front entryway. I squeeze my toes into the soft plush pile of the rug, and it's easy to imagine relaxing here, in this room, with a good book, soft music, and a rich wine.

For these few moments, I allow myself to push aside the disquiet I feel about my parents and my situation. My brain may not recognize this place, but some part of me must. I've harboured a knot of tension in my gut since I slid into Thea Halford's passenger seat. No amount of kindness or generosity from her or Susan or Naomi or even Cass has eased it.

But now, now I can feel the slightest release, just below my ribcage. This is my home. My home base. I take a deep breath. Because I can.

There are so many things I can't control right now. If I hadn't already learned that lesson before, the past few days have proven it once and for all. But having a safe space of my own, somewhere I can let my guard down, away from concerned looks and helpful hands—it makes all the difference.

I have no idea how everything will play out, but for now, being home is enough.

EIGHTEEN

I hear a clatter on my front steps and reach the door in time to open up for Cass. He hands me the first of the suitcases. There's not a lot of room in the small rectangle of entryway, so I pull the case into the living room and leave it next to the armchair for now. I direct Cass to do the same with the second case. He heads back out to fetch his own stuff. After a moment of indecision, I take the groceries into the—*my* kitchen area. The poor battered pear goes into the fridge, but I leave everything else in the bag and the whole thing on top of the island. We'll figure out later where to stash it all, here or . . .

Cass comes back and drops his bag next to our parents' suitcases. I lock the screen door, sliding up the small window in the centre to get more fresh air moving into the house. Cass moves to stand in front of the picture window in the living room, hands on his hips, staring out at the street.

"See something?"

"Just been a long time since I was back." He gestures for me to join him, puts an arm around my shoulders. "It's weird to think we grew up just the other side of that." He points the hand on my shoulder toward the interior wall, sounding . . . wistful, maybe.

I shrug a little, adjusting to the weight of his arm. "You haven't been back since?"

"Nope. You showed me photos after your renos were finished, but this is actually the first time I've ever been inside *here*."

"Have I ever visited you? In Lethbridge?"

"How d'you think I saw the photos? And heard all about every excruciating inch of your renos?" He nods. "Yeah, you've visited plenty of times. You and Etta re-bond over your shared love of the Japanese gardens every time." He gives me a squeeze. "It's strange to be back, but *not* to be back, y'know?"

Tell me about it. I gesture. "Looks like the office doubles as a guest room, complete with a futon sofa bed, I'd guess. The guest bath's just there. It's a three-piece, no tub, no window. But there's a skylight. Hope that's okay."

Cass grins. "I'm starting to appreciate this new you. So considerate."

I duck out from under his arm and give him a shove. "I'm so considerate I'm changing into some not-so-stinky clothes. Don't break anything, smartass."

To my retreating back, he says, "I had a thought. Maybe Mum and Dad's papers are here? You were taking care of that stuff for them, right? Maybe you kept everything here for the sake of convenience. I mean, if you were driving Mum to appointments or whatever, she might've had you keep track of the papers she'd need."

I turn at the threshold to my bedroom. "Okay, I'll try it."

Cass picks up his bag from the floor. "See you in a few. Enjoy your shower."

When I come out again, Cass is nowhere to be seen, and the guest bath door stands open. I hold still, listening, ignoring the leap of unease in my chest. Hearing a murmur from the direction of the kitchen window, I go to the sink and look out, hands tight on the counter's edge.

Cass has earbuds in, their bright white cord linked to the phone in his hand. With his free hand, he trails his fingers over my baby plants and planters as he wanders around the perimeter of my backyard. His expression is pensive, softening into a smile as I watch, unseen. Must be Etta. I leave him to it. I don't dwell on the relief loosening my knees, but I do wonder when I started depending on his soothing presence. Does this mean I'm beginning to trust him? It doesn't sound as scary as I thought it would. Maybe.

I approach the office again, breathing deeply of the fresh air blowing in through the window. The desk is made of pale blond wood, just a rectangular slab on top of four metal cylinders, its surface empty of even so much as a pen holder. I stare at that immaculate desktop, apprehension sliding up my spine. Where's my computer? Or my phone, for that matter? Do I own a tablet?

I give myself a shake. One thing at a time.

I turn to the wall of four waist-high filing cabinets, made of the same blond wood. As I open one cabinet drawer after another, I wonder if my mother would trust me to keep her legal papers if we're arguing about splitting up. I flip nimbly through the hanging folders, reading labels, searching for my parents' stuff. Instead, I discover my old tax information, insurance files for home and vehicle, receipts and bills dating back six years. My accountant must love me.

At the bottom of the filing cabinet closest to my desk, in front of the hanging file folders, I find a scuffed recipe box made of hard brown plastic. Inside, I discover a jumble of business cards, with no discernible order.

A loud laugh rings out and I startle. My hand bangs against the side of the drawer, scraping along the hook of a hanging file folder. I look up to find Cass grinning down at me from the living room, his arms resting atop the partition wall.

"That's funny. Everything in here is immaculate. As in, *everything in its place and a place for everything.* But you have a secret stash of messy shit."

I frown at him as I rub at the shallow pink scratch on the back of my hand. "Guess I don't like Rolodexes. So . . . last century."

"Hey, I'm not criticizing. Everybody needs a weakness, right? Makes you human." He points at the box. "Might have a card for the lawyer in there."

"Yeah, but how do I tell if it's Mum and Dad's lawyer?" I mumble, digging a finger into the bundles of cards.

"Look for Chinese characters. You found Cantonese-speakers for both the lawyer and investment people. Took you a while, too."

I give him a sharp nod, dismayed at the urge to snap at him for coming up with a solution before I did. Instead, I set to work, sorting through a first handful.

"Here, gimme some, too." Cass grabs my proffered clutch of cards, walks to the sofa and sinks down onto the seat.

At the end of it, we have a large discard pile on one end of the coffee table, with cards lying every which way. In front of us, though, Cass arranges five cards along the table's smoothed edge.

"You know, you can just stop here." He taps the card closest to him. "I can take the photos of these and text them to Pendelton. They can do the legwork of figuring out who worked for Mum and Dad."

He's got a point. A good one, in fact.

And yet.

"So, can I ask you something?" I peer at him sidelong.

"Uh, yeah."

"They've already sold this duplex, right?" I wait for his reluctant nod. "So when am I supposed to move out?"

His face tightens, cheeks darkening. "End of the month, close to. Uh, three weeks from . . ." he looks upward, thinking, "today." He winces.

I force myself to speak through the sudden spike in anxiety. "Do I have a place to go? I mean, since I wasn't planning on moving with them."

"Not that I know of. But you wanted to stay in Edmonton. I know that much." He hesitates and I already recognize the determined set of his jaw. "Why don't you just come stay with Etta and me for a while? You can store whatever you don't need from here. Recovering from . . . what you've been through would be a lot without a support system, and that's before we add in anything else. Etta can refer you to someone really good back home." Another pause, this one somehow tense. "Whatever we find out, you'll have family around you. Come, stay with us."

I offer him an attempt at a grin. "You don't trust me to see a therapist on my own, do you?"

He raises an eyebrow. "Well? Would you?"

I let my grin die when I realize something about my imminent home-lessness. I have a moment to worry how it'll sound, but really, there's only one way onward. "So, about the duplex. Who gets the proceeds from the sale?"

"Supposed to be split fifty-fifty between us kids." Cass sounds sad.

I shoot him a confused look. "But wouldn't they need that to buy their condo on the coast? You said Mum already has one picked out."

"Oh no, they're done. Bought and paid for. Well, financed anyway."

"So then . . . how do we get half the proceeds?"

"Okay, so first of all, are you worried about money? 'Cause you won't need to pay rent or anything while you stay with us."

I place a hand on his arm. "No, that's not what I meant. And, of course. Thanks. No, it's that I'm trying to look at this, at *us*, from the cops' point of view."

"Cleo—"

"No, wait, hear me out. I have no alibi. Neither do you, sort of. And it's clear they have to suspect us, like, as a matter of course. It's their job. I just don't want to be caught on my back foot, you know?"

"You're being paranoid."

"It's my life on the line, here, Cass. At least Etta can vouch for you or something, right? She was at home with you all last weekend. Might not be, whatever, an ironclad alibi, but I . . . only have me." I scowl to hide the tremor of fear. "I'm entitled to be cautious, okay? So stop pissing and moaning and help me think this out."

I swear he rolls his eyes. I don't call him on it, though. I need his help. However sarcastically he wants to offer it.

"So, tell me how this splitting the duplex money is supposed to work. I want to know so when the cops ask you to explain it to them, or they ask the lawyer to explain it to them, I'll know where I stand."

"The lawyer won't tell them anything." Cass eyes me for a few more moments, his expression troubled. "But you're right. I'll have to." He sighs, slumping slightly onto the sofa. "Okay, so Mum's going to pay down the rest of our mortgage with half the money from selling this place. My mortgage isn't a lot, luckily, so there'll be some extra, and she'll put that into a trust for us, but we'll have full access. Apparently, the tax burden's easier on us this way. That's what she said, anyway."

"How much did they sell the duplex for?"

"I'm not sure. Mum never told me the exact amount." He hesitates, blushing. "But Etta and I looked up a realty site and, uh, we think maybe around four hundred thousand?"

"And she was going to withhold my half." I stare at him. "Jesus, Cass. This is looking worse and worse for me by the second."

He pushes off the back of the sofa, reaching for my hand. "Whoa. There's no proof she did that. Let's not overreact."

I pull my hands out of reach. "Oh, c'mon, Cass. Keep up. At some point, you're going to be forced to tell the cops that our mother is the type of woman who would be willing to blackmail her daughter. They're not gonna care about *complicated*. They're going to see a motive for me to do something terrible. It's what they're expecting." I steel myself to say it out loud. "They're going to see a big juicy reason for me to want her out of the picture. And I don't have anything to counter their theory." I drop my head into my hands. "I am so fucked."

I grip the sides of my head, shake myself roughly. "And that's before any mention of what we stand to inherit out of the lottery winnings." I scrub at my hair, pulling it completely loose from the ponytail. I sit up, let my head fall back onto the sofa. I stare up at the ceiling, fretting with the hair elastic in my fingers.

Cass moves closer, places a hand on my arm. I don't realize how cold I am until I feel the warmth spreading from his fingers. I turn my head without moving it off the sofa.

"It's only logical. They're going to think I did something to make this happen, Cass. They're going to say I want my inheritance, my money from the duplex. They're going to say I'm angry with her for blackmailing me. They're going to turn what you call a complicated relationship into anger and resentment and . . . worse."

"But you didn't do anything. They can't prove you did something you didn't do."

I stare into his eyes, so dark, so trusting, so much faith in me.

I don't think I've ever felt this exhausted in my life.

"Have *you* ever been able to do that? Prove a negative? 'Cause that's what I'd have to do. The cops aren't going to settle for me repeating *I don't remember*. I mean, it's so totally inconclusive as to be useless." I lift my hands, then let them fall back onto the sofa with a dull thump. "I don't even know if the truth matters."

A car passes by on the street outside. Maybe a truck, judging by the sound of its engine. Not that I care enough to check. I'm struck by how quiet my home is. Not even a ticking clock.

Cass shifts, bumping the sofa against the back of my head. "I'm here for you. Me and Etta both. We're family. We'll get through this together." That voice, so beautifully deep and gentle, letting me know it's okay to despair, just a little.

I consider it, truly I do. But given what I'm learning about myself, about my life with my parents, I'm not sure I can buy into his idea of family. Support? Blind faith? Unconditional love . . . The abrupt threat of tears tells me Cass's concept of family is as alien to me as mine is to him. We may as well be strangers.

I thrust aside the sorrow that realization creates. I can only be myself. Whatever that means. Jesus, I'm tired.

I shift the direction of my spiralling thoughts. "So, like, if I revert 100 percent to my asshole ways, you'll be okay?"

After a brief second of what looks like shock on his face, my brave, decent little brother forces a chuckle. "I've had plenty of training, so yeah, I'll be fine."

"Don't say I never warned you."

He grabs hold of my hand. "However this changes you, or brings back old habits, or whatever, we'll always be family. That's not going to change. We've got your back."

I squeeze his hand, then disentangle, feeling clamminess on my palm. That slither of unease returns, tickling down my spine like a drip of ice water. Resolving to ignore it, I sit up with a deep, steadying breath, pull my hair back into a tight, high tail.

"Okay, my office isn't giving us what we need." I gesture toward the interior wall with my chin as I stand up. "I think I'm ready."

I allow myself a second or two to look out my picture window. I must have seen everything out there a million times over, but right now, I may be truly grateful for it for the first time. Mid-afternoon sunlight, bright and true. Trees, their bright green foliage rustling in the breeze that continues in and through my home. Houses, sturdy, with vinyl siding or stucco or planks, quiet and still in their workday stance. Cars, parked here and there on both sides of the street, colourful and dirty, large and small. A framed snapshot of normal, everyday life. My eyes sting, the skin around them tightening.

I walk over to the window to give myself time to toughen the hell up. I notice the curtains are askew behind the armchair by the door, the heavy cloth poking out sideways at a weird angle. I push it in, but it just springs back. I try again. No change. My heart rate ratchets upward.

Jesus. *Keep it together, Li.* It's just caught on something.

I yank the fabric aside, toward me, reaching awkwardly over the top of the armchair, the seat front digging into my bruised knees. I stop short, my breath pulling into me with a choking sound.

There's a dark hump on the floor.

NINETEEN

My breath quickens, sounding harsh and loud in my ears. "I think it's my purse." I reach out with a trembling hand, the other gripping the armchair for support, and grab hold of two sturdy straps. It's lighter than I expected. I stumble backward, into Cass. He steadies me with his hands on my shoulders.

The bag's more like a small tote, blackish purple, with the look of supple leather and one single zippered opening. "Hidden behind the armchair." I twist the bag by its handles, this way and that, searching for what, I'm not sure.

"—back door?"

I look over my shoulder. Cass's brows are crinkled in puzzlement. "What?" I ask.

"I said, wouldn't you normally leave it by the back door? Like, in the kitchen or something? I mean, if you don't take it into your bedroom, but I don't know if you switch out purses regularly or not. Etta keeps hers in our bedroom."

I take myself and the purse to the sofa, plunk the bag onto the coffee table, avoiding the clutch of business cards. I scooch up, pressing my still-aching knees against the table for ballast, and I unzip the opening. I pull out handfuls of whatever I can grab. A matching leather wallet, a small glass jar of Tiger Balm, two pens, a pack of tissues, lip balm. Impatient, I upend the bag, netting an additional square tube of lipstick, some paper clips, and clumps of fuzz, which drift lazily onto the chestnut-painted wood.

"Do you recall any of this stuff? Can you tell if anything's missing?"

I make another visual inventory. "My phone? I must have a phone, right?" I undo the button clasp on my wallet. No cash. One credit card. Wait, no. It's a points card for somewhere. "Do I have credit cards? There's nothing here."

"Yeah." Cass grimaces.

"No cash, no credit cards. What *do* I still have?" I mutter. My driver's licence. I hesitate, just a little, before pulling it out of its pocket. I don't know what I'm expecting, but I exhale a shaky breath. CLEOPATRA LI. DOB: 12/19/1983.

I give Cass a weak grin as I show him the ID. "Like a mug shot."

"Everybody looks like a criminal in those." He doesn't sound relieved by my attempt at humour. His voice lowers to a worried, tense bass. "Sis, are you okay?"

"Why? 'Cause this proves I left against my will?" I swallow. "Well, we don't know I left without my phone. And there's no money in this. Maybe I was in a hurry? I took the cash and credit cards?" It makes no sense, but I say it anyway.

Cass shakes his head. "If you're in a hurry, you'd just take the whole purse. Faster than rummaging inside to find your wallet and then extract the money or whatever." He takes the wallet, checks its insides. "And no bank card either?"

"Maybe I went clubbing? A purse would be a pain." But I feel taut as a wire. The feeling of relief, at being home, at hearing Cass's words of support even if I don't believe them—now all completely evaporated.

Cass sets the wallet on the table, gathers the other detritus into a pile.

I pick up the lipstick, pull off the cap, turn the tube. It's pale pink. I might have a faint memory of what it feels like to gloss my lips with this colour. I touch my lower lip, feel patches of roughness. I put away the lipstick, use the lip balm instead. My lips tingle. I taste peppermint.

I scoop everything back into the purse, zip it all out of sight again. My chest feels like it's being squeezed, my lungs deflating as the oxygen inexorably escapes. I force a deep, deep breath. "We need to call Miller. Like, now. They'll want to know about this as soon as we do, right?"

Cass picks up my hand again, kneading it gently. "Okay. One thing at a time. We're moving way too fast right now. You need time to adjust." He lets out a slow breath. "We're not in some action movie or whatever. Shit happening at breakneck speed, no time to react. You need to process every bit of new info we find. All right?"

I extricate my hand, gesture at the spread of business cards. "We should send these to Miller. I promised."

Cass gathers the scattered cards. "I'll take care of it, okay? Then we're going to find your doctor's number and call their service. Maybe we can get you in to see someone today. Or over the weekend." He pushes my purse to the far edge of the table, lines up the five cards into two rows.

I watch him for a moment, thoughts whirling, my knees pumping up and down. The phone's camera shutter sound finally prods me to act. I reach out and take hold of his wrist. "Cass, I'm freaking out here. I have to do something."

"Yeah, I get it. You're no good at sitting around. That hasn't changed about you."

"Okay, but wait, please. I know . . ." I gather my wits as best I can. "You were right. I shouldn't assume . . . I mean, we're not white, yeah, but we're also . . . privileged enough that the cops won't actively try to . . . railroad me." I watch to see if he understands. He offers a cautious nod, so I continue. "But I'm scared, Cass. Like, really scared. What if . . . something truly bad's happened to them? To . . . to Mum and Dad? What if *I'm* the only one who knows what happened? What if the reason I don't remember is because . . . I don't want to?"

Cass puts down his phone. He swivels to face me straight-on. "Listen, I'm serious about you getting some professional help. You woke up on the side of the highway with amnesia, for chrissake." He pauses, looking me squarely in the eyes. "Healing from assault takes time and resources and support. You can't do this on your own. More importantly, you don't have to."

I fight the tears that spring to my eyes. "Whoever did this to me, maybe it's this old co-worker, maybe it's not, but . . . I keep thinking, there can't be any other reason they dragged me all the way out there. They wanted something from them, from Mum and Dad. They must have got me to tell them where they were." I bite down on my lip to crush the quivering. "The only thing I can think of someone wanting so bad they'd kidnap and drug me . . . is the lottery ticket." I can't stop wringing my hands. "What would they have done when they discovered Mum didn't have the ticket with her?"

Cass's brave face falters for a moment. "Sis, we have to accept the probability—"

I don't let him finish. "But I can't figure out how anyone would know about the ticket in the first place. You said yourself, Mum and Dad are way too paranoid to tell anyone other than us. And I want to believe there's no way you, me, or Etta would blab." I clutch my arms against my abdomen, feeling sick to my stomach. "None of this makes any sense."

Cass considers me, his eyes opaque. "Someone did this to you. My money's on this asshole you worked with, but whoever it is, we've gotta trust the cops to find them." He rubs his chin, expression taut. I hear the rasp of his stubble. "But for what it's worth, I don't think it was a stranger." His mouth thins. "Maybe Mum or Dad got excited, let something slip. If Mum told anyone, it would be Auntie Annie. Three months is a long time to keep a secret, especially a happy one."

I can feel my face blanch, the blood draining away, pooling in my gut. "No. I can't think that. I won't." I shake my head again. "I would never have told anyone about the lottery ticket."

"I know this is awful, and hard, but . . . why else would they drug you? Deliberately cause your amnesia? If they were willing to . . . harm Mum and Dad, why wouldn't they be willing to . . . get rid of you, too?" His jaw clenches, the muscles bunching alarmingly for a second. "If it is this asshole co-worker, then he might try to dodge suspicion by trying to hide his identity, maybe confuse things by . . . letting you go." His voice trails away.

I shift, unsettled, as I try to read his face. Does he realize he could fall under the same suspicion? Surely, given their inclinations so far, the cops must be considering it. Despite all Cass's words of support, his kindness, his actions so far . . . should I? When do I finally trust him? And yet . . . how can I afford not to? Can I do this on my own?

I don't honestly know. But I can't just sit here, fumbling in my head for answers.

I jump up, as if I've been prodded with electricity. "We have to go over there, Cass. Now." I haul the suitcases, one at a time, into an open bit of floor. "You check that one for a key." The room abruptly fills with the sound of zippers ripping open, of soft thuds as clothes are tossed onto the floor. I check all the interior compartments.

"Wait. Listen." Cass pulls at my arm. "Listen."

I tear my elbow out of his grip. "What?" My breath saws in and out.

"You've got a spare, I know you do. You're always over there. It makes the most sense for you to have a spare. Okay? Do you understand what I'm saying?"

I look at the piles of clothing around me, at my father's suitcase on my floor, gaping open like a fish, slit and gutted. I'm an idiot. "You're right. They wouldn't pack their house keys. They'd take them with." I heave a sigh, rub my eyes. "I don't know what I'm thinking."

"Come on." Cass holds out a hand. "You're . . . not quite yourself, that's all. You're not an idiot."

Oh Christ. I am if I keep saying things out loud when I think I'm only thinking them.

I let him pull me to my feet. He lets go after assessing me intently for a moment, then walks into the kitchen. He stops at the end of a counter, closest to the steps down to the back door, and opens the narrow cupboard above. Three cup hooks are set in a horizontal line on the inside of the cupboard door. Hanging from one of the hooks is a set of keys on a ring with something I can't quite make out. Cass pulls the ring off and hands it to me. I turn over the metal thing attached and see that it's a word, *Queen*, in blinged-out calligraphic letters.

"It's where Mum and Dad always kept spare keys. I figured it was worth a shot, that you'd do the same in your own place."

I run a thumb over the smooth enamelled metal, feel it warm to my touch. I squeeze my hand shut, fighting off the intense flash of fear with the dull pain in my palm.

TWENTY

Three steps down to the back door. I slide into a pair of slip-on sneakers, bracing myself with one hand on the door frame, the keys scraping against its smooth surface. Another pang of familiarity strikes, this time followed by an unaccountable agitation.

I wait with a trembling hand on the doorknob, the other gripping the keys 'til I feel the imprint of each individual tiny glass gem in my palm. Cass comes from closing the front door and sits down on the top step from the kitchen to lace on his well-worn shoes. Then we're out the back and I'm standing in front of the cut-out gate in the shared fence. Gently nudging me aside, Cass pushes the gate open, steps through, and holds it open for me and my pounding heart.

My parents' backyard is just as immaculate as mine. The planters look suspiciously similar as well, though the choice of flowers seems different. The garden here is much more impressive: a rectangular raised bed rather than my small line of pots, with carefully labelled stakes at the end of rows of bumpy soil.

"Dad must've got his seeds in before the trip after all," Cass says quietly, his face turned away from me. "He told me he didn't want to delay. It was beautiful on the May long weekend. . . ."

There's a small garden shed only a few feet away, just where the little concrete pad skirting the back door ends and the lawn begins. I step to the shed, meaning to try the lock, though what clues I think I'll find inside is anybody's guess.

I hear the crunch of glass underfoot, sharp and distinctive. I raise my foot, checking the bottom of my shoe and the ground underneath. A flash of silver catches my eye, close by the shed's edge. I shift, trying to get a bead on the source. I crouch down, heedless of whatever glass I'm grinding into the concrete. I see a corner of something slim and metallic. Is this right?

"It's . . . a phone." I snatch it up from the grass. The screen's cracked, bits of glass missing. I know it must be useless, but I press the power button anyway. "Oh my God. Do you think it's mine?" I look up into my brother's shocked bewilderment. "Mum and Dad had theirs with them. That's what the lodge people said."

"Holy—" he says. "It's trashed."

"Maybe I dropped it? When I was last over here?" It sounds even more improbable said aloud. I hold it gingerly with my fingertips and thumb as I look around the yard with different eyes, uncertain what I'm hoping for. The hairs on the back of my neck stand on end. I kneel, place the phone on the concrete, close to the shed. I wipe my hands on my jeans, staring at the shattered screen, not sure if I want it to light up or stay dark.

I stand, shaking myself loose from the panic that threatens to overwhelm me. I swing the keys round the chain, land them in my palm. Whether or not I'm ready, it's time. I stop at their back door. I match the key to the deadbolt, slide it in, and turn.

"It's not locked." I exchange a worried look with Cass. I pull out the key entirely and try the door handle. The door pushes inward with the same *whoosh* as mine did earlier, breaking the seal with the frame. Christ. I'm half-expecting the hinges to creak, I'm so creeped out. Cass gestures. I nod. We push the door fully open together.

By silent agreement, neither of us steps inside, though Cass does reach in to flick the light switch on. There's a pause, then brightness as a fluorescent bulb kicks on. I see shoes and sandals on a plastic shoe rack fit inside of a low rectangular cut-out in the wall, just like mine. Underneath, a rough black doormat, scuffed and worn in the middle. It sits slightly askew, one corner riding up the rise of the bottom of three steps leading to the kitchen. Above the shoes, a wall-mounted set of five coat hooks, one holding an ugly chartreuse sweater, dragged out of shape.

I'm profoundly grateful in this moment that we have no basement to search. I step into the entryway cautiously, listening for what, I don't know. I hear the hum of the refrigerator ahead of me, the screechy caw of a crow behind, followed by my brother's rapid breathing.

The doormat slips to the side as I put my weight on it. I flail my arms, grab onto the coat hooks for balance. My other hand slaps down on the topmost step, hitting the band of plastic at its edge, mashing my soft palm against the metal keys in my grip.

"Jesus Christ," says Cass. Shouting, really. "Are you okay?"

Cursing, I push myself up, twitching off his hand on my elbow. "Fine. I'm fine." The palm of one hand stings. The fingers on the other twinge. I think I wrenched my shoulder. I straighten out the doormat. We kick off our shoes on autopilot and ascend the stairs.

I stop, unwilling to enter the kitchen fully, my hand moving up to cover my mouth in shock.

Cass halts beside me. He leans forward, as though to enter, then he rocks back onto his heels.

"What the fuck."

I can't blame him. I don't know where to start either.

My parents kept their interior walls intact. From our vantage point, we can see a darkened hallway straight ahead, leading to what I'd guess is a bedroom or den or something. It shares the wall with my office, so it should have a window onto the front lawn. Through an open doorway to our immediate right is my parents' kitchen. Where my island is, they've got a wall, a long counter, and cupboards running farther into the rest of the room. The countertop is stacked with what looks like every plate, dish, and bowl they own.

I lean around the doorway. The drawers gape open and the floor is covered with spilled cutlery, cooking utensils, plastic wrap, aluminum foil, kitchen towels, oven mitts. . . . I step through the doorway so I can look around the corner. A long sheet of paper towels stretches diagonally across the floor, its cardboard tube hanging empty on the under-the-shelf holder by the toaster, which sits on its side next to the sink.

Cass rubs at his face. "We are officially into *holy fuck* territory now."

I tiptoe back, go down the shadowed hallway. Cass calls out to me. I ignore him.

An archway farther down on the right opens into the living room. Where mine is bright and contemporary, my parents have clearly not changed anything since they moved in, in the '80s. Flowered fabric sofa and loveseat with faded cream doilies. A dark wood coffee table, its surface an intricate carving, sprinkled now with broken shards of glass, remnants of the sheet meant to protect the carving from dust and hard use. Above the sofa, a lonely brass nail protrudes from the wall. Beside what remains of the sofa, an embroidered silk portrait of the Three Fates sits on the floor, its heavy lacquered frame broken on one side, the glass cracked from a central impact point like threads in a spider's web.

Beneath the picture window lies a simple wooden shelving unit, the flat boards splintered and smashed, its uprights still intact. Two little orange trees, obviously pruned to fit indoor pots, have been pulled up by their roots, their plain blue planters overturned. A smaller, more elaborate ceramic pot lies in crude jagged pieces on the floor. The orange shrubs plus a jade plant make a sad heap in the corner, their branches stomped and broken. Small oranges litter the mess, though they're mostly squished and rotting. I wrinkle my nose, as though seeing them releases their scent.

Black potting soil mats the carpeting in scattered patches. It lies beneath the stuffing and foam bits torn out of the mangled couch cushions. I suddenly register an insistent buzzing, a black cloud of flies hovering over the ruined fruit.

No wonder the blinds were drawn.

Shivering, I peek into the smaller room at the end of the hall, my knees abruptly unsteady. A rickety-looking desk. A sewing table in the opposite corner. Computer tower lying on its side on the carpet. Monitor with its face smashed in. A laptop with its screen similarly abused, its keyboard misshapen and gapped. Fabric and sewing notions tumble from the open closet doors like they were vomited out.

"Holy fuck," whispers Cass from over my shoulder.

"Everything's trashed." I rub my temple. "Just like my phone." I point at the floor, at the broken slab of sleek gunmetal-grey. "And I bet that's my laptop. It looks expensive."

If Cass notices the wobble in my voice, he keeps it to himself. "We shouldn't touch anything."

I nod.

"We need to call the police."

I rub both temples, let out a shaky pent-up breath. "Here, let me. I know the address. Plus, I can tell them about my situation, and what happened in BC." I hold my hand out.

He pulls the device from his back pocket. "Sis, this is bad. Way worse than anything I imagined . . ." His voice trails away as he studies me intently all of a sudden. "You know the address? You remember?"

TWENTY-ONE

Thoughts ping around inside my head. I feel sweat break out as I blink stupidly at his expectant face. Do I? I take a deep breath and recite my home address, slowly and clearly. "That it? That's it, right?" The bright feeling of accomplishment bursts. "Oh, but I saw my driver's licence. It's on there, isn't it?"

He pulls me in for a tight hug. "I don't care, I'm calling it a win."

I pat him awkwardly on the back. "Let's hope the police feel the same." I pull away, tip my chin downward. My heart beats faster, ramping up the throb at the back of my head. My scalp prickles with sweat. I lower my voice, barely able to say it. "It's not coming back fast enough, Cass. I'm running out of time."

He hugs me again. "We can't control what they think, sis. We've just got to handle what we can. The memories will come back."

I let myself feel comforted. Only for a moment. I nod into his shirt, the waffle weave rough on my nose and forehead. "They better." I disengage, take a step away. "Or else, I'm fu—"

"Stop. Stop right there. What did I just say about worrying?"

"Nothing." I give myself a little more comfort. "You just threw a bunch of pop psych at me and hoped I wouldn't notice."

"Har, har." He holds out his phone, his expression sobering. "We'd better call."

It's a short exchange. I have to ask Cass for his number, explain I'm using a borrowed phone. I change my mind, don't mention my situation, not yet. Whoever shows up can get the story from me in person. I agree to stay in the vicinity and hang up. I open the phone's *Recents* list and tap to make the next call. Cass gives me a curious frown. I hold up my hand to stall his question.

I hear Pendelton answer in my ear.

I try to stanch the sudden tremble in my voice, identifying myself and explaining the situation. I remember to mention my purse, too. "I don't know if you guys are here yet or whatever, but I thought you'd like to know what's going on. We're just waiting for the cops to show." I motion Cass to follow me to the back door.

"All right," says Pendelton. "Just tell the constable in charge to contact me at this number as soon as he's done taking down your statements. We'll get coordinated as quickly as we can. The best thing for you to do is to exit your parents' residence and wait for the local authorities to arrive."

I'm abruptly too tired to play nice. "Yeah, okay, I got it, thanks."

Cass brushes past me as I hang up with Pendelton.

I know it's unwise, maybe even dangerous. I take a long look around as I stand at the entry to the kitchen.

"You okay?" Cass waits for me at the back door.

"This is rage. This . . . destruction, the violence. . . ." I flinch as the chill spreads through me. Was I here? In the middle of all this?

"C'mon." He jams his feet into his shoes, leaves them unlaced. "We need to get out of here." He gestures for me to put on my shoes.

I let him urge me out, then ease the door shut. He strides straight to the internal gate. I pause in the yard as I catch sight of my shattered phone. Squinting at the sudden glare, I leave it, like all the rest, for the cops and whatever later brings.

Inside my side of the duplex, Cass says he'll make some coffee. "It's been a long day already, and it might be a long evening. Plus," he tries a wan smile, "you have the good stuff."

I stare down at my now-bare feet, unwilling to match his forced cheer. I see tiny clumps of soil in between my toes. I crane around, see more dark grains trailing from me to the top step. Will the cops want these? Should we collect them? Put them into an envelope or something? Or a bowl? Maybe there's some of it still in my shoes. I worry at my bottom lip, my hands clenching and unclenching, trying to figure out what best to do.

"Sis?"

I look up. Cass puts out his hand. I watch it near, then land on my upper arm. His hand is warm through my sleeve. I shiver, goose bumps spreading out from where he touches me. An abrupt pain in my hand. I bring it up to eye level. Keys. Sparkling. *Queen.* I offer him the keychain. Cass takes it, his brows furrowing as it releases stickily from my clammy palm.

"We should clean this up." I point down at the dirt I've tracked into my house.

His gaze follows my gesture. "Sure." He draws out the word into an uncertain ending, his frown deepening.

I brush the soil off my feet, thank him, and head for my room, my gaze skittering away from his alarmed expression. I'm exhausted all of a sudden, beyond anything I could've imagined. I clamp my jaws tight together, straining to put one foot in front of the other, feeling like I'm slogging through molasses. I press my soles against the cold flooring and breathe sharply through my nose. I grasp the door frame of my bedroom, reach blindly for the door, scrape it past my arm, 'til it clicks shut.

I stand at the foot of my bed, staring at the smooth sheets and plump pillows, everything invitingly striated by light coming through the slats of my blinds. When did I lower them? I don't rememberrrrr. . . .

I feel myself falling forward, my eyes closing, my brain anticipating the imminent sensation of landing in a soft place—

CRASH.

I startle, jumping back from the bed. Heartbeat loud and racing in my ears. Thumping hard against my ribs. A sensation like hammers in my head. Knees stinging.

I hear Cass curse, and I know he must be angry because I hear it through the door, over the sound of a metal bowl wobbling on my kitchen floorboards. I envision the wobble tightening in a circle as I hear its pitch increase.

I'm breathing like a bellows. I stagger to my bathroom, my entire head ringing at an unbearable frequency. I splash water on my face, run wet hands through my hair, try to sort my thoughts out from the hyped-up tangle of adrenaline shooting through me. I strip off my sweat-damp clothes, get into the shower again, brace for the sharp needles of cold water on my overheated skin.

When my hands stop trembling, I turn up the heat, wash properly, rinse out the sweat and new snags in my hair, ignore every scrape and protesting bruise along my body. My mind is on standby, like a screen of static on a TV when stations used to shut down broadcasting overnight. I know there will be more police, more questions, more skepticism, more pressure on me to remember.

I rinse off and dry myself in a fog of uncertainty. I scrub at my damp hair once more, wind it up to secure into a tight bun, toss the towel back onto the bathroom rack. I stand in front of my closet in my underwear. Does it matter how I look when they come for me? I find capris, T-shirt, long-sleeved pullover. If I bother with makeup, will they think me vain? Heartless? If they see me without, will they think me young and ignorant?

How do I make the police trust me when I've got nothing to back me up?

I scrub at my face. *Big-girl pants, Li.* They're definitely not going to think of me favourably if I'm screaming and tearing my hair out in a frenzy of indecision either.

I dress quickly, allowing myself small diamond stud earrings, and exit my bedroom into the rich, gorgeous aroma of brewing coffee. My steps falter to a standstill.

I place a hand on the back of the sofa and inhale, as deeply as I'm able, closing my eyes to concentrate. That hard little knot within me loosens further, the smallest fraction, and I understand, a little more, what it truly means to feel at home.

It scares me how desperately I hope it lasts.

I squint at Cass at his spot next to my stove. "Is that . . . a percolator?"

He nods. "It's why I was shocked you drank Tim Hortons in Golden. I knew something was way off. These coffee beans are literally from some volcanic mountainside in Hawaii. I'm sure you save them for special occasions, since they cost an arm and a leg, but I thought you might appreciate something familiar." He watches me, shoulders drooping slightly.

"I'm starting to get a certain picture of my personality." I hesitate, trying to calculate how it'll go over with the cops.

"That you enjoy your creature comforts? Oh yeah." He registers the expression on my face. "What?"

"Nothing. Just being paranoid." I shrug.

He studies me for long seconds. I notice the parts of his hair standing up on end, the paleness underlying his tanned face, the shadows beneath his eyes. He gives himself a shake, throws up his hands. "I'm tired. You must be exhausted. Why don't we set aside all the worrying for now? We can't do anything about what the cops think or don't think right now. Or ever, really. We can only do what we can do."

I offer a crooked smile. "That sounds like some bubble-gum pop psych shit for sure." One corner of his mouth rises. "Okay," I say, striving to match his calm. "Let's drink some crazy expensive chichi coffee, get ourselves totally hyped on caffeine, and take whatever comes next as it comes."

"You enjoy the coffee." Cass points to the guest bathroom. "I'll be back after a quick shower."

A flash of worry lights through me. Will the police question why we both showered after coming back here from the crime scene next door? Are we supposed to not? But we didn't have anything to do with that, that destruction. Will they be able to tell? I rub my temples, force my sluggish brain to work. From the looks of those smashed oranges, they'll see it was days ago. Right?

TWENTY-TWO

I exhale sharply. Cass's advice plays through my head. Bubble-gum psych or not, it sounds pretty useful. At the very least, it can stop me from spiralling into a quagmire of doubts. I settle onto a chair at the island and let the soothing smell of really expensive brew permeate my senses.

Still . . . I can't quite get comfortable. Something else tickles at the edges of my mind. I narrow my eyes, trying to figure it out, when it abruptly grabs hold, and before I can examine it closely, I leap up and turn toward the back door. Out into the warm air, through the cut-out gate, and into my parents' backyard.

I snatch up my broken phone, am back in the house in seconds.

I hunt around my bedroom. One nightstand, two nightstands, drawers and shelving. I check the surface of the wide dresser across from the bed, moving aside hair bands, earring stands, books, and magazines. Even though I know from earlier, I check the drawers anyway, running my hands along the sides and underneath my clothes, feeling for a hard lump. Nothing.

I pause at my doorway, scan the kitchen countertops near power outlets. More nothing, though I note the percolator's stopped. I hurry over to my office, eyes focussed on anything that looks like a thin white cable and matching white cube plug.

In my office space, I home in on the desk. An image of the destroyed laptop next door flickers at the edge of my mind, but I turn away from it purposefully. I push aside the chair, which isn't much more than mesh netting over a complicated plastic frame, and I spy a power bar on the floor against the wall underneath the window. It's switched off, its outlets empty.

I slump a little in the surprisingly comfortable chair, staring at the empty desk, at the wall, out the window to my right. I hear two cars pass in quick succession. Guess people are coming home from work.

"Everything okay?"

I acknowledge Cass's concern with a half-hearted smile. "Trying to find a charger for my phone, see if it'll fire up. Maybe I can check my calendar, find something useful. Jog my memory."

His expression turns uneasy. "You picked it up? From next door?"

"If I can get it working and take a look at my calendar, I can see what I've been doing this past week. I mean, the week before." I pause. "I know the police will do the same. I just . . . I just want to know before they do."

"But there'll be evidence on it. You could've messed up the . . . whoever did this, their prints or some—"

"I could've tripped and fallen at the back door, and the phone went flying out of my hand or something. You saw that back doormat. Maybe I went in for something, saw the state of the house, and was running back out to call the cops or something. Maybe I just slipped at the back door, fell, and hit my head."

"Cleopatra."

"Don't take that tone with me. I'm not a child." My face goes hot.

"I'm not. Honest. I can only guess how stressed you must be." He takes a slow, deep breath. "But we both know you didn't get to BC on your own. And the hospital exam didn't show any concussion." He gestures. "Where's your phone?"

I hold it up in my hand.

"The police will need to, whatever, process it for prints and stuff."

"Mine will be all over it anyway."

He tips his head. "Okay, but it might *not* be yours, and if it is, there might be other prints, too. And if we keep handling it, we might end up smearing them or making them unreadable."

"You're using that tone with me again."

Cass makes a face. "And you're being stubborn. You freaked out, made a dumb mistake. Fine. Just admit you screwed up and move on. But now you're doubling down. You could be making it harder for the police to catch whoever trashed Mum and Dad's place and probably ki—"

"I am not." I don't care if I'm shouting. "This is about me recovering my memory, Cass, so I can *help* the police find out what the fuck's going on."

"Jesus." He steps into the office fully, crossing his arms over his chest. "Just admit it, all right? You're not in your right mind and you didn't think it through properly. You fucked up, plain and simple. Why can't you ever fucking admit when you're wrong?"

I feel the sneer forming. I know it's bad, but I can't make it stop.

His entire face darkens, I swear I can see it happening a shade at a time. "I'm thrilled you remembered about your calendar. But. That doesn't change the fact that you did something you shouldn't have. And that you can't admit you fucked up." His voice rises. "Which is one of the reasons you don't have a job right now."

I'm half a heartbeat away from throwing my phone at his head. I know it's a terrible idea. I know we're both just strung out. I know. And still. Well, this fucking proves it, doesn't it?

We *must* be siblings. Nobody makes you lose your head quite like family. My hand twitches.

A sharp rapping sounds on the front door.

Cass wheels around, striding across the living room. I push up off my office chair, sending it crashing against the wall behind me. I jog-step after him, throwing a warning glare over my shoulder as I push past. He holds up his hands. It better be in truce.

I reach the door. There's no shadow on the peephole, no darkened shape through the pebbled glass flanking the door. I open it up, step outside. The concrete is cold on the bottoms of my feet. Gritty.

"Hello?" I call out, leaning out to see the other side of the duplex. I take a first step down, feel raised treads hard against my soles.

Behind me, Cass says, "Here." He hands me my slip-on sneakers. Reluctant, I shake them out and put them on before thinking too hard about it, then jump down the rest of the steps, grimacing at the twinges from my knees and shins as I land. Cass is right with me as I cross the lawn and greet the two men in dark uniforms standing on my parents' stoop. The white officer drops his hand to his side and turns away from the door to face us. The Korean Canadian officer, already positioned to watch the street, wears a stern expression as he gives me the once-over.

I'm sure my angry face is an easy match. "I'm Cleopatra Li. This is my brother, Cassius. I called about the break-in. Our parents live here. I'm next door."

The closer man comes down from the stoop. He's taller even than Cass, with broad shoulders and a long, severe face. His name tag reads *Yoo*. The door-knocker follows, body loose and athletic. I crane to read his tag. *Eastcott*. They both look down at me, expressions hard to interpret.

Yoo says, "Why don't you tell us from the top?"

Where to start? My heart hammers at my chest. "We just got back into town, which I can tell you about a little later. I have a spare key. We entered through the back door." I swallow. "The place was trashed, so we left, and called 911."

Cass fidgets but doesn't correct my white lie.

"And your parents?" says Yoo.

Eastcott eases around us and disappears around the side of the duplex.

I exchange a look with Cass. "Okay, like I said, we just got back from BC. You'll need to speak with the RCMP in Golden. Wait. No, from Serious Crimes in Kelowna. Shae Miller and Chuck Pendelton. Our parents have been missing since Sunday afternoon, maybe evening. No." I pause, try to unscramble my confused narrative. "Sorry. I'm telling it all jumbled." I take a steadying breath. "Our parents went missing from a resort near Field, BC. Inspector Shae Miller and Staff Sergeant Chuck Pendelton are handling the case. Cass has Pendelton's number in his phone. They told us to have you call them for all the details."

My brother stirs. "Speaking of which—"

I talk over him, keeping eye contact with Yoo. "After we came out of the house, I picked up my phone. I think it's mine. It was smashed in the backyard on my parents' side. I'm sorry. I know I should have left it there."

Yoo gives a curt nod. "Can I have that phone number please, sir? And where is this phone now, miss?"

I bring it up in my hand. "I wanted to charge it and see if it was still working. I'm sorry. I don't know what I was thinking."

Yoo ignores my transgression as well as my apology. "Please place it on the step over there. Now your full names and addresses, please." He records everything in a compact notebook, asks us for official ID. Cass shows his. I explain mine's in the house.

I say, "There's something else." Yoo looks at me, his expression pretty close to long-suffering. "The RCMP also have a case open on me." I explain as best I can, but I stop before mentioning the lottery ticket, gesturing for Cass to do it. To his credit, my little brother doesn't miss a beat, and he doesn't show his frustration with me. I'm struck again by his sheer decency. I avert my face to hide my jagged discomfort.

When Cass is done, Yoo squints at me, clearly considering. "So, you were closely involved in your parents' lives?" I nod. He makes a noise low in his throat, says, "I can see why the RCMP are involved. All ri—" He turns as Eastcott comes round from my half of the building. Eastcott gives a short nod, then strides to their SUV. He gets inside and I see him pull up what I guess to be the radio mic or whatever.

"My partner's calling for some techs. They'll see if the perpetrator left any physical evidence. Fingerprints, that sort of thing. They'll need things from you, as well, for elimination purposes, but they'll walk you through all that. In the meantime, I'll get in touch with the RCMP. We'll coordinate with them. I'll have to ask you to stay on the premises for the time being. It may take a few hours to sort everything out."

"What about my phone?" I explain my idea for accessing my calendar. "I think it might somehow jolt my memory, hopefully find something to help my parents."

"Well, as far as the phone's concerned," says Yoo, "we will have to take it as evidence and get it processed. Then—"

I slap a hand to my forehead. "Oh no, I think I have a password on it." I stare at my brother. "And I can't remember what it is."

Cass reaches for my hand, his grip warm and dry, contrasting jarringly with my clammy skin. "Hey, it's all right, sis. They've got resources we don't. Okay?"

"Okay. Right." I straighten my spine, take deep breaths until my heart's no longer banging against my ribs. "Right."

Yoo watches me warily for a moment, says, "It will take some time, of course, but we'll let you know—we or the RCMP, I guess—we'll be in touch with updates. In the meantime, you can wait in your home. Please don't enter your parents' residence again until we give you the go-ahead."

He nods at us both with an air of finality. Cass pulls me gently toward my side of the duplex. I watch Yoo open the trunk of the EPS SUV. I can hear some radio chatter from the open passenger-side window, up by Eastcott. Yoo re-emerges from the trunk end with a large brown envelope. Laying it on the open trunk floor, he uncaps a marker and writes on it carefully. He returns to my parents' stoop in what looks like only a handful of steps. He scoots the phone into the open envelope, using a pen as a prod. He spares me and Cass a flat glance as he rejoins Eastcott.

Cass opens my front door. "We need to call your doctor's weekend service."

I gesture for him to wait as I watch Yoo approach again.

"Can you tell me where you found the phone, Miss Li?"

"It was in the grass by my dad's garden shed. Cass and I came through the gate from my backyard. I heard glass under my shoe, and then I saw the metal of the phone by the shed. There's a concrete pad by their back door. That's where the glass was, that I stepped on." I've jumbled the explanation and I'm babbling, but Yoo only nods, making notes. "Do you want me to show you?"

"No. Thank you." He taps his notebook. "We'll update you before we leave. Can I see that ID of yours, please?"

"Sure. Of course." I hurry inside and grab my purse.

Yoo takes down what he needs, then waits for Cass to pull me back inside, watching me lock my screen door again before returning to his SUV.

I shuck my shoes. "I can't believe they found a spot right out front," I murmur, rubbing my chilled toes over the soft rug. "That should be a good omen, right?" I tap the corner of my driver's licence on my leg.

"Come on. Coffee time."

I replace the licence in my wallet, drop my purse back on the floor next to the coffee table. "So . . . we're good?"

He shrugs, speaking to the backsplash in the kitchen. "You apologized to the cops. What more can I want?" He stands at the island, his back to me, head drooping.

I inject every ounce of sincerity I can muster into my voice. "I'm sorry, Cass. I didn't think about how stressed *you* were about everything . . . over there." I point to the shared wall with my parents' home, but he can't see me. I let my hand drop.

He remains as he is, shoulders tight. After what feels much too long, he straightens up to face me, eyes hard. He crosses his arms over his chest.

"That bad, huh?" My apologetic grin peters out.

His gaze softens, painfully slowly, until he heaves a sigh, face drawn. "You've always been shit at saying sorry. Guess I can't fault the effort now. At least you're trying."

"Thanks . . . ?"

He drops his arms, approaches, and pulls me into a hug. "Like I said, we can only do what we can do."

Hours later, after Yoo has everything he needs from us, wrung out and woolly-headed, I let Cass usher me to bed.

I drop into sleep immediately—only to awaken, panting and clawing at my sheets, trying to get away from the black silhouette lunging for me from the depths of that damned dark car in my messed-up, confused head. The least I could do is see the goddamned face, but no, nothing but sweat and blinding terror.

The bedside clock's subdued digital display reads 4:39. I get up and open both windows by the bed, stumble to the bathroom to splash chilly water on my face and pass a wet hand along the back of my neck, under the heavy length of my hair.

Squinting as I flick the light on, I strip off my damp sleep clothes and turn on the shower. Under the soothing rush of water, I think over everything that might have happened, everything that I can no longer remember—even the things that I can. It's clear this is moving so far out of my control I may never be able to get a handle on it.

But I'm glad I was able to dissuade Cass from making me see a doctor other than my usual GP. I mean, I may not remember her, but at least she'll know me. The mere thought of seeing a therapist, of letting some stranger root around in my psyche, is enough to set my limbs trembling. I'm not going to let some unfamiliar GP refer me to one on top of all that, too. Best to wait for my own physician. At least, that's how I argued it.

The simple truth is, no matter how much I plan and project into the future, I have no idea where any of this will lead. Whether I get back my full memories of that night or not, I have to keep my head in the present. It's the only way I build a future for myself. I take one step at a time, say one thing at a time, wake up one day at a time.

A loud, impatient part of me wants to run ahead of all the uncertainty of the present, just take off and live whatever perfect life looks most appealing. The truth seems a luxury I may never get, so why stress about it? Why not recreate myself from whole cloth and be content? Do I really want to return to being a bitch and a bully?

But the smarter parts of me recognize that for what it is. Wishful thinking. As long as there's uncertainty, as long as I'm under suspicion from the cops, I can't be content.

I can't afford to be passive. I have to act. I have to make whatever stand I can against complacency and fear. There are too many questions hanging over all this to satisfy someone like Miller, and I have no idea if she'll ever accept that some of those questions may be unanswerable. I'm not sure if I can either.

I turn off the shower, brace myself against the tiled wall with both hands, and hang my head for a moment. I watch droplets fall from the ends of my hair, land in the tub with the tiniest of sounds, and slide away down the drain, the trails of their passage forming a small swirl of water that disappears almost as soon as it's created.

I have the heavy feeling there are long, difficult days ahead.

TWENTY-THREE

The weekend is a blur: laundering every stitch of linens for our parents, and cleaning and putting everything to rights in their home. The orange shrubs and jade plant are goners, poor things. We end up piling all the soil into two pots and Cass stows it all in the garden shed. I can't bring myself to do it. For a break, he drags me out to buy a new phone and laptop. Relentlessly cheerful, he refuses to let me obsess over why someone would trash my things like that while he helps me restore everything from cloud backups. Yay for foresight and hiding sticky notes with account passwords in filing cabinets, I guess. He also makes sure I text the cops so they all have my contact info. Only Naomi replies with more than a one-word acknowledgement.

I'm so sorry bout ur parents place.
You ok?

Yeah. Thanks. A huge shock but 🫥
My life is pretty much all kinds of messed up rn.

Well I'm visiting fam in yeg this wkend.

Lemme know if I can help, k?

Off duty as a friend.

Oh wow. Thanks but Cass is taking
pretty good care of me. Despite my objections. 😊
Enjoy your time with your YEG fam.

For real Im around if u need support. 👊

I shove the screen at Cass, pointing out that last text with a laugh while I rub away the sudden tears with my other hand. It's ridiculous to get emotional about a simple emoji. He'd never let me live it down.

I scroll through my calendar for the past month, but nothing sparks any revelations, except that I was definitely not idle. Among near-daily errands for my mother, I scheduled on average three coffees every week-day, trying to network my way into a new position. In between, I met with headhunting agencies and also used online services—a routine I apparently followed for the past five months. I know I must have a non-compete clause as part of my severance, probably for twelve months, but really, people skirt that line all the time. And yet, no one's sent me any leads. Maybe my mother was right. Mediocre men get away with shit all the time, but nobody wants to work with a *difficult woman*.

Late Sunday night, Cass finds me staring out the front picture window.

"Uh, sis, we need to talk."

"What." I clench my jaw. "Sorry." I muster up a lopsided smile as I turn back to him. "What's up?"

"Facebook. People are asking about Mum and Dad. I think . . . I think Miller and Pendelton have been talking to their friends." He gestures to his phone. "Auntie Annie even sent me a private message. She's worried."

Aren't we all. I drop into the armchair. "Shit."

Cass looks discomfited. "I didn't know how much you wanted to say, about your amnesia." He blows out a breath, his face drawn and unhappy. "Plus, I think Miller and Pendelton have been asking what people know about the lottery win."

I shake my head, hard. "I don't care if people are pissed they weren't told. Don't say a word about the lottery. Don't confirm. Don't deny." At his incredulous look, I say, "Do *you* want to spill the beans about the lottery win? Hear complaints about why Mum didn't trust them enough to tell them? Have acquaintances start sidling up to you all of a sudden, wanting to be friends? Or worse, get some reporter on the doorstep?"

"I know all that, sis. I'm not stupid."

"Yeah, well then, stop saying stupid shit." This time, I literally bite my lip. "Fuck. I'm sorry."

It's likely a trick of the light, but his eyes seem to sink even deeper into their sockets. "This sucks."

I count to ten silently to myself. "Look," I say, "I know this is probably not what you want, but let's just ignore all the messages. Don't reply at all. It's not like we're not busy with enough shit as it is. And if someone gets mad about it, they're not being a decent friend anyway, so good riddance."

"I don't treat people like that, sis."

I shrug.

He sighs. "But I'll take your advice. I won't say anything about the lottery or your situation. I'll just reassure them the cops are working the case." He rises. "I'm wiped. Can we just call it a night?"

Sleep lasts just long enough for the nightmare images to wrench me awake in the wee hours. I lie in bed, too weary to wash off the terror sweat, too wired to find sleep again. Eventually, I hear the birds chirping in increasing numbers, so I push myself upright and get on with the day.

By the time Cass is showered, shaved, and ready for breakfast, I've got the moderately priced coffee percolating and my calmest game face on as I lean against the counter next to the fridge. I dodge questions about my night by dialling my GP's office while he's still pouring himself his first mug of coffee. Sipping, he watches me, his expression unreadable.

Between one blink and the next, though, he manages to unplug my earbuds and whisk my phone out of my hands. Fuming, I listen to him guilt-trip the receptionist into squeezing me in at the end of the day.

I can barely restrain myself until he hangs up. "I was trying *not* to mention the assault and amnesia, idiot."

"Which is why she wasn't gonna book you 'til next week." He puts his mug down and gives me a serious look. "Listen, sis, I'm sorry I was gone so long."

I frown. "Uh, what?"

"Mum's totally weird about anything to do with doctors, too. Maybe if I'd been around more, I could've provided a more balanced perspective."

"On going to the doctor?" I stare at him. "I'm fine with going to my doctor, Cass. I've been doing it, on my own, for decades. I don't need anybody to hold my hand."

"Okay, it's like this." He looks deliberately into my eyes. "Remember when Mum had an appendectomy?"

"Of course I do—" His eyes widen. I rear back, heart rate skyrocketing. "Wait. I remember. *I remember*."

He makes a face. "Etta will probably tear a strip off me for trying that."

My hands start to shake. "I remember," I murmur.

His humour fades. "Okay, easy now."

I take several shaky breaths, slowing my heart, trying to ignore the sweat beading at my hairline. Cass utters an apology, alarm clear in his voice. I dismiss it with a wave of my hand. "No, it's okay. I'm okay. This is a good thing, right?" I take another breath, manage a smirk. "Why don't you distract me by telling me what your point is?"

His lips thin for a moment. "Okay, smartass, this was about nine years ago. Auntie Annie had to take Mum into Emergency one morning. She called Dad. He dropped everything and got there in time to find out Mum was already in surgery. But he didn't call you until late that night, after he got home and visiting hours were over."

I meet his expectant look. "And I lost my shit."

The very faintest of grins ghosts across his lean face. "Yeah. But Dad didn't give you any satisfaction. He didn't see anything wrong with not telling you. He was completely sure he did what Mum wanted, even though he never actually spoke with her. He, uh, he told you to go home and calm down. I had to talk you down from moving out, like, right the fuck then."

I rub at my eyes. "Not my finest moment."

"Yeah." He clears his throat. "But my point is, Mum is incredibly, unbelievably, frustratingly old-fashioned about medical stuff—like almost superstitious. Every ailment is a punishment. And she has this twisted idea that if she treats herself poorly, the gods won't strike her down. It's that humility thing, right? Don't be too proud or you'll bring down bad luck."

"Are you . . . trying to tell me to stop being weird about my amnesia? In an incredibly convoluted way?"

"Well, more like stop resisting me when I'm trying to take care of you." He pauses. "And maybe, please don't be so goddamned cranky about it either."

I look across the living room and out the front window. Cass waits for me to join in his attempted mirth. Instead, I examine this memory, dredged up without warning to punch me in the gut. I'm sure Cass thinks I'm over it, the anger and frustration. I probably did, too, but now, I just . . . The thought of my mother, unable to understand why I deserve to know she's in hospital. And my dad, so afraid of Mum's anger that he chose her over me. I don't need to ask my brother. I know there are likely a hundred other examples like this one. Don't they say that dog packs run with one leader? This tangle of emotions must be what you get when you have two bitch alphas in one little family of four.

Betty Wan's downtown law offices have a view stretching southward, across the verdant banks of the North Saskatchewan River and its attendant bridges, and past the University of Alberta campus and its mishmash of new glass architecture sprouting amid dark brick standbys. Wan gestures for us to sit with her at the medium-sized conference table to one side of her corner suite.

"I've never been here before, have I? In your office, I mean." I settle myself into a leather chair, careful to sit forward to avoid bumping my ponytail against the tall back. Cass takes the seat to my right and Wan faces us across the glossy wooden tabletop.

"No, we've never actually met, Miss Li." Wan offers me a cordial smile, then pauses the precise right amount. "The RCMP have been in contact. I'm terribly sorry to hear about your parents. Please let me know what I can do. I'm sure you know I must adhere to client confidentiality, but if I can help, I will."

I share a quick glance with Cass. He says, "Thank you for seeing us on short notice, Mrs. Wan. We know you must be quite busy."

"Please, call me Betty. *Mrs. Wan* is my mother-in-law. I've been married ten years and I still can't get used to that name." The rueful smile on her delicate face makes her unbearably beautiful.

"We're concerned about the lottery winnings." I should probably be trying to ease into this, but I suddenly can't stand the thought of playing at niceties. Despite the sting to my pride, I can admit when I'm out of my league. Everything about the woman across from me reminds me so.

Wan raises her perfectly plucked eyebrows, her full lips flattening the merest bit.

Cass lays a hand on my forearm, stalling any further bumbling from me. "The RCMP are investigating Mum and Dad's disappearance, so we told them about the winning lottery ticket. So now they think maybe it has something to do with all of this." He stops. "Wait. I'm telling it all mixed up. Let me try again."

This time, I gesture to him to wait. "It seems you already know, from the RCMP, but . . . In addition to our parents being missing, I was drugged and kidnapped, and taken out to where our parents were, out in BC. I can't remember any of the details of that night, or a big chunk of anything else, to be honest. I woke up on the side of the highway, a week ago today. It was the morning after our parents disappeared." I explain the discovery of Dad's wallet and the break-in at the house.

Cass takes over. "We know Mum put the ticket in a safety deposit box, and we know she signed it, so it's, I guess, relatively safe. I think Mum would make sure to keep the safety deposit box key safe somewhere, too." He pauses. "Actually, I can even imagine she hid it somehow. But that's just me guessing. To be honest, neither of us knows much of anything else, and . . . well. We're hoping you can help us."

"We know you can't tell us everything they did with you, like, in terms of their estate planning, etc., and we're not asking about that right now," I add, sounding embarrassingly earnest.

"What is it you *are* asking me right now?" Wan's expression remains friendly, but I sense we have to step carefully. So, I start with a definite truth.

"Cass told the police Mum put the ticket in a safety deposit box. And we know you were helping Mum figure out how to claim the winnings and remain anonymous."

Wan watches me, her expression neutral. Afternoon sunlight slanting in through her floor-to-ceiling windows lights up her fitted, pale pink blouse. It's a gorgeous contrast with her charcoal-grey suit skirt. I turn my gaze away at an abrupt flash as she shifts her head—her earrings, delicate diamond drops, reflecting sunlight.

I scrabble for patience as I feel my mood plummet. When I saw the name *Betty* on my mother's papers, I expected a dowdy Chinese woman closer to my parents' age, not this sleek creature with immaculate makeup, glossy hair, and an unbeatable poker face. My cheeks heat at the thought of admitting defeat and slinking away with my tail between my legs. Cass warned me this was a bad idea. No lawyer worth their salt would ever let us winkle out even a scrap of info about a client. But I thought desperate circumstances might sway her.

To my surprise, Cass taps the table and leans in. "We just want to make sure the ticket is properly secured. Someone may have gone to a lot of trouble to find it."

"Is that what the RCMP believe?" asks Wan.

We both nod. Cass continues. "There's got to be a reason someone assaulted my sister and took her all the way out to BC—where Mum and Dad happened to be? For the first time ever in their lives? It can't be

coincidence." His voice roughens. "And let's face it. There's nothing special about them. They're not wealthy or well known. They're just normal
people. Except for this lottery thing. So, we, we want to make sure . . .
even if someone could get into the safety deposit box. I mean . . . if," he
swallows, "if they got the deposit box key from Mum somehow . . ."

"Can't you please tell us?" I lean forward, too. "Did Mum leave a key
with you? For safe keeping?"

Cass turns to me with an expression of utter shock. I take the time
to smooth a hand over his forearm. "You can ask for two keys, right?
From a bank? I don't think she would put that windfall in jeopardy. She
wouldn't carry it around with her. What if she lost it? Or it got wrecked
or mangled? I mean, one of the first things she did was hire a lawyer to
claim the winnings for her so she could remain safe from unscrupulous
people, right? That doesn't sound like someone who'd take that key with
her out of town."

I face Wan again, making sure to sound as rational as I can. "Even
though Mum apparently kept the details from me, I've made some edu-
cated guesses. I figure she could have given you equal authority at the
bank to access that box. Cass tells me the duplex will change ownership
at the end of this month. I think she was going to move to BC first,
her and Dad, then have you claim the winnings. While she's far away,
completely out of the province and out of the picture entirely. If you
also have a key and access, then she wouldn't have to return to fetch the
ticket. No one here would connect the move to the lottery money. It can
be explained with the sale of the duplex."

Wan's smile softens an infinitesimal amount.

"But with the current circumstances . . ." I hesitate, abruptly reluctant
to say it aloud. "I'm worried something's happened to the ticket, that
whoever . . . hurt them—"

"And you," says Cass.

"—somehow came back and stole the ticket after all. I don't know how, precisely. Maybe they got Mum to say where her key is. Maybe they, they forged a letter for the bank, or, or they forced her to sign something, or, I don't know . . ." I let my rambling blather trail away.

Wan considers us both for a moment. "I'm not going to confirm or deny your . . . conjectures. I can, however, say that people in the situation your mother is in, with respect to a lottery win of that magnitude, are always smart to seek legal counsel, in order to reorder their estate plan, redraw their wills, etc., yes, but also in order to consider all the worst-case scenarios, including sudden and unexpected incapacitation or, I'm sorry to say, death." After an appropriately sombre pause, she says, "While I can't tell you any specific details, either by my confirmation or my denial, of anything your parents and I spoke of, I will say I believe your mother wouldn't leave anything of this importance to chance."

"You mean you also have a key?" asks Cass. "My sister's right?"

Wan's smile remains firmly cordial.

I proceed a little frantically down my mental list of items. "What about the condo they bought in North Vancouver? Are you handling that for them, too? Because we don't know anything about that. We don't know what to do about it. Or even if there's anything *to* do about it."

Wan nods. "If the time comes when something needs doing about that condo, I'll make sure I contact the appropriate parties." She pauses, looking at us both in turn before rising. "Now, please let me know if anything else comes up related to your parents. I know we're all praying that they're found safe soon."

"Please, Betty." A bubble of worry, maybe even of desperation, pushes my worst impulses to the fore. I give her my most vulnerable, pleading look. "I know it's asking a lot, but I just feel so much is out of my hands right now. Can you please show us the key at least? I just need confirmation it's real. And protected." I lean forward, touch the edge of table with only my fingers. "Or can you please go check the safety deposit box? Make sure the ticket is safe? You don't even have to tell us. But if it's not there, you could . . . tell the police. Right? You could tell them?"

Wan's lips thin to a line. "I'm afraid my hands are tied in this matter." She looks like she might say more, but after a beat, she only tightens her lips.

My temper ignites. "Did my mother give you explicit instructions to *refuse* me? Is that it? That's why you can't confirm where it is? Why you won't help us?"

Cass cautions me with a touch on my arm. I spare him a scowl and a glance. He's staring at me, wide-eyed and panicky.

Wan's melodious voice firmly pre-empts anything else I might blurt out. "I'm certain your mother had her reasons for the decisions she made concerning her estate. Unfortunately, as I said, I'm not in a position to provide anything more to you at this time on this matter. I'm sorry, truly."

What's that saying? Butter wouldn't melt in her mouth.

TWENTY-FOUR

Back out past the reception desk, Cass holds open the heavy glass door for me. We wait for the elevator in tense silence. When it comes, he jabs the *Lobby* button. The doors glide shut with a soft thud, and we start our slow downward fall. We're not alone, so I keep quiet and focus on keeping my head up and my spine straight. Cass stares at the button panel, his face hard with displeasure.

When the doors open onto the ground floor, we exit with the crush. I step nearer the wall to get my bearings. I'm not sure of the way to the parkade. While I wait for the crowd to thin, I spy a standing sign to one side, for some kind of annual fundraising campaign. I catch on the corporate name, my heart stopping for a millisecond. Jesus, what are the odds. I turn to Cass, unsettled. Surely, he mustn't have known my old company's in the same building as Betty Wan. Or maybe he forgot? He would've warned me. I'm sure of it. I am.

Still, he'll have to convince me it's not a bad omen.

Before I can speak, though, Cass mutters, "Etta texted. Gonna call her back." Without meeting my eyes, he pivots right and strides away toward the building's large rotunda. He passes a set of escalators connected to the second floor of the atrium and takes a seat on the far side, on a bench girding one of the numerous planting arrangements.

He must be pissed because I made a fool of myself with Wan. I can relate.

Sighing, I walk toward a coffee kiosk on the closer edge of the rotunda. To reach it, I have to dodge three different men in suits who apparently expect me to keep out of their paths. I'm tempted each time to make them walk right into me, but that would most likely mean I'd get knocked on my ass. Hard pass.

I get in a long line for coffee. The mid-afternoon rush, apparently.

Someone approaches in my periphery, and I shift to avoid them, my mind focussed on getting my coffee order right because damned if I'm gonna allow this to end in humiliation, too, by hemming and hawing at the cashier.

"What the fuck, Li?"

A white man steps into my personal space, his breath moist in my face. I take a pace back, but he follows, crowding me, violence in his dark blue eyes. Sweat breaks out all over me, my heart rate rocketing upward. I want to look for Cass, but I'm afraid to take my attention off the furious stranger. I sense a space growing around us as people clear away.

"Are you out of your goddamned mind?" The man towers over me, leaning into my space even more, forcing me to crane my neck to stay out of his chest. "Why would you tell the cops I messed with you?"

I step back again. "Hey, back off, buddy. I don't know you." My voice comes out high-pitched, wobbly with fear, completely at odds with the words.

His glare deepens. "I don't know what crazy game you're playing now, Li, but you better tell the cops the truth. I haven't been anywhere near you since I got your psycho ass fired."

I wrinkle my nose at his breath, stale with cigarettes and something sickly-sweet that puts me in mind of apple juice. I take a shallow breath through my mouth, step back slowly another pace. I peer into his face, take in his angular face and strong jaw, note his dark blond hair, curling just slightly at its ends. He has a very slight widow's peak.

It's clear who he is, though I don't remember him. Do I tell him that? Will it help? I'm not sure he'd believe me, not in his condition. Maybe not even if he were calm. This man despises me. I can see it in his eyes.

He presses forward. I feel his knee against my legs. I can't help it. In that moment, I don't care if he's twice my weight. I throw my hands up and shove him, as hard as I can. "Don't touch me. Get off me." The shout echoes around the two-storey, marble-floored rotunda.

He recovers from his stumble and lurches toward me, quick as a snake. My mouth goes dry as I watch his approach, hands like claws. I try to slap them away. He grabs my upper arms and shakes me mercilessly. I feel my teeth cut into my cheek, taste blood. He lifts me off my feet for a moment. I gasp at his bruising grip.

"You better tell the cops the truth, you lying bitch."

Spittle lands on my face as he jams me back on my feet. I can't wipe it away. I can't scream for him to stop. My teeth clatter against themselves, and I feel a stinging slice along the side of my tongue. My hair is suddenly flying around my head, flung out of its ponytail. I can't see his face anymore. I feel the imprint of every single one of his fingers on my arms.

Before I fully register it, I'm airborne. I land on the unforgiving flooring, hard on my left hip. A twang of pain shoots all the way to my ankle. Then another pierces the side of my head. My vision goes grey and black for I don't know how long. Somehow, I find myself prone, staring up at the ceiling. I push a mess of hair out of my face, wincing at the sharp ache in my head.

Through slitted eyes, I see Cass struggling with the man, their hands grappling for purchase, their shoes sliding and shrieking on the slick marble. I try to jump up but manage to rise only a few inches before I fall back down. Fuck, that hurts. I roll over laboriously, pull myself up on all fours, then up onto my haunches. My brain short-circuits for a second, thrown back to the dawn a week ago—only a week?—but I ruthlessly shove the memory away, using the fresh pain to focus. Panting, I try not to vomit.

Cass has a hold on the man's arms at the elbow. I can see the sleeves bunched up tight in his white-knuckled grip. The man is pushing and pulling, trying to get his arms free. He kicks out, but Cass does a small leap to the side, jerking the man with him. It looks like some bizarre dance.

With a hard twist, the man wrestles free, shoving Cass back a number of steps. Then he turns around and runs for the escalators, shoving past people in his haste and disappearing up and out of sight.

Cass whirls around. Seeing my face, his expression shifts from angry focus to deep alarm. He fumbles with his back pocket, bringing up his phone. I blink at him slowly, the lights abruptly unbearably bright. I open my mouth to say . . . something, I don't remember what. I end up closing my eyes instead.

When I reopen them, I'm propped up against Cass, listening to his heart thumping. His voice rumbles within his chest, against my ear. I feel his arm around my back holding me semi-upright, his hand firmly grasping my shoulder. I shift, trying to push off of him. After an initial stiffening, he releases me, gently steadying me as I sit up on my own.

White flashes pop in my vision. I narrow my gaze, to cut the brightness even a little. A cool hand takes hold of my wrist. I lever my head upward just enough to make out the attached body and then face. It's a stranger, a Black woman with deep brown eyes and a golden nose ring set with the tiniest diamond I've ever seen. She stares into my eyes intently. I note her beautiful curly hair. It must be really thick. The high bun she's made of it is big as a softball.

"Pupils look regular size." Her voice is medium pitch and completely no-nonsense. She lets go of my wrist, raising her hand toward my face. I flinch at the shine of a small flashlight, hissing as its light hits my eyes. "Sorry." She speaks over her shoulder. "Dilation normal." She turns back to me. "Does anything hurt?"

"My head," I whisper. "Left hip . . . ankle . . . tailbone."

Cass tenses next to me, muttering, "That fucker."

The EMT prods and palpates my limbs gently, her hands encased in bright purple gloves. "I think just bruising. It's gonna hurt for a few days, but nothing feels broken." She pauses, her expression assessing as she looks around us.

I notice her colleague, an Arab man identically attired in a dark blue, short-sleeved uniform and purple nitrile gloves, standing guard just behind her. Compact and athletic, he rests one hand on a red plastic case set atop one of the tables that dot the perimeter of the rotunda. He alternates between watching us and scanning the area.

"If you can stand," says the woman, pulling my gaze back, "I don't think we need to examine your tailbone right now."

I use Cass shamelessly as a prop. There's way too much hissing, but I manage to stand, only swaying the tiniest bit once I'm upright. It feels like the entirety of my ass has gone numb. But even if it kills me, I'm not saying so. There's no way I'm letting this woman poke at my tailbone in public, doesn't matter how stunning she is.

"You need to sit down," says my brother tightly. He manoeuvres me to a chair at the table presided over by the other EMT. I lower myself on trembling legs and perch gingerly on the edge of the unforgiving metal seat. After a moment, I lean forward to take the weight off my tailbone, blinking away tears.

The woman asks me more questions. No, I'm not dizzy. No, I'm not nauseated. Yes, my head hurts. No, I can't rate the pain on a scale, but I can handle it.

The EMTs agree that I don't need a hospital visit, but only because I already have an appointment to see my doctor this afternoon. They send Cass to fetch me a bottle of water, and they watch me swallow an over-the-counter painkiller. The water is too cold, amplifying the headache for a split-skull second.

I let Cass take in all the instructions. I know he'll do a better job of it than I can.

When I raise my head next, the EMTs are gone. I bite my lip to keep from blurting out my surprise. Cass will sweep me off to a hospital without a second thought if he knows I've lost another patch of time. Clearly, it's only been a few minutes, and I was only zoned out, not actually unconscious, but those details won't matter to him.

I suppose they ought to matter to me, seeing as it's my head and my health. But the thought of being stuck in a hospital waiting room is unacceptable. I struck out with Betty Wan. I just got my ass handed to me by a man who might have something to do with my parents' disappearance. I still can't remember anything that'll help find them. And this headache might just kill me. Is there any way I could be *more* useless?

"C'mon," says Cass. "We're early, but maybe we can get you in to your GP faster once they hear about your concussion." He takes gentle hold of my elbow to help me to standing.

I open my mouth to tell him to stop fussing just as a young Indigenous woman stops about a foot away from us, her expression tentative.

She sidles slightly closer to me, moving into a shaft of weak sunlight from the glass-domed ceiling far above us. Her eyes lighten to the colour of cognac. I can see a few faded pits from acne on her otherwise smooth brown cheeks.

"I—I'm Sara. I filmed the whole thing. If you need it for the cops or whatever, I can share it with you." She fidgets on her feet, her phone clasped in a thick-fingered hand, its glittery silver case winking in and out of the sunlight as she shifts.

Cass thanks her, though I note the flash of irritation from him. She's not much taller than I am, and perhaps even slimmer in the shoulders. I can't fault her for staying on the sidelines. At least she's giving us something useful. I may not remember that asshole's name, or why he hates me, but I'm going to make sure it'll be a long time 'til he forgets me.

"Okay, thanks, Sara, we really appreciate it." Cass taps his phone with a subtle note of satisfaction and gives the woman a kind smile.

She nods awkwardly, then turns to me. "I'm sorry that happened to you. I'll talk to the police, um," she grimaces, "if you need me to. I hope you feel better soon." With that, she wheels around and strides away toward the escalator, turning back once with wide eyes before moving out of view.

I straighten my spine, conscious of the continued stares in this very public space. "Where's security? They'll have cameras in here, right? I want to press charges, Cass."

"Okay, let's think about that later. Right now, we should get you to the doc—" He raises his hand as his phone blares out a song. With a frown, he answers. "Inspector Miller . . . yes, in the atrium. What? Why? No, my sister needs—"

"Please, Dr. Li. Listen to me."

I whirl around, regretting it instantly as my brain sloshes to catch up with the rest of me. Miller comes to a stop a few paces from us, followed by a tall Black man in thick-soled shoes, wearing a collared shirt under a sweater with a security company patch on the left breast.

Miller looks slightly winded. Wisps of hair escape around her forehead, though her posture remains ramrod straight. Other than the slight bulge under her suit jacket, she looks like any of the many other women here, in dark slacks and a pearl-grey blouse. She ends the call on her phone with the press of a thumb.

"I'm sorry to catch you like this, but we need to sort out what happened while we have you here." She gestures to the security guard. "Delson recognized you, so he came to get me while the EMTs were with you. He knew Naomi and I were upstairs, interviewing people at your old company."

I frown, searching the guard's face, round and boyishly appealing. His name tag reads *Adebayo*. He gives me a slight nod, his mouth set in an unyielding line. I duck my head, frowning at the floor. I don't remember him from before . . . and I don't recall seeing him arrive while—

Wait. My frown deepens as I piece together Miller's words. "Did you just say you were at my old company? So, you've talked to this guy? The man who just assaulted me?"

"How do you know that?" Miller grimaces, then gives herself a visible shake. "Okay, one thing at a ti—"

Adebayo interrupts her. "If I may. We need to take this to the security office. This is not the place for this discussion." He gestures with a graceful sweep of his arm. "Please. It's just behind the escalators."

I don't wait for anybody else. The sooner we do this, the sooner I make sure that son of a bitch gets thrown in jail. I will walk wherever I need to, no matter how much it hurts, to make that happen.

Miller places a hand on my arm. "No, we need to take you up to identify the man who assaulted you. Naomi is sitting with him now, making
sure he's available to us."

Adebayo says, "I'm sorry, Inspector Miller, but that is not how we do
things here. I need first to obtain an incident report from Miss Cleopatra
and . . . her companion. That, along with our footage of the incident,
will be provided to the Edmonton Police Service, as is our policy. As is
calling them in to report this. Then you will be at liberty to escort these
people upstairs, accompanied by myself."

Cass pulls me into him with an arm around my shoulders. "I need to
take Cleo to her doctor. She's clearly had a bad knock on the head. The
EMTs cleared her, but she needs to have her own doctor examine her.
That's what's next for us." Cass addresses Adebayo. "I'm Cassius Li, by
the way, Cleo's brother. We'll be happy to help you with a report, but we
have a doctor's appointment we cannot miss. I promise I will call you
with a time we can connect, okay?" He releases me to fish out his wallet
and then a card. "Here. A way to track me down if you need to."

Adebayo reads the card, his smooth brow creasing into a scowl. I feel
badly for him.

Cass gently urges me forward, back toward the elevators, presumably
down to the parkade. I dig my toes into the soles of my shoes, resisting
the hand he's placed in the middle of my back. "No, Cass. I want to go
upstairs. I want to identify this asshole now. I want to know his name."

"You can get that without the theatrics, sis." Cass glowers down at me.
"Inspector Miller can tell you his name right now, right?" He shifts his
dark look to her.

She ignores him, her gaze pinned on me. "We want the same thing,
Cleo. If he's the one who assaulted you, then I want to put him away. The

faster we get that ID, the better." She looks to Adebayo. "We need you to hold off, Delson, please. I or Constable Aoki will be speaking to EPS directly. Soon."

"But what about my—" I flick my gaze to Adebayo for a moment, "situation? What did you get from him about that?"

Adebayo brings his hand into the space between me and Miller, cutting into my line of sight. "As I said, we need to take this into the security office. Now. It is not appropriate to speak of this here." His eyes dart to the curious crowd around us. "You will not want reporters to arrive."

"I'm sorry, Mr. Adebayo," I say clearly. "I need to ID this man. I . . ." I see his face tighten with annoyance. "You see, I have amnesia. I don't remember him. I can only ID him if I see him now." But his expression doesn't loosen. If anything, it hardens to resentment. It might not have the same intensity as the other man's, but I recognize this. Delson Adebayo doesn't like me much.

I spend about a second regretting that I don't recall why, then shove it aside. Fine. It just got that much easier siding with Miller. I meet Adebayo's disapproving frown with a raised chin. "I'm going with the inspector. As my brother said, we promise to talk to you later about your report. And I'm definitely going to press charges, so thank you in advance for your help."

I walk with Miller about ten feet before I realize that Cass isn't with me. I look over my shoulder to see him shaking hands with Adebayo, who's clearly still unhappy. But then he follows alongside Cass with a resigned expression and a disapproving shake of his head. I guess my brother, at least, has a chance to be in his good books. I should count that a win, but I can't stop wondering about myself, about *Cleopatra*.

Is there anyone who knows her who doesn't hate her?

TWENTY-FIVE

Up on the twenty-fourth floor, we push through a double set of glass doors, etched with the company's logo. It pairs precisely and perfectly with the company name, mounted high on the wall behind the reception area within. The wall is at the back of the nook for the receptionist. There's a short wall set at ninety degrees and a waist-high counter that faces the doors. Seated beneath the signage, a curly-haired white woman in a peach blouse and a no-hands headset meets us with wide eyes and a stammered greeting.

Miller says, "Hi again, Becca. Just back for the constable and Mr. Arceneaux."—I frown at the unfamiliar name—"I know the way to the boardroom, thanks. We won't be much longer."

"But—" Becca gapes as Miller stops abruptly.

"Delson," says the inspector, "could you please stay out here in the lobby?"

Adebayo eyes Miller's cool expression, his mouth set into a thin line. But he only replies, "Of course."

Smart man. I think Miller's prepared to steamroll anyone and anything in her way right now. Or maybe she's always this way with people she considers subordinates.

I try to remember this place, but it's a total blank in my mind. I can see an internal door set to the left of the receptionist's nook. I'd guess it leads to interior offices, maybe an open plan of cubicles plus offices along the windows. That's not our destination.

Instead, Miller turns to the right of the nook and leads us into a hallway, previously hidden from view by the angle of our entry. Four doors total, all closed, all dark brown wood veneer with simple brass knobs. We pass three on our left before we stop in front of the final door, set straight-on at the end of the brightly lit corridor.

Miller turns to me with a hard gleam in her eye. "You've dealt with me enough by now to know I'll do what's necessary for the file. So, I'm combining the witness statement with the ID. It's absolutely not SOP, but I acknowledge your concerns, Dr. Li, and this is the most efficient way. I'll take any flak that comes from it. I know you can handle this, Cleo." She hits me with an intent look. "We'll start a video recording before we ask you to make the ID." She flicks a look over my shoulder. "You, as well, Dr. Li. We'll take as many witnesses as we can get on the record."

"*Then* we can go?" Cass fumes, impatient.

Miller shakes her head slightly. "There'll be a few more questions for the interview."

"Inspector, please." Cass steps up next to me. "Shae. Please. My sister needs to see her doctor. I'm certain she has a concussion. I know she blacked out for at least a few seconds. That guy threw her pretty hard."

Another brief headshake. "I meant, I think your sister will have the questions."

They both turn to me. "I won't know until I see him." I swallow. "I think."

Cass huffs out a breath. I know he's angry, but I need to do this. I can give the cops an extra reason to hammer this guy Arceneaux about my parents. I can maybe even jump-start some more memories.

And if I get some personal satisfaction from seeing this man suffer real consequences for tossing me like a rag doll? Why should that be a bad thing? I may have forgotten a lot, but I don't need my personal memories to know how many horrible people get away with too fucking much.

Without another word, Miller opens the door.

As she walks through, I hear his voice.

"Look, I know I lost my head, but honestly, it was just a misunderstanding. I'm sure that once *you* understand why—"

Cass ushers me inside the room, which proves to hold an oblong conference table and eight chairs, all currently blasted by mid-afternoon sunlight coming in through two walls of windows. I stare at the man with his mouth agape and take a seat as far from him as possible, my hands suddenly trembling. My tailbone pulses with pain, even with the padding on this chair. Cass sits next to me, taking the side closer to the others, my bulwark.

"What's she doing here? She's not allowed on the premises." The man—Arceneaux—attempts to keep a level tone, but I can see the sudden rage coursing through him like the deep rumblings of a suddenly active volcano.

Naomi sits to his left, an empty chair between them. Behind her, the city extends toward the western horizon, a jumble of buildings and trees, with a glassy green river snaking through. She stares at us, clearly taken aback. Some strong emotion crosses her face before she corrals it firmly behind a professional mien. She gives me a small nod before fixing her attention on Miller.

The inspector gestures to Naomi. "We're going to record this." She inhales, straightening up to her full height. "Mr. Arceneaux, I'm glad to see you've calmed down. You shouldn't have tried to leave, frankly. Good thing Delson informed us of the incident downstairs."

Naomi pushes back from the table, rummaging in something at her feet.

Arceneaux crosses his arms over his chest, stretching his orange gingham shirt tight over his biceps and shoulders. He leans back, tipping his chair a little, and looks up at Miller while somehow also looking down his nose at her. "If you'd just had the cops busting your balls over some bullshit about someone who made your life a living hell for years, you'd've been pissed too, *Inspector*." If his shoulders get much stiffer, his shirt's gonna rip at its seams.

"As I said, that is an ongoing investigation. There's a lot of information to chase down," says Miller as Naomi, tablet in hand, positions herself so that she can fit us all in the video frame.

Arceneaux responds with a glare.

"Ready," says Naomi.

In her clear, firm voice, Miller recites whatever data she needs to, in order to explain whatever the hell it is I'm about to do that needs recording. I feel my cheeks heating up. I know they must be turning bright pink, and I worry I look overly excited when the truth is I feel like crying.

"This is a little unusual, but please bear with me," continues Miller. "Cleopatra Li is to be taken to her GP as soon as we finish here. We're combining the witness interview with the suspect identification in this recording for the sake of efficiency." She eyes Arceneaux. "You can, of course, object, but it's always in your best interest to cooperate with us, Mr. Arceneaux."

"I've got nothing to hide. It was a misunderstanding, like I've been saying all along." He throws Miller a disdainful look.

I press my fists into my thighs, to push down an abrupt urge to burst into giggles. The pressure on my tailbone shoots white-hot pain, bringing tears to my eyes. I hastily swipe them away. *Game face, Li.* This is not the time to lose your shit. And DO NOT look at Arceneaux until you have to.

"Tell us about the incident in the rotunda, please, Cleo, and be as specific as you can." Miller gives me her best bland expression.

My mouth runs abruptly dry. I swallow, work my jaw, trying to find moisture. It feels like a needle's caught in my throat. "I was waiting in line to order coffee. Cass was across the atrium, on the phone. All of a sudden, he—" I point "—was towering over me and shouting that I was a lying bitch and that I'd better tell the cops the truth. I think everyone around us sort of stepped away. For sure, nobody came to stop what was going on. I told him to get away from me, I didn't know him. But he came closer and he bumped me. I felt a . . . a wave of fear and I pushed him away, in the chest. He jumped at me and started shaking me by the shoulders. I bit the inside of my cheek. And my tongue. I couldn't talk, he was shaking me so hard. Then he picked me up by my arms and threw me onto the floor." I pause, trying to get the order right. "I landed hard, on my hip. I remember that really hurt. But I must have also hit my head because there are bits where suddenly things are different and I don't know how. Like, when the EMTs arrived. I was on the floor, with Cass, but then all of a sudden, one of them was holding my wrist and asking me questions and shining a light into my eyes. I have no recollection of seeing them until that moment."

Miller shifts, turning subtly away from me. "And you're certain Mr. Arceneaux here is the person who was shouting and the one who physically picked you up, shook you, and threw you?"

I nod. "Yes. He was very angry, but I had no idea what he was talking about. I mean, I figured out from some of what he was yelling that he was someone from before. But I didn't recognize him." I risk a glance at him. Still glaring. Still wound tight. "I still don't."

"You said," says Miller quickly, "you don't recognize him as *someone from before*? Before what?"

My breath hitches. I don't want to expose my vulnerable state, not to this asshole. I don't want him to know one goddamned thing about me, I discover.

"I know this must be difficult," says Miller, a study in sympathy. "Take your time. We just want as clear a picture of what happened as possible."

Cass takes hold of my hand, squeezing once before letting go, drawing my attention to his kind face. I take a deep breath.

Nothing comes for free. It always costs *something* to get what I want. And right now, I want to give Miller a reason to put Arceneaux in jail.

I make my voice as calm and steady as I can. "Before last Monday, when I woke up in BC with amnesia."

Arceneaux explodes from his seat, his face contorted and red with rage. "I already told you I had nothing to do with that."

I startle despite my best efforts, scooting back from the table. But my chair only manages to bang into Cass, eliciting a hiss of pain from him.

Miller is beside Arceneaux in an instant, her hands held out wide in a placating stance. "We're going to need you to stay seated, sir." It doesn't escape me that she's also in a position to engage him physically if she has to.

Naomi continues her task, holding the tablet steady as it records, relentless. The only hint of alarm might be the deep furrow between her brows. Maybe she's calculating when to intervene with Miller, or whether she needs to keep recording a potential altercation. Or it could just be a sign of her concentration. I spare a second to marvel at her calm. She was in here with Arceneaux for a long time.

Arceneaux flops back into his chair with a muttered curse. "This is bullshit," he adds. "I didn't do anything wrong. I just—"

"Please wait your turn, Mr. Arceneaux," says Miller coolly. "We'll get to your statement in a few minutes. If you'll keep 'til then, we can get through this initial part faster. Thank you."

Cass stirs beside me. "I have a video, taken by a bystander. I have her name and contact, too. She came over to tell us after he ran off."

"Dr. Li, thanks." Miller gestures with her hand. "Please tell us about the incident from your experience."

Cass sets his phone deliberately on the table, face down. "I got off the phone with my wife and turned to look for my sister. I saw her being . . . attacked by this man, Arceneaux. He had her by her upper arms and was shaking her. It was crazy. I mean, her feet were totally off the floor. So I ran across to them and tried to break it up. That's when he . . . he *threw* my sister to the floor. He tried to run, but I grabbed him, by the arms I think. I guess we . . . wrestled or whatever, but I tried to keep a grip on his shirt. I don't know why, I thought I could hold him until security showed up or something. Which they did. But Arceneaux broke away before Delson, Mr. Adebayo, arrived, and then when I saw Cleo on the floor . . . She looked dazed, so I called 911 and stayed with her." He grabs my hand again, this time holding on tight. "It was scary, seeing her out of it like that."

I can't help it. I glance at Arceneaux then. There's colour high on his cheekbones and he stares out the window, rigid. If I knew him better, I might be tempted to think he's embarrassed. Since I don't know him, for better or worse, I'm going to go with it. He *should* be ashamed. I'm barely half his size.

Miller flicks a sidelong look at Arceneaux. "Let's take a look at the video now, please, Dr. Li. You can send the file, along with the witness's name, to my email afterward."

Arceneaux swallows, his Adam's apple jerking up and down the column of his throat. I steel my expression, unwilling to give anything away. I don't know why. I don't know this man. But something's telling me if I stay coolly level, it will send him through the roof. It's probably a bad idea to needle him. The video will show just how much of a hothead he is . . . and yet. If this man manipulated things to get me fired, I have to think he's smarter than he looks.

Naomi stays at her place, close to the windows, capturing the rest of us as we crowd over Cass's phone. Well, that's not entirely accurate. Miller comes to stand next to Cass, watching over his shoulder, but nobody's invited Arceneaux any closer. He shifts his chair maybe a few inches toward Miller, but it's not near enough to actually see any of the footage.

The audio is terrible from that echoing marble-floored rotunda, but we can hear my screams and all the shouting. The words aren't clear, but the shot of Arceneaux lifting me off my feet by the arms sends the feeling of ants up and down my nape. I flinch when I watch myself land hard on the floor, see my head make contact and bounce. Sara, my witness, gasps sharply on the audio at the same time. I close my eyes.

"What happens next?" I ask shakily, not liking the texture of the silence. I open my eyes to find Naomi standing beside Miller now. Still between Arceneaux and the door, I note. They shift their attention from the tablet screen. Naomi's forehead creases with concern, though she doesn't reply. She looks like she wants to.

"We check your arms and document any visible marks of the assault," Miller says. "Then I take Mr. Arceneaux to the downtown EPS station. He makes his statement. We enter your report. Constable Aoki makes sure you make it to your doctor's appointment, where you can document any bruising in more private areas, or bruises that show up after this interview. Constable Aoki will handle getting those photos to this file. We'll track down the EMTs, too, and get the security footage from Delson."

"If you're taking him into custody, then I don't need babysitting." I grimace at the rudeness of my tone. "Sorry. I mean, surely there's more important stuff for Na—Constable Aoki to be doing than trailing after us." Not that I know why she's here, exactly. I focus on that puzzle, staring out the windows, while Naomi checks my arms. I don't want to watch her assessing my skin. I don't want to watch Miller keeping her eye on Arceneaux.

"Better safe than sorry," Cass murmurs. He raises his gaze from his phone toward Miller. "We can go now? I just sent you the video." He pushes back from the table, holding out a hand for me.

Arceneaux lets out a harsh cough of laughter. "I see she has you all fooled, too."

"Mr. Arceneaux," replies Miller firmly, "you'd be better off saving it for your lawyer."

He stands slowly, carefully manoeuvring his chair until its arms slot beneath the table's surface. He rests his hands on the upholstered chairback as he shifts his gaze from Miller to Naomi and back again. "See, this is the same shit she pulled for years when she worked here. Haven't you been talking to the others here? To Melanie, the HR manager? There's a big fat file full of complaints against *Cleopatra Li*. She manipulated loads of people here.

"Whispering gossip to the newbies, so they sided with her whenever she didn't like something I did. Bullying the code monkeys into prioritizing her projects above the rest of us. All the lies about me undercutting her when I did nothing but compete fair and square. And whenever she got called out on her bullshit, she'd bat her lashes and pull her *little ole me?* routine." His face twists into a parody of innocence, then settles into stony fury. "Every single fucking time. It was insane. She had every-one below her terrified and everyone above totally fooled. She exploited her looks, she took advantage of her . . . size to look vulnerable. When we all knew she was the predator here. Not me." His fingers press into the chair fabric until his knuckles whiten. "How can you know about all of that and still believe *her*?"

"Because we just watched that video, Mr. Arceneaux," Miller answers briskly. "You should be concerned with your immediate future." She gives me a brief, speculative glance. "There are a lot of moving parts, and a number of ongoing files, but rest assured, . . ." she includes Cass in her cool assessing gaze, "we're looking into all potential angles."

TWENTY-SIX

Until this moment, I've just thought of Naomi as the person who helped me when I had nobody else, when I *knew* nobody else, when I was vulnerable and far from home. She's been generous and patient, smart and compassionate, and incredibly kind. Even kitted out that first time I saw her, in her uniform and with a pistol, I felt like I could trust her. I've felt like I was making a new friend—with a generous helping of big sister energy.

But right now, as she stands in my living room, she seems . . . alien. Like a stranger all over again, unknown and unknowable. Maybe it's just the sheer incongruity of seeing her in my home. I mean, she's shed her sturdy boots, she's just in socks. But she looks strangely enormous in my cozy space, her shoulders even broader, those extra inches on me stretched to a whole additional foot. Which is ridiculous. Nobody's shrunk and Naomi hasn't grown. I firmly stop myself from sliding another glance at her from the corner of my eyes.

"How are you holding up?" she asks. Her gaze lands on me briefly before angling down to the floor.

"Okay, I guess." I lower myself gingerly onto the sofa, dragging my legs up to rest on the cushions. Wincing at the biting pressure on my tailbone, I lean a little sideways until it feels halfway comfortable.

In the kitchen, Cass sets the electric kettle on, muttering at me still. "I can't believe you had to wait an hour, sis. I mean, come on, you have a head injury for chrissake."

"Dr. Nguyen squeezed us in at the end of her day as it was. The EMTs cleared me, right? I was in no immediate medical danger. Plus, she pulled a favour to get me into the therapist. Dr. Lalani has a three-month waitlist."

"That doesn't actually make forcing you to wait two weeks any better," Cass replies, cranky. The water in the kettle starts growling. He hovers near it, ready to pounce as soon as it clicks off. "Seriously, sis, Etta could get you in with someone a lot sooner, in Lethbridge. We have markers we can call in, too. You honestly want to go through two more weeks of nightmares without therapy?"

Do I tell him the truth? *I can't bear the thought of anyone prying open my head, let alone someone you might know socially* would sound exactly as paranoid and terrified aloud as silent. So I settle for one truth. "I can't bear the thought of leaving my house right now, not when I only got back, not even in theory. I have so little time left here."

"Yeah." He drops his gaze to the kettle with a sigh. "Yeah, of course." He fusses with a ceramic teapot glazed a lustrous burnt-orange, spoons in loose tea, and gathers mugs. "Do you want it iced?"

I let out a tired breath. "Just water for now? But not too cold?"

"I'll get it," offers Naomi. She seems eager to stay in motion. I've never seen her . . . fidgety like this before.

It feels a bit surreal watching her, though. There's a police constable in my kitchen fetching me water from my fridge spigot, and she's wearing a gun. How is she going to sit down with that thing on her hip? Or is she just going to lean against my kitchen island?

Cass lowers the tray with tea things onto the coffee table, then sits on the floor, facing me at right angles. Naomi hands me a glass from behind the sofa and takes one of the tall kitchen stools. I see another glass of water on the island.

I try to order my thoughts, but instead I get an image of Arceneaux's angular face, snarling with fury. I still don't recall anything about working with him. I can't even remember seeing him on the company website. But something else occurs to me. "Why didn't you tell me you were talking to him, Naomi?"

Her expression flashes with ire before she shutters it up tight into neutral lines. "I'm sorry. That was Shae and Chuck's call."

I search her face, hoping for the person I remember from our first days together.

She sips from her glass, avoiding my gaze. "I got loaned out to them. They're basically my bosses on this. I got the word on Friday, so I came early, over the weekend, to visit family. I wanted to tell you about working your file, but they . . . asked me to wait." Naomi puts her glass down and squares her shoulders. "Listen, I don't want to cross any of Shae's lines, but I owe it to you to explain. At least some part of this. I can tell you why I'm here, for example." She adjusts her shoulders, like she's repositioning a harness. "We talked it over and decided you might feel better with someone more culturally aligned as a liaison with the investigation."

Cass snorts, surprising all of us. "That sounds like something Inspector Miller came up with."

Naomi quirks up one side of her mouth. "Maybe." Her half-grin fades. "I'm not here to keep tabs on either of you. I'm literally here to help with the grunt work and to be your point of contact with the investigation. That's it. Those are my orders."

I consider her explanation, unable after all to ignore her genuine earnestness—the tall, broad-shouldered Asian woman in an RCMP constable's uniform.

I grimace as the insight blooms with an unpleasant taste. "Optics. Someone wants to make sure that the RCMP can point to you and say they've been handling me with . . . cultural sensitivity. When the news stories start."

"Good timing," murmurs Cass, "considering Sara was probably not the only person filming. She was just the only one to offer help."

I examine my realization, turning it this way and that in my mind. "I don't know if I should be flattered or insulted." I glare at Naomi. "Which one are you?"

She tenses, her expression flattening out. Trembling limbs be damned, I try to straighten up, pushing against the sofa cushions. It's impossible to maintain righteous indignation in an exhausted slouch.

"There's nothing sinister going on, Cleo, honest." Naomi sighs. "Chuck noticed that you and I got along well, and under difficult circumstances. Shae thought you might feel better talking to me. And I wanted to stay involved, to help. This was the perfect solution."

"Yeah, well, the optics don't hurt either," I reply drily. "The RCMP isn't known for being real inclusive in its ranks."

Naomi hitches one shoulder. "I'm not going to argue that one. But I *am* going to point out that there are those of us who are changing that. Actively. Don't erase us from the picture."

I flush, shifting my gaze to the tea tray. "Point taken."

Cass squints at her. "They do know you're Japanese and we're *Chinese* . . . right?"

"I said we're working on it." Naomi's cheeks redden.

Maybe I'm just being paranoid. I try to imagine Naomi's side of it, in good faith. She really isn't much more than a grunt, like she said. If someone up the chain gave her an order to tag along to create pretty optics for the media, there's not a lot she can do to object. Not publicly. Maybe not even privately. Not without pissing someone off probably. Which would hurt her standing. And likely her career. And anyway, who would it help for her to refuse that order? It's not a secret that marginalized people aren't well represented. Media stories and commissioned studies come out semi-regularly about that sort of stuff. I can only imagine how little actual power any single one of them actually has. I sigh, slumping back down onto the cushions. White patriarchy sucks. Maybe this is a good thing, to have her here, in my corner.

I watch Cass check the tea and pour himself a mug, the steam curling up and around and drifting into nothingness. The sofa really is quite comfortable, its fabric soft and soothing against my fingertips. My body drags at me, wanting rest, signalling that I should tip my head back and use the upholstered sofa arm as a pillow. It's practically the perfect height, if I just slide down a wee bit more . . . if I just close my eyes.

But my brain revs on, flipping through images and conversations, second-guessing and shouldacouldawoulda. Inevitably, of course, I return again and again to the poshly impersonal conference room with its double wall of windows.

I shove myself upright, hands coiling into fists.

"What is it?" Cass frowns at me, his gaze tight on what I'm certain are my bloodshot eyes. I shake my head at him, unwilling to explain it right now. It's too much.

I look over instead and speak slowly, trying to sound calm despite my clammy palms and aching tailbone. "Naomi, Inspector Miller said you were interviewing everyone, earlier, the people I used to work with. I'd like to see those interviews. Please."

She rotates her glass a quarter-turn on the island. "Why?"

"They might jog my memories."

She hesitates, palpably ill at ease. "You think someone there might help you remember something? Because no one there knew anything about your personal life."

"I'm not expecting them to, per se." I grasp at the right words to make her understand. "I just think . . . maybe I'll recognize someone or even something about what they said."

She stirs from her seat. "We could take another look at the company directory, if you want to see faces."

I frown, searching her careful expression. "Is it against the rules or something? I mean, this is about my case. I'm not going to talk about them with anyone."

"It *is* against my orders, but . . . I trust you to be discreet. It's not that." Yet everything about her shouts of reluctance.

"Then what? Why shouldn't I know what they had to say about me?" That comes out petulantly, but the stakes are too high for me to care if I'm likeable right now.

Naomi's entire body tightens up. "It's not—it's just . . ." She releases a heavy sigh. "They don't have very nice things to say. I'm not sure it's a good idea."

"So?" I squirm a little. "I don't think a lot of people liked me. Even the security guard had a low opinion of me, and it's a mystery to me how I might have ended up in his bad books. It's not like we worked together." I glance at Cass, his eyes wide, like Naomi, who still hesitates.

Maybe a lighter tone might help my cause. I attempt a grin. "It can't be that bad, can it?"

Her expression immediately blanks.

I feel my face heat, the half-assed grin sliding away like runny eggs off a plate. But I'm too committed at this point to care about embarrassment. "Listen, I—" my voice cracks and I swallow against the thickness in my throat, "I owe it to my parents to try this. To *remember*."

Cass rises from the floor, shifting my feet so he can sit on the sofa. "I don't think this is the safest way for—"

"No, Cass, don't baby me. I know it's not ideal, but I can't . . ." To my horror, tears flood my eyes. I feel like an over-inflated balloon, about to explode with emotions I can no longer hide. "I'm scared, Cass. I'm scared that I need to remember something . . . something that could be the key to finding Mum and Dad. Two weeks is too far away to get help from a therapist with this, so I have to try what I can, now." The words squeeze past my throat as though I'm choking on them: "But I'm really scared we're past the point that it matters."

Naomi steps up to the back of the sofa, her phone in hand. "Okay." She sounds agitated but determined. "I made backup recordings, but only audio. That's all I can give you, okay? And if you're serious about it, we should be showing you the photo of each person you hear, so you can match them up in your mind. We can grab them from the website." Naomi peers at me, severe, perhaps hoping I'll balk now. For my own good.

I nod, too apprehensive to speak, swiping at my face with a shirt sleeve. I know they're right. My tailbone throbs as I adjust my position, as though in warning. I can admit this is a bad idea, but that doesn't mean I can ignore a chance to remember something useful.

"I mean, okay, I don't wish, like, kidnapping and what did you say? Assault? Wow, yeah no, I don't wish that on anyone, but

maybe this is, like, karma. I'm sorry this happened, but, like, Cleopatra was a total bitch. She scared people. Playing like that has to
have a price, right?"

"She sucked up to the C-suite, and treated us programmers like
trash, unless she wanted something. If you were at the same level,
like another client manager, then don't even think about being
friends. She talked trash about other CMs all the time, behind
their backs. We all saw it happen. Yeah, she was smart, but we're
all smart, man. She made other people feel dumb. She didn't have
to do that."

"She and Drew were like, I dunno, arch-nemeses or something.
God. If this was a romcom, they'd absolutely be enemies to lovers.
Like, they're both gorgeous . . . except Drew's kind of an entitled
asshole and Cleopatra was mean as a snake. I feel bad this happened to her, but not gonna lie, she was a massive gaslighting
bully. Sorry."

"Cleopatra was an excellent salesperson, top of the heap three years
running. She reported directly to me those years. She was a real ace
with clients, had a great head for the business and the tech side.
Clients were always surprised by her acumen, given how, erm, she
looked. You know what I mean, petite and doll-like."

"I really don't have anything to tell you. I took the advice people
gave me when I started. I pretty much just made sure to avoid
her. . . . I don't know about enemies. People were nice to her, I
think 'cause they were scared of being her next victim, so yeah,

some people kind of hung with her. But she didn't make a lot of friends, I guess I can tell you that."

"If I never hear that fucking bitch's name again, I swear I'll die happy."

"Okay, that's enough." Cass reaches across me and taps Naomi's phone on the coffee table. "Take that away, Naomi, please." He closes my laptop, pushes it to the centre of the table, and turns to me, his movements jerky with anger. "So? Did that help? Did you remember any of them?"

I shake my head. At least I think I do. I can't actually feel the different parts of my body right now. Except my heart. I suddenly feel it pounding against my breastbone. I think I might vomit it out.

He curses under his breath. "So, you put yourself through that for what?" He throws his hands up. "This is insane." He jumps up from the sofa and strides to the large picture window.

I concentrate on slowing my ragged breathing. My hands itch to align the laptop corners with the table edges, but I'm certain I wouldn't be able to hide their trembling. I trap them beneath my legs, curling them into fists, pressing hard knuckles into the underside of my thighs.

Naomi takes Cass's place on the sofa, perching, I think, to accommodate the awkward bulk of her duty belt. "How are you feeling?" she asks softly.

I force the words out, the only truth I can offer right now. "I don't know." My eyes shy away from her concern, dropping downward. My gaze catches, can't slide aside. I scooch away from the black holster at her hip, pushing myself hard into the sofa's corner. I lift my feet up and wrap my arms around my knees, fuck my stinging tailbone.

Naomi tenses, watching me closely. When I do nothing more, she says, "I'm so sorry you had to hear that. I can't imagine what you're feeling right now. If it helps at all . . . we're cross-checking the statements and whereabouts of everyone we interviewed, whether they sounded neutral or hostile." She pauses, as though waiting for a reply. I have no idea what I could say.

"For what it's worth, Cleo . . . what they said, it doesn't have to define you going forward. You can't change what you already did or said, but . . . you can choose to be whoever you want. It's your future. Those people's opinions don't need to box you in."

I slide my gaze to Cass. Back rigid, he stares out the front window, streaked with street dust. He scrubs both hands through his hair with something like a low growl. He turns back toward us, his hands clenched into fists.

Should I be angry, too? Maybe. But I'm bewildered as well. I just can't seem to get a handle on how I can be the same person. And those words . . . I don't remember the people, but those words hurt.

After another moment of fraught silence, Naomi stands. "I'll just do another quick check around your property, then I'll be in my car. Give you some space. I hope you can rest, Cleo." A pause, like she wants to say more, but she only gives Cass a brief nod and heads to the back entry. We listen to her donning her boots, hear the slight creak of leather and the friction of fabrics, then the sound of the back door pulling closed.

Cass sits down in the armchair, elbows braced on thighs. "The irony is that the old you wouldn't have cared. Not even one tiny bit. But you're different. I can see how hard it is on you now, hearing all those shitty things. So maybe you ought to listen to Naomi. You don't have to be the same person." He exhales a harsh breath. "You're *not* the same person."

I blink at him and stay silent. He's too close to my own thoughts.

Close, though still off the mark. I don't know if I can trust him to under-stand yet. I don't know if I can make him.

"But listen." He clasps his hands together. "You've been going through some very real trauma. You can't just dust yourself off and keep going. And you can't keep ignoring your own health for the sake of this . . . thing with Mum and Dad." He holds up his hands, as though I've just burst in with a rebuttal. "I know you'll be okay. You're tough and strong, and most importantly, you have a support system in me and Etta. But it's going to take time. I see what you're doing now. You're burning through your reserves in the hopes of"—I see his throat working, see him gulping—"something that might not happen at all anymore."

I don't really want to say anything at all, but I find I can't stay still at that. "Have you given up? Already?" I ask quietly.

He doesn't reply. A burst of music, wavering and short, blows into the house from a passing car outside. I look out the picture window. It's a shock to see warm sunlight and bright greenery. The lengthening days of June. I'm abruptly aware of the stillness in the room, as though every-thing holds its breath.

"No," he says slowly. "I just think we should be ready for all possibil-ities. That's all. I'm a realist. I hope for the best possible outcome, but I want to be prepared if it doesn't work out, too." He ends so softly I think he might be speaking to himself.

After a beat, he refocusses on me. "I know how much you hate depending on others. Even if I haven't seen it regularly since we were kids, you've definitely given me plenty of proof these past days. But you can't do this alone, sis. Whether you like it or not, whether you agree with me or not, it's not your call if I care about you. We're *family*. We stick with one another, no matter what."

It sounds distressingly like his denial in the car, long days past. True, I *am* his sister, but I'm not sure he knows me at all. Didn't he also say, back in Golden, that we can never fully know other people's hearts?

I feel a deep pinch then in my chest, pushing a gasp of pain out of me as the blood drains out of my face. Memories suddenly drop into my head, like an anvil falling from a rooftop, smashing the sidewalk below. I put up a hand to stop him coming over. "Don't." I can't bear the idea of being comforted.

Wasn't this what I wanted, though? To remember something?

The irony is fucking killing me.

A laugh spills out of me, hard-edged. "That's what she would tell me, too, little brother. Every time we argued. Every time I asked her to stop giving me bullshit tasks to take on for her. 'We're family,' she said, 'and family has responsibilities to one another.'" I gasp, desperate for air to fill my chest and push off some of the weight on my shoulders. "She said it was my duty to repay her for all the money and effort she put into raising me. A girl is only good for marrying well, and since that was clearly not an option, I owed them." My lips twist and I taste spit like bile.

Cass switches armchair for sofa. "You remember," he says, his voice small.

I pull my knees in tighter, drawing on the pain to handle my anger. "Hearing those people say awful things about me . . . It's suddenly come back. Every belittling comment our mother ever threw at me. All the times she reminded me of what I owe her. All the times she criticized any little thing she didn't like." I feel my nails digging into my arms.

Cass shifts, starts to hold his arms out to me.

I brush his sympathy aside. "Do you know Dad never once stood up to her for me? He only ever told me to stay quiet, that her temper would blow over once she had her say. Yeah, right. Because cowering is such a winning formula. Fuck. Be careful what you wish for, eh? Somehow I don't think *these* memories are gonna be good for anything."

"I wish I had something to explain Dad's behaviour," says Cass quietly. "I wish I understood it."

I scoff. "Stephen Li, everybody's favourite good guy, always ready to lend a helping hand—except when it came to me. What a lovely pair they made, eh? Not that anyone else ever saw it. Gotta keep up the rep, right?" I wrench up off the sofa, unable to sit still anymore, exhaustion burned down to a molten needle in my brain.

"I'm so fucking sorry, sis. I . . . I had no idea it was that bad."

"Why would you?" I swing around to face him from across the coffee table. "You weren't around." I cross my arms over my chest, gripping my upper arms. "It wouldn't have made a difference. She used to compare us, you the success, me the failure." I make a noise that might be a laugh, or bitterness made into sound. "You really think she wouldn't have said the same horrible things about me to your face?"

Cass's cheeks turn ruddy.

"She did, didn't she?" I rub my forehead. Of course she did.

"I'm sorry." Cass runs a hand across the back of his neck. "I'm willing to apologize, Cleo, as many times as it takes."

"For what? Running away?" I shake my arms, trying to get rid of the prickling along my skin. "How many times have I wished I'd done exactly the same thing? How many times have I wondered why I didn't just up and leave? That's the kick in the head about it all. You got up the nerve to do it first, and I can't help resenting you for it."

"Why didn't you tell me? I would've helped you, however I could have."

Christ. His earnestness. So fucking precious.

I squeeze my hands into fists, unwilling to let his pain move me. "I know my reputation as a heartless automaton, Cass, but even *I* couldn't abandon them right after you left, their golden boy. They were a mess. Who did you think would pick up the pieces? *Did* you even think about that? While you were making new friends and exploring your identity?"

His face darkens. "You have no idea what I went through. You don't have the right to mock me."

"Then pay me the same respect. Don't you presume to tell me I should've done things differently."

I suppose there might be sounds of late spring coming through my windows, but I can't hear anything save the pounding of my blood. Cass stares at me for several seconds, a veritable movie of emotions flying across his face, until he settles on smoothing everything out with one deep steadying breath.

"Okay," he says cautiously, "it's obvious there's a lot we need to work out, sis." He pauses. "Which is why you should stay with me and Etta for a while. We've spent too much time growing apart. This is the time for family to come together."

I throw my hands up. "Why is everyfuckingbody trying to toss me out of my own goddamned house?"

The screen door bangs. I jump, the hairs on the back of my neck standing on end. Cass rises, jerky with annoyance. I motion for him to stay put. "I'll get it."

"Fine." He follows me closely to the door, but I refuse to give him the satisfaction of arguing about it. I undo the deadbolt and chain, and yank it open.

Naomi's grave face greets me from the other side. Miller and Pendelton stand behind her, one step down. With his hand on the railing, Pendelton takes in my exhausted, pinched face, his gaze opaque as ever, then glances past me to Cass.

Miller watches only me.

Before I have a chance to gesture them inside, Naomi says, "We have some news." She hesitates, her expression a fast-moving panoply of regret and sorrow and determination. "I'm sorry," she says, finally. "They've recovered a body."

O utside myself, there are shouts of alarm as I crumple to the floor. Inside myself, a maelstrom.

Emotions, images, clawing at my foundations.

This time, I know it's a memory.

I am silent though it is not.

Someone behind me screams, terror made vocal, incoherent. I hear the scratch of fingernails on taut cloth, a scrabbling, slippery sound of desperation. I feel a kick against the back of my seat, against the middle of my back. I see glowing green light, black and grey shadows all around. There is the car hood, there the steering wheel. The rear-view mirror is a small black rectangle against the angled windshield.

I sense that a light has just gone out. Everything seems blacker for an inexpressible moment.

I turn, banging into the hard plastic curve of the steering wheel. First an elbow, then my ribs. I see the man, the green light casting his shadow against

the blacker square of the passenger window behind him. I feel my heart ratch-
eting up its rhythm as I throw up my arm to hold off whatever's coming. I see
his hands, one pushing against the glove compartment door, the other gripping
the side of the passenger seat back. He opens his mouth, his eyes yawning shad-
ows. He shouts a curse as he launches himself at me.

In my hand, something I want to strike out with.

I see his face limned in the eerie light.

I know him. God help me, I know him.

Outside the glass, all is darkness.

Salt tears, sweaty clothes, pounding heart, the shakes.

Until I disentangle the flashback from the now, I'll feel the sting of a
banged elbow, the ache of bruising on my ribs, the ringing of screams in
my ears.

I weep, long and hard, inconsolable, for all the things I wish were
different.

But of course it's too late.

There's no going back—and no more forgetting.

TWENTY-SEVEN

I curl into myself, my throat raw from wailing, my face wet and hot, my stomach cramping from the force of the sobs. I press my eyelids tight together, though I can feel the pressure of another body close in front of me. A hand strokes my hair away from my forehead. I don't need to see to know it's my brother. He croons nonsense under his breath, soothing sounds without meaning, drawing more tears than I thought I had. They spill sideways along the contours of my upper cheek and into my hair. Drops splash into my ear. A part of me shouts, *Pull it together*—but it's faint, exhausted by the terrible onslaught of emotions and memories. Pushed far down the unfathomable well within me by fear.

I can't say how long the tumult lasts. It feels like forever. It feels like the blink of an eye. But it's long enough for Cass to say, his voice unyielding, "My sister needs to rest. She's in no condition for this. We need you to leave."

I gasp, sending my diaphragm into spasm.

"Sis, you need to breathe. Breathe, deep as you can, slow and easy." Cass takes my hand. I grip back, trying to sit up and follow his instructions at the same time. My entire body shudders, attempting to overcome the spasms, to bring oxygen into my lungs and replace the panic. At some point, I realize I'm stroking the fabric beneath my hand. I focus on that, too, on the velvety softness of my sofa cushions, and let it lead me to a pale shadow of control.

Cass silently offers me tissues. I clean up my tears and snot, scrub at my face with trembling hands. I have no idea if I'm ready, but I force myself to meet the eyes of the three RCMP officers in my home.

"Is it, I mean, do you know . . ." I trail off, my voice reedy, thin.

Miller clears her throat from her spot next to my armchair across the room. "I'm truly sorry. We believe it's your mother."

A bomb explodes in my chest, silent and invisible, knocking me back against the sofa. The shockwave ripples outward from my heart, spreading sweet numbness. A cold front blankets any remaining turmoil, rendering it distant and inert. *Pull it together*, that part of me says, and this time, it's the only sound in my head.

Cass slides from his squat next to the sofa until he's sitting fully on the floor. Resting his elbows on his upraised knees, he grabs his head in his hands, hair sticking up haphazardly between his fingers. I can feel the tension from his shoulders, like a struck tuning fork filling the last bits of silence with its undercurrents. But he doesn't make a sound. I can see the corner of one eye in profile, squeezed shut.

It feels like a dodgy radio in my head, one minute silent, the next blaring at top volume, and static in between. *I need to think.* Feelings can bloody well wait. There are too many things we need to know.

"Can I have a minute?" I rasp at Miller, gesturing in the direction of my bedroom. "Please don't go yet. I have questions." I try to push off the cushions.

"Sis." Cass turns to me with a frown as he scrambles upward to hold my elbow. "You need rest, not more upset." His voice comes out harsh, like the scraping of metal, words flaking off like rust.

Naomi stirs, catching my attention as she stands in the small square of my foyer. Her mouth parts slightly. I think she's going to agree with my brother, if her concerned frown is any indication. But she snaps her mouth shut instead, gaze flickering to her superiors.

Miller nods. "Of course. Take your time. We'll answer as best we can." She throws a glance at Pendelton, hulking in front of the closet doors of the foyer. His face remains impassive, aloof.

I leave Cass staring after me with silent disapproval. It's better than the alternative. I have no clue how to help with incapacitating grief.

I walk unsteadily toward my bedroom, banging a shoulder hard into the door frame on the way, rebounding with a blink. I stumble, crack a kneecap against the dresser corner, the earrings and knickknacks on its surface sliding every which way. At the bathroom, I carefully latch the door closed behind me and heave up everything from my stomach into the hard bowl of my toilet.

Afterward, I wash my face over and over again with the coldest water I can get from the tap, scrubbing with a facecloth until my skin tightens painfully. My eyes are pink-rimmed, bloodshot, my nose swollen and red. Flakes of dry skin hang from my lips. I brush my teeth with swift, savage strokes, swipe my lips with stinging peppermint balm, and retie my hair up.

When I stumble out of the bathroom, Naomi stands in my bedroom doorway, her features drawn with worry. She looks like she wants to say something again. I brush past, avoiding the care in her eyes.

I join Cass on the sofa and take his hand. It sits limp in my grasp. How strange that my tailbone barely twinges now. I flick a glance at my brother, frowning when I realize he hasn't reacted to my return.

Two glasses of ice water await on the coffee table. Early evening light filters in from the picture window, dappled by the leaves of the enormous elm outside, one of many that line the curbs in my neighbourhood.

Pendelton gently sets a framed photo back down on my bookshelf and sits down in my work chair, pulled out of my office to rest now on the other side of the large window from Miller. He adjusts the height to accommodate his longer legs. Naomi walks across the living room to lean against the entrance to my office. She grips a closed notebook in her hands, her mouth a taut, barely-there line.

Miller's eyes are clear, almost a translucent blue. "I understand this is an extremely difficult time. You've got a lot of questions, understandably, so please let me explain some things first, things I know are useful to families at a time like this, and we'll go from there. All right?"

I shake my head, unwilling to be managed. "Where was she found?" Cass's hand twitches. I feel his dismay, thickening the space between us. "What about our father?" My voice catches on the dryness in my throat. I cough, hacking like a backfiring car, the sound striking the high ceiling and shattering into sharp echoes, dissipating outward.

Miller's gaze flattens. After a beat of hesitation, she gives Naomi a brief nod.

Naomi clears her throat. "A couple of hikers spotted the body"—I flinch—"yesterday morning in the Kicking Horse River, several kilometres downriver from The Lodge at Yoho. It was caught in a side pool. They called 911. Corporal Van der Waal was dispatched from Golden. He visually confirmed the discovery and contacted the regional coroner's office in Kelowna. After preliminary examination in situ and consultation on the phone, the coroner had the body moved to Kelowna for a more complete examination."

My hand tightens inadvertently, betraying my inner agitation. Cass hisses and extricates himself from my hold. He rubs his hand as I murmur an apology, red-faced. I feel a tremor begin in my knees. I wrap my arms around myself to keep from flying apart.

Wait a minute. My brain snags on something Naomi said. *Yesterday?*

"So, you already knew when we saw you earlier." I gaze from Naomi to Miller and back again, my frown darkening into a glare. "How could you keep this from us?" The words tremble, weighted with hurt and disbelief.

Naomi winces.

Miller says coolly, "I'm sorry, really. We weren't at liberty to divulge any of this information at that time. As you can imagine, there were too many things still unknown and unconfirmed." She pauses, her expression softening its edges as she considers us. Her voice gentles. "Our priority is to run the investigation. Sometimes that requires the withholding of information from victims' families until we have more facts in hand. I understand it can be upsetting, please believe me, but it's the best way for us to continue working our file and get closure for everyone."

"And to be fair," Naomi adds, tentative, "it wasn't a good time."

I grimace, knowing she's right. Resenting it. I refuse to look at her.

"So, let me explain how this works," continues Miller, gentle but firm. "Right now, we're waiting on dental records to confirm identity, which we expect to get tomorrow morning. In any death like this, the coroner—in this case, Dr. Helen Rao—performs a coroner's investigation in order to make a ruling on the cause of death."

"Dental records? But couldn't Cass and I make the ID?" I don't know if I can even explain it to myself, but—"It just feels like, like we need to do all this right, you know? That there's no . . . that we know for sure." I rub at the sudden headache creasing my forehead. "Right, Cass?"

He sighs heavily, running a hand over his haggard face. "I don't know, sis."

Pendelton leans forward a little, clearing his throat. Miller subsides and he says, "To be perfectly frank, there's damage and . . . discoloration involved when . . . submersion in water has occurred. In this case, it's been over a week. A visual identification isn't always possible. And," his expression turns grim, "you wouldn't like to see it."

Flushing at my ignorance, I take a drink of water to cool my face.

"There is something you can help with, though," says Miller into the awkward silence. "We need authorization from next of kin to perform an autopsy. It will help Dr. Rao make her ruling." She pauses. "You're listed as next of kin in the system, Cleo."

"Yes," I stammer. "Of course, yes. Anything to help." I place the chilly glass up to my cheek. A strange roiling lightness ignites inside of me. Is this how low the bar is set? To know my mother listed me as next of kin. . . . Did I mean something to her after all? Is *that* why this awful buoyancy, like relief? If I were alone, I'd cry from the pitiful absurdity of it. Or maybe scream. I stuff the raw confusion away instead.

"Good. Thank you. Naomi will coordinate the consent forms with you once we receive confirmation from the dental records."

Naomi nods for my benefit. I can see her jaw clench as her gaze darts back to Miller for a second.

"Is that all for now?" Cass says, curt. "It's been a rough day."

I touch his hand lightly as I address Miller again. "When will the autopsy be done? Is it possible to speak with the coroner? Directly, I mean?"

"What?" Cass stares at me, aghast. "Why?"

Pendelton and Naomi wear similar wide-eyed expressions, but Miller remains unemotional. Her gaze takes on an assessing edge.

She gives a short nod, as though coming to a decision. "It's up to Dr. Rao, but I'll bring it up with her. For what it's worth, I think she'll agree. She's one of our best, and part of why is her compassion." A pause. "She understands the need for answers."

I return her nod, unable to speak past the abrupt tightness in my throat.

Cass stands then, ushering the three others into their assorted shoes and out the front door. It's not until I hear him latch the lock that I realize.

I jump up from the sofa, swaying a little. "Wait, Cass, wait. They didn't say anything about Dad. We have to ge—"

"What the actual fuck are you thinking?"

I startle back from his anger. "About Dad?"

"About that train wreck I just watched." He's so pissed, he's vibrating, his hands fisted at his sides and his face screwed into a deep scowl. "It is not in any way appropriate for us to speak with this coroner. What are you going to ask her, anyway? You really want to know all the fucking details of how our mother *died*?" He throws his hands up. "Swear to God, I don't understand you."

Holding his head, he paces precisely from the foyer to the bookshelf and back again, once. "If you were in your right mind, you would not be advocating for this, sis. You've had a really motherfucking bitch of a day. So have I, in case you've forgotten. We need to eat and rest and grieve and goddamn sleep on it, okay?" Hands on hips, hair standing up on end, Cass faces me wearing a look that dares me to disagree.

He's not wrong. I'm not in my right mind.

It's like there are two of me now, at war over every action and reaction, every emotion and thought, every word I say or don't say. I feel squeezed and wrung out, mentally, emotionally, physically. I'm in no shape to make rational choices, let alone irrational ones.

But making my own choices is the only avenue I have.

I set my body square to him and reach for the most level voice I possess. "I need you to back me up, little brother. Even when it makes no sense. Even when it seems totally insane. Maybe especially then." I meet his incredulous, furious gaze as calmly and directly as I can. "Can you do that for me? Because if you can't," I pause, gathering myself with a deep breath, "you may as well go home now."

We stare at one another. His chest heaves like he's been sprinting full tilt. I watch his face darken, a growing storm I knowingly conjured. I try to tell myself it's not a test, that I'm not pushing him for its own sake, but I know better.

I truly don't understand his idea of family loyalty, of emotional support. And I think I have to because I'll have to rely on it, and soon. So I can't help prodding at its borders, searching for a breach in his commitment.

Will he leave now? And if not now, then when? Where's the line he won't let me cross? What will happen when I try? Watching him struggle against his temper, waiting stiffly for his reply, I wonder if I'm about to find out.

What will I be forced to do then?

TWENTY-EIGHT

June 6, 2018

Field, BC

News Release

On June 3, 2018, the body of a 55-year-old Asian woman was discovered in the Kicking Horse River approximately 23 km downriver of Field, BC. Although an exact cause of death has not yet been determined, an investigation has been initiated by the Kelowna Serious Crimes Unit and is ongoing. The BC Coroners Service is also investigating.

If you have information about this and have not yet spoken to police, you are asked to contact the Kelowna Serious Crimes Unit general information line at 250-555-8963. Or, to leave an anonymous tip, call the Crime Stoppers line at 1-800-555-8477 or visit crimestoppers.net.

File #18-*****

Released by

Cpl. Stan Simkowich

Media Relations Officer

Kelowna RCMP

"What is that?" asks Cass, his voice tight. In fact, he sounds precisely as resentful as when he finally said a begrudging, unhappy yes to this whole scheme of mine yesterday. My little brother sure can hold on to his anger.

I shouldn't be relieved to find something of myself in him, something ugly, should I?

I still the trembling in my hands, but I can't quite manage to banish it from my reply. "Etta sent me a link to the RCMP news release this morning." I glance up from my phone. At Cass's dark look, I add, "About Mum." I tap back to Etta's text, force myself to reread it. "She thought I'd want to know." I look over at him, wincing internally at how furious he still is. "She probably texted you, too," I finish quietly.

He grimaces, his gaze fixed grimly on the road.

It doesn't escape me that we've arrived in the Okanagan Valley on a blindingly beautiful, sun-drenched Wednesday afternoon. If I believed in such things, I'd say someone's having a laugh at us. Inside the car, it's been nothing but terse, grey talk in between long stretches of brooding silences for the past twelve hours.

Blinking against the grittiness of my eyes, I put my phone away. "I guess she's right. Etta, I mean. At some point, some reporter or journalist or whatever is going to find us. We should probably agree on how to handle all that." I press a hand to my uneasy stomach. "I think we'll be okay not to comment for now. That's understandable for an open investigation, right?"

Cass grunts. I swallow my sigh and turn to stare out my window. Not that I register anything I see. I understand why he doesn't agree with me, truly I do. I just wish . . . I wish I could explain it to him. Fully. I wish I knew how to make him feel better. I wish I didn't have to watch everything I say so carefully.

If I'm well and truly honest with myself, I can see how little I've cared in the past for other people's feelings. I see, too, what that's got me. I can't help thinking it's past time I rethink that particular strategy. My brother won't stand for anything less from me. And I need him to stay with me, no matter how incomprehensible I seem. Our parents . . . I can't see this getting any easier over the next days and weeks.

Dread prickles across my skin. We need to stick together.

Eventually, Cass pulls into a parking lot. He pops the gearshift into neutral and clicks the engine off. I think we're in downtown Kelowna.

"I've been up since four and driving since five this morning." He holds himself rigidly, his mouth downturned. "So, before we really go through with this, I need you to tell me this isn't some . . . whim. That you haven't lost it. Because there are better ways to deal with your grief than—"

I click the window switch, a little frantically. "Look, can you open the window? Please? I'm feeling carsick. I don't want to throw up."

Movements rough with irritation, he switches the car back on. Before I have a chance to manage my window, he runs them all down halfway, then turns the electrical off again. Grudgingly, he asks, "Do you need water?"

I wave him off, wishing my window were all the way down. I turn to make Cass help again, but I stop short instead. Maybe it's the angle of light, maybe it's my conscience. I realize how haggard he looks around the edges of his anger. He deeply, *deeply* hates the corner I've backed him into.

And yet, he's here. It strikes me, not for the first or even the tenth time, that my brother truly is a kind and decent person. I don't think I can say the same about myself.

For the first time I can ever recall, I wish I could.

I shake off any further emotional awakenings. Looking over my shoulder at the building behind us, I force myself to focus. I need armour if I'm going to make it through this. I cannot be a walking wound.

"Cleopatra." Impatience hones his voice. "You owe me an explanation, goddamnit. Why do we have to be here in person?"

I bristle. *"Because."*

His eyes widen in disbelief. "Are we really doing this now? You picked a great fucking time to revert to your bitchy cold-hearted self, sis."

"So sue me," I retort. "You want to know why we're here? I will tell you." I swivel to face him square-on, biting off every single word. "I won't believe it until I see for myself."

Cass's face twists with angry bewilderment. His mouth gapes open for a second before he clamps it shut. "Is this . . . is this like you trying to get Betty Wan to show you the safety deposit box key? Like, that kind of irrational?"

I sag, the fight abruptly gone out of me. "You don't understand, Cass. Having amnesia, listening to *other people* tell you about yourself and it . . . it's not a person you even recognize. Do I take everyone else's word at face value? How do I know what's true?" I swallow, hard. "It's getting harder and harder to rely on others to say what's real."

"I can understand even if I don't know exactly how it feels," he replies, unbending a little. "But we don't have to do this alone, sis. I—"

A clatter of footsteps stops abruptly next to my window. A middle-aged woman with curled grey-blond hair looks sideways at us as she opens the door of the dusty maroon car to my right and slides inside. She ignores my gaze as I hear her engage her locks. She deftly backs out of her spot, zooming away with a little spit of gravel.

I swipe impatiently at my wet eyes. "We should go." I unclick my seat belt and push open my door, talking over Cass's attempt to speak. "We don't want to be late."

The parking lot, a rectangle of pitted and patched asphalt marked with faded yellow lines, empties of two more cars as I wait by the trunk. Arms crossed, I stare at the two-storey building that houses the regional BC Coroners Service. Behind me, I hear the telltale dinging of the car electricals coming back on, then the sound of the windows rolling closed. Cass slams his door and locks the station wagon. I avoid eye contact as we walk over the bumpy lot surface, a foot of space between us.

"We're not done talking," he mutters as we go up a wheelchair ramp, flanked by a long built-in planter filled with bright pansies and large hostas with marbled leaves in green and cream. "It's important."

"It's all important," I retort. "Put it on the list." I can *not* think of all the things I need to track right now. I might not keep going if I do.

We enter through glass double doors into a medium-sized lobby, its floor tiled in terracotta-coloured squares. A silver-faced elevator awaits us straight ahead. I double-check the listings on the small wall-mounted directory.

The jerky elevator tosses us out directly into a space with pale grey walls and dark patterned carpeting. A reception counter divides the space into a few chairs' worth of public waiting room on our side, and the staff area on the other. It's an open-plan office, with two rows of cubicles stretching toward a far bank of windows.

Cass gives our names and asks for Dr. Rao. I can barely make out the receptionist's thick eyebrows and the top of their head over the counter. Why would they make it so every person looks down on the receptionist? I refuse to go on my tiptoes. I hear the clatter of a phone being picked up, then Dr. Rao's name and the announcement of visitors.

I stand in the empty space between the hard-looking chairs, rocking from foot to foot, trying to keep my blood pumping, my mind alert. I don't know whether to laugh or cry. I settle for pulling my hair out of its messy bun and remaking it into a high ponytail. The number of things I can control is shrinking rapidly.

A low *bzzt* sounds to my left, a door opens, and out walks a short, thin South Asian woman wearing an impersonal smile and her thick black hair in a braided bun at the nape of her neck. For some reason, I can't stop myself from examining her white lab coat for stains. It's stupid, I know. Naomi assured us when we dealt with the consent forms late yesterday morning that the autopsy would be completed long before we met with Dr. Rao today. And yet, my eyes keep straying, searching for anything amiss on the white fabric.

Stop it. Keep it together, for the love of—

"I'm Dr. Helen Rao. You must be the Lis." She shakes our hands, her gaze direct and open. "Please accept my condolences. I'm sorry for your loss. If you'll follow me, we can speak in private."

We end up in a room like any other bland meeting space: central table, chairs, a telephone, a wall-mounted whiteboard/screen, a couple of dry erase markers. There's a laptop in matte grey at the far end of the table. Also a sideboard with a box of tissues, compostable cups, and a pitcher of water. I release a shaky breath. I don't know what Rao's office is like and I don't want to find out.

She gestures for us to take seats across from the laptop as she fetches the pitcher, cups, and the box of tissues. She sits behind the laptop, facing us with something like sad composure. "Let's begin with your questions."

I swallow, suddenly uncertain with nerves. "What can you tell us about . . . about what you found? About the results of the . . . autopsy?"

Cass asks, voice raspy, "What did she die of?"

"Technically, your mother drowned. Her body showed signs consistent with being in the river for some days." Rao pauses, perhaps allowing us to absorb the news.

From the corner of my eye, I see Cass ball his hands underneath the table.

My mind abruptly fills with the memory of boulders in the Kicking Horse River, sharp and implacable. I shove the images away, frantic to unsee them and to hide that I can't.

After a drawn-out silence, Rao gently asks, "May I ask you about your mother's medical history? Of course, I have requested her full medical records from her personal physician, but it will help to ensure my report is thorough if I can ask you some things right now."

I fidget. "Mum was intensely private, especially with her health stuff. A lot of Chinese people think it's bad luck to talk about it." I hesitate. "Also, it's shameful to be sick. In their eyes." I flick a look at Rao. "I don't know how much I can tell you. She didn't share a lot with me. Dad was her main go-to."

Rao nods, as though I've just settled a question for her. "Your mother was found with her purse still slung across her torso. As part of the investigation, we of course made a survey of the contents. The reason I ask about her medical history is that a glucometer and insulin pen were a part of that inventory." She pauses. "Also, the physical examination revealed signs of chronic blood glucose testing."

I frown, unsettled by the thought of the purse. "I . . . um, is this part of your investigation? The coroner's investigation?"

"Yes. I collect as many facts as I can, related to the remains and the area and circumstances where they were found. I interpret records and interview people, as needed. My job is to rule on the cause and the manner of death."

"And what is . . . glucose testing?" asks Cass quietly. "Or a, a glucometer?"

"A glucometer is used to measure blood glucose levels, mostly for people with diabetes." Rao glances at me. "One draws blood using a small lancet and applies the blood drop to a test strip, which is inserted into a glucometer. The resulting reading helps a patient figure out if they're in healthy parameters or if they need to change medication, etc. At any rate, people most commonly prick for blood on the sides of the fingertips. Frequent and prolonged testing usually results in callouses there. Which is what I found in your mother's examination. It's clear to me she was likely diabetic, but I prefer confirmation from multiple sources, whenever possible."

My brain blips. I know she's finished speaking, but it's like I see her mouth shaping the words in slow motion. Like my synapses are clicking over and over, unable to catch fire and connect.

"I never . . . I don't know . . ." I look from Rao's raised brows to Cass's puzzled frown. "She . . . but I thought—and then I didn't—" I fight the churning tangle of thoughts in my head. I need to piece something together for them, something they'll understand. My mouth works uselessly.

Cass leans into me, alarm colouring his face. "Sis. What's wrong? You're not making any sense. Sis!"

A bolt of ice shoots through my brain and slides down my spine. I grab my aching head, swivel toward my brother. "I should've told you. Oh God, I'm so sorry. But she made me and . . . I think I remembered, before, but I'm all jumbled. And things were happening so fast. And, but—I should've said something sooner."

How could I possibly have forgotten?

TWENTY-NINE

Cass eyes me, panicked. "What? *What is it?*"

I force air past the invisible band around my chest. This is not the time to lose my head. *Keep it together, for fuck's sake, Li.*

I fist my hands in my lap, as though it might help gather my will. "Doctor, you're right. My mother . . . our mother is diabetic—was."

Cass grabs the table edge, his fingertips turning white with the pressure. "I don't know what . . . Since when?"

I glance at Rao briefly. "With everything going on . . . I didn't remember before, talking to Miller and Pendelton or even Naomi. I didn't tell anyone who was searching. I'm sorry." I know I'm not making my case very well, but I push forward, lurching words and all. I grip the arms of my chair. "Cass. She . . . Mum. She didn't want me to tell anyone. Not even you. She made me promise."

"So you can confirm that your mother did, in fact, have diabetes?" Rao asks in her measured voice.

I bob my head, feeling like it's in danger of snapping off.

"And was she Type 1? And taking insulin?"

I tear my gaze from Cass's angry profile. "I'm sorry. I don't know. Diagnosed, I guess six years ago? But I don't know anything about the . . . the insulin. She didn't tell me about her medications."

"If she was diagnosed recently, then it's likely it was Type 2. Used to be called *adult-onset diabetes*. It's more commonly treated with oral medications, but . . ." Rao types rapidly on her laptop. "I'll confirm with her doctor. There are some Type 2s who use insulin."

"How could you not know?" Cass scowls at me. "You must've helped her fill prescriptions and stuff. You helped her with everything."

"She had Dad for that. You know he did whatever she asked. No questions asked. Always." It's totally inappropriate, the bitterness in my voice, but damned if I can take it back now. I hope Rao will chalk it up to stress. We can't be the first family she's watched ripping at the seams.

"I don't think that's true," counters Cass. "He's not perfect, but I know he wasn't like that when we were growing up."

I grimace, forcing my furious reply back down my throat. Stoking that anger won't help. "I don't want to argue, Cass. You're just gonna have to take my word for it." I huff out a breath. "Mum didn't want to tell me at all. The day she got diagnosed. I only know because I had, like, three meetings that morning. I was pissed she'd waited until the last minute to tell me. I told her I needed a damned good reason—" I flush at how that sounds "—to reschedule my whole morning to chauffeur her to yet another doctor's appointment. I had no idea. . . . She said her GP made the appointment for her on short notice, once the test results of her blood work returned. It was urgent." My voice sounds small, wobbly. I swipe my eyes with the heel of a hand. "And Dad was in Calgary."

Cass runs his hands through his already mussed hair. "Jesus Fucking Christ." He shoots Rao a fast, sheepish glance. "Sorry."

"I'm sorry you're hearing the news this way, Mr. Li." After a pause, she addresses me again. "As I said, I will check her files to see if insulin was a normal part of her diabetes management plan."

I shiver at the continued chill along my spine. "Why do you keep asking about insulin? Are you saying insulin was involved in . . . in her death?"

Rao speaks with gentle calm. "It's a possibility, yes. Too much insulin at once can cause a person to fall into a coma. If your mother was incapacitated like that, she might have fallen into the water—"

"And drowned," says Cass, "because she was unconscious." His voice comes out raw, anguished.

Rao nods. "Yes. I'm sorry."

"But," I say slowly, carefully, "how does that change the cause of death? You said it was drowning." I swallow. Feeling fidgety, I pour water for Cass and myself. But I don't drink. I can't.

"As part of my investigation, I'm required to understand any additional information I discover. This will help me determine if, in my opinion, a death requires an inquest *over and above* an investigation. So, in this case, knowing your mother was diabetic, I need to follow up to discover if an insulin overdose was involved."

I rub tiredly at my temples. "What's the difference between an inquest and an investigation then?"

"An inquest is a public court proceeding, with a jury who listens to the evidence regarding the facts surrounding a death. It's the job of the jury at an inquest to determine the formal verdict, which is their official classification of the death."

"But . . ." Cass frowns. "As the coroner, aren't you the person who decides if an inquest is needed?"

Another patient nod. "There are certain times when an inquest is mandatory and automatic, which I won't go into. Right now, I do not recommend an inquest in this case, but the circumstances do require an *investigation*. This interview we're having right now is a part of that." Rao sits back a little. "My ruling on this death will directly impact how the RCMP handles the rest of your mother's file."

"You mean"—I shift in my seat—"if it's accidental? Or, or otherwise? You can tell?"

"Yes, and," she makes a noise in the back of her throat, "I'll do my best to determine that."

"So, this ruling," I say hoarsely, "do we get notified? Or is it just the police?"

"It's public record," she replies. "But families often request that we send them the report or the results at least. I can do the same for you, of course."

"Thank you."

Cass says nothing. I sip the water in my cup. It tastes like damp cardboard.

Cold continues to seep into me, spearing from spine to head, down into my legs. I feel my knees start to tremble.

"Doctor," I say, wrangling my voice to hide my apprehension. "I'd like to view my mother's body. Please."

Cass goes rigid.

Rao hesitates, her professional mien slipping for a second. "I'm afraid that's not a good idea, Miss Li. You see, the water—"

"Staff Sergeant Pendelton explained it to us. The discoloration and stuff." I push down hard on the fluttering in my gut. "It's just that . . . none of this seems real, you see. The last time I saw my mother . . . well, the amnesia, um, makes it . . . but in my mind, she's still . . . alive." I flush, flustered and self-conscious. "I don't know how else to make sense of all this." I aim to appeal to her compassion by being earnest, but my fear betrays me. I sound curiously flat, my emotions too tightly reined in.

Rao assesses me, her gaze guileless and kind despite what must be her very real objections. After a beat, she switches her attention to my brother. "And you, sir? Do you share your sister's preference in this matter?"

"No." Cass inhales, long and slow, before releasing his breath in one quick huff. "But I'll stick with her, if you say yes." He flexes his hands, openclosed, openclosed, beneath the table's edge.

In a flood of gratitude, I reach out. Cass makes no move toward me. I retract my hand, abruptly timid. I need the support, badly, but am I relying on him too much?

What I recall of my life with my mother . . . It's not nice, not tidy. Is this grief, then, this deep queasiness within me? Like the ground beneath my feet keeps shifting. And me, repeatedly shocked by these tides of feeling.

I should know what kind of person I am. I see it reflected in the eyes of the people I've disdained. Cold-hearted, arrogant, untouchable. I've apparently spent a lot of my time *not* feeling. On purpose. All the more reason not to push Cass even more now.

Emotional beggars can't be choosers.

I shift to meet Rao's gaze again. She nods, curt and decisive, and picks up the telephone in the middle of the conference table. She murmurs instructions as I try to gauge my brother's internal state from his refusal to speak to me.

Minutes later, Rao leads us to an internal stairwell and has us go back down to the first floor, our footsteps echoing in the concrete-walled space. Cass walks ahead of me, the *clink* of his wedding ring against the metal handrail echoing strangely. He leaves off clasping the rail.

My heart pumps faster and faster as we exit into a nondescript hallway. Rao opens a door for us, and we file into a beige room with a curtained window, framed in black. There are uncomfortable-looking upholstered chairs, but no table, just a vertical shelf unit with a box of tissues. An open-top trash bin, lined with a plastic bag, sits next to the door we came through. I stop in the middle of the space, uncertain if I should sit or stand. Cass looks around, face tight. His cheeks look too sharp.

Rao closes the door behind us with a soft click, walks to the curtained window, and turns to address us, her dark skin now looking harsh and dry under the fluorescent lighting. "Whenever you're ready, I'll draw this open. The body is in the adjoining room, with my colleague, Dr. Mendoza, in attendance. She will uncover only the face." Rao pauses. "You've heard this already, but I have to warn you, because of the time in the water, the features will be quite distorted. It will be distressing. Are you certain you want to go ahead?"

I'm sure if I try to speak my heart will jump out of my mouth. I jerk my head up and down. Cass looks even paler than he did just seconds ago. I squeeze his hand, feel our palms slip in our commingled sweat. I move to unclasp so I can wipe the wetness away, but Cass won't let me go.

His voice comes out a strangled whisper. "Yes."

Rao pulls on something behind a panel of the curtains. The fabric slides open to the left, away from where she stands, revealing a sheet of glass with wire work sandwiched inside of it. Now that the curtain has moved, I see a wall-mounted telephone over Rao's shoulder.

Through the reinforced window, on the far wall, a placard hangs on a hook just above eye level, inscribed with a large black "D." A woman with heavy red-framed glasses, wearing pale green scrubs, a cap, and a face mask, stands next to a gurney set a few feet from the window, positioned with its long side toward us. Atop the gurney, a . . . form draped in a medium-blue cloth.

I rest a hand at my throat, feeling the manic thrum of my heartbeat. I hear a soft sound escape Cass's mouth. He shifts his feet.

The woman in the other room, Dr. Mendoza, acknowledges Rao with a nod before moving her attention to us. Her expression is impossible to make out. She turns to the gurney, stepping behind it. She grips the cloth sheeting at the left end and pulls up and away, folding it down in one tidy movement. She wears bright purple gloves.

I breathe shallowly, force my eyes to move, to look.

I see a thin neck, dark hair, skin mottled blue-grey and black. My attention skitters away from the puckered stitches just visible at the fold of the cloth. Tears sting my eyes, sudden, surprising. Sharp.

Cass pulls his hand out of my grasp, falling to his knees beside the trash bin. The sounds of retching come to me as though filtered, from a distance.

Halting steps. Tremors through my body. Blink the tears away.

I stop so close to the window, I can smell the glass cleaner last used on it. I pull in the harsh ammonia scent. I ignore my poor brother's state. This is what I came here for. I can't let emotions or a weak stomach break my resolve. I cannot afford to fuck this up.

My eyes rest first on her thin eyebrows, though the cosmetic tattoos no longer stand out so much. Slanted, elongated eyelids, now puffy, bloated. Cheekbones, no longer high or taut, but misshapen, and flat in the wrong places. Skin, waxy . . . distended and all the wrong colours.

I think of the boulders in the river, edged and hard. I think of bones breaking and skin tearing against them.

I clutch at my neck, pressing hard enough to feel the crescents of my nails against my collarbone. My head feels light, insubstantial. I imagine it detaching, floating upward to bump against the pale ceiling.

From above, I see Rao raise her hand at her colleague, pull the curtains closed with three rapid jerks of the string. Cass stands, muttering apologies. Rao offers him tissues from the box. Once he wipes his mouth, she murmurs something at us and ushers us out of the room.

I walk behind Cass, my steps automatic, clumsy, as though my feet aren't all here. Maybe none of me is. I stare at my shoes while I walk, unsure how they're moving at all.

"I'll give you a few moments, shall I?"

I raise my head. We're back at the other room.

Rao waits for us to enter, one hand still on the doorknob. "Please drink some water. Take your time. I know this is a discomfiting experience. When you're ready, just press 319 on the phone and I will come escort you out." She closes the door gently before either of us replies.

My knees give out as I reach the same chair I took earlier. A thousand ants explode in my chest, burning their way up my throat, pouring out in a torrent of racking sobs. I try to force my eyes open. I don't want to see that horrifying face again in my mind, but I can't stop it. I try to keep hold of the chair, but my fingers won't obey. Muscles slack, I slide out of the seat and onto the floor. I feel the nubbly roughness of industrial carpet against my cheek. I feel my mouth moving mechanically like a fish gasping for water.

Of course, my kind and decent brother is having none of that. He gently raises me up and sets me into a chair, pillowing my head on my arms atop the table. Tears quickly soak my sleeves. What is this? Why can't I stop?

Eventually, the tears dry up, leaving behind a wrung-out, hollow feeling right behind my breastbone. I don't like it. In fact, I fucking hate it.

"Your idea of closure sucks, sister mine." Cass's words come, still weary, but unexpectedly light. He sighs, slumping into the chair next to me. "Are you all right?"

I sniffle, straightening up. My cheek is on fire from chafing against my wet sleeve. "Are you?"

He shakes his head. "Stupid question. From both of us." He pushes the tissue box toward me, then downs a cup of water in one go. "I can't believe we just did . . . that."

I clean my face up gingerly and pull another tissue out, playing with its corners until it rips. "I'm sorry I forced you here, Cass. But I'm grateful you came with me. I needed . . ." I look up at him, trying to order my thoughts, trying to understand before it all gets too far out of hand. "I don't know how to handle this, these . . . how I feel. They're all over the place." Oh, the arrogance, thinking I could just waltz in, say *That's her*, and swan out again, closure complete. What was I thinking?

"I think," he replies quietly, "it's natural to have conflicting emotions. You and Mum had a really complicated relationship, right? It makes sense that your . . . grief is complicated, too." He touches my hand. "You didn't force me here. I *chose* to come. I choose to support you. Always, sis. No matter how hard it gets. That's what family means to me. It's a deliberate choice."

I don't know how to process that right now. It's too overwhelming. Or maybe I just feel too much right now. More than I bargained for. Deeper than I believed possible, if I'm honest. I'm all but unrecognizable to myself, and I'm not sure how to process that either. Some days, I barely know how to feel.

A truth presses against my heart like an anvil. I don't want to share it. I'm no good with doling out fairness. But I just put Cass through a horrific experience, one he'd never have gone through on his own. One I forced him to choose to do. Me and my implacable compulsions.

I've heard it said that grief makes people strange . . . but can it make you be better?

I search my brother's face, tear-streaked and haggard, his mouth turned down at its corners, his eyes red-rimmed and bloodshot. He is wrecked and beautiful and *here*. I owe him. I owe him more than I might be willing to give. I owe him this truth. We may be family, but we'll never be the same. He needs to understand that. For his own good.

"I'm a fraud, Cass. I don't have the right to grieve." I crumple the tissue in my hand. "All I caused her was heartache and trouble. All we ever did was fight." I squeeze my fist as tightly as I can, compressing the tissue into a hard little ball. "If I'd tried harder to get along, or to keep my head down, to just do things her way . . . she and Dad wouldn't have been in this situation."

"You're not to blame for this," replies Cass fiercely. "I won't let you do that to yourself."

My startled gaze slides away from him, from his earnestness, his blazing belief in me. "We had totally different relationships with her, little brother. I don't know if I can ever make you understand."

His lips thin. "We're both her children. You don't have to *earn* the right to grieve." I can feel his searching gaze on me, like butterfly wings against my skin. "Listen, maybe you're worried she didn't, but . . . I know she loved you, okay? It's not your fault she was hard on you or that she wasn't very . . . affectionate. There is nothing wrong with *you*. If anything," I hear him swallow, "Mum is the one with the problem expressing her love in a way that worked for *us*."

"That's a pretty thought," I say carefully. "But it doesn't matter now, does it? She's gone. Dad's . . . disappeared. They aren't here to tell us any different. All we have now is our past together."

I turn my eyes away from him, feeling utterly scored and raw on the inside, unwilling to let him see the terrible yawning sorrow, the dark guilt, blooming in me. There's no going back. No changing the past. No making things better. No amount of talk or touches or hugs to paper over the hurt.

My mother is dead and I know it's my fault.

THIRTY

The RCMP awaits us when we exit back into the reception area.

Rao greets Naomi with a professional smile and handshake, then takes her leave of us with a final utterance of condolences. I find myself staring at the white sliver of her lab coat as it disappears with the closing of the door behind her.

"I'm sorry to surprise you like this," Naomi says, "but we wanted to catch you while you're still in Kelowna. Shae has a few more questions for you." She stands in a crisp uniform, her shoulders square, legs braced, her cap tightly stashed between her elbow and side, her sombre expression all business.

Behind her, the receptionist taps loudly at their keyboard.

"That doesn't sound like a request," says Cass, narrowing his eyes.

Naomi has the grace to look apologetic. "It's actually not far, but let's not leave your car here. I'll ride with you and navigate." Her gaze barely lands on me before skimming back to Cass. I don't like the tense feeling in my gut. Naomi shifts her feet, her expression determined and polite. The distance yawns between us.

Cass glances at me, raising a brow. He knows as well as I do there's no refusing. If he has any doubts about Naomi's loyalties, though, he doesn't show it. Then again, he didn't spend as much time with her as I did. He didn't rely on her like I did. She wasn't an anchor for him during a dark, engulfing storm.

Never mind. Plenty of time later to marvel at how quickly I made and lost a friend. I should probably feel more . . . betrayed. Or something. But the truth is, Naomi never lied to me. Protecting me is part of her job. Nothing more. I know next to nothing about her. It's pretty much been a one-way street, I realize.

If I happen to feel a fierce stab in my chest at the reminder, well . . . more fool me.

I shove away all the untidy emotions swirling around inside me. I say, "We have questions, too. Because I haven't heard a single thing about our father. Or anything about how Drew Arceneaux or anyone else at my old firm fits into all this. Or what I need to do regarding the assault charges." I keep my chin up and my gaze steady.

Naomi looks briefly uncertain before her expression clears, and she tips *her* chin up a little as well. "Of course. I understand. Why don't we wait until we get to the detachment? I know Inspector Miller will do her best to address your concerns."

I know a brushoff when I hear one, and that use of Miller's formal title sounds like a reproach—I shouldn't be so disturbed to hear it, however. Hiding my displeasure behind a blank face, I acquiesce with a nod and allow Naomi to lead us into the elevator. She assures us it's just a matter of three or so blocks.

At the car, I take a back seat without a word. I see Cass tapping out a fast text while Naomi slides into the front passenger seat, her attention elsewhere. He doesn't mention anything, though, so I add it to the things I have no idea are important or not but need to be addressed anyway. It's a long fucking list. On the drive, I leave them to their halting, inconsequential small talk, my mind awhirl with more important matters.

Was there any sign of my dad when they found Mum? What are they thinking about him now? Are they still searching for him? Have they widened the search area, given where they found Mum? What do they think the probability is he's still out there, unharmed? It *has* been over a week. Isn't it more likely they think he's gone, swept away by the roaring river? I swallow at that, abruptly queasy again. I scrabble for another item on my ever-lengthening list, desperate to dim the images of body parts battered against boulders, of blue-grey skin and too-still faces. Even the panic blooming at the thought of another police interview seems a better option. . . .

Are they still working on my former co-workers? They must've cleared some of them by now, but how many? And Arceneaux. Did they arrest him? Is he in jail? Out on bail? Or is it called bond? They have to charge him, right? We have video proof of the assault. I hope Miller used it to pressure him about his alibi on the weekend my parents disappeared. I wonder where he was, if Miller thinks he's a credible suspect. I should consider taking out a restraining order—

God. Maybe I should be considering hiring a lawyer anyway. Shouldn't I be looking out for my rights? I don't know the first thing about the criminal justice system. A good thing, in another life. Now, it seems idiotically naive all of a sudden. And overwhelming. I bet Naomi would tell me where to start, though. Dizzy with mounting nerves, I realize I haven't the first goddamned clue how to trust a complete stranger with my story.

We pull into another surface lot, and Cass parks the car facing a single-storey, windowless brown building. I follow the lines of it to our left, find it attaches to a three-storey square of glass and off-white walls and the same dark brown brick. I squint. See *City of Kelowna Police Services* in large plain silver lettering aligned with the second storey.

Cass receives a buzz on his phone as Naomi clambers out and closes her door softly. I have one foot on the pavement. Still seated, Cass types rapidly on his phone. Before I have a chance to ask him about it, he's out of the car, sliding the phone into a pocket. He walks to the back of the station wagon and retrieves what looks like a laptop case. Uh . . . Is he planning on taking notes? He offers no explanation, doesn't even glance at me, just locks up, motioning for Naomi to lead the way. Rigid with unease, I stay behind him and his hard-eyed expression. I don't know what *my* face looks like, but I doubt this is the time to test him.

Naomi takes us inside briskly. Once ID and signatures and visitor badges are dealt with, she ushers us down a bland interior hallway lit with ceiling fluorescents and into yet another nondescript conference room. This one isn't graced with any windows, and I wonder if we're just a few inches of drywall and brick away from Cass's station wagon. The orientation would be about right.

Miller and Pendelton greet us sombrely, standing as we enter. It's late afternoon, almost evening, but they both look freshly pressed. I note, with a sudden, wildly inappropriate urge to snicker, that save for the tailoring, they're actually wearing identical outfits: dark grey trousers and pale blue shirts.

I sit, scrubbing at my face to stop from breaking out into giggles. The last thing I need is to play the hysterical woman. Pendelton places bottles of off-brand water in front of both me and Cass. I take advantage of the distraction and take a long pull of the chilly water to subdue all traces of unwanted levity. Hysteria's probably what they expect of me, frankly, after seeing my poor mother, but I refuse to break now.

Naomi seats herself at the short end of the table, while Cass and I face the other two across the surface of pale blond wood. I try not to read anything in Naomi's position.

Miller glances at Cass's laptop with a raised brow, but she only says, "Thank you for agreeing to this interview. Please let me say again, we're very sorry for your loss." She pauses, her expression shifting as she sees me stir, impatient to speak. "I'm sure you have questions, but there are some additional details I'd like to tell you about first."

I subside, as she wishes. She acknowledges my obedience with a small upturn of her lips before turning grave once more. "Unfortunately, we have no news at this time regarding your father, I'm sorry. The Search and Rescue teams have been called off, given the discovery of your mother's remains. For your sake, I don't wish to get into the grisly details of it, but there are a lot of possibilities with a body in the river in such circumstances. If your father also fell into the water, they think it likely he's been carried even farther downriver. I'm sorry, but the chances of him being found are decreasing."

I grip the water bottle, rubbing a grubby thumb along one of the ridges. I inhale slowly, wrestling against the sudden pressure in my chest until I can exhale without shouting. I feel Cass slump beside me, his breathing hitching, before he straightens himself up again. Neither of us flinches anymore when they say *body*.

Pendelton adds, "We still have your father listed as missing, and his photo and details will remain up on the national and regional boards until further notice. We're also updating the public statement on his status to reflect the probability that he was in the water, and to ask for people in the communities downstream along the Kicking Horse River to contact us with any new information or possible sightings."

"But that's purely based on conjecture," I say, softly. "That he fell in, too."

Pendelton assesses me for a second, his eyes unreadable. "We have to make some guesses, yes, but the search teams came up with nothing other than his wallet when they concentrated on land. It seems probable, given where they found the wallet, how we found your mother, and the fact that he still hasn't turned up, that the river is the best place to focus now."

I frown, forcing myself to let go of the water bottle before I crush it. "But what if the person who kidnapped me took him, too? Or . . . or did something else with him?"

"Which brings us to another, very important point." Miller leans forward, clasping her hands on top of the table, her expression resolved and somehow earnest. "You're right, Cleo. There are still too many questions about what happened to your parents. About what happened to you. I believe, as does Chuck, that you hold the key to those questions. Even Naomi agrees. We think you know exactly what happened."

I've said as much myself, but it feels infinitely different when it's the police saying it now. I feel my heart leap into my throat. I flick a look at Cass. He grabs hold of my hand. I clasp back tightly.

"We know you must be as anxious to recover your memories as anyone. And now, with the added stress of your mother's discovery . . ." Pendelton pauses, shifting in his seat. "Have you considered something that might be a bit outside the box? Like hypnosis?"

"What about it?" I reply warily. Naomi must've mentioned it—but did she tell them about my fears?

"I've seen it done," he says, intent. "Under professional supervision and recorded so that the person going under can see everything that happened during the session, after the fact. It's all aboveboard."

I marshal my objections carefully. I want to seem reasonable, not terrified. "Look, like I told Naomi, I'm just not comfortable—"

"I can understand if you're feeling skittish, but there's no reason to be. Honest. There's a therapist in town who's done this with us before. It got us good results. And the person who went under, they actually felt better for it. Afterward."

I speak over the end of Pendelton's declaration. "No. No way. I can't just . . . submit to being vulnerable like that. And to a stranger?" I shake my head, sending tendrils of hair flying around my face.

Miller's expression sharpens. "Cleo, please consider this from our perspective. The further away we get from the time of the disappearance, the less likely we'll find the truth of what happened." Pausing, her expression takes on a grim cast. "Someone would be getting away with a terrible crime."

I squeeze my eyes closed, trying to get a handle on the burst of wild emotions pushing up my throat, wanting out. I need to concentrate. I need to *think*.

I reopen my eyes on another slow exhalation, reaching for a calm, rational rebuttal. "Dr. Rao hasn't decided on the ruling yet. She said, so far, it looks accidental. If that's true, then why do I have to go through something like that?" I wince at the taut note of desperation in my voice. It fills the space in the room, broadcasting just how badly I want all this to go away, to be done. I can see it in their reactions. Miller, Pendelton, Naomi—each with some version of pity on their faces.

"I just want to move on. Can't you understand that?"

Miller replies, low and urgent, "There are just too many questions. What about your father, Cleo? We don't know why your parents were up at that viewpoint. When did they leave their cabin that night? Did they leave at night? Or was it earlier? And you? Why were *you* there, so far from home? Who assaulted you? What happened between your parents leaving Edmonton and you waking up in BC? Who broke into their home? What were they searching for? Did they find it? Are they the same person who kidnapped and assaulted you?" She sits back, her expression sharpening. "Can't *you* understand? These things can't be coincidence. Even if the ruling comes back that your mother's death is accidental, there's still your file and your father's disappearance. It's our duty to pursue this."

"But it's impossible." Cass runs his hands through his hair, glaring at all three of them. "I don't see a way to solve this and keep my sister safe."

Quietly, Naomi says, "I can only imagine how exhausted you both are, and the toll grief must be taking on you." She pauses, her sympathetic gaze landing on each of us in turn. "But, I'm sorry, ignoring these out-standing issues won't make the grieving any easier."

Noting how I stiffen at Naomi's words, Miller continues. "Think about this, Cleo. Wouldn't you prefer to know, for certain, what truly happened?" She looks to Cass. "Wouldn't it be an important part of the healing process, to recover those memories?"

I shudder, fear a dry hiss clawing up my spine. Cass replaces his hand over mine. Looking at him, I force myself to manage a whisper, "What if I'm involved? I don't know if I can live with that."

Miller makes an impatient noise, startling me. "It's too late, Cleo. You already are." I stare at her, my heartbeat once more roaring in my ears. "You were found mere kilometres from the last place they were seen. You, and no one else."

I snatch my hand from Cass's damp grasp and pull my knees up to my chin, wrapping my arms around myself. My voice trembles as I shape the terror into words, small and wounded. "You think I did this? You think I hurt my parents?"

THIRTY-ONE

Cass bolts upright in the chair, his momentum sending it rocking. "Okay, that's enough. Stop right there." He grabs the case in front of him on the table, unzipping it with jerky motions. "I'm calling our lawyer."

"What?" I stare at my brother, thoughts frozen with shock. "What are you talking about?"

His lips thin for a moment as he extricates a matte silver laptop from the case. He pulls out a power cord and square adaptor, connects it to the laptop. "I may be innocent about this stuff, not being a career criminal or whatever, but I'm not stupid. This is way beyond the two of us, sis." He feels along the underside of the table, cranes his neck, searching with restless eyes. He asks Naomi, "Where can I plug in?"

"Uh . . ." She looks to Pendelton, clearly caught off-guard.

Cass scowls. "Never mind." He sets the power cord down and opens the laptop cover. "I can connect with them for now, and we'll plug in when we need it."

"Who are you taking about?" My head begins to ache, I'm frowning so hard.

Miller shifts in her chair. "Yes, Dr. Li, who are you contacting?"

Cass ignores the questions. "Do you have public wi-fi? No?" He fiddles with the connection menu on the laptop. I watch him choose his phone and rapidly type in a complicated password from memory. Is he using his phone as a hotspot? I don't know why that's bothering me now, of all things.

Cass brings up a browser and types in a URL. A landing page for something called Zoom pops up on the open window. I know this site from my working days. It's video conferencing, like . . . Skype, but newer. Who is Cass calling? Since when do we have a lawyer? Surely, he doesn't mean Betty Wan. She handles estates and stuff, not criminal cases. Maybe Cass got a referral from her?

But . . . why didn't he talk to me about this?

"Gimme a sec," he replies evenly, "and they'll be able to speak for themselves soon enough. Oh, and please pay attention to their pronouns. Not *he* or *she*. Use *they* and *them*, please."

The cops share a wary look among themselves.

Cass finishes setting up a—I think it's called a "room," air quotes and all. Then he fiddles with some menus and sends an email. He addresses the police. "This is a secure online meeting platform. Our lawyer's calling in from Calgary. I didn't know if we for sure would need Karmen, but I thought this was the most expedient way to ensure our rights." He pauses, his expression hardening. "If you're accusing my sister—or me—of being involved in our mother's death, I'd say this qualifies."

I should care how the cops react to that, but honestly, I don't give a fuck. My stomach squirms, chilly and unsettled. "Cass, you better explain right fucking now. Or I might just throw up all over your shoes."

My brother meets my panicky gaze in silence for a few interminable seconds. He gentles his voice. "I texted Kong last night. They suggested this as a way to keep them available for us. They didn't have the time to come in person." He has the gall to shrug. "I signed their retainer when we stopped for gas outside of Calgary. All digital."

I close my eyes briefly, give my head a shake. "Kong? Auntie Annie's Kong? Her youngest?"

Cass clears his throat. "They made partner last year. We keep in touch."

Fuck me. I can only hope they don't share their mother's disdain for me.

"Hush," says Cass. "Don't worry. They're gonna help."

I drag at my face with both hands. If ever there were a time to keep my thoughts *internal*, sitting in an interrogation room with three cops who think I'm guilty would be it.

Before I force myself to check the cops' reaction, though, Cass tips up his chin as he faces Miller. "This might be . . . unorthodox, Inspector, but I know you're open to it if it gets the job done. As you've said."

Miller concedes the point with a cool nod. "I can live with it. For now." She gestures at the laptop. "So, how about you explain who's joining us today."

"Karmen Ong." The voice comes from the laptop, crisp and clear, like its owner is sitting right next to me. I startle, my heart kicking against my breastbone.

Onscreen, a round face with a shrewd gaze and artfully spiked, short black hair stares out at us from the large square of the browser window. A little line of white text shows below and to the left: *Karmen Ong, they/them.* Above their video image, in a black strip, I see a smaller square showing me and Cass. I wince at the dumbfounded expression on my pinched face.

"Hi Cleopatra, Cass. I'm really sorry about Auntie Glinda. I know this is a hard time for you both." Their brow furrows for a moment. "Just let me get settled with the officers and then we'll talk." Karmen offers a sombre nod. "Cass."

I stammer out a greeting past the thickening in my throat. Stiffly, Cass swivels the laptop screen, fussing with it a little until he captures all three RCMP in the frame for Karmen. He punches the volume button a few times, too.

"Inspector Miller?" Karmen asks, voice now distorted a bit.

She raises a hand calmly. "Nice to meet you, Mr. Ong."

"I prefer Karmen or Counsellor, thanks," they reply smoothly. "I understand that neither Cass nor Cleopatra are under arrest? Is that accurate?"

"Yes."

"So, this is an interview with them as . . . persons of interest?"

"Yes."

"All right. I'd like to confer with my clients, please. Please ensure that all recording equipment is turned off for the duration of our consultation. I've learned over the years, better safe than sorry."

Miller hesitates, her eyes narrowing as she considers. She aims a short nod at Pendleton before answering. "You have an hour, Counsellor." She gathers up the papers and file folders in front of her. Without another word, she strides out the door.

Uncertainty crosses Naomi's face as she grabs her notes and pen before following Miller out into the corridor.

Pendleton checks a wristwatch. "I'll give you 'til 6:45. Don't leave this room on your own. If you need something from us," he jerks a thumb, "you can tell the constable waiting outside."

I think about asking for another bottle of water, but Pendleton's gone before I can stop dithering. I turn a wide-eyed gaze to my brother. After a beat, he stands and opens his arms, his eyes tight at the edges and bright with wetness.

I tell myself my brother needs the reassurance. That he needs to feel like he's caring for me. That we're . . . grieving. I step into the offered hug.

"It's gonna be okay, sis," he whispers, rubbing my shoulder. "We haven't done anything wrong. Karmen will make sure we're okay."

My nose twitches. I push away before the sniffle escapes. "Let's get started then."

He cocks his head, wary. "You don't want to ask me anything? Or yell at me?"

I pluck at my purse zipper. "Do I wish you'd told me, or even maybe conferred with me about it? Fuck yes, but . . . you're right." I grimace at the admission. "This isn't something I can figure out on my own." I fetch tissues from my purse and swipe at my nose. "The clock's ticking, little brother." I sit and include Karmen with a nod. "Let's talk."

"Wait." Cass gets down on one knee, peering beneath the conference table. "I need to plug in. Sorry."

As I watch Cass hunt for an outlet, Karmen's earlier comment strikes me.

"Cass?"

"Mmm?"

"Do you have earbuds we can share?"

"Uh, yeah. Why?" He looks over at me, then at the room. His attention catches on the bubble in the high corner of the room. I know he recognizes it. Cameras like that are everywhere nowadays.

I shrug to hide my nerves. "Just in case."

"Okay. Check in there." He points at the laptop case as he reels out the power cord to reach across the table. I rummage and find what I want in an interior pocket. I hastily plug in the earbuds and offer Cass the one marked *L*. We have to sit awkwardly close, but feeling some bit of control is worth it.

"All right," says Karmen, as though picking up a conversation, "you're going to give me as much context as you can. Then we'll get back with the inspector and her crew, so I can get a sense of what they want to know from you. From now on, I'm your go-between. They'll want you to answer them directly, but you won't say anything to them unless it's through me. Got it?"

Cass nods immediately. I hesitate, painfully aware that I'm still in freefall. I don't know how Karmen fits into this. Their job is to help, but I'm no good at playing with others.

"Cleopatra?" they prompt.

Nothing's the same anymore, is it? Not the awkward hulking teen we used to call *Kong*, not me.

"I'm Cleo now," I reply, rubbing at my gritty eyes. "And yes. I got it."

"Okay, good. And again, I'm sorry for your loss. I'm sorry we don't have time to mourn Auntie properly right now."

Cass gestures vaguely. "We'll talk personal stuff another time, okay? I can't . . . I can't deal with that now."

Karmen concedes with a graceful nod. "I understand." Their gaze sharpens, and though they aren't looking directly into the camera, I sense their attention on me. Acutely. "So, what can you tell me?"

I pick through the past nine days, careful to prune away conjectures, to stick as closely to the verifiable, to the things I said to others, to the places I went, accompanied and protected. And though it's so goddamned fresh, Cass and I both tell Karmen of our appointment with Dr Rao. If I expected them to disapprove of my insistence on seeing our mother's body, I'd've been sorely disappointed. Karmen absorbs that bit of information with nothing more than a soft *hmm*.

Then they promptly summarize everything we've told them, laying out our story in a neat timeline of events, all guesses and emotions handily stripped away. I'm incredibly envious.

Karmen says, "So, it sounds like the RCMP should also be looking into other former co-workers, if, as you admit, you were generally characterized as a bully. Arceneaux may have been your most vocal critic, but there might be others with equally strong feelings."

They make a few more notes, their eyes focussed on what I guess must be a pad on their desk. They weren't typing while we spoke. Karmen inhales briskly. I hear a tapping sound, like a pen against a desk. They raise their gaze again.

"Let's talk about your dad."

I jerk, inadvertently yanking the earbud out of Cass's left ear. I flush, mumbling an apology, my fingers fumbling at the cord. Cass lays a firm hand on mine, stilling my clumsiness. He plucks up his errant earbud deftly and replaces it, giving me a sidelong glance.

"What do you mean?" he asks Karmen.

They take a moment, assessing the two of us in silence. I only now notice the fine grey pinstripes in their pale lilac shirt. Karmen rubs a hand against their chin. "Look, I'm going to bring everything I can to this. There'll be some really hard things for you to hear, but my job is to protect you, both of you. If that means telling you unpleasant things, I will do it with as much compassion as I can. But the truth is, I'm not here to safeguard your parents' reputations. I'm sorry."

I hold my breath, afraid and yet strangely expectant. I'm smart, I know I am, but . . . they have expertise here that far outweighs anything I can muster in my own defence. I ought to be terrified, being forced to rely on them. I should be concerned that I can't gauge our relationship well enough to influence Karmen's actions on my behalf. I may agree with them. I may not. What happens when it's the latter?

"Jesus, Kong, you're scaring me," says Cass abruptly.

"Maybe that's a good thing," Karmen replies. "You shouldn't go into this lightly. Or in ignorance."

I exhale, wobbly.

"You need to be prepared for me to narrow the focus onto your father," Karmen says gently. "I know your parents had a rough relationship. You know it, too. We all saw it. Maybe as kids we thought it was normal. But as adults, we *know*. Glinda bullied your father. He put on a brave front, because gotta save face, right? But let me be real here, among the three of us. I saw how he flinched. I saw how he kept his mouth shut so tight, the muscles in his neck corded. And that was just when I saw them together in public. You can't tell me things were better in private. I won't believe you, and you are literally paying me to believe you, for better or worse."

Cass falls back against the chair, tugging me toward him by our shared cord. "I . . ."

Karmen doesn't stop, though. "Now your mother's dead, and he's disappeared. I know this is hard, but you have to hear me out. I'm sorry, truly, but . . . what if Stephen finally had enough? What if he wanted that ticket for himself? What if he got his hands on that safety deposit box key? He could add his signature to the ticket, with no one the wiser, and no one to object."

Another shudder racks me. The hairs at my nape stand on end.

They ask, "Neither of you actually, literally, saw the back of the ticket, right? You couldn't swear that only your mum's signature was on it before she stored it?"

An almost electric shock jolts through me. I can imagine it so clearly it hurts. The reverse side of a lotto ticket, and a hand signing an additional name. Blue ballpoint on a thin black line, next to my mother's sprawling signature. Goosebumps sprout along my arms, like pinpricks poking from the underside of my skin.

"What about Cleo?" Cass sounds like a drowning man, his voice garbled and thick. "If he . . . why leave her with amnesia?"

"That's not a question we need to answer," replies Karmen. "I don't need to fill in all the blanks here, Cass. That's not my job. I just need to expand Inspector Miller's focus until she's not fixated only on you, or on Cleo, as the main persons of interest."

Cass wrenches to face me. "You honestly think Dad could—"

I shake my head, trying to keep the earbud cord untangled with one hand. "Don't ask me that, Cass, please. I don't . . . I can't answer."

"But remember, too," says Karmen into the charged silence, "this isn't a criminal case yet, your mum's death. That coroner's report will be key."

They make our fucked-up circumstances sound so straightforward. If this, then that. If not this, then not that. *If the cops suspect our father, then we're off the hook.*

I can practically taste the temptation to tell Cass. . . . Like rock candy on my tongue, jagged and sweet.

THIRTY-TWO

When the cops return, Naomi surprises Cass with access to the detachment wi-fi.

"I'll type in the password and then unclick *Remember this network*," she explains. "The network will remain secure and you won't have to keep using your phone as a hotspot. See?"

Pendelton, meanwhile, gets his own laptop ready and Miller organizes her notes. They seem suspiciously studious about it all.

I deduce we're in for a long night. At least there's water again.

Once Cass has the laptop situated properly to let Karmen see all of us, they say, "Inspector Miller, thank you for allowing us time to confer. I really appreciate it. Now, what would you like to ask my clients?"

"No problem, Mr. Ong. We'd like—"

"Karmen or Counsellor, please," interrupts Karmen firmly.

Miller hesitates a microsecond. "Of course . . . Counsellor. As I was saying, we'd like to tell you how we see things. To lay out why we think Cleo should seriously reconsider her objections to hypnosis. Before we dig into more questions, of course."

She exchanges a quick look with Pendelton. "I know it'll be difficult to hear, and painful. We *are* sorry." Her expression is difficult to translate, something akin to reluctance and yet, also . . . doggedness. "But you have to try, Cleo, for your own sake."

My own sake? Who does this woman think she is?

As Naomi catches sight of my silent fuming, her professional mask shifts. Her brow furrows with concern, and regret. I cut my gaze away, uninterested in her compassion. Too late anyway. I know where she stands.

The clacking of keys comes from Cass's laptop, loud and fast. Apparently, Karmen's typing notes now rather than writing things down, as they did with us. I have to admit, the extra noise is distracting.

Miller continues, "We know you're in potential financial straits, Cleo. As soon as we knew your identity, we requested all the records we could get on you. Including banking." She pauses. I clench my hands to keep from speaking. "You paid down your debts, which was admirable, but now the funds from your severance package are running out. What you don't know is that you're on the blacklist of every IT shop in Edmonton. That's why you haven't been able to find another position. We don't know if it's Drew Arceneaux per se, but someone's been talking about your time at that company." She hesitates, perhaps giving me time to react.

I don't even know what to say. Those assholes. I should never have counted on their word. I clamp my jaw tight as possible, unwilling to reveal any damned reaction now.

"We know no extra money has been transferred to you since the duplex sale finalized last month," says Miller, "so your parents didn't share the proceeds with you, Cleo. However, a lump sum payment to your brother's bank cleared his mortgage and all fees. Since we know you were arguing over relocating to BC, we can deduce that your parents were probably holding the money from the sale as incentive to force you to move with them."

"Are you asking my client to undergo hypnosis to confirm this . . . deduction?" asks Karmen blandly.

I barely register their question in the rush of intense rage. I turn to Cass. I pull out each word like splinters of glass. "You told me they were *going to*. You didn't say they already did. Why?" I want nothing more than to scream, to vent my fury. My shame. Why did I think I could trust him?

I deliberately lower my voice instead. "Why did you lie to me?"

"Cleo," cautions Karmen.

But Cass meets my accusation with unfeigned, wide-eyed shock. "I didn't. They didn't." He asks Miller, bewildered and angry, "What are you talking about?"

"It happened yesterday, the paperwork is still on its way to you," replies Pendelton. "I confirmed it this morning."

Cass gapes at me. "I swear, sis, I had no idea." He covers his mouth with a hand. I can practically see the gears whirling behind his eyes.

"Listen," says Karmen, "don't worry about that now. We can work—"

But Miller doesn't wait for us to catch up with this revelation.

"Cleo, I'm sorry, but we also know you had ready access to a way to incapacitate your mother. Her insulin comes in self-contained pens that only require the attachment of small needles, like screwing on a cap, to be ready for injection. There's an incredibly narrow window for insulin to show up in post-mortems. It can be a dangerous weapon under certain circumstances. Dangerous and untraceable."

"Access is irrelevant to your theory," says Karmen calmly. "By that token, Stephen Li should also be under investigation, regardless of his current whereabouts. Is he? And are you currently accusing Cleo of homicide? When the coroner still hasn't officially ruled on Glinda's death?"

My skin flashes cold. I shiver, feeling like someone's walking over my grave.

"No," says Cass, shaking his head in vehemence. "There's no way. My sister is not a murderer. Neither is our father." His voice grows louder with outraged incredulity. "You're making all of this up, trying to frighten us. None of it's true. I won't believe it. No fucking way. I refuse."

"Hey," interjects Karmen firmly. "Let's take a moment to calm things down, okay? Inspector, stop riling things up. It's counterproductive."

"We know they argued all the time, Counsellor." Pendelton spares my brother a brief look of pity. "Dr. Li, we have dozens of statements from former co-workers. They said your mother called you almost daily, Cleo. They could tell when it was your mother because you always argued with her. Loudly."

I frown, jumping on the inconsistency. "None of those people speak Cantonese. How would they know what I was saying?"

"If you happen to have recordings of these conversations between my client and Glinda Li," says Karmen, "please do send them to me. We can find third-party certified translators for you."

"They weren't recorded, Counsellor." Miller eyes me intently. "But everyone who mentioned them all mentioned your tone, Cleo, as well as your raised voice. It's a tonal language, isn't it?"

I look, disbelieving, from one to the other. I even glance at Karmen, who uncharacteristically seems at a loss. "Did she just—" I return my attention to Miller and Pendelton. "That just means saying the right word depends on producing the right tone." They stare back at me, blankly. I scowl. "Listen closely, this is the word for dog: gauw. But if I stress it slightly differently—gauw—it's the word for the number nine. And if different again—gauw—it's the verb, to rescue." They exchange confused glances with one another.

I continue, "I doubt you can hear the difference. Your ears aren't trained to. But that's what it means when someone says Cantonese is tonal. They don't mean *tone of voice*." For fuck's sake. I rub my fists against the chair arms, trying to settle my anger.

Because they still seem baffled, I add, "Growing up, my white friends always said Cantonese sounded like arguing. And maybe it does. But it doesn't mean I, I, I *hurt* people." I glare at them, hard, belying the frantic pummelling of my heart.

Karmen's rapid-fire typing fills the space.

After another beat, Pendelton gives a minuscule shrug. "I also interviewed your neighbours, Cleo, and I have a recorded interview with Anna Ong. Your mother, right, Counsellor, and Glinda Li's best friend?"

Karmen appears unperturbed by the obvious nettling. "You'll make that available to us, of course?"

With a short nod, Pendelton continues, "Everyone we spoke with, *every one*, corroborated that picture of you and your mother. She was a real"—he makes air quotes—"'Tiger Mom' and you were a typical immigrants' daughter, striving to succeed in two worlds. They all said you two argued constantly."

I refuse to rise to the bait. Gritting my teeth, I slowly wring the arms of my chair.

"For the record," says Cass darkly, "that Tiger Mom shit is a racist stereotype."

"Cass," warns Karmen.

"Be that as it may," Miller replies firmly, "resentment like that has a way of building a real head of steam over the years. Add in the recent discord over the duplex money, plus the move to BC, and then a huge money motive, like a $47.3 million jackpot. . . . It's easy to see what might have pushed you over the edge, Cleo." She manages to sound sympathetic.

"Again, I have to ask," says Karmen patiently, cutting through Miller's grating solicitousness, "what *edge* are you talking about here? You seem to be insisting that my client perpetrated a crime," they gesture with one hand, "that hasn't happened."

"Karmen's right." Cass says tightly. "Until we hear from Dr. Rao, this . . . discussion is cruel and upsetting. Pointless."

I can't help a glance at Naomi, trying to gauge how serious this theory truly is. She's scribbling rapidly in her notebook. I think she might be avoiding my gaze. She's gripping her pen so tightly I can see the ligaments in her hand in stark relief.

An awful suffocating dread creeps over me. My thoughts scramble, then go blank, like dead air over a radio. I press my fists over my eyes, trying to focus, using the almost-pain to force something into my head. All I get when I open my eyes are white spots dancing in my field of view.

"Not only is there no current ruling of homicide," says Karmen steadily, "we have yet to hear about any results in Cleo's assault file. What about her assailant? Have you leads on an identity?"

"A fair point, Counsellor," Pendelton replies, voice flat. "We're getting to that."

Miller doesn't seem to hear them, her attention singularly concentrated on my face. She reaches out a hand, though she's too far across the table to touch me. "If you truly did these things, Cleo, even if you don't remember doing them, you need to own up to them. You need to pay your debt to society. How long that means will depend on how a judge weighs your extenuating circumstances, but I have to think that it *will* weigh in your favour if you help us now, if you agree to having a hypnotherapist recover those memories." She offers what I think is meant to be a kind smile. "I know it's frightening in the immediate term, Cleo, but in the long run, I think you'll find it will be good for you."

THIRTY-THREE

My brain stutters, wanting to shut down, even just a few seconds, to reboot and get a fresh angle to tackle this nightmare. Fuck. How do normal people deal with this constant onslaught of feelings? Horribly, a panic attack seems appealing at this point. . . .

I know if I allow myself to fall into one, though, I'll lose all control of this conversation—and possibly the rest of my life. It doesn't matter right now that Mum's death hasn't even been ruled on. It doesn't matter how often Karmen reminds her. Miller's decided I'm guilty.

C'mon, Li. You know how to do this. You've been doing it your whole fucking life. Get it together right the fuck now. Or they will destroy you.

Right. I sweep the entire mess of emotions and fearful self-doubts and timid second-guesses under the proverbial carpet in my over-stuffed head. I have an inkling, new-found and unwanted, that it won't be sustainable, but for now, it will have to do.

I will have to do.

"Really, Inspector," Karmen chides in the meantime.

"Do you understand what I'm telling you, Cleo?" Miller leans forward to emphasize her point, utterly uninterested in anyone else. "You have a chance at a future, if you cooperate now. We can help you retrieve those memories of yours. Granted, it may not be an ideal future, but don't you think it's better than spending the rest of your life with doubts? We're all on the same side here, Cleo. We all want the truth," she finishes softly, clear-eyed and guileless.

Who the *fuck*? The rage reverberates inside my head, needling me to lash out at Miller and her patronizing attitude. Of all the overbearing, paternalistic bullshit—

"Can we return to the issues at hand, Inspector?" says Karmen steadily. "Without the extraneous comments, please?"

I see Cass's glazed eyes and the coiled fury in his taut fists. He's itching to defend his sister, with his bare hands if needed. Karmen watches Cass with a considering expression, likely calculating how to de-escalate.

But I need it. I need this anger, icy and sharp, to centre me, to help me lock on to what's actually important right now. Miller thinks she knows best. I think, if I'm being fair, she truly believes this will help me. Well, her good intentions can go fuck themselves.

Karmen steps in before I say it out loud. On purpose.

"Your request for my client to undergo hypnosis is duly noted. Your . . . opinions, as well. Let's set that aside for the moment and focus on facts."

"Sure." Miller sits back, her expression politely bland once more. "Where do you want to start?"

"Wait." Cass settles a fist on the table. "I still don't get it. Why are you pushing for my sister to confess to something if we don't even know if a . . . if a crime's been committed?"

"But a crime *has* been committed, Dr. Li," replies Miller. "At least three, in fact. Your parents' home was invaded and vandalized. Your sister was assaulted and possibly kidnapped. Your father is missing under suspicious circumstances. That's not a crime, technically, but I have to tell you, in my professional opinion . . . it sure smells like one."

"Inspector," Karmen interjects, "Stephen Li is missing, of course, but what makes you automatically place him in the victim category?"

"What makes you suspect otherwise?" retorts Pendelton.

Miller eyes both Cass and me, with deliberation. "Ultimately, we are in pursuit of justice for your mother—and your father if it comes to that. And, of course, for you, Cleo. How does it serve your family to leave all those dangling questions unanswered? Believe me, I've been on the force for over twenty years, and an investigator for almost eight. Somewhere down the road, you'll find yourself wishing you'd pursued every last one of them to a proper resolution."

Cass subsides then, his expression deeply troubled. He shoots me a quick glance, but I don't have anything reassuring to tell him. I'm surprised that I wish I did. But frankly, I can't spare the emotional distraction. I need to get this investigation pointed in another direction. For both our sakes.

"May we begin now?" Karmen's placid cordiality breaks the strained quiet.

"Of course," Miller replies, gesturing magnanimously.

Karmen tips their gaze downward, checking notes. "First, what have you discovered about Drew Arceneaux's alibi regarding the weekend of May 26–27?"

"It checked out," replies Pendelton. "We have multiple corroborating witnesses, plus the key card logs and video logs. He was at the office that weekend. A huge project with multiple teams. Apparently, it was all hands on deck, so everyone there has been cleared." He watches me, his face unreadable.

Miller adds, "Also, I apologize, I should've said sooner. Drew Arceneaux has been charged with assault. He's out on bail. No date on his trial yet, but Naomi can let you know. You'll be contacted by a provincial prosecutor, too."

Naomi clears her throat. "Given the video evidence, I think he'll plead guilty. That might only involve a judge, but yes, I'll keep you in the loop."

"Thank you for that." Karmen finishes a spate of typing. "Next, do you have any evidence of how Cleo arrived in Field, BC, on May 28?"

Pendelton replies, his voice without inflection, "It's a long bus ride, but doable. We checked video from the Greyhound stations in Edmonton and Lake Louise, the closest station to Field. It's not a hundred percent conclusive, but there is someone who could be Ms. Li in the Edmonton video. Small stature, hoodie, ball cap, knapsack."

"But you're not sure," Karmen clarifies.

Pendelton concedes with a nod.

"You just described the standard uniform of teenagers everywhere," retorts Cass. "Not to mention every man in a state of arrested development." He resolutely keeps his gaze on Pendelton, ignoring Karmen's possible censure. "If you can't confirm Cleo's face in the video, then you're just trying to scare her by bringing it up."

"How far," I ask, hearing Karmen sigh, "is it from Lake Louise to Field?"

"About thirty kilometres," says Miller confidently. "Walking it would be hard, yes, but not impossible. Maybe six hours, give or take. Depending on the fitness of the person."

She runs a finger along the edge of the table, her expression turning speculative. I wait for Karmen to jump in again, but they stay silent, watching us all with a thoughtful expression.

Miller says, "You conveniently sent your parents on their trip on a Friday, Cleo. I think you wanted to search their home for that lotto ticket. You see, Anna Ong confirmed for us that your mother told you where she put the ticket for safekeeping. According to her, your mother hinted that she hid the key to the safety deposit box, too. So, say you spent Saturday turning their house upside down looking for that key, the key to getting your hands on a $47.3 million lotto ticket."

Cass startles, reaching out for my hand again, squeezing hard. He gives a tiny shake of his head. I know, I know—*don't say anything. Let Miller lay it all out first*. I slide my gaze toward the laptop. We were so sure Mum wouldn't risk telling such a huge gossip like Auntie Annie, but . . . how much does she know? Would Karmen be able to convince Auntie to talk to me? Would she even tell me the truth?

I bite down on the inside of my lower lip, fighting to stay silent. Miller's already pinned this on me as it is. Betraying fresh doubts will only make it worse.

Miller continues once it's clear I'm not reacting. "That would still leave Sunday for the bus ride and the hike. The Greyhound schedule corroborates the possible timing. Maybe you also hitched a ride part of the way." She gestures at me. "No one seeing you with a thumb out on the highway would think twice about helping you. Small and dainty and Asian. Perfect damsel-in-distress bait for any self-respecting Canadian. Let's be honest here. A *stripper* even stopped for you, and she should know better."

Pendelton adds, "We know your vehicle, a 2016 Prius, remained in your neighbourhood. We saw it. We also know you didn't hotwire a car because we found no reports of abandoned vehicles in the vicinity of Field or the lodge."

"We're moving into conjecture again," says Karmen calmly. "What I hear is that you have no hard evidence that Cleo made her own way to Field. Correct?"

Miller's mouth purses for a second. "Correct." I let myself relax a fraction.

"What about anything that proves Cleo broke into her parents' home the weekend of May 26–27?"

"Forensics found plenty proving she'd been there," replies Miller.

"Which is to be expected, given her role in Glinda and Stephen's daily life," concludes Karmen.

Pendelton sits back in his chair, his hands lacing over his abdomen.

"It seems to me," says Karmen slowly, with a sideways glance at Cass, "that one could as easily theorize that Stephen Li drove back to Edmonton from Field. Cleo said there was mention of him asking the lodge staff about pharmacies, I believe? Perhaps Glinda had forgotten her insulin. That's not something she could spend a week without. Say she didn't want the hassle of filling a prescription out-of-province. From what we know of her . . . she could very well have bullied Stephen into making the ten-hour round trip to fetch her medication. That's a long time to nurse resentment, to grow it into something harsher."

They pause, their eyes moving to each of us in turn. "It could as easily have been Stephen who searched the duplex to look for that key, the one his wife could've hid from him for her own reasons." They shift. "Say Cleo discovered him in the act. It can't have been hard, their homes are connected after all. Perhaps he incapacitated her, or even deceived her into returning with him to Field. Perhaps he made her drive." They shot Miller a pointed look. "If you're entertaining theories, Inspector."

Miller shrugs, but I can see the skin around her eyes go taut. Naomi clears her throat delicately. Cass clenches his hands, over and over again. His mouth tightens.

Checking their notes, Karmen makes a mark with a pen, then continues in a sombre tone. "Dr. Rao told my clients that the cause of

Glinda Li's death was drowning. What evidence do you have that Cleo caused an insulin overdose in Glinda Li? Or that insulin was even involved at all in her death?"

"We're still investigating," Miller replies, her voice flat.

Beneath the table, I pinch my thigh to fight off a wave of light-headedness. I think it's relief, but at this point, I'm not certain anymore why I feel anything.

"I'll take that as a no then," says Karmen briskly. "All right. Let's move on to Cleo's assault."

"Yes, let's, Counsellor." Miller leans in, her eyes glinting. "Because something's been bothering me about that. Don't you think it's strange, Cleo, that your older memories still haven't returned? Rohypnol is well documented to affect *short-term* memories only, maybe only twelve hours, give or take."

"Your point, Inspector?" asks Karmen politely.

"What else is causing you to repress those other, older memories?" Miller tilts her head to one side, zeroing in on me, ignoring Karmen entirely. "The long-term ones?"

I tighten my arms over my chest.

Naomi flips a page over on her notebook, flattens it with a crackle of sound as she speaks gravely. "Traumatic experiences, things people don't want to remember because they're overwhelming. The brain can block them to help you survive."

"We are trying," says Miller forcefully, "to piece together a puzzle, Cleo. For your benefit. Not to pin a crime on you." She hesitates, her focus turning inward for a moment. "Like I said, it's not quite correct to say we *suspect* you. It's like . . ."

Pendelton leans in. "It's like there are two people, one guilty and one innocent, but they're both . . . you."

I make a face. "There's only one person. *I'd* be facing prosecution. Me."
I don't care if Karmen's displeased. I *will* speak up for myself against this
nonsense.

Cass pushes up from his seat, pacing the short width of the suddenly
claustrophobic room. Karmen watches him, unease sliding briefly across
their face. I'm not sure Cass even notices. He says, "You're putting the
cart before the horse here. Again. There's been no ruling on our mum's
death, and therefore, no indication of, of . . . foul play. Aside from which,"
he halts, facing the cops, both hands flat against the table's smooth blond
surface, *"my sister is not a murderer."*

Implacable, Miller replies, "Our job is to discover facts, not rely on
opinion, Dr. Li. It's understandable that you're loyal to your sister. Admirable, even. But we have to remain objective."

Cass straightens up, crossing his arms with a scowl.

"Speaking of facts." Karmen's cool voice breaks Miller's intensity. "Hospital results confirmed Rohypnol, and the exam suggested possible physical assault. Do you have any evidence pertaining to the perpetrator?"

"As a matter of fact," says Pendelton, "we haven't found any sign of
such person. The only prints inside and out of the Lis' car, the one currently in our forensics lab here, belong to Stephen, Glinda, and Cleopatra. No one saw her arrive. No one can speak to her being under duress."
He pauses, deliberately. "Or arriving with another person at all."

Karmen raises a forefinger. "If Cleo were brought by Stephen, oh, as
another theory might have it, they would've arrived in the middle of the
night."

Still, the hairs at the back of my neck prickle. I look from Pendelton's careful impassivity to Miller's close scrutiny. I try to collate
all the pieces of info we've talked over so far, ignoring the heaviness
threatening to crush the careful walls inside of me. I know Karmen

might very well lose it, but how can I be expected not to say something?

"You think *I* dosed myself with Rohypnol?"

"It would give you a legitimate way to avoid suspicion," replies Pendelton, matter-of-fact. "You wouldn't remember what you did to your parents. And you'd have the benefit of actually telling the truth."

"Speculation again," retorts Karmen. "Do you have evidence my client purchased Rohypnol?"

"There's a possibility," says Pendelton, voice gruff, "she found out about it through her old work." He regards me again, his eyes opaque. "One of your former co-workers was drugged and raped last year after a work party at a nightclub, a club well known to EPS as a hot spot for scoring drugs of all kinds," he finishes, "including Rohypnol."

"That doesn't sound like evidence." Karmen raises their brows. "Frankly, none of this sounds like definitive evidence for your theories about Cleo. I feel compelled to point out, there's another possible person of interest here. As I've said." They hesitate for a split second, glancing at Cass's stony expression, before finishing. "Stephen Li."

Cass all but explodes, throwing his arms up in the air. "That doesn't make any sense! What possible reason could there be for any of this?" His hip collides with his chair, rattling the table.

"Motive, you mean?" asks Miller, gaze bright. I get a sinking feeling in my gut.

Karmen sighs audibly. "Cass, please. This isn't the time."

"No," my brother shoots back. "Why aren't any of you listening to me? You don't know shit about my family."

"We know more than you'd like." Miller clasps her hands together on the table, her expression grim. "Your mother likely tried to coerce Cleo into moving. The sort of person who would easily resort to financial blackmail with *her own daughter* would surely also consider the threat of cutting her out of a will entirely." She gestures to Pendelton beside her. "We believe that's the case here. Your mother could have used that threat, Cleo, to make sure you did whatever she wanted."

She raises a hand, to stall my arguments, though I haven't made a noise. "Now I'm not saying you're greedy, but a multi-million-dollar inheritance is not nothing. In all the years I've investigated serious crimes, money has been at the root of . . . at least 85 percent of my files. It can turn good people bad, and bad situations worse. I've seen it happen. Too many times to count."

"Again," Karmen interjects, "where's your evidence?"

Speaking over them, Pendelton directs a serious gaze at Cass. "You know your mother better than anyone else in this room right now, Dr. Li. Was she capable of cutting your sister out of her will? Would she have threatened that, to get her way?"

Cass lets loose a deep, desperate growl, startling everyone into recoiling. "I can't believe this. Our mother is *dead,* and you want me to—" He whirls away, pacing to the far end of the room. "No, I will not be a party to this . . . character assassination. I can't believe you want me to *confirm* that my own mother was a horrible, cruel . . ."

He falters to a stop. A look of dawning horror replaces his scowl.

"What is it?" asks Naomi sharply. "Are you all right?"

Cass looks to me, his face blanching.

"What?" I try to interpret the sudden fear in his eyes, my heart racing again.

"I'm sorry, sis. But you said it yourself. You remembered what Mum was like . . ."

"Stop," warns Karmen. "Cass, stop talking."

I still, every part of me going cold. "You think . . . I did what they say?"

Cass hesitates, a split-split second of doubt, gone with a blink—but

I saw it. He may as well have shouted. I gasp at the needle of fear that pierces my chest.

My brother's face crumples as he cries, "No, no, no. Never." He strides to me, falling to his knees in front of my chair, and grabs my hands. "No, Cleo. I will never believe you did it. Never." He embraces me, awkward and tight, then releases me, looking fiercely into my eyes. "No, I mean . . . Mum *was* cruel sometimes. Especially to you. You told me so. Remember?"

"What?" Miller gives us each a dark look. "What did you remember, Cleo?"

Too much. Too fast. Why is Cass such a goddamned Boy Scout? I suppress a frustrated growl. God help me, I'm so twisted up, I'm looking to Karmen for guidance.

They make a face. "You should talk to me privately first."

But that will only take up more time. I'm so fucking exhausted, I want to cry.

"Cleo?" prompts Naomi gently.

Despite everything I fear about Naomi's priorities, I know she's still the most sympathetic cop in the room. She knows how hard this hit me. She was there, at my old work, in my home. . . . So I speak to her. I don't think this is going to surprise anyone. Karmen will just have to deal.

"All those people you interviewed, they're right. We didn't get along because . . . Mum was always nitpicking me. I tried to please her. I ran her errands and played chauffeur. I tried to keep my tongue, really I did, but . . . nothing I did was ever right for her. I told Cass I remembered the hurtful things Mum said to me. That's all."

Cass drops his head, ashamed, I think. "I can't help thinking how bad it must have been for Cleo. And I never knew."

Quietly, Naomi says, "I can't know what you went through, Cleo, none of us can, but I think . . . given my training in domestic violence and my experiences on the force . . . have you ever considered that what you went through was long-term emotional abuse?"

"What? No," I reply automatically, ignoring the abrupt tremor in my limbs. "She never hit me. I mean, beyond a few spankings when we were both kids, right, Cass? That was just traditional Chinese parenting. Just like criticism is normal because they wanted me to succeed and no one else was going to be as honest with me. I learned to take it. I even learned to stand up for myself *because* of it. I didn't . . ." I stammer, "cower in a corner or anything. You heard, I argued with her all the time. I'm nobody's *victim*."

Next to me, Cass fumbles for his chair and sinks into it, his face dark and furrowed into a deep, unsettling frown. He doesn't meet my eyes.

"Cass, no." I frown at him. "They don't understand. They can't. Not even Naomi. Asians aren't all the same. You know that." I can't hide my contempt at the very idea. "There was no . . . *abuse*," I repeat. I can't believe my brother is taking this seriously. "Mum could be an asshole, fine. From everything I'm learning, so could I. But . . . abuse? Really?"

"Being an asshole," says Naomi firmly, "doesn't equal deserving—"

Miller stirs abruptly. "It's natural for you to want to defend her, Cleo. She was your mother, after all. Even if not, it's been known that some-times an abused person will start to feel an . . . affinity or sympathy for their abuser. Like a sort of survival mechanism."

I grimace at her, shaking my head. Naomi gapes at Miller, though she swiftly tucks it away when she catches me watching.

"Stockholm Syndrome," murmurs Pendelton, as though just recalling the term.

Cass starts forward, gesturing broadly with his hands. "Come *on*, that's been debunked for years now. Some misogynist therapist made it up because he preferred to spread the lie that a woman hostage had a mental disorder. When the truth was, she was smarter and more level-headed than he and all the other men involved in the situation had been. He just couldn't admit it." Cass glares at Pendelton with disdain.

Pendelton stares back, unperturbed. Miller blinks. Naomi keeps her head down, eyes on her notebook.

Karmen speaks into the silence. "I feel compelled to point out two things. One, no one in this room is qualified to assess my client's mental health or the parameters of her relationship with the deceased. Having said that, my second point is that the characterization offered by Constable Aoki could also very well apply to Stephen Li."

"I'm sorry," replies Naomi softly. My hackles rise at the note of contrite submission in her voice. I flick my gaze at Miller, who watches me closely. Nothing indicates she's even heard. Maybe she takes Naomi's apology as her due. I don't know. And I don't care. I shouldn't. Naomi might've been a good friend, but now it's pretty goddamned clear she has to be a cop.

Naomi continues, "I thought it an appropriate consideration to bring up. Not just for a criminal investigation, but also for your mental health, Cleo. I'm not claiming a professional diagnosis."

"Damn straight you're not." Cass shoots Naomi a disapproving glare. "I don't care if I'm a broken record. Cleo needs to see a therapist, not be manipulated with psychobabble and unsubstantiated theories." His lip curls on the last word.

Miller straightens up in her seat, cool and composed. "We understand your concerns, Dr. Li, but to be honest," she aims a narrow look at me, "right now, I'm more interested in the fact that you lied to us, Cleo."

THIRTY-FOUR

Karmen lets out a sigh. "Cass, Cleo, not another word. I mean it." They shift their gaze a little to the left on the screen. "I need to speak with my clients privately again, Inspector. Please stop recording."

I expect her to refuse. Hell, I expect Cass to refuse, too, but he only crosses his arms over his chest, his face set in belligerent lines.

Surprisingly, Miller only gives a curt nod. "Get us when you're done, like last time." The three cops shuffle out of the room, leaving behind only a faint, acrid scent—frustration.

It's impossible to tell for sure, from the angle of their eyes on the screen, but I know without a doubt that Karmen's frowning at me. "What part of *don't talk to them directly* don't you understand?"

"That was so much bullshit," I retort. "I can't just sit still and take it, Karmen."

"Well, you'd better start practising, Cleo. That inspector has a target ready and she's dying to slap it on you. Stop shooting off your mouth and let me do the talking. That's what Cass hired me for. Let me do my job. Try not to be such a hard-ass about it."

"Don't take that tone with me, *Kong*." I bare my teeth in a fake smile.

"As if." Karmen rolls their eyes. "Sheathe your claws, Cleo. Now, I asked for this time so you two could simmer down before we continue. It won't do any good if you let them rile you up." Their gaze shifts subtly. "Cass? Are you okay? Can you keep your cool?"

"No," answers my brother, defiant. "The cops are accusing Cleo of murdering Mum, while *you're* accusing our dad. How the fuck am I supposed to be okay with any of that?"

"They've got nothing but guesses," counters Karmen calmly. "They're dangling theories like bait, hoping to hook you with something. Stay calm. Listen for the subtext. It doesn't matter how plausible they sound. If they don't have facts . . ." Karmen shrugs. "They're just fishing."

"You make it sound so cut and dried, Karmen," I reply, "but I don't trust it. I can't. Miller's fixed on my supposed guilt. They're not even talking about Cass anymore. Not that I want them to," I add hastily.

"We'll ask them about that," Karmen replies, "in due course. Don't worry. My guess is they've cleared Cass as far as May 26–27 is concerned."

Cass pushes up from his chair. "No, this isn't happening." He paces along one wall.

I share a worried look with Karmen. "Cass." I sigh. "Talk to me."

He glowers at my put-upon, impatient tone.

I am so bloody tired. Why am I fighting with him? Why am I struggling so hard with what to say, when to say it, and how? When can this relentless, cautious parsing of my words and thoughts finally end?

Temptation hits me again, the urge to talk without the careful filters. Oh God, the sheer relief of unburdening. If there were ever a time, this might be it. Karmen's bound by confidentiality. Cass . . . well, it's not the same, but he'd never believe the worst of me, right?

Cass continues his pacing, muttering under his breath now. He won't look at me.

I squeeze the nape of my neck, trying to relax the building headache. No. Never mind. He looks about two seconds from falling apart. I can't risk it. *We* can't risk it.

Besides, it's pretty fucking clear he needs *my* support right now.

So I shove every scrap of complaint, of exhaustion and whiny if-only into some dark mental corner. For fuel, I grab onto that anger Miller so carelessly conjured. I push up to standing. I remind myself of who I am.

I intercept Cass halfway back from the end of the room, grabbing gentle hold of his hands. He tries to make fists, to pull away. He tries to hide how hard he's trembling.

I tighten my grip. I lean toward his weary, panicked eyes. I stay silent, waiting. When I see his eyes finally focus on my face, I make sure to enunciate clearly.

"Get it the fuck together, Cass."

It's a gamble, I know it is, but this is the sister he knows. Perversely, it may be the sister he trusts best. All this time, I've been worried about how far I could trust him. It never occurred to me 'til this moment. He needs to know he can trust me, too. We can't stick together, not for the long haul, unless he does.

So here it is. The moment of truth. Not the way I'd've wanted it, but let's be honest. This isn't anything one can plan for.

"Cass," I repeat, "are you listening? Can you stop freaking the fuck out for a moment and hear this?"

He stares at me, blinking, blinking, blinking, rigid and silent. His brain's resetting, I don't know. "We don't have time for this. C'mere." I lead him back to our chairs, where Karmen can see us again. I flick a glance at them, praying they're smart enough to let me handle this. Cass follows reluctantly, his feet literally dragging over the industrial carpeting.

I tug on his hands. "This will be hard for you to hear, but I need you to understand, okay? You need to be able to choose, freely."

That pulls a startled frown from him. "What are you talking about?"

"Cleo," says Karmen carefully, "what are you doing?"

I can't overthink this, I'll lose my nerve. I can't unload every single truth I have, but I can do this for him. I can help him choose his own limits.

I leap off the proverbial cliff.

"If my memories returned, if Dr. Rao rules homicide, if I did what Miller believes . . ." Cass's face grows more horrified with each phrase. He twitches his hands, but I won't let go. "Karmen, what would you advise?"

In my periphery, I see Karmen shift, distancing from the screen. "That would depend," they answer with deliberate caution, "on how much the RCMP get as far as evidence goes." After a delicate pause, "And what they can prove."

Cass's mouth drops open, his bloodshot eyes wide with shock. "No, you . . . What are you saying, sis?" The words tremble in the air between us.

"I'm talking about the worst case, little brother. The time for avoidance is way over. It's time to face it. I might be guilty. My memories might return." I huff out an exhalation, hoping it settles the flutters in my heart. "What do you want to do if that happens?"

"But it won't," he retorts. "How could it? How could you possibly—"

"This is about giving you a choice, Cass. I know all about the opposite, trust me, and I can't do the same to you. I *can't*." I cock my head toward the laptop. I try not to dwell on all the things I might fuck up even more. I can *feel* my throat quivering as I say, "Karmen, hypothetically, if that happened, would it be better to admit to remembering? Or to play dumb until—"

Cass wrenches his hands out of my grasp, shoving away from the table. "Stop. Stop talking. Now. I don't want to hear it."

"You can't keep your head in the sand," I say, exasperation hardening my voice. "And I won't force you to stand by me if—"

"I don't want to know the worst," he interrupts, voice pitched low. Like he's talking to himself. He grabs handfuls of hair, pulling upward until his face distorts.

I exchange a look of alarm with Karmen, but we both remain silent.

Cass turns on his heel, as though he might leave altogether. Throwing his hands up, he whirls back around. He grips the top of the upholstered chair beside me, knuckles whitening as he kneads the fabric.

"It's too fucking late to pretend I don't know what the cops and Karmen think about all this," he tells me intently. The chair fabric squeaks beneath his fingers. "Maybe it's cold and heartless, but what difference does that make? Really? All these . . . theories and . . . and guesses and insane speculation. I just—I can be here for you, I *will* support you, but this . . . this is the only way I can do it." He stills, then takes a deep breath. "The dead are gone, sis. I have to be concerned with the *living*. Do you understand?" He stares hard at me, unyielding, demanding I leave off.

We lock gazes for an eternity. The fan in Cass's laptop whirrs on, like a mosquito hovering in the otherwise silent room.

Pressure builds in my head. Tension knots in my shoulders, my gut, my hands. I watch my brother's lean face slowly tighten, his internal agony disappearing by microns behind a mask of stone. His laugh lines morph and mutate, become signs of his distress instead. That, more than anything, breaks my resolve.

"Okay," I reply quietly. Even I can recognize I've pushed him to his limit. I guess the difference is, now I care. I reach out and touch his wrist, a feeble attempt at solace.

Cass deflates, the harshness on his face dissipating. He drops his head into his hands for a moment, then rallies to grab his chair and sit. "Okay." I hear the tremor in his voice.

Karmen clears their throat. "Do you still want me to answer?"

I close my eyes and take a deep breath, shoring up my strength. Cass has chosen what he can live with. I'm glad for it, glad to know, but the rest is still up to me.

"No," I say softly, "never mind. I'm not thinking straight, sorry."

"Good," Karmen agrees briskly. "Let's not get distracted. They're testing you pretty hard, Cleo, but I don't hear a lot of actual evidence. Until the coroner rules on your mother's death, this line of questioning is nothing but a fishing expedition."

"It feels more like a fox hunt," I mutter, trying to shake off the returning weight of exhaustion. How much longer will this drag on?

"Cleo has a point," Cass adds, his voice tired. "Miller seems hellbent on getting some kind of confession. Do you think she'll let it go? If Dr. Rao rules . . . it accidental?" His cheeks darken.

Karmen nods confidently. "They don't have the budget for investigations into accidental deaths, I'm afraid. If anything, they should be concentrating on your assault file, Cleo."

I consider Miller's attitude so far. I shake my head. "But it's basically all connected—in their minds." I shiver. "They'll keep hammering on about hypnosis, but they'll say it's for my case. . . ."

Karmen makes a face. "They know as well as I do it wouldn't hold water. No court in Canada will accept evidence or statements garnered from hypnosis. I wanted to understand their approach, so I kept quiet on this point earlier."

Cass scowls. "So, what *is* their approach with pushing hypnosis then? To dig up leads?"

"It seems likely," says Karmen evenly. "I didn't hear either of them actually say it was for official testimony."

"Those fuckers." It sounds hollow, though, as scraped-out as I feel. I scrabble for my earlier fury, hoping to restoke a bit of righteous indignation or some such. I pretend the roiling in my guts is only weariness. I pretend I can trust Karmen to correctly predict Miller's next steps.

None of it quells this restless, relentless anxiety.

Miller's already proven her persistence, several times over. In her eyes, I'm far from innocent. If there's no crime against my mother, if Rao rules the death accidental, I don't think Miller will simply let it go. She's *invested* in her theory. She thinks I have a guilty conscience that needs clearing—whether I remember it or not. Hell, she thinks the memory loss proves her point. She's certain she's helping me because, of course, she knows better. God help us when a well-meaning white person wants to play saviour.

Too bad for her, waiting for a rescue will never be in my nature. I need to *do* something.

Miller controls the narrative. She reels out the story. Karmen's job is to react, to point out the gaps. The framework's set for them, their respective roles laid out by the rules of the system.

I *cannot* sit on the margins and hope for the best. Better than anyone, Cass understands that about me. He'll back me up, no matter what. I know that now. But he doesn't have the stomach for what we need, and I can't even blame him. I wish I had the privilege of choice, too.

I need a way forward, one that doesn't risk prison or leave me peering over my shoulder for the rest of my life. I need to prove to Miller I'm cooperating in good faith. I've been careful with my boundaries, but I think . . . I think she wants to see me pushed to my limit. What satisfaction is there for a self-appointed "saviour" to rescue someone from mere inconvenience? No. They want to see trauma, front and centre.

Inspiration strikes, desperate and twisted, turning my knees to jelly. I shove my fears aside. I need to be clinical, like Helen Rao in her pristine white lab coat, bulwarked against death and misery. I force myself to think carefully through the terror, to consider all the possible angles, to weigh the risks.

I turn my focus outward again, back to the room. Karmen's watching me, narrow-eyed and contemplative. They're not the one I need to convince, however.

"I . . . I have an idea."

Cass draws his brows together at my abrupt pronouncement. I take a breath to steady the sudden squirming of my conscience, like chilly fingers grabbing my guts.

"I'm sorry." I wince. "You're going to hate it, little brother."

THIRTY-FIVE

Naturally, Miller champions me putting myself at risk for a good cause, while Cass argues, Karmen demands reassurances from Miller, and Naomi's brow furrows deeper and deeper in silence. Pendelton didn't return with them this time. Who knows what he'd think.

It takes ten increasingly angry minutes for Cass to realize I won't budge. Then Miller bids us farewell with a promise to Karmen that Naomi will connect with them to confirm the arrangements for tomorrow.

Karmen gives me one long assessing look before they disappear from the screen.

Outside, I realize with a jolt that it's a glorious evening, with the sun still on its way down and a light breeze smelling of fresh water. I stumble along beside Cass, his strides longer than mine anyway, but now worse so because he is well and truly *pissed*.

He reaches the station wagon and unlocks the doors, sliding into the driver's side without waiting for me. I hurry, forcing myself to jog to the passenger side in case he's furious enough to take off without me.

Sitting silent as Cass jerks the car into traffic, I tell myself to be present, to focus on what's in front of me, my brother's fuming excepted. Tomorrow will come soon enough, and with it, my possibly harmful, definitely crazy idea. Or rather, going through with it. My knees start trembling again.

So I think of hotel room service and a hot bath, of a fluffy bathrobe and solitude. The hotel's on the lake, which is only a few blocks away. I can be in my own space in less than twenty minutes. I mean, it will be borrowed, but at least I'll be alone. I almost let myself smile in anticipation. It's better than crying.

But there's no lake in sight when Cass parks on the curb a few short minutes later.

"I thought the parking lot was right beside the hotel." I crane my neck every which way, trying to figure out where we are.

"We need to talk, sis, and I'd rather do it where I won't be tempted to completely lose my shit on you." I can see the effort it takes him to relax his stiffened jaw. "I really need some noise and people, normal ones. Food will help us both. Food and a drink," he mutters.

He opens his door without further discussion. I consider refusing to cooperate, but I recognize the unfair position I've put him in. It doesn't feel right to be a child about this now. I scrub at my face, pushing aside the lure of that hot bath, of peace and quiet. I scramble out of the car.

Halfway down the next block, he gestures for me to precede him through the open doorway of a pub-type restaurant, its two doors of heavy carved wood propped open with stones the size of basketballs. Smooth and prettily multicoloured, they could've come straight from the lakeshore. Or a river.

If Cass sees my shudder, he doesn't comment, ushering me through to the inside with a touch to my shoulder. The interior is open and bright, with windows standing open onto the sidewalk. Early evening sunlight gleams off polished brass railings and sparkling glassware. The room hums with lively conversation.

A group of five East Asians mills around in front of the hostess stand in the foyer. I see small Korean flags on two of their immaculate athletic jackets. From the interior of the restaurant, a short teenager with bobbed blond hair approaches the stand, a stack of folio menus in hand. Her gaze flicks over us, counting heads. "For seven?"

I scowl. Cass coughs, gesturing to the tourists. "We're just two. But they were here first."

The white girl shifts her attention to the larger group. "Five?" She raises her hand, fingers splayed. "This way, please." She doesn't wait for an acknowledgement. The Koreans give us quick nods of thanks before following her, swivelling their heads to take in the buffed and shining decor as they walk.

Seconds later, a tall smiling waiter, all blue eyes and charming black curls, shows us to a table for two by one of the many open windows. As he passes our menus to us, Cass asks for a pint of something or other. I ask for ice water with lemon. Skimming the menu, I choose something at random when our drinks arrive.

Cass watches the waiter retreat out of earshot, gritting his teeth. "I still don't understand why you're risking a major setback to satisfy the cops' curiosity. You could suffer serious mental and emotional damage. Maybe irreparable." He lowers his voice to a pointed whisper as people walk past on the sidewalk outside. "It's irresponsible. I can't fucking believe Karmen didn't have an aneurism over it."

"Karmen trusts that I've considered the risks." *I hope.* "Aside from which, this won't be for the cops, Cass. It's for me." I pause, trying to work past my exhaustion, and his. Does he really not get it? Do I truly have to spell it out?

I look at him, really look, searching past his drawn features. I think I see something of the little brother I remember, before he grew up and moved on, before everything turned to shit. Even if I don't recall every last detail of our childhood together, I can remember his many kindnesses these past days, his unwavering loyalty, his choice to stick with me.

So, if I'm doing this, if I want to build a future for myself, with my brother and Etta and baby nieces or nephews in it, I owe him more than derision. A pang of remorse hits me square in the chest. This thing I'm doing tomorrow . . . Things will never be the same for my little brother again. He might end up hating me because of it. If this is our last civil conversation, I owe him as much of the truth as he can take.

Scanning the tables around us, I keep my voice lowered. "It doesn't matter what the police think, Cass, we've been through this. Miller's not going to let this go, not as long as there are no other alternative . . . suspects." I pause, giving him time to reply, but he won't meet my gaze. "And we both know innocent people can get convicted. I don't want to be that kind of historical footnote."

Cass shakes his head, vehement. "You won't because they have no case against you. There's no way." He leans toward me over the table, his eyes somehow blazing. *"No fucking way."*

A burst of laughter draws my attention away, saving Cass from a tirade, and possibly both of us from being tossed from the pub altogether for making a scene.

Across the restaurant, I spy the Koreans laughing and taking selfies with their food. Their clipped speech is musical, full of playfulness. It reminds me of Miller's wild misconceptions about Cantonese. I pull a frown, thinking once more of all the ways she—and Pendelton—could get so much wrong about me. My knees start pumping, trying to burn off the sudden anxiety bouncing around my insides. It's either the knees, or I vomit.

Cass and I sit in tense silence, studiously staring out the window in opposite directions until our food arrives. I take a few bites of my fish fry. It's perfectly done, crisp and flaky and moist, but I can't stop thinking of rushing waters. Of rivers. My appetite dries up. I push the rest of my meal around on the plate.

I consider how to handle my brother. From where I sit, he's being a pain in the ass. If he doesn't want to know all the details, he should bloody well trust me to know the risks. Christ. Will I have to test him every single time something difficult comes up? The enormity of that threatens to sink me.

·I give up on my dinner. I fold my paper napkin, set it under one side of my plate. Cass swallows his bite of cheeseburger, eyes me silently as he chases it with a mouthful of some craft beer or other, golden and clear. Abruptly, he squints as his eyes are hit by the reflecting sunlight from a passing car. I track the bar of light as it scythes across the rest of the restaurant behind him.

My eyes prickle, maybe with tears, maybe with grit blown in by the lovely evening breeze. I can't begin to describe how tired I feel. I swipe at my eyes with a rumpled sleeve. I just wish I had some certainty.

"Me, too, sis, me too," murmurs Cass.

Oh fuck me. Again?

It suddenly feels such an insurmountable burden to keep everything to myself, to keep all the lines of conversation straight, to keep track of internal thoughts and fears versus the all-important external show of confidence. I sigh, and almost laugh at how long-suffering I sound. It pulls me out of the threatening funk.

Trust runs both ways. It has to.

"They're right, you know." I look up at Cass, keeping my voice low. "Mum threatened to keep my money from the duplex if I didn't move with them." I fidget with my napkin, put it back on my lap. "And she threatened to cut me out of her will. Both their wills." I pause. "I don't know if she went through with it." I slide my gaze away, pressing at my temples. "Not that I want to celebrate remembering this," I mutter.

He curses under his breath. "I don't know what to say."

Figures. I drop my gaze to my plate. The one time I'm actually hoping for comfort. The one time I'm willing to accept it. The plate blurs in front of me. Why can't things be easy? I bite my lip, holding back the tears. *Why couldn't Mum just leave me be?*

"What would you do?" The words spill out before I even know they were waiting. Before I have a chance to rethink them. "If I'm out of the will, but you're not?"

Cass reels back as though I've slapped him, his expression flitting from shocked to hurt, before hardening into granite.

I blink, wide-eyed, my stomach roiling with alarm. "Never mind. I don't even know why I asked that. Forget I said anything."

"I can't," he says, biting off each word. "You can't take back an accusation like that. I can't *un*-hear it."

"What? What accusation?" Sweat breaks out along my hairline. My shoulders jerk, spastic. "I didn't accuse you of anything."

"You may as well have. Do you honestly think I'd be okay if Mum cut you out of her will?" He curls his lip. "Maybe you really do remember everything now. You sound just like your old self."

I see four heads at a neighbouring table swivel to stare at me. I cover my chilly fear with fury. "What the fuck are you talking about?" I whisper heatedly.

"What kind of person do you think I am, that I'd just go along with Mum's crazy-ass threats? That as long as I'm taken care of, I'm good?"

"But that's not—"

Cass cuts through the air between us with a hand. "It may as well have been. For fuck's sake, I shouldn't be surprised, though, right? You're always only out for number one. And you always assumed everybody else did likewise. Maybe you're just not capable of considering other people."

My temper snaps back before I can reconsider. I am so fucking tired of his goody-two-shoes act. "Does it really matter? I assume she's giving you more than whatever she was originally giving me, anyway, since you're the boy. That's how it works, right? Daughters are second class."

Cass pushes his plate away, balling up his napkin and tossing it on top of his half-finished burger. "That's not my fault, sis."

"But if you benefit, it makes you part of the problem." Why am I pushing him? I can't seem to make my tongue still. I sit on my hands, as if it might make a difference.

He lowers his voice to an angry buzz. "Are you expecting me to refuse an inheritance in the millions? Seriously? Don't even try to tell me *you* would." He leans in, tapping the table with a finger. "That money will set up generations beyond me. Etta and I would be able to do some real good in the world, too. Charitable foundations for women and children, for queer communities. It's not just about our little fucked-up family, sis."

"But it's not fair, Cass." I rear back, blinking, startled by my outburst, by the venom in my words.

The waiter approaches. "Everything all right?" He eyes Cass narrowly, before turning a concerned smile on me. "Do you need anything?"

I free my hands, take up my napkin, and indicate I'm done with my food, giving a tiny shake of my head. Cass asks for another pint. The waiter's mouth purses for a blink of an eye, but he bustles away, our plates in hand. I sit, folding and refolding my napkin, watching my brother refuse to look at me, his jaw stiff with fury. The silence stretches, tension snapping between us, until the waiter returns with the second pint.

"Nothing for you, miss? You sure?" he asks, a white knight interested in rescuing the poor damsel he sees in me.

"No, thanks, I'm fine," I reply clearly. "Really."

"Okay, well, if you need me," the waiter gives me a pointed look, "just give a wave. I'll keep an eye on your table."

Cass watches the waiter's retreating back for a second, his expression sour, before regarding me with tired eyes. "Life isn't fair, sis. We've all learned that lesson by now." His mouth turns down at the corners. "It's not about the will. We both know that." At my disbelieving expression, he raises his hands to chest level, palms out. "Fine, it's partially about the will, but you and I both know you've been waiting to unload on me for years. Right?"

I can't stop the blast of resentment. "You were lucky you got out, Cass. Don't deny it. And don't pretend you wouldn't be as bitter if our situations were reversed."

"I could argue equally that you have no idea what it's like to be disowned. To have your father refuse to take your phone calls. To have to explain why your parents aren't at your wedding. To have him ignore you *to your face* when you try to speak to him. As if you're invisible to him. As if you don't exist. As if you mean nothing."

"So what?" My hand fists on the tabletop. "We had shitty parents and now we're fighting over who had it worse? It's a fool's game, don't you see? I just want you to understand it was horrible for me, being left to take care of their every stupid little need, like a servant. When you left, I had no one to back me up."

"When I left, *I* had no one to back me up."

"It's not the same. Mum was still talking to you. So was I."

He shakes his head, the corners of his eyes tight with sorrow. "The saddest thing, sis, is they would've treated you the same fucking way even if I *had* stayed. That's the shittiest truth there is about all this. And I hate to even think it, but Naomi might not have been far off the mark about long-term abuse and trauma."

I narrow my eyes at him.

He huffs out a breath, smelling of yeast and hops. "But let's get one thing straight between us. Whatever fucked-up traditionalist attitudes Mum and Dad held, and put into their wills, I had nothing to do with it. How they treated you was insanely shitty. How Dad treated me, also fucked up. In a strange, messed-up way, we're even on that score. What's not fair, sis, is you resenting me for your own lack of courage."

My entire body flushes hot. "What *lack of courage*? What are you talking about?"

"You could have left. Once you started making your own money. You could've moved out, like any regular grown-up would do." A forefinger taps the table's glossy top with every word. "Why didn't you?"

I blink at him, frowning now, feeling truly bewildered. "I couldn't. Who would've taken care of them?"

"Jesus, sis. Denial, much? Be honest with yourself, like *really* honest. How old were Mum and Dad when you started your first high-paying salaried job? Barely in their fifties? Far from old and infirm." He pins me with a glower. "They emigrated when they were in their twenties. You don't think they had enough English to get by? Come *on*. Dad's a mechanical engineer, for fuck's sake. He's plenty capable. And Mum works a service job, dealing with people. In English."

"But . . . I . . . it was hard for them. That's why they had me write up their cheques and fill out government forms. They were afraid of making mistakes."

"Because it was easier *for you* to do it. Not because they *couldn't*. I mean, use your head. There's nothing you did for them that they outright couldn't do for themselves. Or ask friends to help with. They know plenty of Chinese professionals. If I were really honest—" He holds up his hands. "Never mind."

I glare. "As if they'd ever let their Chinese friends know their private business."

"You're missing the point. I'm not saying you should have cut them off. Which I didn't do, for the record. *Dad* disowned *me*, remember? I'm saying there's some part of you that enjoys feeling indispensable." He jabs a finger in my direction. "*That's* why you stay. You like the feeling of being needed. And Mum gave you that fix, every single day."

Now *I* feel as though I've been slapped full in the face. I swear my ears are even ringing. I look down at the table, press my fingers to the sides of my face. My jaw feels hard as stone beneath my fingertips.

"They treated me like a maid when I was a child." I lift my head to meet his eyes. "When I didn't clean something right, Mum whipped me with that fucking bamboo feather duster. Don't you remember that?" More blood fills my face, hot and prickling.

"She caned me, too, sis." Cass's face darkens. "Of course I fucking remember it."

"Then how can you say I was a coward? I stayed to be the best daughter I could. I tried, hard. It took bravery for me to stand my ground whenever Mum shouted insults at me. I didn't just take it, like Dad. I told her—" I shake my head abruptly.

"What's the use? She never hit you as hard or as often. She never got on your case as bad. She never shit on you—because you happened to be born with a penis. You'll never know what it was like, between her and me. *That's* the point I'm making, Cass. It's not fair she cut me out of her will, especially after everything I put up with. It's not fair that you come waltzing back into the fold, and everything's forgiven, just because you're having a baby. As though you were never gone. As though Dad didn't lose his fucking mind when you came out to them."

"What the fuck do you want me to say? I'm not apologizing for being bisexual. I'm not apologizing for being a man. I'm not apologizing for our parents' backward views. Those are not choices I made. They're just facts."

"So where does that leave me? And what about all your talk about sticking together? If you get the lion's share of that inheritance . . ."

"Then what? You'll disown me? Trust me, I'll survive." He gestures to the waiter, requests our cheque. Coldly, he says to me, "Something's come up, with Etta and the baby. She needs me to get home tomorrow. After you finish up . . . whatever the hell you're doing at the police lab tomorrow morning, we're driving to Lethbridge." He takes care of our tab with a few bills and hands it all to the waiter with a terse thanks. "I wanted to talk it over, work out our plan for the next few days, but this didn't go the way I hoped."

"But we haven't even talked about Dad. Cass, we need them to keep looking for him. We need to know if he's still alive, or, or . . ." I grip the table's edge. "It's important."

"Why? Because you're worried about the will?" He mutters a curse. "Let me recap where we are right now in this conversation. *You* resent me for something that's got nothing to do with me. *I* think you've got your head up your ass. This is not a *let's agree to disagree and move on* kind of moment."

I stiffen in my seat. "Fine. I can make my own way home."

Cass shakes his head before I'm even done talking. "And have you accuse me of abandoning you? What kind of a sucker do you think I am?"

I don't trust myself to reply with a civil tongue.

THIRTY-SIX

Cass—

I'm not going with you to Lethbridge tomorrow. I'm going straight home by myself in the morning. Thank you for everything you've already done for me. I know I'll be asking for more in the weeks and months to come. I'm not running away, please trust me on this. I just feel like I haven't had a second alone for days now and I can't deal with all the noise anymore. I don't have much more time left in my home and I miss my space.

I'm sorry I pushed so hard. I'm sorry I'm such an asshole. We both know I can't promise it'll be the last time, but I can promise that it doesn't mean anything. We're still family. You're still the better man. I'm still stuck with you.

Etta and the baby need you. They don't need me to tag along. I'm sure Etta wouldn't have called you back home unless she's worried about something important. You should be with them. I can deal with the Edmonton stuff.

Also, I've decided to put myself out of my misery tonight. I can't wait. I'll drive myself nuts thinking about it all night. I've called Miller and she's setting everything up now, instead of in the morning. Don't worry,

*I can handle myself. I'll text you when I get home. I'm still welcome to
stay with you at the end of the month, right?*

*(And don't send me angry texts or leave angry voicemails all day
tomorrow!)*

Cleo.

Through the glass doors of the plain brick building that houses the
regional forensics lab, I see Pendelton raise a hand in greeting. He waves
a pale grey key card along the door frame. One door slides open and he
gestures for me to enter. I watch him as he gives the closed door a tap,
making sure it's properly shut behind me once I'm inside.

I follow as he leads me deeper into the small lobby. "Thanks for doing
this now, and on short notice."

He shrugs. "If you think now is the best time, then we're all for it.
We're lucky Shae's on such good terms with everybody here."

"But not you?" Am I making small talk? Really? I curse myself silently.

"I get along just fine."

There's too much else to say, it seems, and all dangerous territory, so I
save my breath. Pendelton seems to agree, ushering me without another
word out of the lobby through a plain, old-fashioned door—it even has
a knob.

Miller's waiting for us on the other side, down a no-frills hallway,
with fluorescent lights, walls painted a flat grey, and industrial carpeting
in a weirdly indeterminate shade of blue. Not the sort of place to have
wall sconces or framed paintings. I recognize the low hum of a quiet
office building with practically no people in it, its ventilation systems and
lights working in the background.

"Hi." Miller sounds matter-of-fact, not at all bothered that I've dragged her out here at almost nine o'clock in the evening. She's in the same clothes as earlier. Like her partner, still a matching pair. Pendelton brushes past me and taps his key card against the small black reader mounted next to the door beside Miller.

He holds the door open, eyeing me with his dark, flat gaze. I peer into the room as I enter, noting high ceilings, dark grey flooring, more fluorescent lighting.

It's a large warehouse of a room, just like I've seen on TV shows about crime labs. Though the lighting here is of course much less dramatically contrived. A wide pull-down garage door is at the far left, about thirty feet away. Our footsteps echo off what looks and feels like poured-concrete flooring, smooth and hard and unforgiving. To the right of me, maybe ten feet away, I see a line of rooms, each one fronted and separated from its neighbour by full-glass walls. Desks, counters, stools, and lab equipment sit ready for tomorrow's workload, or so I presume.

"This way." Miller leads me toward the left, where I see two people waiting, chatting in low tones. Behind them is my parents' silver RAV4.

My steps falter. My heart picks up the slack, triple-time.

Pendelton makes brief, cordial introductions to the two lab technicians. I forget their names as soon as I hear them. Distracted, uncertain why they're here, I thank them anyway. Habit, I suppose. You never know what white people will hold against you.

I can't stop staring at the car. Its metallic exterior and tinted windows are dulled by streaks of dust and dirt, though the tires look freshly washed, their rubber gleaming darkly in the overhead lights. I walk toward the little silver SUV, strangely reluctant, the straps of my purse seeming to drag at my shoulder all of a sudden.

Slowly, I put my hand out toward the driver-side door, then snatch it back. Fuck. I don't know if I'm ready for this. I thought I'd gone over it enough in my head, but the reality . . .

Whirling away, I stand with hands fisted, swallowing against the surge up my throat. I thought I had myself under control. God*damn*it. I need to handle this just right or I might never get the chance to go home.

Maybe I should've waited 'til morning after all, not rushed out while my head's a maelstrom from arguing with Cass. Not while my heart— my poor fracturing heart's nevertheless working like hell to break right out of my chest.

"Cleo?" Miller's voice seems so far away. "Are you sure about this?"

Jesus. I think she's sincerely concerned.

I scrub at my face with both hands, pushing back my shoulders. I can do this. I have to. Forward is the only way. I pivot on my heels, facing the car again, trying to tame my breathing. I stride stiffly to the driver-side door and snatch it open.

The smell of chemicals, acrid in my nostrils, and also an underlying mustiness.

I search the interior with what feel like painfully new eyes. In the flashback, the seat covers are invisible in the dark. Now, they're a plain medium grey, with thin pinstriping in one shade darker. I touch the side of the driver's seat, a sense of unreality vying with a feeling of familiarity as comforting as pulling my hair up into a ponytail. The seat fabric glides, soft and slightly fuzzy beneath my fingertips.

Light-headedness threatens at the edges of my skull. I ignore it by climbing up and inside the car, my purse strap pulling down on one shoulder. I extricate myself from its double loop handles and drop it onto the passenger seat.

I ratchet the driver's seat forward and close the door, then open it again, looking at Pendelton. "Key?"

Miller gestures with her chin. "Should be in there." She walks around the front hood, her stride neither hurried nor slow, her gaze locked on me.

I look around the centre console area, find the black rectangular key in the small cubby below the radio/CD player combo. I hit the START button to turn on the electricals so I can roll down the windows and air the staleness out a little. A burst of chilly air hits me in the forehead, teasing out strands of hair. I feel them tickling the contours of my face.

Miller opens the passenger-side door and slides in before I have a chance to have an opinion about it. She moves my purse from the seat into the footwell. With a shiver, I hit the AC off, roll down the windows, close the driver-side door.

She says, "You doing all right in here? You still sure this is where your flashback takes place?"

I manage a quick nod, my hands fisting momentarily until I force them to relax.

Three feet away, Pendelton stands with his hands in his pockets, watching me with his partner. The lab techs remain behind him, whispering to one another, curiosity clear in the way they peer around Pendelton to catch sight of me.

A bubble of irrational laughter lodges in my throat. I think if I try to swallow it, it'll just come right back up, with interest. So I let it out, masking it as a harsh cough.

Miller swivels until she's sitting sideways in her seat, one ankle tucked neatly beneath the other knee. I notice her one concession to the late hour: ballerina flats in black leather. Her foot looks neat and slim. She waits for me to meet her gaze. "I know this is your idea, Cleo, but if it's too overwhelming, we can stop any time. There's no shame in knowing your limits."

"No, I'm fine." My guts churn so much with nerves, I don't even bother rising to the bait of her condescension. *Concentrate.* "I want to do this," I tell her earnestly. "I need to."

Miller wears a strange expression, like *atta-girl*, like she's . . . proud of me?

I clench my jaw. Maybe I'm not that impervious to her condescension after all.

"Okay, we'll go slow," she says. "You tell me what you remember, and I'll ask questions to clarify as needed." She quirks her mouth into a reassuring smile. "That's how you want to do this, right?"

"Yes," I croak. I try again, clearing my throat. "I think, maybe if I'm here, in this seat, I can try to . . . place myself back to that time and . . . I might be able to remember."

"Well, it's really brave of you to try this, Cleo. I'm ready whenever you are. Just say the word." She fishes her phone from a pocket. Frowning, I watch her tap to open the camera app.

"Wait, no, you can't record this." I gulp.

"We need an official record. Your lawyer agreed, remember? Insisted, really. As they should have." Miller sounds like an elementary school teacher, using an exaggeratedly patient tone. "This is a pretty risky gambit you've chosen, Cleo. We need to make sure it's properly documented. So everything's aboveboard. For everyone's protection."

Right. There's no way I'm putting myself on video for this, though. The thought of close scrutiny like that, recorded for anyone to dissect—

"Okay . . . what if it's only audio? Just an audio recording?" My voice shakes, but only a little.

"I can live with that." She flashes a small smile of satisfaction.

As I settle deeper into the driver's seat and rest my hands lightly on the steering wheel, my heart rate abruptly skyrockets once more. I feel it pounding in my throat, flushing my face. My back and armpits dampen again, though I'm not even sure the last bout has even dried yet.

If Miller notices the sudden sour tang of stress sweat, she makes no mention of it. If she had any doubts my nightmares about a man attacking me took place here, my instinctive reaction now should quell them all. Oh fuck me, my hands are even shaking. I must look completely out of my head. I try to swallow the sudden lump in my throat.

Miller turns to me with an expectant face, her eyes somehow warmly blue now.

I catch sight of Pendelton in the rear-view mirror as he crosses behind us. In the reflection of my side mirror, he consults with the two lab techs, his back to me. The techs bob their heads, a little reluctantly. Neither looks over at the car. I still don't know what they're here for. Maybe they have to supervise? Though it's clear they've been awaiting directions. . . .

I shake my head. Never mind. I'm only trying to distract myself. I mean, it's probably important to know, but at the same time . . . I'm sure I'll find out soon enough.

There's no going back now. This is my plan. I have to see it through.

Miller speaks clearly into her phone, listing all the details she needs for official documentation.

I interrupt as she takes a breath, praying I sound confident and sure. "I just want it on the record that I don't consent to having any of this, uh, interview filmed, but I do consent to an audio recording."

"Noted." Miller pauses for a moment. "Tell us what you remember from your flashbacks, Cleo. This is the car in those memories. You're sure of that now?"

"Yes, um." I shift to look out through the windshield. "I'm sitting right here. In the driver's seat. It's night. I don't know what time. Everything is dark outside the car." I move my gaze to the hood, blinking as a slice of light reflects off the silver surface into my eyes. The lights are awfully bright here, tinged greenish. I note the large garage door of dirty steel, slatted lengthwise, made to slide up and down, operated by a simple chain-and-pulley system attached on either side, its small wheels running along thin rails. I wonder if it squeaks. I wonder why we're parked facing that door, and at an angle. Frowning, I realize there are no other vehicles around us.

I lose my train of thought. "Um, yeah."

"Would you like to close your eyes? To help you remember?" says Miller. "And let's close the windows, too, okay?"

"Uh . . . okay. I guess." I comply with jerky movements, then reluctantly close my eyes, feeling supremely self-conscious.

"Please continue, Cleo."

For the first time since this whole horrifying train wreck began, I purposefully reach for the images, the ones which've been scrabbling at the edges of my mind for what feels like forever but has only been nine horrifying days. God. I mean, I *know* what happened. I remember every detail from those nightmares now. How could I forget? Waking in the middle of all those harrowing nights, soaked with sweat, my ears ringing with the echo of screams, my heart hammering so hard I think it's going to burst like an overripe tomato.

But the flashbacks can't hurt me. I know them for what they were. I remember the truth now. It should be easy to tell Miller what she needs to know. Shouldn't it?

I blow out a breath, opening my eyes. "I'm sorry. I can't." I gesture vaguely. "Everything's too distracting. I just . . . I don't know if I can describe it."

Miller gives a short nod, as though I've confirmed something for her.

"That's all right. Take your time." We sit in silence for a few beats as I try to wrestle my breathing back to normal. Maybe once I do, my heartbeat will follow.

Then, gently, Miller says, "Maybe it's the lights. You said it was night-time. Maybe these lights make it too bright. Too much like daytime."

I shrug, look down at my hands. "I'm not really sure it matters." I can't bring myself to admit I don't know if I can do this without freaking the fuck out completely. I clasp my hands together, to still their quivering.

"Okay," Miller says, drawing it out. "How about I ask you a few questions then?"

I nod.

"First, I guess, is, do you want to do this? Like, really want to? I mean, I'm clearly no psychiatrist, but perhaps the problem isn't your memory. It's your will."

I feel my hands shaking again for an entirely different reason. "I *don't* want to do this. At all. Losing my memory's been . . . difficult, but it's also shielded me from the worst parts of what happened. How many assault victims have you encountered who *wouldn't* prefer to forget?"

She flushes slightly. "Point taken. Sorry."

I ignore that, continuing in a huff. "But I'm here, and it's important, so I'll do the best I can." I snatch the righteous anger and hold it tight, channelling it to refocus. Miller is *not* going to manipulate me into any corners. Not now, not ever.

"All right." Miller's face softens for a split second before she pulls on a mask of brisk professionalism. "I think this will work better if you keep your eyes closed for as long as possible. Why don't you go through your memory of the flashback and simply list out everything you see in your mind's eye? Maybe beginning with the small details will yield larger ones. We'll take it one detail at a time, okay?"

I try to set aside my exhaustion, I really do, but it only settles more acutely into my bones inside the darkness behind my eyelids. I struggle to stay awake all of a sudden. Maybe this is a really bad idea, after all. I should've waited 'til morning.

Too fucking late now. Suck it up, Li.

I hear Miller's clothing rustle, then something on the outside of the car. A scratching sound, soft, then gone, so quick. Conjured from my memory? Or is it just something going on outside, in the lab?

I squeeze my eyelids together. No. I can't get distracted again. I can't afford to stretch this out any longer. I'm not sure I can last.

I concentrate on my breathing. Slow ... steady ... regular. Relying on it to help me walk the tightrope. I have to open myself up to the terror of that night, but also remain calm enough to tell Miller what she needs to hear.

The space behind my eyelids darkens to black. The silence in the car deepens.

Where to begin?

"I'm scared. Scared and sweating. It's pitch-black outside the car. It feels late. I'm sitting in the driver's seat. It's dark inside the car, too. There's the barest of illumination from the dash lights. The row of— what're they called? Uh ... icons, that's right. I see the row of icons on the dashboard, in green and amber. A few are in amber. They blink out."

I swallow. "There's someone in the back seat. I can't see anything in the rear-view mirror. It's just ... blank. There are ... there are screams coming from behind me and it, it sounds like a woman. She's screaming, high and—and terrified. She's screaming, *No*. Over and over. It all runs together, one endless word."

I shiver, tempted to open my eyes, to leave this memory behind, quickly, but I don't. I curl up slightly, searching for some shred of warmth. My knee hits the bottom of the steering wheel. I curse, some-how manage to keep my eyes closed, and shove myself into another part of the memory.

"A shadow moves to my right. I turn, feeling like something bad's gonna happen, and I better be ready." I hesitate, reaching for a way to translate into words, forcing myself to continue through the familiar, growing dread. "Maybe I feel the touch of clothing or the movement of the air as he moves. I don't know. Whatever signals his . . . intent, I feel it as a threat. The steering wheel digs into my left side. I hear a small sound, like a short *zzzip* as my elbow bangs and slides against it. It feels like I bruise my elbow and then my ribs. On my left side. I shove up against it, the steering wheel, trying to squeeze past, trying to turn to face the threat coming from my right, from the passenger seat. The space is too tight. There's a dark . . . shape. My eyes are still adjusting, so I'm not entirely certain. I think the overhead light's just gone out. There's a dark shape in the passenger seat."

I swivel my torso, my hands held out in front of me. I recoil as my palms brush the cold plastic of the steering wheel. The car horn blares, though its usual beep seems muffled. My heart tries to leap right out of my mouth.

"Easy there," says Miller softly. "You're perfectly safe. We're just talking. No one's going to hurt you, Cleo."

I take a few moments to catch my breath, to slow it down, to break the spell of terror and memory. When the silence in the car reaches me again, I continue.

"The man, he . . . he lunges for me. His hands are pale shapes in the darkness. I see one hand on the glove compartment, and the other, it's holding the side of the passenger seat. It—his hand looks like a claw, curling around the chair back."

My hands spasm, rising up off my lap a little before I force them down again.

"The shape . . . the man, he . . . he's angry. I can see his face, just a pale shape, too, and his teeth . . . they're bared like an animal, a wild dog. An angry dog. Maybe he's shouting something, I don't know. I can't hear anything over the screams. All I see are his teeth and the rage on his face. His eyes flash with it. Even in the dark. He looks like he could kill me."

Tears again, goddamnit, sudden and unrelenting. I swallow, over and over again, trying to get past the thickness in my throat. Trying to get a handle on this unreasoning emotion. And yet, my mouth is so dry, my tongue so swollen. I'm scared to close my jaw for fear of biting through to blood.

Miller breathes a word: "Cleopatra?"

I realize with a jolt that I'm panting. Short, ugly breaths sawing through my gaping mouth.

"Tell me what you see, Cleo. You can do it. You've mentioned it before, remember? The man's face. What can you see of his facial features?" I feel Miller's hunger for more, and decades of internalized obedience make me want to please her.

I release my hands, swipe at my still-closed eyes, then cup my face. My breath smells stale and, yes, bitter.

"You're doing so great, Cleo. I know you can do this. I know you can stick with me just a little longer. Concentrate, okay? Just concentrate a little longer and we'll be done in no time."

I sense the slight tremor of excitement in her voice. She feels how close this is, too, though for reasons so utterly different from mine. It should make me sympathetic. Or is it empathetic?

"Who is he, Cleo? Who is the man?"

I want to tell her, I truly, deeply do. It's the only fucking reason I'm here, tearing myself open for her. But the words stick in my chest, right behind my breastbone. Like a bone jammed crosswise in my windpipe. I shake my head, confused, hurting.

Why does this hurt so much?

"Tell me." Miller presses. "You can see him, can't you, in your memory? Who is he? Tell me and we can be done. Tell me, Cleo. Tell me and you can be free of him."

"No." I'm trembling again. "I can't. I can't tell you." What is wrong with me? I know I have to tell her. There are no other options.

"You're stronger than you know, Cleo. You can tell me and then you'll be free. You just need to be brave. You need to be brave and tell me, okay? Who is he? Who is the man who attacked you?"

She's right, damn me. I need to be brave. Not just for me, but for Cass, too. The only family I can claim. He deserves the best from me, however broken that may be. However short I may fall. My brother is all I have left. I won't abandon him.

I open my eyes, finally ready to tell Miller what she needs to know.

It's dark, truly dark. I feel my breath rasping my throat, blood rushing to my face and neck. Heat presses in on me, squeezing rivulets of sweat from my flushed skin. I swear I feel a sharp twinge in my ribs and elbow. My ears fill with a low thread of white noise, as though I'm trapped in a thick covering of cotton. I wince, anticipating the piercing shrieks sure to come—

A shadow rises to my right and I turn, raising my arms up to fend him off.

"No! No! Dad, don't!"

THIRTY-SEVEN

But it's not my father in the passenger seat. Not anymore.

I lower my arms, thumping my left elbow against the steering wheel, sending my heart into another stammer. My mouth feels dry, painfully stale. A jagged pinch in my throat sets me gagging. I cover my mouth with ice-cold hands.

Miller seems only inches away, her head blurred and shadowed. Her gaze roams my face, reading me as my disorientation fades. Before I can think of what to say, she clears her throat.

"It was Stephen Li who attacked you? Your father?"

Even now, I hesitate.

"Cleo, we need you to make a verbal reply, for the recording."

"Yes," I whisper, dropping my hands.

"I'm sorry, Cleo, louder, please."

"Yes."

"And your mother was in the back seat? It was Glinda Li?"

"I . . . I can't see her. I don't know."

"Do you recognize her voice?"

I shake my head, as much to rid myself of those screams as to answer. "Please, Cleo, I'm sorry. Can you reply verbally?"

"No. I . . . I don't know that it's her. I . . . I've never heard her sound like that before. . . ." I look down at my hands, nothing more than pallid lumps in the dark.

Wait.

I lift my head, surveying the murky interior. "What?" I scrabble for the door release. It unlatches, but the door won't open past a few inches. I shove it against something that feels springy but weighted, heavy. I whirl on Miller, hiding my heart's panicked fluttering behind a dark scowl. "What the fuck is going on?"

She reaches toward me. I recoil, spooked now, my throat spasming with fright. She taps the horn in a three-burst pattern, the equivalent of a door knock. A slash of light in the rear-view mirror startles another gasp from me.

I contort my body to stare out the back of the car. I watch with wild eyes as the light grows in the rear window, the darkness retreating from the bottom toward the top in a moving line. The car rocks slightly from side to side as the gloom surrounding us breaks up. Twisting, I see the lab techs, one on either side of the car, rolling up a heavy black fabric. I realize with growing shock it must have been covering the whole car, creating a false night inside.

The techs continue rolling up the industrial fabric until they pull the last of it across the hood, away from us. I squint in the brightness, watching as they hoist the awkward cylinder of fabric onto a large flat dolly. The woman returns to my side of the car, where a squat boxy device sits on the floor, maybe a foot away. She unplugs the whatever-it-is from an extension cord and carries it to the dolly, setting it next to the tube of fabric. They trundle the two items away, toward a corner to the right of the garage door, filled, I see now, with items on blue metal shelving.

I shift my disbelieving gaze to Miller's face.

"I'm sorry, Cleo, really sorry. It was no small thing for you to even suggest trying to relive this terrible experience. I thought there might be a good chance it would be too difficult. So Chuck and I worked this out, to recreate conditions similar to what you described, in case we needed something stronger to jog your memory."

Miller points at the departing techs. "We used the noise-cancelling machine to cut out any external noises. It also helped cover up the sound of the fabric being rolled over the car. We didn't want it to distract you."

I shudder involuntarily. Images crash and tumble through my mind, with no regard for time or place. I know it's really fucking bad when the same thing spools over and over: a small, pale figure tossed and smashed against eons-old boulders jutting out of black water. It feels like a feverish, nightmare imagining. I don't want it to be a true memory.

"Does your brother know?" asks Miller, her voice as gentle as I've ever heard it. "About your father?"

Groping for the latch again, I open the door and stumble out.

"Cleo!"

I raise my head at the cry. Not two feet from the car, my brother tears out of Pendelton's grip, his face dark with fury. Cass runs to me, pulling me in tight to him. I briefly feel the tremors in him before he rears back, peering into my face.

"What happened? Are you okay?"

I flail my head, unable to manage a nod, and extricate myself. I set my back against the car. Through my spine and the hands I've pressed against the gritty metal panelling, I feel Miller get out on the other side, the passenger door closing with a soft click. She rounds the hood, coming at me from my right.

"Did you tell your brother, Cleo?" she asks gravely. "Did you know, Dr. Li?"

Cass steps to my side, standing between Miller and me. "What the fuck could you possibly be talking about?"

"No." I cough, trying to dislodge the lump in my throat. "No. I had nothing to tell him. Cass hasn't done anything wrong." Fresh moisture drips down my cheeks. Fuck me. I'm crying again.

Miller halts, close to Pendelton, her eyes narrowing. "But *you* have?"

I press harder against the car, bumping the hard knot of my ponytail against the window. "No. That's not—" My gaze swings wildly from Miller to Pendelton to Cass. I use my shirt to scrub at my face, the cuff scratching me raw from eyes to jawline. I need to stop crying. I need to be strong, confident. I need them to believe me.

My eyes pop as I see Naomi now, standing in street clothes next to Pendelton. She frowns, wrath and worry fighting for dominance on her face before she settles on a familiar blank stiffness. She wants to help me, but she can't. I have no idea how I feel about that. Fuck. I shouldn't feel anything about it at all.

My heart thrashes with panic, sending too much blood into my head, filling my ears with the roar in my veins, making it hard to think. The tears won't stop, my diaphragm catches with every other breath, the signals shoot to my lungs in erratic fits and starts. The less air I get, the harder I try to breathe, the more I can feel myself freaking out. Suddenly, the overhead lighting glows and fades in strange patterns.

"Whoa there," says Pendelton, eyes flaring in alarm. "Easy now. You're gonna pass out if you don't calm down. Whoa."

Fuck you, buddy, I'm not a horse.

My knees give way. I slide downward against the car's side, dropping onto my ass with a thud. My eyes start to roll up, back into their sockets. I feel hands on me, manipulating my body like I'm a marionette on strings. Feet flat on the floor, knees up and apart, head downward between knees. Someone lays a steadying hand on the middle of my back.

"That's it," murmurs my brother. "Breathe nice and slow. You're okay, sis. You're going to be fine. Just keep breathing nice and slow."

Second by second, the thunder in my ears subsides.

". . . some fucking nerve, taking advantage of my sister like this. You knew she was already exhausted from a long day. You should've convinced her to wait until the morning. Can't you see how dangerous this was?"

"It was her choice," retorts Miller. "She doesn't need permission from anyone else. She's a grown woman."

"She's not in her right mind," says Cass tightly. "She can't give proper consent like this."

I pull away from the reassuring hand on my spine. Biting my lip, I twist myself to one side, getting my knees underneath me, then straightening my torso to sit back on my haunches. Panting a little, I pull one leg up, bent at the knee, so that I can push myself up to standing.

"Jesus." Cass takes my left elbow, pulling me up the rest of the way, while his other hand supports me at the small of my back. Through my sweat-soaked shirt, his palm feels hot as a brand pressing on a fresh bruise. I twitch him off.

"Why are you here, Cass?" I ask wearily.

"After your stupid fucking note? What did you think I'd do?" He scowls at me. I stare back. "I was coming to find you anyway when I found that idiotic note slipped under my door. Dr. Rao called. She tried you first but couldn't reach you." His scowl deepens. "I had to cuss Naomi out to bring me here."

I blink away the white spots in my vision.

"Are you all right?" Miller bends down to peer into my eyes. "Do you want some water? Chuck, go find some water, would you?"

Shaking my head makes me dizzy, light-headed. I grip Cass's hands so tightly he winces. "What did she say? Cass? What did Rao say?"

He takes hold of my hands, his gaze softening as he lowers his voice. "She ruled it an accidental death, sis."

I sag. Oh my fucking God. It's over. *It's finally over.* I could scream from sheer relief. Or collapse.

Then the implications land, jolting through me like electricity down my spine.

"Did you already know?" I ask the cops, my bleary gaze landing on each one of them in turn. "Before you set this up? You must've heard from Rao first, right?"

"I did, yes," replies Miller coolly, "but not Chuck."

Pendelton stares at his partner. I can't read his expression for shit.

"What about you?" I ask Naomi roughly.

She shakes her head, her shoulders taut with something I'd like to interpret is indignation. But the truth is, I don't quite care. Her loyalties are none of my business anymore.

Miller adds, "I was going to tell them both tomorrow. When you called me about doing this tonight, I recruited Chuck's help, but I thought it better to leave Naomi out of it. Frankly, if there was fallout, we could shoulder it better as senior officers."

I want desperately to sit down, but I'm afraid I won't be able to get back up.

Miller continues. "I knew you'd hear from Dr. Rao anyway, Cleo. It was important to support you in this," she waves her hand at the RAV4. "With you being the one pushing for this, it seemed likely you'd be able to break through your block and remember for real. Whatever the outcome, we honestly believed you'd heal better if you came clean." She hesitates, a frown settling on her features. "But now, with this new piece of information . . ."

"What? What new information?" Cass jumps on Miller's murmured afterthought, his entire body vibrating again.

I shake his hands, pulling his attention back. "No, Cass, it's nothing we need to worry over now. We can talk about it later." I let him see my true state, knowing it hits home when his brow furrows in distress. "I'm exhausted. I need to crash. Please."

"He deserves to know," says Miller, relentless. "This can't wait, Cleo."

I squeeze my eyes shut, cursing the stubborn unmitigated arrogance of well-meaning white women.

Cass sounds hesitant now, his voice low and close. "Sis? What's going on? Did you remember something after all?"

"Fine," I say to Miller, too wrung out to play nice, "but this is my news to share." I tug gently at Cass's hands, leading him to the door behind the driver's side of the RAV4. I stumble once on the way. "Need to sit," I mumble.

"You did remember something, then?" He opens the door for me, helps me inside, to sit sideways. I stop him from closing the door so I can leave my legs dangling out. I do not want to be trapped in here any longer.

Cass frowns. "Is it bad? Are you okay? You're worrying me."

I rustle up a wan smile for his concern, but it can't stand up to the enormity of what I'm about to do, the terrible thing I'm about to share. It will destroy any last illusions he might still hold about our parents. It was hard for him to hear how much worse my mother was than he thought. But . . .

I tried to prepare him. I tried so hard. And yet . . . he *must* know, at some deep, visceral level. Otherwise, why protest so hard?

Still, I hesitate. Fuck, I hate being the bad guy.

Because this is betrayal. This is doubt and fury and potentially poisonous hatred. There'll be no un-saying it, no un-doing it.

"Sis? It's okay. You can tell me anything." He offers me a lopsided half-smile, though the shadows in his eyes tell me how fragile he truly feels.

I take a steadying breath. "Cass . . . little brother . . . I remember who attacked me in the car." I shudder. "In this car."

His mouth stiffens. He looks outright frightened now, his face pale. I can't blame him. It surprises me how much I wish I could protect him from this. But he needs to know. *I* need him to know. He's the only family I have left.

So I tell him. Dad, enraged. Mum, screaming. Me, in the middle of a maelstrom.

Oh, Cass, poor Cass. He takes it all in, his body turning to stone sentence by sentence, his face darkening, his eyes becoming sunken and dull. When I'm done, he stares at me, speechless, his gaze blasted and out of focus.

The terrible screaming silence grows heavier moment by moment.

I brush the wetness from my face. "I am never doing anything like that ever again, little brother. You were right. It was stupid and risky and I should've listened to you."

"Too late now," he whispers. Then, as if waking, he blinks several times, and stumbles back a few steps, away from me. "Too late." His voice grows in volume as he turns to face the cops, all three watching with wary gazes and rigid stances.

"So now, it's my father who's the murderer? That's your newest theory?" he asks them. "He killed my mother? Tried to kill my sister?" He reels back to me. "But you're still alive. So, he *didn't* try to kill you? He drugged you so you'd, what? Be unable to identify him?" He drags his hands down his face, pulling it into a grotesque mask for a second. "You're saying he might still be alive? None of this makes any goddamned sense."

My insides squirm at his anguish. I clench my hands tight on my legs, unsure if he wants comfort, or space to rage.

"Perhaps," Naomi offers, cautiously, "he . . . he found he couldn't go through with it after all. He changed his mind, about Cleo."

Cass lets out a harsh, bitter laugh. "Next thing you'll tell me is that my parents were in on it together. They lured Cleo out here to deal with her once and for all, but Dad couldn't bear to go through with it. So, he what? Left Cleo, hurt and dosed up? She would've wandered around all night in the fucking dark for hours." Tears drip down his cheeks. Unheeding, Cass continues, "Which means . . . Dad turned on our mother instead? They struggled and fell into the river together, then?" He spits out the words like gunfire, hard and meant to injure. "You're all *fucking nuts*. My family are the victims, not the perpetrators." He sounds wild, untethered. My heart aches.

Naomi makes another tentative effort. "Perhaps Cleo's presence was unexpected. One of the lodge staff mentioned your father asking about nearby pharmacies. Maybe your mother needed her medication. Maybe she . . . forced Cleo to bring it to her, from home." She pauses, eyeing Miller diffidently. "It doesn't explain the Rohypnol, or how Cleo got to Field, but . . ."

Miller takes her hands off her hips, ignoring Naomi. "Your father's still missing, regardless of the original circumstances. But since we now know one more definitive thing, thanks to Cleo's courage, we do have other firm leads to investigate."

I can feel her considering gaze on me, but I'm busy watching my brother. He stands, loss and anguish stamped on his haggard face, his hands hanging at his sides, restless. I realize he's rubbing his thumbs along his fingertips, back and forth, back and forth, over and over and over. A habit I recognize from memories of our childhood, from all the times he had to stop and figure out what to do for himself.

I feel a sharp prick in my chest, bringing fresh tears to my eyes. I push myself out of the car before I consciously decide on it. The time for distance has passed. My brother is hurting. He needs comfort. It's as plain as if he's just spoken aloud, though I'm only reading the pain on his features.

But that clinical, unemotional part of me won't quite shut up. It nags at me, about unfinished business, about accountability.

I stop before him, suddenly quivering with doubt. "I'm sorry, Cass. I'm sorry I . . . remembered. I'm sorry about Dad. I . . . I messed everything up." It's awkward as fuck, but it feels . . . right somehow, to say it. To acknowledge that I've shattered his illusions and any lingering, improbable dreams of a happy family, where one parent isn't, possibly, a murderer . . .

So many emotions flit across his face. I can't begin to interpret them all, so I let them cascade without comment or reaction. I've said my bit. It's his turn now.

Nevertheless, I tense, anticipating the barrage of anger or confusion or some nasty combination to spew from him. I remind myself, no matter how bad it gets, he deserves to have his say. He deserves to feel whatever he feels. I brace myself.

Without a word, Cass grabs me to him, mashing my face into his chest. His arms band around my shoulders, hugging me so tightly I can only manage shallow breaths.

"Thank God," he murmurs. "Thank God you're alive. I'm so glad you're okay. So fucking glad." He squeezes even harder, forcing a cough from me. "It's only us now, sis." With a cracked noise, he starts sobbing, great heaving cries that he muffles against the top of my head.

I remember this sound, the confusion and impotence and desperate desire for someone to fix what's broken, someone who never comes. We both cried too often like this as children. I remember.

Even though he's loosened his hold, I let him cry into my hair. I let him prop himself up by my shoulders. I let him grieve.

And I gasp with a painful resonance, right where my heart should be. I think I've finally tuned in to it, after all these difficult years. It's terrible and terrifying, sounding the truth through me like the vibration of a struck tuning fork.

Our family is gone now. I'm responsible for destroying it.

If Cass and I want any chance of building something new, something *better*, then we have to stick together. Against all comers. For all our sakes.

This is what family means to me now.

THIRTY-EIGHT

Two weeks later

I s it easier to leave this place now, if it's on my own terms?

In so many ways, I believed I already had. I've been living on my own for over a decade, earning my own money, learning how to navigate life as a full-grown woman, enjoying the perks of self-sufficiency.

And yet—*living on my own* only meant living just a few inches away from my childhood. That invisible tether, braided of obligations and habit and sometimes, maybe, of something my parents called love, it kept some part of me still caught on *this* side of the dividing wall. I stare at it, at the fake wood panelling, bring my face up against it, find the innumerable scrapes and dimples picked out by the light and this new perspective.

I touch it lightly, saying a final, blessed goodbye.

I look around me as I walk through my parents' empty rooms, touching window locks and pushing open internal doors. All I see are old, tired surfaces, given a new coat of cleanliness by the three-person crew I hired last week, sure to fade with the heat and dust of approaching summer.

I don't know what the new owners plan for this place. I don't want to know.

In the kitchen, my phone sounds Vader's "Imperial March."

"Inspector Miller, what's up?"

"Hi, Cleo. I just thought I should be the one to let you know, Dr. Rao won't be reopening the investigation into your mother's death. There's been no further info discovered to make any definitive determination as to your father's role in your mother's death. Her death stands as accidental."

"Okay."

"Also. Your father's status will remain as Missing until and unless something happens to prove either his death or . . . that he's still alive."

"Okay, I understand."

I hear her take a deep breath.

"Please accept our condolences again, mine and Chuck's. We're very sorry about your mother's death."

"Wait. What about Arceneaux? I was about to call my EPS person, but since I have you on the line. When will the trial be? Will you be served a subpoena, too?"

Her hesitation is palpable. "You can't quote me on this, but . . . I'm hearing he's going to plead guilty. That video is hard to argue with, and it sounds like he's got a decent lawyer."

I frown. "Okay, but what happens then?"

"The judge will sentence him. For this charge, the max is eighteen months in jail. The minimum is community service up to eighteen months. At the sentencing, you have the option to give a victim impact statement, if you want."

I hear a pulse of reluctance underneath the facts. "But? I can hear it in your voice."

"But . . . if he's got a good lawyer, they'll bring up your history at that company, HR reports, statements from former co-workers, the works. Mitigating circumstances. It's more than possible he'll get community service rather than jail time."

"I get it. He plays well to the audience." I don't bother hiding my snark. The white man's world order. "Whatever. I'm still thinking of getting a permanent restraining order against him."

"That's your choice, of course. I understand."

I just bet she does. "Goodbye, Shae. Take care," I say flippantly, then ring off before she replies. What more would she have to say to me?

But her call reminds me of the text from Aoki this morning. I pull it up on my phone, finally ready to reply.

**Safe travels and good luck
in Lethbridge. Hope you get what
you need there.**

Take care, Naomi

Slipping my phone into my purse, I hesitate as I spy a familiar tattered square of paper. I shoved it in here forever ago, putting it off until I had my head on straight. Strange that it's been practically invisible all this time.

I unfold the square, fuzzy along its edges now. Thea Halford's immaculate handwriting greets me. I barely recall the woman who needed this, frightened and trembling in a building full of strangers. Thea's role in all this ended weeks ago. There's no need to reconnect now. I refold the paper with the tiniest twinge of guilt and drop it onto the worn counter.

I walk to the back door, readying to lock up with the keys in my hand. My gaze catches on the "key cupboard" next to the back steps. The door sits slightly ajar. I tap it closed. It scrapes, making a sound like a low *brrrrp*, then springs back a little. I run my eyes up the opening and spy a bit of tape at the very top corner, preventing a tight fit.

I allow myself one sigh, but I know I can't ignore it. Even if the cleaning crew did. I mean to leave this place spotless and in perfect order. That was my promise to Cass.

In a huff, I drop my purse and keys on the top step and climb up onto the counter to reach the top of the cupboard door. It looks like someone used coloured duct tape on this corner. It's just about the exact shade of brown as the door. Their mistake was wrapping it around the edge. I grump internally. Now I have to peel it off with nothing but my too-short fingernails. There's probably a hole underneath and my fa—they figured it was cheaper to cover it up than to replace the door or fix it properly.

I should leave it. Serves the new owners right for not noticing. But that promise I made to Cass . . . Jesus, what a pain.

I don't care to count the minutes it takes me to curl off one tiny edge of the tape. But it happens, finally, and I rip and pull impatiently until the whole mess comes off. At which point, I discover it's not just one layer of duct tape. It's three.

But the surface of the door is intact, pristine even. I stare at the smooth wood with a growing frown.

Jesus, Joseph, and Mary . . . why would anyone need—

I look down.

Nestled against the sticky triangle of tape in my hand is a small, delicate key.

I've never seen this key before in my life, but I recognize it instantly.

My head goes a little wonky, images popping into my mind's eye, a bewildering rewind. I see flashes of this place, filled still with its broken furnishings and the aftermath of mayhem, with fury and frustration and an overwhelming, crashing madness. . . .

I scramble down before the buzzing dizziness sends me tumbling to the floor. I do not want to crack my head open. Fuck, and definitely not here. Not trusting my suddenly weak knees, I slide all the way onto the worn linoleum. I place the flats of my hands on the chilly flooring, willing myself to stay in the present. The past is done. It has no place in my new life. It will not dictate my choices for my future.

A small insistent prick of pain brings me back to myself. I lift my hurting hand upward. I stare down at the smooth brown tape. I rub at the red spot of irritation on my palm. I unpeel the tape from the floor, then fold it back on one side.

I force the key from its sticky trap. I let the ugly triangle of duct tape fall to the floor. The key adheres to my fingertip. I let it hang there as I raise it to eye level.

There's no ring, just this tiny scrap of shaped metal. It could be for a box at the post office, or a mailbox in an apartment building foyer.

But I know better.

And all I can think is—

How differently everything might have turned out.

EPILOGUE

July 11, 2018
Golden, BC
News Release

On June 30, 2018, human remains were discovered in the vicinity of Wapta Falls. Pending ruling by the BC Coroners Service, an investigation by the Kelowna Serious Crimes Unit has credible information that the deceased may be related to File #18-***** pertaining to the death of Glinda Li, 55, of Edmonton, Alberta.

If you have information about these remains, you are asked to contact the Kelowna Serious Crimes Unit general information line at 250-555-8963. Or, to leave an anonymous tip, call the Crime Stoppers line at 1-800-555-8477 or visit crimestoppers.net.

File #18-*****
Released by
Cpl. Stan Simkowich
Media Relations Officer
Kelowna RCMP

July 25, 2018

Claiming "extraordinary circumstances," the Western Canadian Lottery Corporation (WCLC) has agreed to allow the winner of a $47.3M jackpot, drawn February 16, 2018, to remain anonymous. Information on the WCLC website confirms that lottery corporation rules in Canada stipulate that winners must agree to have their prizes, names, likenesses, and places of residence published, in order to claim lottery winnings.

WCLC spokesperson Rachelle Marchand explained this current development via emailed statement: "The unusual step of allowing winner anonymity occurs solely at the discretion of lottery corporations, which consider such requests on a case-by-case basis. Anonymity is granted only if an investigation finds credible and independently verifiable evidence of the claimant's assertions for anonymity."

No further details were provided on the $47.3M winner, or on the nature of the "extraordinary circumstances," though WCLC officials did confirm that the winning ticket was purchased on February 14, 2018, at the Lucky 88 grocery store in Edmonton, AB. Additionally, the winnings were claimed by Edmonton lawyer Betty Wan, of Chen Wan LLC, on behalf of the winner. Wan declined to comment.

June 4, 2018, Excerpted Interview
ONG, ANNA: Glinda is a good mother. She didn't throw Cassius out, Stephen did that. Glinda's happy to give him money for their house, for the new baby. She's excited to be a grandmother. Of course. Cleopatra's not doing that for her. That girl, acting so smart. Who cares? Smart girls scare everyone, especially the men. No man, no husband, no grandbabies. Glinda told her to pretend more, not always show people they're dumb. But [noise] Glinda must drag

her to a better future, selfish stupid girl, so stubborn. Can you believe it? No common sense. Glinda hid the ticket and the key, for the bank box, yes. Not even Stephen knows where. Glinda's smart. She loves her children, but like any good mother, she knows. You spoil them if you love them too much. Especially the girls.

Author's Note

If you've had the pleasure of visiting Yoho National Park, or of travelling along the Trans-Canada Highway in the eastern parts of British Columbia, you may already know that Yoho Valley Road is real. If you've enjoyed the additional pleasure of heading up that road to The Meeting of the Waters and Takakkaw Falls, you will also know that there is indeed a luxury resort across the street, so to speak, from a Parks Canada campground. While the Cathedral Mountain Lodge shares many striking physical characteristics with the fictional Lodge at Yoho of this story, including a lovely situation next to the Kicking Horse River, the happenings at The Lodge at Yoho remain firmly and wholly in the world of imagination.

Acknowledgements

I'm humbled and grateful to live as an immigrant settler on Treaty 6 land, as part of the vibrant community of Amiskwacîwâskahikan (Edmonton).

Heartfelt thanks to Lauren Abramo for understanding Cleo from the start, for getting what I was trying to do with this story, and for coming up with the perfect title for this novel. I also adore that she patiently abets my nerdy enthusiasm for shoptalk. She deserves all the saskatoon berry jam I can make.

I'm grateful to Iris Tupholme for her sharp insights, wit, and kindness, and for being a delight to work with.

Thanks to the mighty HarperCollins Canada team (staff as well as freelancers) who contributed their talents, time, and cheer: Cory Beatty, Lisa Bettencourt, Dominic Farrell, Michael Guy-Haddock, Julia McDowell, Natalie Meditsky, Judy Phillips, Lisa Rundle, Neil Wadhwa, and Noelle Zitzer. Thanks to the ace HarperCollins 360 team for their talents and energy on U.S. distribution and promotion: Meredith Dowling, Jean Marie Kelly, Alex Serrano, and Emma Sullivan.

And, of course, my thanks to all the others at HarperCollins who also worked on this book but whose names I wasn't quite able to sleuth out. I appreciate you all.

Thank you to Tyner Gillies for answering questions early in my process about the RCMP in the BC interior. Any inaccuracies herein are either by design or human error on my part.

Thanks to Dr. Kristen Hutchinson, who kindly pointed out a few gaps in Cass's characterization of himself as bisexual. If there are any lingering mistakes, they're on me.

Thank you to the Crime Writers of Color! It's so lovely to belong to this welcoming, empowering community. What a blessing to know that support and perspective are only a single message away.

It's an utter privilege to serve on the national board of Sisters in Crime (SinC), and to do it as the first-ever vice president/president/immediate past president from the Asian diaspora community. Thank you to all the generous volunteers, and to Valerie Burns, Tracee de Hahn, Kellye Garrett, Edwin Hill, Cynthia Kuhn, Vanessa Lillie, Alec Peche, Shari Randall, and Barb Ross for being *amazing* board members during my term as president. I'm especially grateful to Stephanie Gayle, Faye Snowden, and Jacki York for their brilliance and for making the work so much fun.

Many hugs full of love and gratitude to Lori Rader-Day for all the things—cheerleading, laughs, and, of course, the juicy shoptalk. All hail publishing nerds!

Very special, loving thanks to Julie Hennrikus for all the laughter, the many words of wisdom, and for sharing of her incredible, gorgeous self. Virgos rule.

Thanks to my Lola Starke/Crescent City readers, who have been so lovely and patient, and lively when I needed it. (I'm working on more Lola, I promise!)

Thanks to Rhonda Parrish, who read a verrrrry early draft of this novel and encouraged me with her honest feedback.

Thanks to my mum and to all of my extended family who lovingly cheer me on from afar. Extra shout-out to my brother for early research help plus a few late-in-the-process answers about criminal defence lawyering. Any inaccuracies on this are mine, either by design or by mistake.

Thanks to my teen children, beautiful, funny, loving souls who always seem to know when I need to be called out and when I need to be hugged.

Big, beautiful, infinite thank-yous to Kevin, who loves me well enough to know that my preoccupation with imaginary murder and mishaps during a milestone anniversary trip in Yoho National Park in no way detracts from how deeply I cherish him and how madly I adore that smile. (He knows the one.)